The Winterpoor

A Novel

George Michelsen Foy

Sea Crow Press

For my Family
and
for the Crew at the Abode

Also by George Michelsen Foy

fiction:

The Last Green Light: A Novel of the Jazz Age

(as GF Michelsen):

Mettle

Hard Bottom

The Art and Practice of Explosion

Asia Rip

nonfiction:

Run the Storm: A Savage Hurricane, a Brave Crew, and the Wreck of the SS El Faro

Finding North: How Navigation Makes Us Human

Zero Decibels: The Quest for Absolute Silence

Book One
Spring

Murdo squeezes the trigger but the screw won't bite. When he pulls the trigger hard the drill whines to top speed; the bit slips out of the screw's slot, carves into his left index finger which was pinching the screw in place.

"*Vai-te foder.*" Murdo hurls his drill into the barge's side. The movement jinks him right, pushes the rolling chair he stands on leftward, and before Murdo knows what has happened he's in midair: each assumption, all pretensions, suspended for this brief instant of flight.

He lands on the floor butt-first. When he lifts his elbow from the deck the joint bends and nerves there fire off pain signals that read as red distress flares in his brain.

From this viewpoint the joists of the boat shop, lined up to support the roof's peak, change shape. For a second, though he's seen them five hundred times before, they look like dark architecture to Murdo: angles joined to store evil the way a battery hoards electricity—wired backwards, negative to positive, they will fry the world once connected, not join but blast it all apart: this project, how he lives with Una, the skin of change on her and why Speed is never here so that he, Murdo, is the one who must screw planks into this barge to meet the director's deadline.

"*Vai-te foder*": Murdo, who curses in Portuguese when shocked, says it clearly, and this time finishes the curse as his grandfather would have, "*no cu da puta da tua mãe!*"

The boat shop snorts.

Murdo rolls right, taking weight on his unhurt elbow. He finds his spectacles, prongs them to his face and looks about him, confused.

Boat shops don't snort. The nineteenth-century harbor scow that he's working on, this barge with scalloped bow and the absurd, *belle époque* yacht's cabin grafted on its deck, all propped on more fell timbers, stayed with rust and jack stands, is too sad and rotted to get jokes. He sits up, adjusts his glasses.

Something stirs beside the door, the people-door set into the bigger, corrugated tin boat-door that will not roll open till this wreck is healed.

Murdo's heart thuds faster: No one is in here, no one came in but the smaller door is cracked open and something could have entered, a raccoon probably, maybe Pancho, would Pancho follow him this far? He spots movement again, under a broken band saw covered with a Korean tarp.

He gets up, groaning only a little; crosses the shop, lifts the tarp's corner and sees a hump that shouldn't be there, under a grimy hoodie. Too big for a raccoon he thinks; anyway raccoons, even Pancho with his gangbanger ways, do not wear hoodies. No it's a kid, hiding under the saw's steel table. A window in Murdo's head scrapes open and lets in light to scatter his whim of evil in the rafters, the Lovecraft umbrage of his fantasies, his "excursions" Una calls them.

"Hey," he says. And louder: "*Hey*—what're you *doin'* in there?"

The nylon twitches. Sneakers budge, trawling laces. Murdo waits. Finally:

"Well you got to come out, right?"

Still the child doesn't move. Murdo grows aware of a crawling down his left hand. He grabs gauze from the first-aid box and wraps it 'round the wound. He cuts it short with his rigging knife and the gauze at once turns scarlet—pain starting to gather, find pace, throb to the bluesy systole of his pulse.

When he looks back the kid has shifted, one cheek now pressed against the steel stand, eyes fixed on Murdo.

The hair is bushy, too short for most girls. Ten-eleven years old, chubby still in chin and neck though his skin pulls back from the cheekbones as if he's otherwise thin, and hungry. His mouth is crooked, half open on one side, top lip pulled over bottom on the other, buckteeth marking the divide: eyes wide as if he just said something, then took it back.

What he really looks like, Murdo thinks suddenly, is someone who has asked a question but expects no response, ever. Murdo stares at the boy as if he wants to draw him, as he most likely does. The skin on face and neck is the hue of Murdo's—swamp-cedar, north of tan, south of cream. The nose is broad in the middle as if a tool had scraped its bridge down at a formative stage, leaving it fine around the nostrils. The eyes are of a blue so deep it's almost shocking. Here the genes of the Mediterranean, of Europe and Africa, have mixed and spilled in different directions from Murdo's, whose irises are dark as tar. The kid's body, like the face, is chubby-lank, puppy fat glued on baling wire. It's not just his fingernails: His hands and half his forearms, what you can see under the rolled-up sweatshirt sleeves, are grayed with grime.

Murdo sighs. Irritation creeps in. He has nothing against kids, hell he not Una is the one who wanted children, he admires them for the surprises they're good at, stunts like this but not now—the adult speaking with all his locked-down time and deadlines.

Murdo runs a project that depends on a town grant managed by the Cape Realtors Action Consortium and the grant specifies certain "watersheds," they call them that in the contract, Director Cooper calls 'em that, and the douche of dislike sprays Murdo's guts, he can't help it: something about Russell Cooper, his padlocked smirk, the sheen off cheeks he shaves (Una claims) twice a day—Murdo's history with the Coopers—yeah Cooper calls 'em watersheds, dates by which a fixed percentage of the work must be done.

This sea-chewed scow will anchor a new marine-art school and workshop centered on the rebirth of Eby Noble's floating studio that was a rigging barge for forty years and sat in a parking lot for another twelve and the chief boatwright for this job now vanished like the *Mary Celeste*'s crew. At the thought of Speed, Murdo jerks, one foot to the other, and the kid eyes him nervously.

Then Murdo squats, to the level of those eyes the color of winter sunlight, of the top stripe on a kingfisher's wing.

"What's your name?" Keeping his voice low and easy, the way you'd talk to a skittish pup.

Kid lifts his hand, sticks a finger in his right nostril, brings it back out bearing a small, greenish worm on the end.

He glances at the snot, and back at Murdo.

Boy, Murdo thinks. Definitely.

"Well, I can't wait till you decide."

The boy eats the worm. Murdo walks back to the hull.

What he's been doing to the barge: what he has no business doing if the hull will ever be a waterfront art school that floats again and even moves under its own diesel, as Cooper specified; is daubing caulk on the sixth and seventh strakes, the scow's rib-bones, and screwing in a new plank, an inch-thick board of white oak that Speed previously measured, sawed and steamed neatly to fit this bend.

But Murdo is not a carpenter, far less a boutique boatwright as the contract also demands. Murdo is a boutique art-printer who makes the kind of precise, detailed etchings the ex-owner of this hulk once made. They are drawings that he scratches with fine steel tools on copperplate coated with a tarry substance, called etching ground, then dunks in a bath of acid. The acid cannot penetrate the ground but it eats into the copper wherever he scratched through, chewing his images into metal. Just to think of the process, even sideways, ricochets to daydreams of the work Murdo should be doing and makes his fists clench from the bite of what? Frustration? Anger? Lust, for the strong yet held-back motions his work involves—the power it takes to restrain power, the use of each muscle in arm and wrist to scratch a line a half-millimeter long and three microns across, that will bring in through the miracle of association some aspect of the greater world he draws?

He longs for the absorption, or escape perhaps, those processes confer.

From the workbench he pinches a screw between bandage and thumb. He plugs the screw into a starter hole. His cut stings, his elbow twinges. Murdo stands there, not quite defeated, wondering why this shop feels so full of change ... that greater force he felt before plus 220 volts writhing through this drill cord, and he so fucking blocked.

"My dad-dy showed me."

The kid has surfaced. His face is level with Murdo's breast-bone. The sweatshirt hangs almost to his knees. From one pocket loll the head and arms of a stuffed animal, something so beat up and moldy it's hard to identify: bear? groundhog? rat? The boy slouches a bit, same way Murdo does, somewhere between peering forward and shrugging. He'll think later this might have come into it, an early concordance of angles, a stance they shared.

"What. Showed you what?"

"Screw." A finger points. "My dad-dy showed me dah *screw*."

Though he is looking up at him the boy's eyes are not on Murdo's. Rather, they are five degrees off to one side, and again he has that air of expecting his words to find no response. That's when Murdo for the first time senses this child is not normal, whatever "normal" means for children, humans still in the act of gel. The snot-finger cruises closer now, skims the drill's casing, and Murdo starts to jerk the tool away, then brakes his action.

"He showed you—" Murdo shakes his head. "Listen, who—I mean, what's your name?"

The eyes edge closer, though still east of Murdo's gaze.

"Boy," he says.

"Yeah I know, but who are you, your name."

"Boy." (Insistent.)

"Boy?" Staring at him. "Your *name* is Boy?"

"I, Boy." The blue touches Murdo's gaze. Cold as snow country, Murdo thinks, though he also feels an opposite there on the order of quilts, wood-fire, warmth anyway, does it come from his own mind or what he somehow scries deep inside this kid?

"My dad—dy showed me."

Not my daddy; my dad, *he. He* showed me.

Murdo holds the drill away from the boy as if he cares, as if he himself is any damn good at this, OK then. The decision sudden: It's only afterward that he remembers that this boat-art school, his workshop, are supposed to do exactly this, *inform*; teach schoolchildren how boats are made and used and how art can even grow from harbor hulks. Maybe the CRAC will like it, Cooper and his "core values," Murdo starting lessons early.

"Here," he says, and hands the kid the drill.

Winter flounders are flatfish, but likely they were not always flat. This causes identity issues when first the fish is born for just after birth, at the larval stage, the winter flounder looks like a regular if tiny fish, with gills and one eye on each side as it swims upright like cod or shark.

After a few weeks one of the eyes migrates. It moves from the left side of the fish's head—or what would be left if the flounder were still swimming "upright," like other fish—to the right side. This allows it, when lying on its left flank on the bottom as flounders will, to aim both eyes upward toward both predator and prey. It has become what fishers call "right-eyed."

Young winter flounder are also known as "blackback" when they are less than three pounds in weight, and "lemon sole" when bigger. They earned their more common name from a habit of swimming inshore when the water cools, spending the cold months in shallow lagoons and estuaries such as Hyannis Harbor and nearby Eel Pond, on Cape Cod. The flounders spawn in these saltwater bays when water temperatures are lowest in February and early March. The females pump out between 500,000 and a million and a half eggs that clump on the bottom, adhering to rocks, weed and sunken moorings.

The winter flounder has an idea of home; it will return to the same body of water all its life to spend the winter and produce the next generation of flatfish, which also will return to that harbor only.

Once they have spawned, however; once the temperature starts to climb as the sun tarries and warms Nantucket Sound, the winter flounder of Hyannis and Eel Pond are motivated only to leave harbor. It would be foolish to suggest that these fish, with brains no bigger than a pea, hold any concept of freedom. But it's also true that their drive to leave, to swim out of the bight of harbor into the Sound, to fin deeper and deeper, seems as powerful as it is obsessive.

It usually happens in mid-March. Cued by warmth and increasing daylight, they strongly, deliberately make their way down muddy channels to closer reaches of the Sound. Some swim farther, threading sandbars between Nantucket and Martha's Vineyard, past shoals and channels to the south of these islands, into sectors of continental shelf that sink past thirty fathoms. Dragger captains who depend on blackback catches know to haunt the areas between Hallets and Hodges Rocks off Hyannis Harbor in March, waiting for the flounder to leave sanctuary and start their yearly voyage to the deep.

Someone *has* taught the boy—Boy. The drill is heavy for him but he holds it well, hunching one shoulder up to aim it true. Murdo points to a different hole and with his left hand starts a screw. The kid fucks up first time but no worse than Murdo—the bit slides off and with kid-weak pressure behind misses Murdo's finger and only makes a light score, and the boy immediately shouts, "I know, I *know!*" though Murdo has not said a word. Jumping with a weird intensity, three hops, while Murdo again starts the screw.

"I *know*," Boy repeats. He fits the bit into the screw's head, squeezes the trigger, squinting like a sniper and *filho da puta* if the screw doesn't squirm into that hole like it belongs there and the kid stops the drill at just the right instant, screw-head shining flush with the oak. "Yay," he yells and does the same manic hop, pogo-ing two inches off the floor in a circle, one arm half raised, "Yay-yay!" Eyes screwed shut, mouth stretched so wide in joy that everything in it, hills, buck teeth and valley, flattens to a sea horizon.

He sinks the next three just as clean and by the fourth Murdo is starting to have faith in that killer squint, the intensity of desire, if maybe less so in the jig he still performs with each success. He's gone past wondering about the boy and his handy dad, he's thinking elsewhere now, following his own eyes around the shop, workbench, sink/chemicals counter, hotplate, coffee machine; past the cabinet that hides his whiskey gear; to a bench at the northeast corner where he set up his etching tools, needles, pencils, *échoppes*; the ranked bottles of exotic inks, the American-French Tool Co. press with the hundred-inch flatbed—his most prized, and valuable, possession, bought distressed after a printing shop fire in Providence, and carefully restored with the help of Mass. College of Art's industrial-design geeks.

He's not really thinking the boy could help. It's simply that the low but constant stress Murdo's been feeling over the last few months, because he is foreman of this project and the scheme is not going well, means he spends less and less time on the work he aches to do and that he also is *supposed* to do, his side of the program: etchings. Tension from all of that is steady and rising, not crazy high but close—so that when it drops suddenly, when someone not himself actually makes a half-ounce-worth of progress on the hulk and he can think elsewhere for a few seconds, his thoughts zoom where the gravity of his trade draws them, to desk lamp and print table; where this morning, before barge-work got in the way, he scoured clean, rinsed, and set on the hot plate a nine-by-twelve-inch sheet of perfectly flat copper on which he would apply a thick black ground made in Paris, France.

It's not the ground Eby Noble used, a homemade medium he described as combining the qualities of "hard" ground, which accepts a very fine clean line, and "soft," which normally does not hold detail but can be drawn upon more freely with a pencil. No one is sure what Noble's medium was: He called it his "true" medium, and there's another project hanging fire, to recreate "true ground." But the hard ground Murdo's using now, a Charbonnel black, provides a good base to sketch Noble's barge as he's paid to do. This drawing will show the scow in chiaroscuro with a figure, Speed, measuring a frame, and the workshop door behind him open to the marsh.

He will use one of the finest tools he owns, a wood-handled etching needle sharpened to a tiny point, to scratch in details of the cattails and spartina grass you can see through the boat-door, just over the road's camber. He'll add scarves of mist, hinted like today, which will echo shadow in the workshop corners, dark calling to dark; plus shine upon the planks, on Speed's face, from work lamps.

Murdo's hands, without his knowing, tighten. The idea of drawing fills him with such energy that his heart rate jumps and it feels as if his arms might burst with the pressure of blood, and is this the source of the current he imagined, the stopped-up impulse to draw, to—

A bang, and rattle from the door. To one side, a clank as power drill hits deck. Boy, interrupted. From stacked tarpaulins behind the scow, a flick of plastic. The thought zips through: He goes to ground in tarps.

Murdo opens the people-door.

It is late afternoon and mist has clotted what light is left. A pine across the road ducks for cover, branches fuzzed. Up close the man seems solid by contrast, or maybe it's how he stands—Officer Gutzeit, known as "Gut" for reasons obvious even under his uniform jacket, the eyes of blue a different shade from the boy's, a pretty almost violet color that between long lashes transmits false codes of softness.

The eyes slide left and right, searching the shop. They gather steel to them, gauging what could go bad or has already soured. Murdo sees the still-hatch in his head, padlock and hasp, all snicked shut he's sure. Gut could have a warrant if someone talked, ah who has talked? But cops don't serve warrants alone, not Gut, especially not Gut—headlights from the idling cruiser braze Murdo's truck. And now a blue-gray SUV with a state police badge hushes past. Murdo watches it pull over a hundred yards down Fresh Holes Road. No one gets out.

"Gut," Murdo says. Flexes his hands twice. The cut throbs.

The cop looks at him now, chewing gum. Three chews, a pause, three chews, till Murdo cuts the rhythm: "Whassup?"

Two chews.

"Juvenile," Gut says finally. His voice is high considering the resonance his belly must provide. He pauses again, and seems to wince as he ponders whether to allow more info into the public domain. Another statie cruiser lurkdrives from the far end of Fresh Holes, sixty-nines with the first. *Filho da puta*, Murdo thinks.

"Behind Sea Street," Gutzeit says finally. "Kid attacked someone's car." Gut runs his hands behind him, he has white fingers like breakfast sausages on one of which their high school ring squats like a brass cockroach. Thumbs slide inside his belt to ease the strain. The cruiser's radio makes frog sounds. A pair of yellow rubber ducks hang from the rearview mirror.

"Said he came this way."

Murdo watches Gut's jaw. The rhythm of it interests him beyond reason. Relief is strong, this has nothing to do with him it seems, but relief seems less powerful than the tempo of Gutzeit's jaw. Two chews, a pause, another chew.

"Whaddya mean, attacked a car? And who, and what"—Murdo waves at the cruisers up the road—"is up with the staties? 'Cause of a *kid*?"

"You seen him?"

Chew. Pause. Chew.

"What do you mean," Murdo asks again, and shifts his glasses as if to see Gut better, hating himself for this, it's a gesture of nervousness, Gut always makes him antsy and while there's a reason behind it also feels like something jellied and weak has filled Murdo's joints when he does it—"attacked a car?"

Gut's jaw stops. It's in the pauses, Murdo thinks, that decisions are made.

"You seen the kid or not?"

Murdo's fists clench again. His left index feels like the bit is still embedded. Blood greases the near digits. He thinks of how the boy aimed that drill, lining it up with his eyes to sink it true.

"Kids ain't allowed in here," he says finally. "Look somewhere else."

Behind Gutzeit the harbor's lack of definition, without changing in volume, alters in quality. Scraps of sunlight litter water on the boatyard's southern side, though other pockets of Eel Pond still lack focus. On the pond's far shore a figure moves among the cattails. Some of the homeless, Murdo remembers, set up camp there once winter slacks its grip.

On the lagoon itself a wide, low skiff floats to one edge of the sun's reflection. It has the straight waist and stem of old-fashioned quahog skiffs. Murdo would have recognized it as Brian Fuller's even without the eel pots, the clam-rake handles sticking up like masts askew, the cloud of smoke from Phil's senile outboard; the figure, thin as a spider leg, jerking as he changes course for another quahog patch; the wedge of white plastic lurking on the edges of mist where shellfish warden Macabru, a former Army Ranger, keeps his target of choice under observation from the town's twenty-foot patrol craft.

In the foreground Gut shifts, peering at the workshop windows but not asking to come in as Murdo feared. Then he turns and climbs back in the cruiser. The yellow ducks bank and dance. Gut steers left and drives toward the statie cars.

11

Murdo keeps his eyes on Fuller, whose boat still lies within the tunnel of focus. The white wedge picks up speed, Fuller turns his head. Now the fisherman's boat changes aspect ratio as he guns his engine. Foam unfurls from the bow, reeling in smooth, converging lines from the harbor surface—it loses pixels in the side effect of fog. The force of contrast between soft focus and sharp sunlight does not reinforce the sense of held-back power that Murdo got when he fell off the chair, nor tweak the charge from his delayed etchings—but maintains them both, the way a transfer station keeps the current high along a powerline. He wrests his gaze from Eel Pond, walks back into the shop.

It's past dark and the house is hot with lights, the sense of high temperature always swelled in Murdo by the South Sea details, the twin "Fijian" archways like swords crossed in front, the ersatz Easter Island stelae flanking the wide Maugham-esque porch that is Murdo's chief argument against adding a lanai, it's the wrong exotic surely, Malaysian not Polynesian? But Una wants it and Murdo has always said she's got the right, she anted up down payment for the place, brings in the bulk of cash plus health insurance, vacation dough. She works hard as a spawning alewife and shoulders many burdens while he pursues what in bad times she calls "your gosh-darn arts 'n crafts." She twisted Cooper's arm to score the boat-shop gig for Murdo, against all history.

Anyway on cold late-March evenings with the first buds gloved in freezing rain it's not so bad to get a taste, looking at your alleged home, of coco-palms and sea so clear that fish five fathoms down look trapped in polyurethane.

He shakes his head to trash the image and checks the dashboard clock. He's forty-five minutes late and the drive is stuffed with cars: her Swedish SUV and Ken-Ken's German, Dog's big pickup with his dog, lowercase, barking at Murdo from the cab—and fucking Speed's creampuff van with the porthole, and varnished quarterboards announcing "Charles N. Herreshoff, Boatwright."

Another Audi to one side must be the architect's. Murdo is glad Dog and Ken-Ken are here, it will water down Una's annoyance, dilute his own now building against Speed, fucker can't come to work ever but when Una calls with a cocktails invite he shows up stat. She wants only the best for home improvement and Speed's skill with tools near matches his skill at vanishing. Murdo watches them for a few seconds through the living-room windows, Una with that oil-spill hair sweeping forward, half-tint glasses perched on up-tilt nose, lips pulled up to smile but not too much. When she laughs though her lips break through control and open her face like a shucked clam. Speed sprawls on the couch in a crash of yacht club semiotics—slacks, deck-shoes, button-down, martini glass—fumbling vaguely for the pack of smokes he's always giving up.

Ken-Ken, in side view, fools with the drinks table. Even the paparazzi shoot him from that angle, Kennedys drinking, whoring or both, but always at the bar: that hair-wave women of a certain age melt over because it's like Jack's, the sun-faded yellow shirt and jeans.

The matinee idol in slicked gray hair and hornrims must be the architect. Jesus, Murdo thinks, is he actually wearing a Hawaiian shirt? Woodsmoke stings Murdo's nose, she's lit the fire. It's raining harder. Walking in he finds Dog in the foyer rooting through a basket of DVDs, titles with women's names and words like "passion," "heart" and "eyes": Dog and Una share a taste for antediluvian chick-flicks.

"Murdo," Dog says, not looking up. "I seen most of these?"

"Call the manager." (Dog's middle finger.) "They been here long—I mean, that's the architect, right? C. Fairfield Tuttle?"

"You call him that."

"C.? Fairfield?"

"Architect."

Murdo cracks a knuckle.

"He'll do your lanai up real good," Dog says, grinning. "Along with the second airport terminal, the rotary fly-over, it's gonna look like fuckin' Honolulu 'round here pretty soon." He squints to read the fine print on a film called *Leaving Cairo*. Cairo is a redhead with breasts bountiful as the Nile.

"You wanna shot?" Murdo asks. "Not that," he adds, pointing at Dog's half-finished bourbon, "I mean the good stuff. I'm cracking the last run."

The basement stairs are off the kitchen, the counter of which opens into the living-dining area. Knowing he'll be spotted anyway, Murdo leans through, calls "Aloha, be right in, sorry I'm late." Everyone looks at him but Una, and Speed who's not in the living room, must be in the toilet. Ken-Ken calls, "Bettah hurry, Murdo, we're gettin' low on vodka." Murdo's foot crunches something, there are Cat-Starz all over the floor. And Vortex never spills her food—

Pancho, he thinks, just what I need. This is not topmost on his list of problems (but how the hell did he get in?).

Into the mold/cement/Tide fug of basement. Dog tromps down the stairs behind him, to the row of jugs lined on a pine shelf like fat constables, Murdo pushes away that hint of Gutzeit. Checks the labels, heaves a jug labeled "Olde Bilgewater Number 7" to the discarded dining table that he uses for this task.

"You'll like this one."

The cap does not come off easily at first and the bandage on his finger gets in the way but when he finally gets a grip, it opens with a bang and hootch gushes out, on his sleeves, over the table.

"What's that," Dog says, "Olde Premature Ejaculation?"

"*Funny.*" Murdo wipes himself.

"E-Z Cum," Dog continues, snortling at his own crack. "Old Jizzum." He opens the freezer, frees ice-rimed shot glasses from Devonian steak, eyes the maple-colored liquor. "Damn," he says, "my momma always said bathtub booze would kill me but right now it looks purty darn good."

"It is good," Murdo agrees. "Heavy on the malt maybe."

"How's the hangover."

Murdo shrugs. "How's Ellen Sofia."

Dog shrugs. "Can't live with 'em, can't shoot 'em." He takes a gulp of Number 7 and grunts, "Aaah. You know the new pastor at the Federated Church? I mean have you *seen* her?"

Una claims that married men, and women, like talking to Dog because it lets them live vicariously in the stories Dog tells of his frequent, often parallel affairs. Until recently Dog was trying to bed a wiry marine biologist who does research in Eel Pond, someone he met when he stopped by Murdo's workshop at the same time she did. Now Murdo sees in his head the Norman Rockwell steeple, worn and empty pews, Dog sitting on hard oak: the lissome pastor, robes hitched, riding him. Methodists in rut—he shakes his head.

Dog is heavy, slightly wall-eyed and his face is over-broad; not movie-star grade, and his lack of Me-Too ethics is a problem, but he makes jokes that bite like etching acid and above all does not pretend to look for much beyond fucking and boozy companionship, a discreet service that women, married or not, have small hesitation in ordering fast and easy as take-out pie. As Murdo turns toward the stairs Dog says, "Wait," and pulls from his pocket a thick fold of paper.

"The mooring petition, like I tole you."

Murdo sighs.

"I'm gonna get my permit back. And everyone who town council kicked out when they restricted mooring space. *And* to protest them hiring that Army Ranger to enforce—"

"Macabru?"

"He calls everyone who tries to moor their boats without a permit a boat Jihadi. Boat *Jihadi*! Can you believe that?"

Murdo notes his signature is fourth behind Joe Barboza and Eugenia Gomes from the Winterpoor area behind Sea Street, but thinks mostly of Una waiting, and Speed locked in for once. "Better go up," he says. Dog snaps his right arm up and down: whip crack.

In the living room only Una, Ken-Ken and the architect remain. Speed has gone. Piss-off churns Murdo's stomach once more but far less strongly than earlier with the cop, in a way he's been expecting this, in a way he'd be let down if Speed, unaccountably, were still here. On the local shopper butterflied by his empty seat a headline reads:

Police: Hyannis Ties
To Winslow Murder

As if summoned by the headline, sirens now yelp and wail, dragging up Greenwood it sounds like. "Somethin' going on tonight," Ken-Ken grunts, peering sideways through a window behind the drinks table. "I saw an ICE van on School Street?" He walks his drink outside. Smile like a T-square on Una's face, on this woman who until eight months ago still held Murdo naked, though not often; who promised to love him till death do us etc.

"So what happened," she says.

"I'm sorry, I had to take this kid home, you wou'nt believe, it was—complicated."

C. Fairfield is fly, he feels the currents. With paws delicate as a hamster's he unrolls a blueprint and points out details.

"This follows the contour of that rise to the north on your property."

Una has seen all this, she had it explained earlier but her eyes, which are the blue-gray of a statie cruiser, show a lot of white as they trace the turns of teak and tropical woods; her lips move in synchrony with the architect's. "Mister Herreshoff has said he can carve these totem motifs, um, they are modeled on Gauguin's wood carvings, you know? He even decorated his rifle butt."

He decorated butts? Murdo wants to ask, but refrains. C. Fairfield touches his earlobe with one finger when he makes a point. "Are you Hawaiian?" Murdo asks, and Una's head snaps round. She hitches her dress up, it had slid off one shoulder almost, Murdo reflects, as if she had started to disrobe for C. Fairfield—although

C. Fairfield, neat and presentable as she likes men to be, is also short. She has never been drawn to short men. Murdo at five-ten is on the low end for her. The architect's smile is a shutter folding open, closing again.

"No, I'm from Wilmington, North Carolina, originally." He touches his earlobe.

"I'm sorry," Murdo says, "the shirt, um, lanais, you seem to know a lot about—" he waves his hands and Olde Bilgewater sloshes on the kilim. C. Fairfield leaves soon after. And then there is only Dog, but Dog is as good as C. Fairfield when it comes to spotting the tidal rips that swirl up between Murdo and Una. His dog, whose name is erwinrommel, one word, lower case, ruffs a welcome as he goes outside.

A rumble of V8; another siren in the distance; and then the relative silence of South Hyannis at 7 p.m. in late March rolls over them like a motel wall-to-wall.

"A kid you said," Una says, ferrying martini glasses to the kitchen island. She brought out the Cahoon, Murdo thinks, noticing the painting hung where one of his own etchings usually holds pride of place over the sideboard. A pulse of rage tautens his abdomen. He hates faux-naïf but it's the priciest piece of art, if you can call it that, they own: a legacy, or curse depending on your point of view, from his mother's side. Una moves it from her study to the living room when she seeks to impress. The balance of power is in her favor though: because of his tardiness he cannot use that weapon now. He says, too eagerly, he hears nerves in the woodiness of his vocal chords, senses them in how he tweaks his glasses, in how he stands, "Yeah, it was weird, this kid just snuck into the workshop—I think he's retarded, okay maybe not retarded—"

"Differently abled." (The correction is automatic.)

"Whatever, a sandwich short of a picnic, right? But he wants to help put in a plank and shit I'll take anyone, nice enough kid anyway an' you know, he didn't do too bad! But then Gut showed up—"

"Who?"

"Gut. Ernie Gutzeit. The cop. An'—"

"The guy who, like, busted you when you were—"

"That one."

Another coast best steered clear of, Murdo thinks, and adds, "The kid attacked someone's car."

"He attacked a *car*?"

"What he said."

"The kid said?"

"No. The cop."

"So he arrested him? Gutzeit?"

"No."

"What happened to him?"

"The kid?"

"No, the cop. Duh."

"The kid. ... I took him home. I mean, I tried."

Murdo talks faster, his hands moving quicker also, he wants that slip in assumption to carry on, the idea that he took Boy home *before* Gutzeit showed up. Murdo would rather not lie to her but if she fools herself it's not his fault.

"He wouldn't tell me where he lived, for the longest time."

He sees the kid hunched deeper into his hoodie in the pickup seat, staring at the tools Murdo leaves lying around the front. The filthy cloth groundhog or whatever it is droops from one pocket, rain turns to glass eels on the windshield. Finally Murdo, losing patience, says "I'll have to take you to the police station" and *then* the boy—Boy—reacts, almost shrieking, "Cat-lee! *Fugg*! Cat-lee! *Fugg*!"

Boy guides him then, a quarter mile by road but only a few hundred yards if you walked the wetland to the area of rotting cottages off Sea Street that they call the Winterpoor: to a low ranch with vinyl siding, a patch of dead squash and runner beans, kids' gear—trampoline, swing set, bikes, lawnmower, most rusted to hell —plus a new van with a starred side-window and dents and scratches on the shotgun door.

The woman who comes out is a surprise. He was expecting Boy's mother but this woman is white-Irish and looks nothing like him. He expected also, because of the neighborhood, some cliché of American hardscrabble: soap-watching, nip-guzzling, lotto-playing, oxy-popping trailer trash, cellphone surgically attached, gaming-slackjaw much in evidence. But this woman has energy coming off her in waves and her mouth is set like a time-lock and her green eyes are so sharp that you look away for fear of getting cut, or he does at any rate.

Boy gets out and stands there, hunched forward, hoodie closing down his face. Murdo says, looking at the van, "Is this," and she says "Fuck *yes* goddammit and who the fuck are you," and he explains and she says, "Cops are looking for him, *I* didn't call 'em it was that bitch next door.

"He's in foster care with me," she adds, green searchlights raking him again. "Or was, family wants him home now god bless 'em they can have him." She says "family" the way she might say "diarrhea" only with more disgust, but she has her hand on Boy's shoulder as she says it and now he stands with head docked to a comfy-looking cove between her breasts and convex stomach.

The ranch is in poor shape but to the south of it stands a fine blue spruce. It is fifty feet high and probably as many years old and Murdo finds himself staring at the tree as she sheepdogs Boy into the house. The kid will get a cup of hot chocolate and most likely, Murdo thinks, if those eyes mean what they seem to, the rough side of her tongue before she drives him home. Fixing his own eyes on strata upon strata of black-green needles, dark limbs, squaw wood, and the degrees of shadow in between, he could cut them into coated copper later. ...

Una says nothing more about his being late. In the upstairs bathroom the waste bin holds exploded tampon wrappers and in the neat basket where she stashes them the stack of maxipads is down. As he pisses, Murdo looks out the small window, eastward where the moon clambers up the roofs of beach McMansions, expecting what he sees: nothing. It's overcast anyway but Una's period comes at dark of moon, there's some slippage but that is how it's been for close to a year. It does not affect this situation since Una's moods, unlike the ocean, are not much pulled by deeper rhythms.

He sits on the bed. Sips at his whiskey. She says, very calmly, "You know this lanai means a lot to me. I wanted to involve you but if you don't think improving this house is, like, worth your time I'll just do it myself."

He tells her he wants to get involved, he didn't mean to be late, and she replies, "Murdo you have to *learn*, you can't live like a college student."

He says, "Speed lives like a college student, it's four days he hasn't shown up for work this week at all;" and, too loud, "but he comes to your party and disappears soon as I show—"

She interrupts him, "Well you've done boatwork haven't you? You'll have to, like, keep filling in, it's part of the contract, your contract with CRAC." (Accent on the "your.") Her lips fine and set like a straightedge again. He is reminded, unexpectedly, of Boy's foster parent.

"That's not what I was s'posed to do on this project. I was supposed to make etchings, I was s'posed to teach etchings, it's about Eby Noble, it's about—"

"*Murdo*," she places a hand on his arm. "Listen."

She grips his arm harder, moving the elbow that hit the boat-shop's concrete; he tries not to wince. She looks at him level—sitting two feet away now. Murdo's wife wears lotion that smells of citrus, aluminum, root beer. He feels, without warning, utterly alone. Murdo has friends who have known him all his life, he has Dog, he has a raccoon who used to be a pet and now stalks him like a pervert. He has a wife, although for almost nine months they have been "reexamining" their relationship which means that he sleeps in the guest room now. He "has a life," as the Influencers say; he got skills.

Yet he feels, if he disappeared right now, no one would notice because he has somehow been changed, separated from the very people who until then made up that life. Almost as if the dark force he dreamed up in the workshop has taken power over this small stretch of Cape Cod and polarized him out. Isolated as he has been, no one would miss him much; there would be some rearrangement of schedules and Junie might wonder, eventually, what happened to her brother.

Otherwise it would be as if he'd never lived.

He shakes his head to lose that feeling. Was it her calm that shoved him off-balance? Una claims tardiness is symptom of a deep refusal in his character to become part of what she calls the real world. That's what she says when she rages at him. But what would it mean if she quit raging? Not forgiveness he's sure, not deeper understanding or acceptance. Like most people she rages about what she cares for. Her hand tightens on his arm again, releases.

"There's a watershed coming up, right? Like what, May twentieth?" This is part of her technique, she went to law school before switching to an MBA program, she asks only questions to which she already knows the answer to seek her witness's help in building the very trap that will ensnare him. "The hull has to be all done, right? Cooper's getting strict about this, he's like an animal sometimes, he wasn't a big fan of the marine-art school to begin with, I can't hold him off forever."

She sighs, withdraws her arm.

"I have to tell you," she adds. "Daisy called."

"Daisy?" His voice thins in surprise. Una's sister and his wife do not get along. The last time she visited, Murdo found Daisy drove him crazier even than she drove Una. It was long enough ago that his memory of her has grown hazy, a wash, not ugly—she doesn't look like Una up front but there is a shadow of resemblance, as if they had different nose and cheeks glued on identical bones. What beauty she possesses hides behind piercings and kohl; she gets up late, chain-smokes, waits on her husband, Cooch. Cooch is English and (Daisy says) does not have time for cleaning, shopping, or washing up since he spends fifteen hours a day on his laptop tweaking programs that control other programs that perform what he calls "flying quantum-encryption raids" to test the data-vaults in finance shops in London's City. These tweaks buy the sports car, the Willesden flat, the interactive video-worlds over which they both obsess when he's not online working.

"Next week," Una adds.

So this is why she did not punish him. She has favors to ask, herself. Murdo in turn feels calmer, though the taste of separation does not fade.

"She and Cooch," Una says—"thank god, they broke up."

"Really," Murdo says, and then, "Why? I mean, why have her stay, it's not as if—" but no answer comes.

There are battles half-engaged here, trucial issues to resolve, but in the standoff now achieved they can relax. She slips off her shoes with care. The pumps are blue and high-heeled, of leather with thin golden straps. She was in high spirits tonight, he can tell by the shoes. She wraps them in tissue paper before stowing them in a hanging shoe-caddy, then claims the bathroom.

He goes down to the cellar and gushes himself another Olde Bilgewater Number 7. Wonders now if Gut was using the Boy excuse as a way into his shop; and would the portly cop know a whiskey still if he tripped over one?

He asks himself again why the hell does Una put up with her sullen sis. How Pancho broke in; now there, he thinks, is a problem he must deal with soon. The raccoon, as far as he knows, lives in a stand of scrub pine and poison ivy just down the street. The thought of scrub pine brings back the Winterpoor spruce, and all the colors of that part of town: broken cars, lights coming on, kids yelling in the cemetery as they do fuck knows what.

"Cat-lee," if that is her name, he never asked, lives on Ridgewood, a thin asphalt track which straggles off to join smaller lanes behind the East Hyannisport Co-operative Market and Package Store. After dropping off Boy, he followed the dirt roads all the way around, and back to the main drag. On the market's porch, as he stopped for traffic, he saw Harold Crew, the old guy in a porkpie hat who lives in the rooming house on Camp Street; and Swear, who for three weeks after he gets his federal check spends his time at the dark end of the Foc'sle bar, sniffing oxygen from a green tank at his side. When the bar closes Swear just disappears, like Speed. Maybe he and Speed live together? Murdo smiles at the thought.

In Murdo's memory a cop car passes, very slowly, the pale face of its driver, not Gutzeit, turned toward Murdo. The wrecks, Una calls them, Swear and Crewe and the people like them who drift around Sea and Main, to the consternation of the Cape Realtors Action Consortium.

Leaning on the table, sipping Number 7, Murdo sees them all: Boy and Swear and Crewe, himself as well, alone yet together, sailing on the fucked black hull of his barge—drifting into the thickened fog, pursued by shellfish warden and coppers both, pulled by currents he has no knowledge of, into the salty spin-cycle of Nantucket Sound.

What do they dream of, these long, transparent fish? Put one in a petri dish and you can see through the glassy membrane each internal organ, heart pumping, gills pulsing. And if they dream—if dreams have substance you should be able to catch one there, behind the neural node, at the head of the 110 vertebrae characteristic of anguilla rostrata, the American eel—a dot shaded blue and green that perhaps, in sense, color or context, mimics (and it's this process that is relevant here) the place for which they're bound.

They are ten millimeters long, recently spawned with a million siblings in the limbic system of the Atlantic, deep Sargasso, northeast of the Leeward Islands. But for this larval eel, this elver, the dream paints a stream 2,000 miles away that smells deliciously of rotting sea lettuce, spit of oyster, resin of pine and maple, a smash of August sun. Sand too, quartz-limestone, mud. And how this glass eel longs for the riverplace and snaps its tail, spasmodically at first, and then with cleaner rhythm—the dream is lodestone, the means a

George Michelsen Foy

current, hot Gulf Stream flowing past Hispaniola, past Hatteras. The dream is love: love as defiance shouted, love as acceptance also of the tension between a more perfect union and a force arrayed to kill.

The glass eel grows as it drifts north and west while its siblings, by the hundreds of thousands, are devoured by ravenous dorado, bonito, skate. Survival is a matter of chance; of being, for no fathomable reason, an inch to one side of the silver rush, the shadowed maw.

Vaster risks accrue. The Gulf Stream is slower now than the eel's dream allowed for. The current's vast pump, fueled on wind, sun and salinity—trade winds pushing seawater up the coast, wind and sun evaporating the water, water growing more saline and thus heavier and colder, then sinking southward as lighter, warmer seawater flows north to replace it—the pump runs less smoothly. A rise in the climate's average temperature melts more ice to the north, which dilutes saline layers and fouls the contrast fueling the current's drive.

But the dream does not die. Late, but not yet too late—it's still March at this point—off Georges Bank the colors in the eel's neural node start to match the shade of bottom mud, the smack of flounder and what remains of cod, of glacial waste and spartina grass and winter-culled blue crab. Without knowing why, aware only that this is right, as right as it gets, the glass eel flicks its tail more strongly right, heads west; sniffing for the precise alkalinity of marsh love, crab sex, of tidal stream.

Into Nantucket Sound it swims, around Bishop and Clerks rocks. The tiny eel is churned but not destroyed by the propellers of an island ferry, rides in and out with the sigh of tides, the dream now thumping strong as joy in its system, past the Hyannis breakwater. Now taste is everything, the alkalinities must match. Other such flows have been betrayed by landfill, dams, bulkheads, but not this one. Glass eels have run this stream for thousands of years, ever since Cape Cod was formed by glaciers, and formed in turn this riverplace.

Well into Hyannis Harbor, under the drawbridge, through the pond and up Eel River beyond, a dream ecstatically and against all odds resolves into a morning's peace. Nitrates from septic tanks and golf courses, poisons from pharma waste and gasoline, dog shit from road runoff, cocaine and Dilaudid dumped five steps ahead of the Heat; if this eel lives, if the streams survive, perhaps the dream will alter to include these tags? They are tags only for now, not strong enough to kill with any speed, and in the ponds upstream the weeds are plentiful and good.

How do you start with this

How do you start this

How do you start the day with this? Una parks her car in the load-and-unload-only zone. She unholsters her smartphone, checks the time, and gets out, walking around clean planes of the new transportation center to the bus bays. Two aluminum mastodons, Plymouth & Brockton commuter buses, are lined up at the bays but no one's getting out.

Late as always. Traffic, probably. If they would just build that flyover she has written six proposals for already. She checks the P&B site online but they never list delays; walks restless, back to the car. Una has always been what they call a morning person, up early. When they lived in Silver Spring she was awake by five, curled up like a cat in the window-seat overlooking the azaleas, reading while everyone still slept. Being up before them all gave her a sense of independence, power even, she could take care of things while others were in bed: homework, makeup, laundry. She is like that still, or was until a few weeks ago. A restlessness has crept into her since then, maybe it's just plain lack of sleep, too much going on, too much of her life up in the air, these days she's comatose till the alarm rings at six. And now this.

This Daisy. (*How do you start with this?*) Una takes a twelve-pack of gum from her handbag, slips a stick from its foil wrapper.

She folds the foil and holds the stick briefly like a cigarette between two fingers until she pops it in. Chews briefly, gum is for breath only, she dislikes people who masticate while doing other tasks; once she has chewed the sweetness out she wraps the green wad in its cowl and drops it in a waste bin. Daisy on the other hand you couldn't get out of bed with a hand-grenade till maybe noon or 2 p.m. and likely that won't have changed.

Cold, this wind, it has a bite like a diamondback. In April, Maryland would be warm by now. Una groundhogs her hands deep into the pockets of her down vest—and with a snort and sneeze of brakes the Logan bus is here, trundling up an access road to the terminal. Thanks in part to Coop, the town finally put this place up to replace the old bus station at the foot of Elm. The contrast between the older building: dingy, jury-rigged, a combination of garage and hotsheet motel; and this large, modern temple to transport designed by Fairfield (the Polynesian archway is his signature), reminds Una of similar transitions in her life. How hard it has proved to cut the ties to previous versions of herself.

She used to arrive at Elm Street, summers, on the bus from D.C. via New York. The tiny waiting room was jammed with t-shirted, hungover students. Families with bawling kids sucked fried food into distended stomachs. Coop wants the old terminal knocked down to make way for a shopping arcade centered around a high-end seafood restaurant, an online retail-fulfillment hub, a marine-antiques and -art gallery. But the bus firm owns the property and will only sell for a price no one so far has been prepared to pay. They park their off-line buses on the apron.

She takes out her cell again; she'll text Coop, tell him she's running late—Hi b there in half hr, she prefers to text shorthand for the speed—and there, walking across the concrete, Daisy is. That thin form like a willow grown straight yet leaned against the wind; black hair dragged back, long ponytail; the cowboy boots and that eternal motorcycle jacket (could it be the same one she wore, what, seven years ago?) and the British Army haversack she uses as a handbag—it all feels just like the old bus station to Una. She experiences a rush of familiarity, simmered strong, and something harsher: something that feels like choking for air, as if the life she has built for herself here were a world in oxygen, and everything before and beside that was Una buried alive.

They hug, leaving a couple of inches of air between. Daisy looks exhausted. Her lips, top one slightly wider than the lower creating shade in the twin curves on either side of her mouth, always make her look vulnerable, as if she has just been beaten up; but today on top of that effect they are dragged down around the corners as well. Her eyelids sag with weariness. Through all the irritation, big sister still comes through, Una speaks with care in her tone, "You're tired."

Daisy shrugs.

"Long trip. Been a long month I guess."

"Daisy, I—".

"—well."

They both shrug, shoulders high, a little hunched. Because their shrugs are so similar they don't even notice how each duplicates the other. In the car Daisy says, "I mean, you putting up with, I know. Well."

"Well that's okay." Una puts the Volvo in gear. "We'll manage." Driving with one hand, with the other she fires her cell, chooses "drafts," sends Russ the text message she typed earlier.

"I was in London three days ago," Daisy says. "Then Brooklyn —place I tole you about, in Bed-Stuy? We were s'posed to split it but, like I said, Carol's boyfriend moved in."

"You told me."

"Yeah."

—

—

...

"So, Cooch," Una says finally.

"Cooch," Daisy agrees.

She looks out the window. The north end of the transportation complex is built beside the old railyards: A derelict locomotive and five passenger cars rust on weed-drunk sidings. A police cruiser stands beside the locomotive. A man sits on what looks like a pile of blankets near a train-car that reads "Erie Lackawanna." The cop stands over him, punching data into a computerized ticket-writer. Una's lips straighten to a line and relax almost at once.

"Cooch, believe it or not," Daisy says, "I'm not allowed to discuss fully." She stage-winks. "Official Secrets Act."

"You're joking?"

"Nope." Daisy runs her tongue over her lips, stretches bent arms behind her head. Her breasts push aside the lapels of her open jacket. They are medium-sized with small nipples and still firm under a t-shirt that reads "Sex and Drugs and Sausage Rolls." Una, whose own breasts are small, has always been envious of her sister's and she realizes that in some spelunked pocket of her psyche she has been hoping that Daisy's breasts would have begun to age by now, to sag like rotting plums.

"Well, I'm only exaggerating a little," Daisy adds.

For a second Una has to think back to what Daisy was talking about, to figure out what she's saying now.

"He did some encryption work for GCHQ, he sent me emails from his work computer" ... She shrugs again. "It's ... weird."

"I'm gonna have to go back to work," Una says, "I'll drop you off first. Murdo's off-Cape, you'll have the place to yourself, like, all day. You can sleep—"

"How is Murdo." Daisy's tone is like Indiana, mostly flat.

"Busy," Una says and her tone, Daisy notices, is like the part of Indiana where, amazingly, there are dunes. There is grit in it. "He's, like, way behind on a contract," she continues. "*Way* behind."

Daisy glances at Una. She is about to say something, then looks away, her lips nearly as straight as her sister's.

"I gave up smoking," Daisy says, a few minutes later.

"About time," her sister replies.

Outside the clouds have the color and solidity of gray forklifts, lifting and moving precipitation in numbing sequence, but within the Cape Realtors Action Consortium's offices on Main Street the mango color scheme makes the place resemble an ad for sun-cooked islands. It took longer than planned to show Daisy her room and equip her with towels, shampoo, toothbrush and soap; another aspect of Daisy she's forgotten, her sister never owns toiletries and relies on others to supply them. Anyway because of being late for work Una has two dozen text and email messages to sort. She is no more than halfway through emails when the door to her office opens, no knock. Una looks up, frowning; but it's him.

"Got a minute?" Cooper says.

"Not really." But now she smiles. Cooper tends to make her smile. He played volleyball in college and still plays at age 38 and he is lean, and tall—six foot two, he says, though she reckons he adds an inch, for effect—and taut in his motions, as if he's about to leap for a smashing drive. A personality always set to jump, always believing in the shot he must lunge to make, though he's missed it before; sure this time he'll "nail" it, swing the game.

He is handsome, she thinks, as well—a short exact nose, fore-head high and broad, chin that's just big enough to build a founda-tion for lips which are, she now reflects, the opposite of Daisy's. While his eyes sit maybe a tad too close together the lower lip is broad as a ledge, as solid as Daisy's is unsure, while the upper lip is thin enough to cut, with words if not in fact. He is good with words, almost as good as Una. He smiles, he was smiling as he came in, making dimples in an odd place, near the top of his cheek. She has known him long enough to recognize the dimples as a mark of excitement. His dark hair is thick and cut with great precision to mask thinning areas on top; his only white hair, at the temples, fans out 45 degrees as if designed that way. He shuts the door.

"Take a break. I won't tell."

"Coop—"

He leans over her desk. She smells Italian roast, plus something chemical and clean.

"It's the model," he whispers, faking conspiracy, which reminds her, against her will, of Daisy—*Official Secrets Act?*—she shakes her head.

"The *secret* model. It's ready."

They take the elevator to Lower Level 2, the cellar. The cellar conference room is rarely used except to store office supplies. The CRAC operations manager, a squinty, crew-cut man almost as tall as Coop, comes out its door as they approach. "Link," Una says; he nods at her, squints at Coop, and enters the elevator they just vacated. The cleaning lady, a thin, stooped, very brown Brazilian woman named Elsa Soares, is emptying an industrial shredder at the hallway's end. Cooper jokes with her: "Fourth time this week, Ellie, you can take a break once in a while," and the old woman's face folds into wrinkles, a shy smile.

When Ellie has disappeared they enter the conference room and Cooper locks the door behind them. He does not switch on lights. In thin illumination cut from gaps around the door she sees that conference tables have been shoved together. Something lies on top, covered with a drop cloth. "Chris's assistants brought it over last night," Coop says, still whispering. "They set it up."

"Chris?"

"Fairfield. Fairfield Tuttle."

She feels ridiculously jealous, of whom she's not quite sure.

"You didn't tell me."

Coop is rolling up the drop cloth.

"You ready? Turn on the lights."

She hits a switch, and draws her breath in hard. The model is much more realistic than she would have thought possible. It is an entire town, or the center of one at least, built of balsa houses three to five inches tall and carefully painted: miniature trees, in full plastic leaf because everyone wants every day to be summer on Cape Cod, harbor of blue-stained plexiglass. On Main Street one-inch people walk, enter shops, or simply stand around in awe of all the perfection. How happy models are, Una thinks, how optimistic. This is Hyannis from the airport all the way down to the outer harbor. Not Hyannis now but Hyannis in the future, Hyannis in some bling-struck dawn when all tackiness and squalor have been sucked away as by a giant vacuum. The Obama-era airport terminal is gone, replaced with what looks like a giant Tahitian hangar built of stainless steel. A five-story steel beach umbrella stuck in the lawn beside is the control tower.

The traffic jams of Iyannough Road are history in this land-scape. Instead Una sees an elevated roadway lobbing tourist cars like volleyballs from the Mid-Cape Highway straight to the transport hub, from which all corrupted tracks, shattered rolling stock and hobos magically have been expunged. Further south, the cheap cottages and shacks off the stretch of Sea Street that parallels Eel River marsh have disappeared, along with the half-assed Stewart Creek golf course just north of Winterpoor. In their place stands a complex of elegant mock-Colonial condos linked by parkland in oval shapes and sine-curve drives.

She walks to one side of the model, away from Cooper, touching with her right hand the plastic roofs, the cotton-ball bushes, while her left hand in the pocket of her skirt fingers her tepid smartphone. Her fingers brush the screen, wanting to form letters, but whom would she wish to text when Coop is right beside her? She breathes deeply again, wondering why a simple architect's model should make her feel better, subvert the coddled rage against her sister: at how Daisy basically invites herself, how she lives in general, fighting with all her might for goals no one else can formulate or care about.

Now, looking at this model, Una *doesn't care*. Something has cut her loose from Daisy's problems. The feeling has separate effects, or maybe it's her reaction toward the cutting loose but she also feels wetness start, a weight in her panties, a languor of cotton.

"So," Cooper says. Una looks up at him. It takes her seconds to recall what he's asking.

"It's beautiful."

"But? I can hear a 'but'."

She shakes her head. The image of his naked chest, zoomed in wide, flashes like a popup. Even around the crotch he has almost no body hair.

"Just ... something." Una shallows her breath, still trying to gauge her own reaction to the model. Touches another bush. "Well, town council hasn't approved this yet, the 40-B housing is, like, much bigger than what the zoning board saw and the airport flyover, the new runway, well you *know* about the funding—"

The dimples are like gopher holes. He walks around the table to her. He stops, twisting to its proper height a bush she bent. He leans to examine closely one of the townhouses, takes a CRAC ballpoint from his pocket and winkles out a strand of spider web, wrapping it around the pen's clip. He throws the pen, clean shot, into a corner waste bin. In almost the same motion he takes out a travel canister of Zap! bug spray and aerosols the townhouse, roof to cellar.

"When we announce the plan," he says.

"The plan. What you submitted—but town council didn't have," she waves her hand at the model, "all this. Even the Business Improvement District people didn't go this far." She shifts her weight to tauten her inner thighs against each other.

"No," he says.

"Then you mean—"

"The *new* Plan. What you and I talked about. Where we get everything we want. There's a way to do it."

He is behind her now. She is conscious of his smell: coffee, Zap! and laundry soap. Her pulse works faster. She starts to say something, her voice catches, she clears her throat, understanding now a further absence, one matched in various ways inside her.

"Also—the marine-art school? The school isn't on Eel River. Even in our plan, like, the *secret* one—"

"It's in this townhouse, here. On Gosnold Street."

He points, then folds his arms around her shoulders. She stiffens. Murdo will hate that, she wants to tell him. The school is meant to be near his barge, on the water, as it should be really.

"But," she begins.

"But what?"

"Nothing."

He is frowning.

"That's prime waterfront, Una," he tells her. "We're not gonna reserve dock space for some fucked-up barge and, you know, its half-assed school."

She looks away, wills her muscles to loosen. Thinking: this is not Murdo's project, after all. He is only a contractor, and if he drops another deadline he won't even be that, he'll have only himself to blame. The barge school is only there because she lobbied for it. Cooper didn't want him from the start, for a bunch of reasons.

Cooper's crotch is hard against her buttocks. Her eyes scan the model again, following Main Street, the shiny shops, the banners hung to flaunt the new Hyannis. The old bus station, too, is gone.

Una leans back against Cooper's chest.

Murdo walks in toxic fumes.

His eyes smart from varied chemicals with which the factory galvanizes or otherwise coats the nails, screws and fastenings forged in this place. He breathes through a scarf of Una's that he borrowed for the occasion. All flamingos and mountains, this one, but very soft, silky as her hair on his chest; the thought comes from no-place, stings somewhere, and is gone.

Bud Amaral strides mask-less beside him, down a concrete strip between the vats, cracking insults at his crew who lift racks of dripping steel plate from one vat and work the overhead crane to position them, still dripping, over another. The crane engine whines, metal plunges, more mist rises. The space is split between neon, gray mist, hellish shadows, and the men move in and out of darkness and light like the damned in Gustave Doré's etchings of Inferno. Hopping behind to keep up, the boy coughs, though Murdo did force him to wear a mask as well as a hardhat. The cough causes his hardhat to slip over his eyes, Boy leans backward to reposition it, the hat falls off.

"Your nephew, you said?" Bud yells over the hiss of molten zinc and the wayward banter of the men.

"No," Murdo yells back, "I didn't say." He coughs into the scarf. "It's like, a Big Brother arrangement" (though it isn't really, not officially). "Boy," he adds, his "name is—" but Bud has stopped at the heavy sliding door to the paint lab and, using all his weight, rolls it aside.

The Mattapoisett Marine Paint & Nail Factory Inc. should not exist anymore. It was built in the early 1900s and still produces boat varnish and fasteners in roughly the same way it did a century before, while similar industries have long since shut down or farmed out their production to Asian countries where labor's cheap and safety rules negotiable. Bud can hardly be reckoned a stickler for rules himself, he never wears a hardhat in defiance of orange "No Entry Without" notices on every door; was twice fined for this violation by OSHA. Bud makes the factory work by producing traditional boat nails, high-tech super-glossy spar varnish, and racing finishes for the tiny subset of boating population who can afford to own and maintain antique boats or wooden craft built in obsolescent styles. He demands top dollar for his products and because what he makes is of top quality, and because no one else bothers competing for such a niche market, gets what he asks for.

Behind the door hangs a thick fireproof curtain, which Bud shoulders aside. Murdo waits for Boy, who is still struggling with the hardhat. He steers him through the curtain, one hand on each shoulder.

The room beyond is long and narrow, built along the brick wall of the factory's end. A huge window set high is half covered in ivy and bittersweet but the vines let in enough leaf-stained daylight to color green the myriad glass jars of chemicals lined up on shelves hung over soapstone sinks. Tall glass-fronted cabinets, made of wood so thickly coated in varnish they must date from the factory's founding, line the end farthest from the door. They are crammed

34

with specimen bottles, each ID'd by its own yellowing label. In one corner stands an emergency wash-down sink plus shower. A long table in the center sags under its burden of pipettes, wiring, Bunsen burners, laptop computers, a state-of-the-art gas chromatograph, and numerous specimen bottles; also a coffee machine, toaster oven, newspapers, a baseball calendar.

"Gotta tell ya, I din get to this till yesterday," Bud yells—then, remembering he doesn't need to yell in here, repeats at a lower volume, "till yesterday. But I think it's close."

He takes a stack of cans labeled "Tung Oil/Alkyd Varnish 227," and sets it on the floor. He lights the burner under a clear retort half-filled with muck as black as devil-snot, as the night-sweats of dark energy. Boy hitches his pants high with one hand, leans over the table toward the retort, so far that Bud has to nudge him clear of the flame with one hand.

Murdo, watching the boy, feels a volunteer affection wash over him, which he's aware is in part fondness for himself because as a kid he too would have loved this gimcrack laboratory—hell he loves it now, all the "Igor, hook up the *deathray!*" chimes it rings, the fascination that seems coded into the DNA of males, young ones anyway, for things you can affect by trick and fire: stuff that mixes and changes colors; that bubbles, steams, blows up. Fascination for power, he reckons—but also a love of how the world fits together and how a boy, in turn, fits into that.

Maybe that nostalgia for how he once was explains in part why he let the kid back into his workshop two days after the Gutzeit incident; has let him in almost every afternoon since then—doesn't want to think about it. He can already sense there will be complications. Doesn't want to dilute the pleasure he takes in coming to grips with printing—the search for Eby Noble's "true ground," the substance he spread from 1926 onward on copper plates to etch in such detail the ships he loved; that Murdo loves, too; boats for sure but above all the visual iambics of etching, stealing a chunk of the waterfront and translating it, hard line by thin dash onto ground and metal and then, through acid and ink and a process of negative transference, to paper. Not just any paper either, but thick sheets of hand-pressed linen rag, of a texture that excites fingers and soaks up the ink exactly and no more ...

Much faster than Murdo expected, the dark glop starts to quiver and bubble. The excitement in him resonates with the beaker, it quivers in his stomach. A smell of road tar, piss, and chestnuts wafts from the retort. Boy, leaning surreptitiously toward the beaker, gets a noseful of the smell, jerks back in disgust. The hardhat's visor falls on his nose again. Bud picks up the retort and pours a half-cup of the mix into a glass tray.

"Try it." Bud hands over a mixing paddle.

Murdo pokes the devil-snot. It is the consistency of loose toffee. He drips it onto a second tray and spreads it thin. The ground hardens fast, within twenty seconds Murdo's stick gets stuck on the tray's bottom.

"Too hard? Okay." Bud searches around the clutter. He opens a can and pours clear liquid into the retort, which he then mixes and sets on the burner. Boy is hitching up his trousers with both hands now, head thrown back so he can peer at what the two men are doing from under the hardhat's fallen visor; hopping slightly, one foot to the other.

"Bathroom's in the office," Bud tells him.

"It's not that," Murdo says. "He's just excited."

"Whatever," Bud says. "It's forty-eight percent bitumen."

"With the rosin?"

"Like you said." Bud points to a jar labeled McMurdo's Ground/AR/No. 23.

"The resin is what's making it harden up so fast." Bud takes another paddle and stirs the mixture in the retort. "Need more time to get that even—"

"I kin do that!" The boy points to Bud's paddle. He is almost shouting.

"No," Murdo tells him, his voice low, already he knows the kid listens best to lower tones. "This is hot. *Dan*-gerous."

"I kin *do* that!" Boy hopping harder now. Bud leaves the paddle in the beaker. He takes out a pack of cigarettes and lights one, watching Boy curiously through the bloom of smoke.

"Kinda excitable, ain't he?"

Boy takes one hand off his trousers and pushes the hardhat so far back it falls off his head. Murdo should see it coming but he is distracted by the crack the hardhat makes hitting the floor. By the time he realizes what's going on, Boy has lunged forward to grab the hot retort. Murdo, reflexively, thrusts out a hand to stop him. Boy's hand, deflected, knocks the retort off the burner's stand. By some miracle when it hits the table it does not break, but gobs of molten ground splurt through its wide mouth onto table, floor, and nearby trays and beakers.

The boy freezes, staring at the mess. His forelock veils one eye. Then he spins, stumbles, almost falls, and runs toward the lab's far end. He squats against a cabinet, head sunk, hair over both eyes now, hood pulled over his hair, rocking back and forth. Bud picks up the beaker with a hot pad. He looks at Murdo, frowning.

"What is he, a retahd?"

Murdo is angry at Boy for making this happen; pissed at Bud for the word "retard." He is about to snap at the plant manager, but holds back—realizing even before he does so that Bud probably didn't mean it literally since Bud calls everyone "retard," as well as moron, idiot, maggot, and shit-for-brains, it's part of the Bud lexicon.

Plus, Murdo has to admit, Boy *is* a "retard," or "mentally challenged" as Una would say, although neither term paints a true picture of whatever crashed this kid's brain, probably as an infant. Murdo walks over to the boy and as he gets closer hears a sound, half breath half tone, that resolves when he kneels beside the kid into a soft, staccato keening.

"Hey," he says. "What?"

Boy's cheeks bear a film of curved water. He clutches with both hands the gopher-bear, holding it so hard that if it were a real animal its neck would break. Internal stuffing is visible through a half-open zipper, the animal has a pouch; is it, Murdo wonders with no relevance at all, a *marsupial* gopher-bear? Dark streaks of ground, half wiped away, alternate with bands of red and scalded skin on Boy's left wrist, just below the palm.

"Shit." Murdo adjusts his glasses to look closer, and touches the boy's wrist. "That hurt?"

"Shid," Boy repeats in the same staccato tone. "Shid-shid-shid!"

Murdo pulls him upright and half steers, half pushes him, the kid does not want to go, to the half-shower half-sink of the washdown station. Boy, spotting the oversized showerhead and chain and lever, putting two and two together his way, yanks the chain and both he and Murdo are immediately drenched in freezing water, Murdo gasping and cursing, Boy keening twice as loud and gasping too while Bud, one hand still holding his cigarette, starts to laugh, and coughs, and laughs and coughs again.

Excerpt from Eby Noble's notebooks, 3 March 1935

All of my life I have tried to preserve the texture of a life that is disappearing, the work and people of the northeast coast. I do not want only to record the beautiful hulls and masts and rigging, the perilous and elegant movements of men and sea, but also the most basic textures: the rankness of salt water filling bilges, the soupiness of hot tar, the rawness of skin around the knuckles of men who haul soaked manila, furl rough canvas, heave baulks of timber for a living in the depths of a New England winter. How to convey in copper and ink the thrum of a line that holds the giant, heavy-grained mainsails of a three-masted schooner against thirty knots of wind. That is why I spend my days in the dinghy, sculling from wreck to wreck, sketching gray, weathered wood and broken capstans, rowing back to my barge to transfer the sketches to copper by the light of lanterns. I am considered mad by the watchmen on the docks ...

My difficulties in transcribing these lost ships before they disappear forever are matched by the continuing problem of what ground to use. I have tried so many different compounds this winter, so many mismatched materials, from English beeswax to gum Arabic to road tar. They coat the copperplate, and on all of them I find a drawing surface, but I have not yet found the mix that gives me both the crispness and the versatility I need to best represent the complexity of these ships. The grounds go up and down the spectrum, some so hard they stiffen my line, some so soft I lose definition. Just this morning I was performing another experiment, adding 2 oz. of violinist's rosin and 1 of bookbinder's glue to the mix I used yesterday: asphaltum, linseed oil and mutton tallow. The glue contains shellac, which will harden well. Yesterday's batch, # 32, was a little soft, and I fear what will happen to the running rigging on the "Sarah Anne Winslow" if I use it again. The whole point of that etching was to bring out a second level of patterns in the web of rotting cordage by her mainmast.

I fear it is all blurring together. I dread losing my deep sense of the work, which lies in how such tragedy—the elegance in hulls that found a third way between strong wind and violent sea now left to fall apart in a disused harbor—can turn to grace; the way their lines change, bringing out the hidden ridges in oak, the arc of sagging shrouds. ...

Different forms of bookkeeping exist, Murdo reflects as he drives back to the Cape, and he has just used three of them with Bud Amaral. On-the-record accounts: In the bed of the pickup he carries three boxes of boat nails, the kind cut in wedges from the galvy plates he saw dipped earlier, they look like pointed rectangles in cross-section. These are for the scow, of course, and will be billed to the boat-school.

Then, the accounting of affinity and mutual interest, because Murdo and Bud have known each other since high school. Bud does not charge for fooling around with printer's ground. He got hooked on the Eby Noble project because he's interested in boats or he wouldn't be doing the job he does; and of course the boat-art school is a customer.

And finally there is off-the-books accounting. Murdo brought Bud two bottles of Olde Bilgewater Number 5, the vintage from three summers past, of which Bud is fond. Sometimes Bud gives him money for the hootch and sometimes not. Sometimes Murdo barters it for stuff he needs, glass tubing or beakers for the still. Both understand how this accounting works and keep track of it in an area of their brain, not too far from the subconscious, where lurk the occult thoughts.

Boy slumps in the shotgun seat, sniffling. He holds his left wrist, carefully salved and bandaged by Bud, with his right hand, stares fixedly at the bandages. Something in how he looks at the wound, Murdo thinks, indicates he is proud of it, as one would be of a scar earned in battle. As he steers the truck through a cool April evening and over the Sagamore Bridge, Murdo realizes he doesn't know how to work Boy into his accounting categories. In the workshop he exploits this kid who, for the first hour at least, is happy to help out with little stuff, sweeping, humping planks, as long as he can get a crack at the power drill.

Murdo has talked to the boy's uncle, the only adult he found at home, to let him know the kid hangs around his shop. The uncle didn't seem to care, so Murdo assumes this unofficial internship helps the kid's family by giving Boy something to do. Free babysitting. Maybe Boy learns something as well—

A ringtone cuts that line of thought. Another text from Una. "Late mtg can u pikup mlk, egs." He wonders for the thousandth time why Una has to use this telegraphese when she types as fast on her cellphone as any high-school kid; wonders also why the hell

Daisy can't pick up mlk, egs. Una's sister has been here ten days now and he has barely laid eyes on the woman. She's asleep when he goes to the workshop, and when he comes home all he sees is a shadowy form, wrapped in a black, hooded poncho, a garment of black cashmere so long it looks like a cloak, playing a videogame called "Nekropolis" with cans of English ale lined up beside her. She never wants dinner or talk, which is a good thing he supposes because Una's always at the CRAC office and Murdo's hours, split between scow repairs and printmaking and occasional whiskey business, are as full as a bookie's in Super Bowl season.

"Sell a phone?" Boy says.

"What?"

"Sell-a-phone?"

"Oh. Yes. Cellphone," Murdo says, stashing it in his pocket. "Mine."

"My hand, it hurts."

"I know, Boy. It'll get better."

He'll have to enter Boy's house this time, explain what happened. The uncle's lack of interest will probably extend even to this but maybe the mom's around—although Boy, when questioned, never seems to know exactly where. Murdo wonders how he will explain it: "I took Boy to a hundred-year-old paint-and-nails factory run by a guy I supply bathtub whiskey to in Mattapoisett and your kid knocked over a hot beaker of experimental printing ground"?

Probably not. He glances at Boy.

"How come you do that?" he asks, but gently.

The boy says nothing.

"I mean, just jump? You jump at stuff, like that—that pot of hot stuff?"

Murdo's irritation has not dissipated but now that it has washed through the mental gears he realizes he is mostly pissed off at himself. With the exception of print-drawing and etching he is not very efficient in his own life but on top of that he lets people get away with things. He lets Speed disappear, he lets Una turn their house into a set for *Blue Hawaii*, he lets her sister camp like a foreign army in the living room, he lets Boy play with hot equipment. Just three days ago, when Murdo showed him how the flatbed press worked (he even printed out an image using a scrap plate—a portrait of Una, drawn from memory, unsuccessful), Boy pulled at one spoke of the star-shaped wheel that turns the roller; it was sheer luck no one's fingers were on the bed.

The kid shifts in his seat, still holding left wrist in right hand.

"I just," Boy says, "I just seen it. I kin *do* it."

He starts crying again. His hair, like Murdo's, is still wet.

"Shit," Murdo says. There are no streetlights on this stretch of freeway, his headlamps tunnel into void; and Murdo gets that feeling once more, of forces lined up in the dark, waiting to go into motion, he has no idea how or why but he is sure it will not end well when it happens.

"Shid," the boy repeats, sniffling. "Shid."

Murdo fishes out his cellphone and hands it to the kid.

Boy lives in the area of cottages—to the south of Walton Avenue and west of Sea Street, between Our Lady of the Pines cemetery and the marsh separating Eel River from habitable land—known as "the Winterpoor." Here small half-Capes and pre-fab ranch houses lie scattered around ravaged lawns, rusted cars, rotten fencing. Power cables swing from crooked telephone poles to sagging eaves. Some of the satellite dishes are green with mold. Closest to the marsh, armies of cattails in golden, military ranks invade play areas, vegetable patches; lanes of potholed asphalt peter out in seawrack. The nation right now rides an upswing after pandemics and rougher economic times but cycles such as that don't affect this stratum of Cape society, for in summer there are always vacationers, albeit of varying income brackets, and therefore always work, if only shit-work: house-cleaning crews, construction help, waiters and bar-backs, motel night-clerks.

In winter, the work dries up.

Otherwise, all the time and in between, there is survival, whatever it takes: Goodwill sneakers, SNAP and WIC vouchers, the dole, the ER, booze, B&E, meth and opioids and dope dealing. For those pursuing illegal activities the area is optimal for it combines a fair density of inhabitants, few of whom much like cops, with a backstory of cattails and cemetery and (closer to Hyannis) a ratty golf course across which one could, if need be, flee on foot.

No one remembers exactly how Winterpoor Lane, which runs west of Hiramar Drive in the heart of south Hyannis, originally got its name. One optimistic story claims it refers to an ancient and little-known herb. That the name came to define the area because of how it fit the neighborhood's realities is contested by no one. The Winterpoor, to the rest of the town, conjures an image that mixes a marshland apt to flood in winter storms with a perceived baseness of the people here. The Barnstable Police Department pays more attention to what goes on in the Winterpoor than to activities in other parts of town, and neighborhood kids sometimes play the window game: counting how many lights abruptly blink out along the lane when a police car whoops up its siren nearby.

The ethnic flavor of the Winterpoor changes on its surface. The latest influx is usually obvious: most recently, refugees from Syria, Somalia, Ukraine and Mexico, plus a handful of Macedonians. But spend time here and every day becomes a core sample drilled into the history of the nothing-left-to-lose: Guatemalan, Jamaican, Brazilian, Cantonese, Cape Verdean, Alabama black, Portuguese-Azorean, bog Irish, swamp Yankee, Acadian French, British zealot, Wôpanâak Indian.

A blue-white cruiser is parked, lights out, in the cemetery near the East Hyannisport Cooperative Market and Package Store. Murdo takes a right onto Ridgewood, the road of broken asphalt leading to Hiramar and Winterpoor Lane. He follows the lane west to Lusitania Circle and the boy's home. The cop is lost to view behind patch-paint fences and middle-aged maples long before Murdo's truck pulls into Lusitania. The circle is a track of sand and weeds surrounding crabgrass and ringed in turn by three half-Cape-style cottages. All of these, Murdo gathers, belong to Boy's relatives. Two of the cottages are cedar-shingled, not a bad job, with white trim and asphalt roof. The third is vinyl-sided, with an old-fashioned tin roof and a small, one-window addition that is all tarpaper.

Boy's house is the farthest shingled half-cape. Its trim peels off in curls. A Tacoma on concrete blocks occupies half the driveway and a fiberglass boat with a gash in its side the rest. The boat's name is spelled out in PO-box letters glued on the transom: DIXIE DUE. Three kids' bikes, two of them rusted out, a plastic wading pool, a lawnmower with the top taken off. Murdo knocks on the storm door, cracked plexiglass falters under his knock. The door behind it opens fast and suddenly.

"Where the *hell*—oh."

It's dark now, the inside is lit from an adjoining room; a lean man in a white t-shirt and jeans stands in the doorway. He has a thin dark beard and a high forehead roofed with hair that has been dyed red and greased back.

"It's you." The uncle cants sideways, right shoulder against the doorframe. He holds one hand delicately before him, like an instrument too precious to use; the other holds a smartphone. "Where's pain-in-the-ass."

"I'm sorry?"

The man's head doesn't move.

"Pain-in-the-ass. Mow-ron. Right? You know."

Murdo pauses for a second. He is getting angry for the second time in two hours. He does not enjoy getting angry, he has no talent for it.

"Sonny," the uncle says finally. "Calls hisself Boy."

"I took Boy with me, he came over. You said it was okay."

"I did?"

"Well, yeah." Murdo takes his glasses off, polishes them on his shirt, puts them back on. "I talked to you, right here, I asked you if he could hang out, gave you my cell number—"

44

The man looks him up and down.

"She-it," he says finally, "cool with me I guess."

Murdo forces himself not to cross his arms, which he also tends to do when he's angry.

"Better 'n what he usually does when he's upset," the uncle continues. "Goes 'n hides with some homeless asshole in the marsh?"

The uncle turns and walks into the next room, lifting the phone to his ear. "It's Sonny," he says. "Call ya back." A light comes on: clock in the shape of a golf bag, seahorse wallpaper, dishes in a plastic drying rack. He turns around to face the door. Boy steps around Murdo, shuffles inside without a word, head down, left hand still holding right. He banks left around a partition. Footsteps clomp heavily upward.

"Ya got yer stuffy?" the uncle yells up the stairs.

Murmur back. Murdo thrusts his hands in his pockets.

"Just need to tell you," Murdo says, "ah, he scalded his hand."

The man is looking at his smartphone screen.

(After several seconds): "Wah?"

"His hand. It got burned. Not serious. I was using a hot liquid—"

"He burned it?"

"Yes. Or scalded. Not serious, as I said—"

"It's never serious," the uncle says, head still bent, gazing at the phone. "Till he has to go to the ER. Right? Then it's serious—thousand bucks worth o' serious."

"He won't need the ER." Murdo's voice is level, cool; he is proud of his ability to keep it that way, though the sense of dark forces he felt earlier never left his consciousness, and now they have multiplied to include this rotten house and the kind of man who calls a kid "moron" within earshot. It's the feeling he got in the shop right before Boy showed up the first time, he knows it's the same now by the way it floods him all at once, more lavishly than it did while he was driving, brutal as a levee break, a tide of black wrongness that shorts and misuses power. It electrocutes his life, this idea he has of it.

"It's just a burn." Murdo has to make an effort to talk loudly enough. "Is his mom around?" The uncle's head snaps up, swivels to stare at Murdo straight. He has a chest tattoo, some sort of claw that disappears down his shirt.

"I got your number, in case," the uncle says and without warning shuts the door three inches shy of Murdo's nose.

Murdo stands there for a few seconds. Finally he draws a long breath and goes back to the pickup. He looks back at Boy's home; upstairs, one window is now lit. He drives halfway around Lusitania Circle, and brakes. By the cottage of vinyl-siding, between the house and a tiny vegetable patch, a late '80s American sedan is parked, and beside that a pickup new enough to stand out in this zone of $3,999 "pre-owned" cars. Murdo recognizes Dog's truck before he clocks SNOW LANDSCAPING painted on the door.

Without thinking more he turns onto the nearest patch of grass and switches off the engine. He gets out and walks to the front door, wondering at himself; he rarely barges in on friends, let alone strangers. But he needs to cut away the black architecture and seeing Dog will help. And, while he dislikes anger and all its shadows, he ought to learn something about this family that seems to treat its backward child with disinterest if not outright neglect and this is the grandfather's house, Boy said that a few days ago, the way Boy says things, real short: "Gan'pa"—pointing.

Murdo also is aware that the sense of seeking home, of snapping back to base like a rubber band loosed backwards, is not in him tonight. It's too early for Una to be home. Instead he'd only see her weird sister profiled against the laptop screen, and when Una does come home she too will have her screen lit, diving straight back into email. Or else he or Una will each trip up on some idiosyncrasy of the other's and they will squabble; it seems as if their relationship can be boiled down to what they fight about now and how, with agonizing slowness, they climb out of squabbles after.

They used to end up in bed after fights, the arousal of anger in them having triggered other drives. Murdo cannot remember the last time that happened. He and Una haven't had sex for almost a year. He shakes his head to clear his thoughts. Voices sound inside the cottage, loud, in argument; it feels for a moment as if this cottage echoes Murdo's thoughts about his own house. He knocks, too loudly.

The man who opens is very tall and stooped, with skin the color of Boy's, of Murdo's own, though the color is complicated by a profusion of wrinkles. His hair is lush, white and shiny as zinc pigment. A gray mustache, very thin, roofs a thin judgmental mouth. He has librarian's spectacles and half-opened eyelids with eyes of blue-jay hue, like Boy's. Murdo knows this man. Joe Barboza once owned Twin Joes' Villa and Bar on Old Mill Road where Murdo and his buddies drank before they were legal. Joe looks at him with bartenders' eyes—can't remember the name, exactly, but he'll recall what Murdo drinks, or used to: vodka and cranberry, Black Russians. Rolling Rock.

"I'm McMurdo Peters," he begins, "I," and Dog's voice breaks in from the room behind, "It's okay, Joe, let him in."

"This is a private meeting," Joe says slowly.

"It's okay," Murdo says, "I only came—"

"Joe," Dog calls again. His voice is thick. "You know him: Murdo?"

The tall man does not move.

"I'm sorry," he says.

"I don't want to come in, I just wanted to ask about Boy—about Sonny."

Joe looks at him for a few seconds. He has white eyebrows too. They lift, very slowly.

"You're the fella Boy's been visiting," he says finally.

"The boat-school guy," Dog says. Another voice cuts in, high and sharp, "Tell him come in for god's sake, you're lettin' in the cold."

Finally, Joe steps aside.

The room Murdo enters takes up more than half the cottage. It is low and wide and crowded. Two couches, one of plush chintz that looks as if someone slashed it with a knife, the other of sprung wicker with mismatched cushions, take up two walls. More wicker in armchair form; hook rugs, a large, flat-screen TV tuned to a reality show, are angled to honor a monstrous bar made of fat bamboo that blockades the room's far end. The bar's counter holds a cash register, multiple bottles, and Murdo's eyes widen slightly as he recognizes one of his Olde Bilgewaters, the Number 5, half full.

An enormous stuffed swordfish hangs overhead, a dry aquarium behind the bar is filled with plastic fish. Dog stands at the bar next to a short black man Murdo recognizes from Twin Joes': Harold Crewe. Crewe's buddy Swear, another Twin Joes' veteran, sits on the wicker couch, hunched over as if unused to the comfort of cushions. With one hand he holds to his nose the shiny tubing that carries oxygen from a green steel bottle nestled cozy beside him on a cushion printed with mallards.

The biggest wicker armchair enfolds in its shadows a tiny woman with hair whiter and skin darker than Joe Barboza's. She reminds Murdo of a thin squirrel, if a squirrel's face could carry wrinkles deeper than a topographic map of Nepal; if its body could wear nylon slacks the color of marsh mud and a red wool sweater with Santa's sleigh knitted in. She rocks back and forth in the armchair, her feet eight inches off the floor. The rhythm reminds Murdo of Boy's hopping except that there is nothing backward or as Murdo's grandma used to say "obligated" about Eugenia Gomes. His grandmother knew Eugenia from growing up, in their early years, not far from here, on Great Western Drive.

Most people in Barnstable know Eugenia. She is an amateur politician and professional gadfly who rarely misses a public meeting or the opportunity to voice her views, which usually veer toward conspiracy theory and the belief, not entirely unjustified, that town council is perpetually and secretly trying to screw the poor, the dark, the Lusophones. Una hates her guts and so does Cooper. This would make her more interesting to Murdo if he ever thought about her, which he does not. Joe Barboza says, "Time for a break anyway." Dog is saying to Eugenia, "We can *talk* to him, I mean, he's been in on the mooring revolt from the start."

"You gonna talk trouble," Crewe announces; he slowly pushes back the straw porkpie on his bald head, and takes an even more relaxed sip of his drink; "talk *soft*."

It brings Murdo back, all this: Twin Joes' Villa, where Crewe and Swear sat at the bar, evenings, for as long as Murdo can remember. An ancient wooden phone booth stood beside their corner, at the end of a counter made of elbow-polished oak. The joint was all shadow, of an umber deeper and more delaminated even than the counter or its occupants. Crewe's statements often sounded as if he were repeating lines by Faulkner out of Brer Rabbit, but they were sharp like thorns in that they grabbed your mental sleeve after you passed and made you pause, made you think about them a bit. "Ain't no problem not solved by a good drink," he once told Murdo, "ain't nothing solved by it either." The end result of your thinking usually meshed with that kind of wisdom in that it propelled you toward another drink even as you sought to figure it out. The fact that Crewe was well aware of the "homespun philosopher" cliché never bothered him or anyone else. Even Una thought Crewe was smart, an understated genius she called him in the days she too frequented Twin Joes'. And here, by some miracle of magic and nostalgia, is a Black Russian in a highball glass, with a green plastic palm tree to stir it. "*Min skål*," Swear cackles, holding his tube out of the way so he can take a sip of his own drink, "*din skål, alle vakre pikers skål*."

"What?" Eugenia says.

"Norwegian," Joe explains.

He moves away, favoring his left leg. Dog reaches high to touch Joe's shoulder.

"He signed the petition."

"People always welcome from the old days," Barboza says in doubt-soaked tones. Slowly he turns again, leaving open the question of which people he's referring to. He raises his arms, almost like a blessing, like some swamp pope Murdo thinks, except that

Joe Barboza never does anything quite like anyone else. ... "But here we're talking about breaking the law," Joe continues. "I'm not sure I agree with that as yet. An' if he's with the boat school," he continues cryptically, "ain't he with the people you're talking about?"

"He's married to 'em," Eugenia offers. "Una Bell, that's his wife. That Cooper guy she works for, at CRAC—never seen a man so scared of bugs, he sprays everything with that spray, one with the gas mask on the mosquito? You know?"

"Zap!" Joe Barboza says softly. "Zap."

"You can win three million dollars, as long as you jump that turnstile *before* the Dobermann—and answer *this* question!" the TV blares.

After a minute has passed, during which the Dobermann gains the upper hand, Murdo says, "I just wondered where his mom and dad are. Boy. Sonny, whatever."

Joe Barboza stares at him, then looks away.

"He come see me sometime, in da marsh," Swear says. "Boy—yust, when he's scared 'n stuff ..." The oxygen dispenser burbles.

"*Who* ... won the top prize on the show, *Screw Your Co-Worker*, in its third season?"

"That guy got three hundred thousand," Crewe comments. "Greed makes you forget what you got already."

"It's just cuttin' off buoys on the moorings." Dog turns to Murdo now. "Switching some of the fat-cats' boats around, right? Maybe put a little rope around Macabru's prop?" Dog chuckles, takes a swig of his drink, which looks like straight Bilgewater; chokes, starts coughing—it reminds Murdo of Bud.

"Din go through the right channels, didja," Eugenia says, and jams a thumb in the side of her mouth to hold her dentures in. "There'sh a waiting list, an' registration—"

"That's not the point." Dog clears his throat, puts his glass on the bar noisily enough to attract attention. "So many people have moved here from off-Cape, the waiting list's so long by the time they get to you you're *dead*. Anyways, my Dad—"

"Of *coursh* it's not the point." Her dentures now solid, Eugenia removes thumb from mouth and leans so far she nearly does a forward roll off the armchair, and catches herself. "Point is, that's a whole campaign they got themselves, you know they do, clean up downtown, get rid of people can't afford the rents or marina moorings. Harbor's part of that. You think"—she leans back almost as far as she leaned forward and repositions her spectacles, staring at Murdo now—"you think yer little boat-artist school isn't part of that too? What's your wife tell you, anyhoo?"

Murdo stares back. A vibration happens in his pants, followed by a quick text jingle: Una. He ignores it. ("Gt mlk?" most probably). He picks up the Black Russian now. It's as if he was waiting to feel welcome here before he accepted the drink and in truth he must be in a way, not welcome but involved, because Eugenia mentioned the school; because Joe does not seem to agree with Dog, which is how Murdo himself often feels about Dog's projects.

The drink is three-quarters vodka, lubricated with coffee liqueur, it goes down like a mouse down a snake's gullet, kicking all the way. Almost immediately he feels reckless. "I got to admit," he says—it's the part of him that wants to be social, wants to be liked or at least respected, it happens when he drinks Black Russians—"there's a different feel to this town all of a sudden." And Dog says, "Damn right!" and Swear exclaims, "I don' believe it, he go for da tree meel-yon!"

"Greedy," Crewe knocks back his porkpie, "greedy."

Murdo, thinking of Gutzeit, and staties suddenly lurking for no good reason—thinking also that he'd wanted to say something completely different, something in the back of his head that he came here to say that had nothing to do with moorings or whatever paranoid theory Eugenia is spouting, and it was why he came here. Boy? For a second the thought of Boy seems to cohabitate with the scene in front of him, the bamboo bar and cash register and Barboza tilting the Bilgewater bottle, saying "I got to order another one of these, tell your friend"; understanding by this Dog kept his name out of it as Murdo asked him, to keep the town from learning about the bootleg still, about a hobby that would likely make him far better known and respected in Barnstable, at least the old Barnstable, maybe not the flashy clean Main Street Eugenia is talking about, than setting up the waterfront art school and etching workshop—understanding (and the back-of-the-head thought strengthens with the realization about Dog) that he really *does* want to know how Boy lives. It's a question that has been growing like mold in a Cape cottage until it changes the color of his wallpaper, his idled memory, that zone of recall in which the kid has come to squat.

Cellphone shakes again, then rings. He swipes it to "answer." Una seldom rings right after messaging. He mumbles, "Sorry, better take this," and leans around the corner to a hallway hung with cheap-framed photos, furled beach parasol, heat grid on the floor pumping out warm air that smells sweetly of LNG—"Una?"

"Where the heck've you been, jeez!"

He can guess the urgency by her use of blasphemy. Una equates cursing with incompetence.

"What's wrong? What—"

"What's wrong? My god"—orange to red alert, Murdo thinks—"that gosh-darn, darned—gosh-darned omigod there they *are* again, he's—"

"*Who's* there? What's wrong, Una?"

"You don't have to *repeat* everything! Murdo please, he's loose, we're trapped here! He's got, like, he's got his whole goddam *family!*"

The call cuts out.

Crewe is watching him carefully. "If you gotta go," he says, "don't stand around."

Murdo looks at them—Eugenia rocking, Swear sucking at his oxygen tube, staring at the TV screen where someone is betting big on the German dog. Dog picking up the bottle and Joe, frowning, making notes on his liquor list, for all the world as if he still commanded the dark brown freighter of his bar.

"Gotta go," Murdo agrees.

The Winterpoor

East of Cape Cod, on Georges Bank, a system thousands of square miles in size is powering up. Driven by the tides which, washing over the bank's shallower ground to the northeast, flow faster there, cause a vacuum on the nether side the southern currents strive to fill, a clockwise gyre has formed that circles the entire area of muddy channels, rocks, sand, and ships sunk among them over centuries. In springtime the flow is boosted by an increase in fresh water running into the Gulf of Maine. The fresh water, being less dense than salt water, must rise over it—a version of the Gulf Stream's pumping that, twisted by the tidal gyre, adds itself to the Bank's overall dynamic. The increased flow boosts the stir of nutrients just as the seawater's average temperature climbs, waking life that until then has been larval, or dormant.

Eel Pond, though more than one hundred miles to the west of Georges Bank, in many ways replicates that system in miniature. Fresh water running down Eel River, from scarce snowmelt first and then from April rains, adds energy to the diurnal flow of tides, pulling in nutrients from the land, stirring up food from the bottom. Phytoplankton—tiny plants, algae, diatoms—are jolted into activity by the increasing warmth. They feed on minerals and decomposed matter, through photosynthesis they burn the strengthening octane of light, they bloom and cloud the water.

This spring, as for the last quarter century, the nutrients banquet is augmented by an artificial dessert of nitrates washed off lawns and an adjacent golf course, which certain types of algae—in particular, a long, kelp-like, bright orange seaweed that found its way into the ecosystem via a discarded box of Japanese specialty foods—find easily digestible. The phytoplankton and weeds are scarfed in their billions by copepods, a tiny crustacean that looks like a shrimp clutching a microscopic bouquet of feelers.

Jostled by warmth from polyp status, hibernating jellyfish, known as moon jellies for their round shape and the four U-shaped gonads resembling craters in their center, dilate like balloons. Their *tentacles ensnare the copepods and, stunning them with slight poison, ferry the plankton to gastric cavities. The moon jellies are in turn devoured by the alewife herring migrating to their spawning grounds, by scoter ducks as well as by larger species of fish that April tempts into the lagoon. The remains of digested fish, jellyfish, copepods and phytoplankton sink to the bottom to join ten thousand years of similar debris, all of which are stirred up by spring's increasing energy to continue the cycle; all of which will settle into relative dormancy when the cycle wanes.*

The homeostasis of Eel Pond in mid-April is a system, it is a force that includes adventure, feedback, catastrophe; it is, in many ways, a brute intelligence, an organic calculating mechanism that, when it works well, seems to throb with joy and fecund smells.

Right now—despite the added nitrates, which the golf course owners insist are due to cesspool leakage and private lawns, and which the marine biologist who is researching hippocampi in Eel Pond swears come mostly from fertilizer used on the greens—the pond's intelligence is high. It throbs with weed, rich mud, young mussels and the burst of grass. If it was a brain, it would be humming Coltrane to itself.

He hears it before he sees it—banging, Una's voice in shriek register at first, then settling down but still at turbine strength. It's all off the track of how things usually stand. Una seldom raises her voice, even or especially when angry; she considers high volume, like cusswords, to be what you use when you don't know how to use language to best effect. Murdo often wonders why, since this is by way of being a coherent philosophy with her, she uses "like" so much, the ultimate waste-word—but when even in the driveway, in the truck he hears her yelling, his adrenaline calls in special forces and he jumps the steps to the kitchen door, which is locked. He pounds on it with balled fist.

Una falls silent. He becomes conscious of a different sound, as of someone sobbing. He imagines her on the floor, pinned and struggling; a burglar, a rapist, a family she said, a family of burglar-rapists, but if that were so how did she manage a phone call and a text? And why call him and not 911? He bangs again. *"Una?"*

Nothing but the wind.

"I'm on the *phone*," he hears, finally.

"You're—listen, Una, it's locked! What's going on? Let me in."

Something bangs again, and Una squeals. The sobs are louder now. Murdo runs around front, where the lanai will be, and through the Fijian arch. The front door is unlocked. He trots through the living room, the kitchen is half lit.

A box of frosted double-glazed cereal ejects, as if powered by servo-rockets, from a higher cupboard.

Una and another woman. Both sitting atop the kitchen counter, legs tucked under them on the granite surface, surrounded on each side by ramparts built of espresso machine, toaster, bread-box. The other woman is Daisy, she has her head tucked between her knees, she's the one crying, her back vibrates in sync with sobs. Una has her back to the wall, head bent under the expensive cabinets of guaranteed genuine *ōhiʻa lehua* hardwood. The cell is clutched to her ear, as usual Murdo might say, except that her eyes are not normally so white-rimmed in panic, nor staring upward as another box of cereal comes zooming through the air to crash-land on the *moa* flooring.

Boogiewheats.

"What the," Murdo whispers, though he already knows.

He rounds the butcher-block island, and stops. The floor is crazed with objects, none of which should be there: Una is obsessed with clean space, empty space, it's part of her lanai obsession but this is the opposite of empty, it's inches deep in cardboard boxes of cereal as well as cereal unboxed, Star Chex, Fruit Blam!, Raisin-Oats, Bran Shimmy, Fiber So-Prize, sugar in multiple hues sparkles and shapes—cat food too, the Kitty Yums that Vector likes. Automatically he glances at the space between fridge and upper cabinets where the cat seeks refuge. Within twin circles of darkness he sees a hint of gold, first fixed on him, then flicking rightward.

"It's an e-*mer*-gency," Una says loudly. "He must have, like, a different number for emergencies?"

Murdo switches on the counter light.

Daisy's back is vibrating harder. She looks up suddenly, drawn by the surge of light. Murdo is surprised to see no moisture on her face. Her lips are usually full, especially the upper, but now she is biting the lower lip, which makes her mouth curve downward as if in grief. A bottle of the English ale she drinks sits half-empty beside her.

"Oh, Murdo," she gasps, and puts her face between her knees again and howls, "at last! Our hero! Come to save" (hiccough) "us."

Daisy is *laughing*. He feels almost cheated. This hero perhaps wished for danger so he could save the day? He feels, almost, a fool. He frowns, steps 'round the corner. Cereal crunches scrumptious underfoot. He opens wide the cabinet doors from which the last box came flying. Immediately a face pokes out at him, like a housewife peering indignantly at whomever would disturb her domestic peace. It's a face alive with curiosity: long nose, pointed black ears, eyes like polished agates, a mustache of pale fur on the muzzle; brown-gray fur with a black band drawn across the eyes, the archetypal bad-actor/burglar mask—but the element really defining this intruder and B&E artist is what grips the torn corner of a box of cereal, a small hand bearing five long, artistic raccoon fingers tipped with black claws, the knuckles sweetly defined and caught in the act of ripping open Honey Rays, which were always his favorite.

"Pancho," Murdo says. "Jesus fucking Christ."

"Oh yeah," Una interrupts her call. "Like potty-mouth's gonna, like, *solve* this. Where the hell *were* you, anyway?"

A dark-brown and furry wheel rolls at high speed from under the sink. Knocking aside bottles of detergent and scrubbing pads, it slips in a puddle of non-fat milk appropriately mixed with Raisin-Oats, caroms into another cupboard and lies doggo, its four paws splayed around a plump body, a ringed tail. Then, getting to its feet, it sprint-waddles past the counter into a storage closet; climbing now, agile as an alpinist, one shelf, three, front paws gripping the boards on which cans are stored, its Cyrano nose counterbalancing the fat butt and seesawing tail—all the way to the top shelf and a vent window, half open, through which it waddles, then vanishes like a lost thought.

Pancho has been observing his comrade's disappearance. Now he peers down at Murdo.

"You crazy 'coon," Murdo says, trying to sound stern but Daisy's giggles are still perkling as from a coffeemaker from between her knees and he's relieved enough at this point—he really thought something was amiss—that the lightness of his relief and the helium effect of her giggles seem to mix, creating a secondary lightness that makes him giggle as well.

Pancho makes his noise, which is somewhere between a growl and the word "rubble."

Rubble, Murdo thinks. Man, isn't that what you created here.

"Okay," Una says, "15 Harbor Way, no there's like two of 'em now, one just left."

"I'll get the rest out," Murdo says, eyeing the fridge, "all it takes—"

"No!" Una says sharply. "Murdo, the animal control guy, he's coming *now*."

"We don't need the animal control guy," Murdo tells her but in a conciliatory tone, for Una does not bend when challenged.

"Animal control guy," Daisy says, and giggles flood her voice again. "Our *hero*."

Murdo moves to the fridge. "Murdo," Una says urgently, "don't even think about it."

"Murdo's got a tranquilizer gun?" Daisy asks hopefully. "You need to keep the darts cold, innit?"

"Shut up, Daisy," Una says. "Not—"

He finds it, a large, flattish pack of waxed paper.

"Not the organic salmon!" she says.

"I'll just use a piece."

"Murdo," Una says, louder and in a menacing tone.

"Wouldn't he prefer it with dill aioli?" Daisy asks. Una looks at her.

"I said shut the fuck *up*, Dais'," she says.

Murdo stops what he's doing to stare at his wife. A scrabbling comes across the kitchen. Pancho rappels across the cabinet fronts, looking down to see where he's going. He lets himself fall, with a solid thump, on the counter three feet from Una, who shrieks. She truly is afraid of Pancho and for a few seconds Murdo feels bad. Then again, the Salmon Solution is the only surefire way to draw him.

He opens the package on the counter, three feet from Pancho, takes a carving knife from its rack, settles his glasses more firmly on his nose. Another much smaller raccoon appears from behind the fridge and squats on its haunches, nose high in the air and sniffing. Murdo lifts the knife, judging where to slice. Pancho watches him for a beat or two then walks over, ass high raccoon-style, on the granite. He seizes the package with both paws and tugs. Murdo pins the fillet to the butcher-block with the knife. The image of Luca Brasi's hand pinned to Tattaglia's counter in *The Godfather* flashes incongruously to mind. The soft flesh tears. Pancho makes a noise somewhere between a dog's growl and a squirrel's chatter and jumps off the counter with two-thirds of the fish in his mouth. He scampers around the corner, salmon flesh dragging orange between his legs, and disappears toward the front door, and the smaller raccoon scampers after him.

It is Una now who holds her face between her knees.

"I guess they like organic fish, huh?" Daisy says, and sniffles.

"I guess," Murdo agrees, kicking aside boxes with one foot. Una's voice is calm and low at this point but it sounds like something round and slippery is rolling around the plumbing of her throat as she says, "I can't take this anymore, you know I really can't." Her phone warbles, the overture to *Don Giovanni*, a text message. A siren howl-whoops far away, then closer. The animal control officer must have been nearby.

"He's gone," Murdo says.

"I told you, always," his wife replies. "That raccoon goes, or I go."

"But I threw him out two years ago."

"And that worked, like, *really* well."

"She has a point," Daisy agrees, and yawns.

Una tears a square of paper towel from the dispenser and wipes her face. So *someone* was crying, Murdo thinks. The siren makes that satisfied, downbeat wail cop cars give off when the car is stopped and the officer gets out.

"They sent a *cop*?"

"They'll send whomever I ask," Una replies. Her voice is even calmer than before, fat with a confidence that in this kitchen full of exploded cereal packaging and the pungency of purloined salmon seems to Murdo out of place at best and, at worst, as inexplicable as so much of the other stuff that's been happening in his life of late.

When the wind is low or absent, around three in the morning on the hinge between April and May, Eel Pond feels like a pool of secrets, its surface flat and black as the smoked glass of a mobster's limo; it sucks in light instead of reflecting it. The stars should be bright and visible for there is only a quarter moon, but most are hidden behind a quilt of clouds slow-drifting west to east. The silence is near perfect. A juvenile striped bass, surfacing, flips water; a jet high overhead on its way to Germany makes a sound like tissue paper being slowly unwrapped in the next room.

The pond is surrounded by crab condos; much-tunneled mud on top of which grow eelgrass, spartina grass and then cattails. The cattails, which prefer less salty water, lie thicker and taller on the western end, where a tidal creek grandly named Eel River reaches inland toward the Scudder Avenue culvert.

Looking toward the east, toward Hyannis Harbor, a few houses crowd the right-hand, southern side of the drawbridge; on its other side stand the high wooden panels of the boatyard's main shed, the tracks of a marine railway dipping without fuss into the pond, a Quonset hut used for storing boats. A snack bar, more of a shack really, hugs the road. All the buildings are black against the thick night except for a security light, egg-yolk yellow, over the boatyard office; and a lit window in a large summerhouse by the bridge. Someone there lies sleepless, or ill—or more probably, at this hour, it's a light switched on by a timer to give the illusion the house is occupied, to fool the B&E artists of the Winterpoor.

On the deeper end of Eel Pond, boats lie still and dark but pointed, in the absence of wind, toward the greater force of tide, which is on the flood. You would have to look as closely as a sniper to notice that one of the boats, an eighteen-foot fiberglass outboard with a canvas dodger, is not still anymore, but slowly shifts position; no, two boats. The flat wedge-shape of a wooden quahog skiff tows the eighteen-footer toward the drawbridge. A light flashes twice from the skiff, seaward; then again, three times.

A night bird croaks.

Swear Bjørken, camped under a green tarp beside the thickest cattails, snores loudly, grunts awake. He scratches at a bite that has given him, from the virus carried by deer ticks, a disease that will further stiffen his joints. He fumbles around, finds a half-empty bottle, checks the cap is twisted tight, and falls asleep again.

The flat hiss of tires from a cruising police SUV changes from high to low frequency as its wheels leave the tarmac briefly for the drawbridge's steel gridwork. The cop continues down Ocean Avenue toward Hyannisport.

A sound happens, like a big stick breaking. It is wrong, out of place in this cove of silence. It echoes off the boat-shed wall.

Another car passes. Kathleen, Boy's former foster parent, is working the second of her three jobs. A rolled newspaper thuds flatly as it hits a porch. The idea of a third cousin of a girlfriend of light touches a fringe of clouds to the east. The cattails, as if to shun the threat of morning, seem to grow thicker and more black.

Two windows shine from the Winterpoor. Soon a pickup starts up. Its headlights sweep north up Sea Street, toward the distant highway. A twelve-year old sedan chooses the other direction; south down Sea, left at Gosnold Street. Further north it takes a right on South Street toward the Cape Cod Hospital complex. The vehicles, before dawn, have more presence than humans, they seem to sheepdog their drivers, one toward a construction site in Waltham, the other to a gig mopping blood off operating-room tiles.

Walkers: the old, the recovering, the health-conscious. Groups of the sane and not so sane from the Old People's Institute off Gosnold; the home's housemother believes in walking therapy. The gray, pearl, peach colors of dawn soften the aniline hues of sports clothes. Unnatural, too, the blue and white strobe of police cars, the banshee yelp of sirens, flashing down Main Street toward West Main, toward the high school. The red and white lights of ambulances follow.

Well to the west, on Ken-Ken's porch, Speed and Ken-Ken notice the strobes and automatically take mental stock of class D substances in their possession: peyote buttons in the freezer, Olde Bilgewater in the liquor cabinet, pharma coke in Jack's back-up rocker, to check the upholstery of which would be a crime against America. All surely safe from search?

It crosses Ken-Ken's mind that in ensuring a supply of illicit substances he is only continuing a family tradition his great-grand-father started, when Joe Kennedy went into the rum-running trade with Joe Barboza's father, and the two stashed their contraband in what would later become Twin Joes' Villa and Bar.

And finally, like a klieg light firing up to close the drama of night, the sun climbs, lust-free, over hospital roofs.

Murdo wakes early from dreams that were not bad, scenes from a holiday in Nantucket when Wrong-Way Warny Ormesson flew them to the island. In real life not dreams Una was furious because Warny flew a few tricks with his souped-up Skyhawk, a barrel roll over Nantucket Sound, a strafing run on Wade Behlman's conch-boat. It soured the whole weekend. She insisted on taking the fast ferry back; in the dream, though, she was nothing but happy with the aluminum fog and shingled quaintness and twenty-dollar-a-glass wine bars of the island.

Murdo, full of sleep endorphins, decides he will break fast with his wife of six and a half years but as he leaves the den where he now sleeps (Daisy having made the guest bedroom her own) he hears Una's car start and does not race downstairs to stop her. The engine's noise dwindles in the calm of Harbor Way in the middle of spring. The fog spreads Nantucket gray in his chest but he will not lose his bearings today for he's had good sleep. He showers, dresses, stops by the Over Easy Diner for a watery java and he's in the shop by eight and there is Noble's barge waiting for him: thirty by twenty feet of scow, built thickly of white-oak planks, most of them new but four of the old planks, gone soft with dry rot, still to replace. Bollards, tiller, small crane for hoisting a dinghy, stand on deck. Inside the structure Noble tacked on the barge's top, like a gazebo on a garbage truck, lies a lovely double stateroom of mahogany, cherrywood and teak, with brass portholes and fittings and four large skylights. It holds a tiny galley and a sleeping loft and looks like a miniature house from outside, with a stovepipe chimney and a tinier house tacked on top to hold the loft. The stateroom was once part of the German Kaiser's yacht before she was broken up in a Staten Island scrapyard. In the main cabin, gilt bas-relief, finials and Persian carpets; a giant easel and benches of carved mahogany around the edges that carry, as well as jars full of Eby Noble's inks, needles, and brushes, a woodstove for heat and for warming his "true" ground.

The hull was once painted black but now is stripped to bare wood. Darkness gapes below the waterline, a void between rebuilt frames and trusses marking the last section of planking to be replaced—Murdo feels it start again, his excursion, the fog of that cursed trip to Nantucket and all the questions unanswered between him and Una since they have "taken a break from" (her term, a recent departure from "re-examining") their marriage: no change, no answers or questions even—just the sense of foreboding he's had for weeks now, always linked somehow to black gaps below the barge's waterline, to those fucked dark beams above.

But today he will not knuckle under. Today he will not even try to do this boatwork that brings him down.

Instead, once he has switched the shop's heater to high, he walks to the prints worktable and shrugs on the apron that hangs on a nail beside it. Then he opens his last six-pack of pre-beveled nine-by-twelve copper sheets and carefully peels off half. He locates, in a stores cabinet that camouflages the hatch under which he hides his whiskey still, a tarry ball of basic hard ground, not Charbonnel; he won't get fancy today. It is time, it is time he followed his hands for a change. His conscious mind says No, you should get your basics right: it insists, Stop, if you miss the CRAC watershed you will have neither job to support your habit nor studio to work in, and never mind high art. But his hands want to hold a needle to scratch on smoked metal the images that have built up and burned in his brain for weeks now, *weeks* since he drew anything. He selects one of the plates, cleans the copper with Comet and steel wool; rinses it in the sink using a vinegar solution, polishes it with a stiff cloth and finally, careful not to touch the etching surface, sets it on the hotplate. There he rubs the ball of ground over the metal and, when the ground melts, rolls it with a brayer until the surface is perfectly black and smooth.

And Boy comes in, plump apology against the light, hunched forward in his hoodie, walking sideways like a crab. Murdo, who has lit a kerosene lamp and, using a cloth to hold the copper by the edges, is passing the metal back and forth over greasy smoke to further darken the waxy coating, does not stop what he's doing but asks, "How come you're here?"

"Boy," the boy says.

"Okay." Murdo is not pissed off. He really would have preferred to work alone. But anger belongs to the country of rafters and island fog: that empire of shade, hegemonic but not powered up today or not yet. He forces himself to talk all calm and low. "What about school?"

"Closed," the boy says, and then: "close-close-closed."

"How come?" Memorial Day is three weeks away, Murdo thinks, schools cannot be out yet.

Boy stands still. Then hops as he answers. "I" (hop). "Don't" (hop). "Know" (hop). He sits on a chair by the heater. The door smacks open again and Dog walks in, followed by erwinrommel.

"Saw him come in," he says, pointing at Boy. "Yer workin' early." He stands over Murdo, looking at the copper, pointing: "You missed a spot."

"You lookin' for the marine biologist?"

"Nah, I heard she's bangin' that writer guy on the Hill. You got coffee?"

Murdo points an elbow at the Java-Mate.

Dog is dressed in work clothes: pants that once were khaki, Picasso'ed with house paint, a sweater with holes in one sleeve, a down waistcoat, work boots. He is unshaven and has a fresh bandage on his jaw. erwinrommel, a shaggy mutt with retriever tendencies, hops up on the couch, yawns hugely, and sets to the difficult and endless task of licking his balls. Dog fills a paper cup with coffee, stands beside Murdo. Runs his fingers through his hair, announces hoarsely, "*Did* it, babe!"

"Did what?"

"Mooring revolt." Dog is tense with the effort it takes not to strut. "Vince Hamblin is avenged!" He pumps a fist.

"You're not serious."

"'Course I am."

"I mean, Vince Hamblin? That crock?"

Dog crosses his arms defensively.

"We took thirty-two buoys off legal moorings, let the pennants sink, it'll take 'em weeks to salvage 'em."

"You're gonna be *real* popular." Murdo shakes his head. Dog ignores him.

"And we towed the harbormaster's boat to Yarmouth. And the police boat, it's got fifty feet of trapline wound around its prop. Insurance, yeh?"

He snorts.

"Nobody saw us. I think." Dog looks at Boy, but Boy is peeling a square of copper off the six-pack, looking pensive.

Oh shid, Murdo thinks.

"He won't talk," Dog says. "You won't talk, right, Boy?"

"Won' talk." Boy nods, too hard.

"Don't cut yourself on that," Murdo warns him.

Dog talks more softly.

"Pulling that creep Cooper's Jetcraft next to—"

"You got *Coop's* boat?"

"Yeah." Dog stares at him. "You got a problem with that? I would think—"

"My boss?" Murdo shrugs, careful not to smile.

"Anyways," Dog continues, after a beat, "there's cop flashers speedin' everywhere, I thought we were screwed but they weren't looking for us, or not then. Someone got shot near the high school—"

Murdo lets the plate down carefully and stares at Dog.

The door opens again. Gutzeit! Murdo thinks—realizing immediately it's not. A thin, medium-sized form wrapped in a long black poncho hesitates on the doorstep, then walks in. He figures, with a sudden lark of hope warbling in his forebrain, it's Una, she has that arc in her turn, the cant forward as she moves; but Una does not wear cloaks and would not be caught dead carrying an army-surplus haversack.

"Ah," Murdo says. "Daisy?" and touches the hotplate in surprise; his finger, hand and arm shoot back on their own, pure reflex, seared. "Jesus ow!" he yelps. "You're—"

"Up?"

Daisy walks deeper into the shop. Lamplight catches her face. She's out of place in here, Murdo thinks, with her snappy answers, her way of anticipating what you think, same way Una does. Yet for all her edge she also seems tired, dissonant, that bruised upper lip pulled down over the lower as if in doubt. Probably for the first time, Murdo feels a little sorry for Una's sister.

"Bloody lanai," Daisy says, lowering the haversack to a workbench, "the workmen started at seven this morning." And mingled with his nascent anger, because Speed apparently has seen fit to send a crew to work for Una though he'll not do the same for him, comes a spasm of triumph, for he recognizes in Daisy someone who might hate the lanai as much as he does.

Excerpt from Eby Noble's notebooks, 2 May 1934

Six years working on these coastal schooners: hauling granite from Maine to Queens, NY, where they became tombstones for the great cemeteries there. Or coal from Baltimore to Manhattan, to heat the city. 700 schooners, some of them five-masted, were built in 1919 in the US alone! Lumber from New Brunswick to Boston, sewing machines to Cuba once. I have been nearly sunk in a storm, but gales are not half as dangerous to these ships as hard times, and competition from oil-fired tugs and trucks. As fast as they were built a dozen years ago these beautiful ships are being laid up and abandoned to rot. Even in Hyannis Harbor the bulkhead is lined with schooners that have no cargoes to haul and nowhere to go.

Certainly I do not suffer from lack of material. I have been occupied, paradoxically, by a large etching of the Vineyard schooner "Alice B. Wentworth" and her crew making ready

to leave harbor. They have just been contracted to haul
paving stones from Stonington, Maine, to New York, for one
of the President's reconstruction projects. A. has secured for
me the promise of an exhibition at a gallery in Provincetown, where Father once showed paintings of Paris and Le
Touquet, but it may be that my personal life is tied to the
rhythm of moribund sailing ships more than it is to the
rarely beneficent tides of art ...

Penny has tired of living on the barge. Our life aboard,
marred by too little space, and by personal disagreements
that so often turn into fights, has become untenable. Annie's
energy is taken up with grammar school. The strain of
making sure that Johnny is occupied yet does not wander
around the decks and fall overboard takes its toll on all of us.
We agreed, with the rest of the money from my Boston show,
to rent a cottage in town, on Sea Street, where Penny would
have a room in which to write. The kids would have a large
room to themselves. For a few weeks everything seemed
better ...

Our aims in life are very different though, and I believe this
is causing Penny to rethink her plans. Certainly we possess
very different personalities, though each of us shares a need
at times to be solitary. She likes sitting in a room with type-
writer and paper and cigarettes, I prefer living in my
seaborne workshop with a different sort of paper, and inks
and acid and the other tools of my craft. We both require
forays outside but in this too our tastes diverge. For me, a
day spent sculling around the harbor: sketching, drifting
with the tide, stopping at Eel Pond dock to talk to boatyard
workers or to the fishermen, soaking in smells of cod and
salt, being caressed by the wind which today is quite warm
for December and from the southwest; this fills me with ease
and a sense of being alive and a part of the world. For

*Penny, however, the rhythm of the harbor and its denizens
does not count for much. She wants to return to New York,
to the hum of streets and trolleys and rushing crowds.*

*She has taken to boarding the tram to Boston once a week.
She has a friend on one of the newspapers there, a Mr.
Wiley, of whom she seems fond. I cannot object to this, for
she has faithfully followed me and my work from Paris to
Staten Island to Provincetown and now to this insignificant
harbor. The solution as she sees it is to move back to the city
entirely. Sometimes she says we should not move together
and then the terror of losing her, of losing Johnny and
Annie, fills me with a black mood that is not lifted or even
diluted until next morning, when I climb into the dinghy
again and run among the hulls, wondering if there is truly
something wrong with me that my soul is eased by sinking
ships, and mud, and all the stench and rot of a dying harbor
town.*

None of this should work out, Murdo reflects later. But Dog does
not seem keen to go back on the streets anytime soon. Murdo will
not push him; he probably wants to lie low awhile in case the cops,
or Macabru, have figured out a way to link him to the harbor high-
jinx and vandalism last night. To the shooting, why not, if that
really happened, he has no way of finding out here short of
searching news sites on his cellphone, which he has no desire to do.
Still it's part of the alternate accounting Murdo thought about
coming back from Mattapoisett that Dog should pick up tools and
start fitting new planks to the scow's hull on his own; and when he
has caulked and fastened the two that were left from Speed's last
working day some weeks ago now, he figures out which planks go
next—the last gap in the hull!— and fires up the steambox.

Daisy, of course, has her laptop, and a password for the wifi

Cooper insisted, against Murdo's wishes, be installed here; and soon she adopts her usual attitude, hunched in that poncho over the febrile screen, earphones clamped under her Death Eater hood, tracking what monsters lurk in the burning cities of her game. Boy has his Screwmaster and Dog is showing him how he will cut a plank on the table saw, which is not a great idea, but this works for a few minutes until Boy spots Daisy's laptop. He sidles over immediately to stand at her elbow. She notices him after thirty seconds, turns. A few words, and then the fatal mistake; she hands the console to Boy. Murdo tries not to smile—Dog can work quickly now, without distractions, he has already screwed in the last garboard plank. Daisy will not be able to shake the kid.

And Murdo, careful as a hostage escaping his cellar of confinement—not walking backwards exactly but making as little noise as he can—loads his pants pockets dangerously with etching needles, holds the prepped copper plate horizontal in his left hand like a waiter bearing his tray in a fancy restaurant, and eases over to the barge. Using his right hand to steady himself on the ladder he climbs to the deck, opens the stateroom door and enters Eby Noble's workshop.

What he loves most about this cabin is the smell: a combination of the world Noble drew and the medium through which he drew it. In one breath Murdo detects tar, printer's ink, wood caulk, ship's paint, hemp, metal, turpentine, asphaltum, mold, salt and soap. He smells also the perfume of gas heater, the beginnings of steam from the steambox, coffee; hears Dog moving wood about, a hint of breeze in the rafters; but outside input is damped in here.

He places the plate on Noble's workbench, adjusts the desk light. Nothing is as sweet as a flat field, perfection lives in and at that point: The first line, even if it's good, must inevitably bring it down—and yet without the line the field cannot live. Murdo takes a breath that goes all the way to the bilge of his lungs. He wonders why he chose to start a new plate now: even his preliminary drawings of the barge, with the sliding door half opened to marsh, are unfinished; still, this feels right. He is not sure what he'll do today but he wants to, he *needs* to start something new, something untainted by earlier days, by all his trammeled life. And he does not have much time to work on ground freshly smoothed on the etching plate.

Murdo takes from a locker a folder full of Eby Noble data, notes on his biography, and shuffles through the papers. The artist came to Cape Cod several times; right after World War I when his father Jack Noble, aka "Abilene Jack," a successful painter in his own right, left Paris for the States and moved to Provincetown, which was where Noble first watched schooners come and go or anchor in the crooked elbow of Race Point while waiting for fair wind. Later, as a crewman, Eby sailed on schooners to and around the Cape. Finally, approaching middle age, when the schooners were being laid up right and left, he came to Hyannis. His wife took a cottage off Sea Street. She was a writer. Their marriage was by then more broken-down than the barge and they separated the following year.

Noble chose to live where he worked. He paid a small tug, deadheading from Brooklyn to a job in Boston, to tow his aging work-barge, slowly, to Hyannis, and Eel Pond.

Murdo's eyes rest on a photo of Noble sketching in this very stateroom. The face is square in structure but thin, worn looking. It bears a stubborn nose and chin, the tendons of its neck break out like bridge cables, the skin is crinkling with age. A swag of graying hair curves over his brow. His pupils in shade look almost silver, they shine in reflection or empathy with the bright square of paper on which his hands crouch like a hunting lynx. His face is that of an inquisitor, or a saint, though Noble did not have the character to match. He was a quiet man, the scant biographies and a collection of his letters suggest; someone who did the best he could for his kids and loved them well by all accounts—asked only for enough time to make his art. A decent guy, Murdo thought, which was maybe why he never hit the big leagues of the art world, where decent family men seldom generated the kind of notoriety that garnered a saleable fame.

Not stupid though. He hired a former detective in the Boston police department to deal with gallery owners and museums, figuring an ex-cop from Boston would know how to get stuff—shows, percentages, money—out of people who did not want to part with them.

Murdo starts to sketch the face and neck on his rectangle of ground. It is well lit by skylights. He uses his finest needle, a 0.02 millimeter: very very thin parallel lines, which the hard ground can handle, with light between the lines to further convey the idea of light. Behind them the image requires deep black so he switches tools, choosing a wider échoppe, and cuts fat strokes closer together to catch more ink where darkness lives: under the coal stove, below a barometer, in an open locker beneath workbenches.

When he needs really large lines he unfolds his rigging knife and uses its wide blade. The lower left portions of the scene are filled with Noble, while the upper right will be white where sunlight strikes the barge's upper cabin: He leaves that area unscored. It is good to sketch in here—he can use the photo of Noble to draw the man himself. To reproduce the grain of mahogany of which the workbench ledge is made he merely has to swivel slightly to see the actual ledge, draw a notion of grain from the original wood. The portholes on the cabin's starboard side are open; open here, in this life, not Noble's, and halfway through sketching the table-easel—sketching the easel while he sketches *on* the easel!—he notices a sound that's wrong, behind the noises he has even in such a short time grown used to and factored in: quick shriek of power drill, "thock" of planks being moved, pop-songs cricketing from the boombox, the little whistle Dog makes when his work goes smoothly, a clank from the steambox as wood shifts, beeps from Una's HDMI pod; notices Boy-sound. "*Shid!*" A crack of concrete and "Shid! *Shid!*"

Murdo sighs, puts down his needle, walks out onto the narrow deck.

Boy, hopping again. Daisy has turned to watch him. She does not look sad, Murdo thinks, but sick—as if something was deeply wrong with her, that this weird behavior on the part of her fellow "Nekropolis" player brings out. Murdo climbs down the ladder, walks over and puts his hands on Boy's shoulders. The kid twists away, still holding the console, the wire tautens, pulls her laptop half off the workbench and Daisy cries out. Murdo shouts, "Boy!"

His voice is too loud, too rough. The kid drops the pod, and runs off to the printshop area.

"Shid."

"He can't," Daisy says, and pushes a strand of hair off her face —her eyes are the color of asphaltum, they hoard light as if filled with tears but that can't be what's happening, surely Daisy is not one to cry over the disappointment of a child?

"You know, there's something seriously wrong with him," she continues in a lowered tone, "he just doesn't have the motor skills—"

"I know," Murdo interrupts. "I should—"

"He shouldn't—"

"You—"

"I—"

"Oh, bloody hell." She picks up the pod, slumps in her chair, wipes at her eyes. On the laptop screen a shattered city is engulfed in fire and ash. A mad-haired woman on a white horse holds a lance with eight antennas on the tip. The woman, the horse, are surrounded by machines with metal snouts, all aimed at her.

"He lost my whole district to Enforcers."

Almost whispering now.

But Daisy's world is not Murdo's and even if it does make her cry for some reason—because of some fantasy fight played with usernames in London, Ljubljana, or Libreville, whose affect she was thick enough to allow in—he does not have time to headshrink Una's sister. Maybe, he thinks, he should not hide so well when Boy's around. Isolating himself, though useful in the short run, finally will cost him time. Murdo goes back to the scow and, even more carefully than when he went up, brings down his gear. He places his etching on the printshop table, turns on the work light.

And Boy, after a few more minutes of rocking and saying "shid," though not so loudly, at length gets to his feet and shuffles nearer. Murdo's jaw tightens, but this is what he bargained for; Boy looks over Murdo's shoulder at Eby Noble.

"I can do that. My Dad, he showed me."

"Yeah, I know."

"My Dad, he's coming back."

(This is new. Murdo turns to look at him.)

"Your Dad—he's there? I mean, he's home?"

Headshake. No.

"Your uncle? Mom?" The knowledge already in his voice. "Why can't you stay at home, Boy?" The kid looks at him as if this were a novel concept and Murdo says, only half kidding, "Oh, boy," and raises his hands in the air. He will *not* let this stop his working and so he takes the quick route out, grabs what's left of the six-pack of copper, finds a pad of tracing paper and a ball of soft ground in the stores cabinet. He cleans copper sheets, heats them on the hotplate, rubs them with ground and brayers them; he'll use two of these plates himself, he hasn't used soft ground in a while, it's time he experimented with the rougher wash effect ... When the plates have cooled he picks one, tapes a sheet of tracing paper flat against the ground, and carefully tapes that paper-covered plate to the workbench.

"Here." He hands Boy a sharpened pencil plus a couple of blunter ones. The kid's hands are grimy as always but that won't matter here.

"Do what I'm doing." Murdo picks up a needle and adds more crosshatch of wood on his own plate. He gestures to the tracing paper. "Draw. Try not to touch it with your fingers, just draw with the pencil, okay?"

The boy looks at him, and smiles. Murdo finds himself wishing the smile could last; it is wide-open, no holds barred, the kind of smile anyone would enjoy coming home to, oh to any ease at all in this forsaken child. He knows Boy will work at it for five minutes and then screw up, displace the paper, scrape the ground half off or knock the plate into the coffeepot or something else; cry Shid! and hop—but for now Murdo has five minutes or, with luck, maybe even fifteen and after that he'll ask Dog to give him the Screwmaster or assign some other task that will buy more time.

They don't have a warrant. He does *not* have to go anywhere with them. Just a few questions is what they tell him—but he does not know how much they know. Lucky Maria-Luisa's kid isn't back yet. Spending half the day with that faggot artist as always, not yet gone where Sonny fuckin' *knows* he should always be at one-thirty.

There's Sherrick, the thin plainclothes guy, and a female cop, Carvalho, overweight but not bad looking, most chick cops look like tractor-trailers. Something, tho, about cute women cops and the semi-automatic pistol just does something to a guy, he'd like to stand her against the counter with but her belt on and that M9 and fuck her brains out.

Standing in the kitchen now, maybe he shouldna let them in, he worries too much sometimes about being agreeable, always the nice guy, Lariat tells him that. Looking around at everything it feels like he's bein' groped by both of them and man, growing up with ole Papito, he knows something about that. But he's got nothing to hide, or more like what he has to hide is so well hidden in the crawl-space insulation he can look at them with some degree of righteousness, some dredge-up of his usual pride and 'tude and say, "You got grounds for this? I mean, what're your grounds? I have done nothing wrong and you know it." The art of bluff is believing in it one *thousand* fuckin' percent, Lariat Wilson says that too. And it works, yet again; the lady cop puts her hands up—*she* puts her hands up, he almost chuckles at that—the "let's all calm down here" gesture.

The man says, "We're just lookin' for information, Danny."

Carvalho says, "The kid that was killed last night, your number was on his cellphone."

Sherrick frowns at her.

"Devan Douglas," she adds. "We're figurin' out what happened. Where he was, kinda thing."

Fuckin *idiot* Devan, he thinks. You can rely on him for some things, like fuckin' up even when he's dead.

"He had a bunch of oxy's in one of his pockets?" Sherrick says, like it's a question.

And he can tell them what happened, which is nothing, because he was nowhere near the place they won't tell him at the time they won't tell him either, but he was here all night and his cellphone calls, which were legit, to Domino's and that blonde he met at BAR-ista, Britney whatsername, they'll all back him up. The truth of what he says is like sunshine warming your neck on a winter day when the rest of you's cold, and after a while he gets genuinely annoyed and starts to mention lawyers. Thinking all the while it's lucky he's got the back route to Wilson; he'll have to send all messages that way now.

They give him a card and tell him not to be so touchy and come to police headquarters for more questions, at his convenience they say. Playing nice, now he mentioned lawyers.

When they go he sits at the kitchen table under the golf clock, relief flooding him, lightening him like helium in a balloon. And out of nowhere, in that lightness, he finds himself wishing she were here, Mari-Lu: her sassy dark eyes and hair falling down her back like a frosted waterfall, and her way of hanging onto him with her arms around his neck, pulling him down one side—Danny, she tells him, my lil brother Danny (even though she *knows* how he uses the moron, knows he's got no time otherwise for the kid who looks anyway not just like a moron but also like her dead boring-fuck carpenter husband Jeff, the Barboza side)—but he misses her way of holding him, arm around his shoulders, whispering Hey Danny it ain't your fault, that's how things go Danny, hey Danny, yo Danny, hey my bro.

OPINION: Cape Cod's 'Mooring Revolt'

To understand the reasons behind the so-called "mooring revolt" in which a person or persons unknown recently sank moorings, swapped boats, and sabotaged town equipment in Barnstable's harbors, it helps to examine the case of Vince Hamblin.

Let's be clear: Vincent J. Hamblin, 56, of Marstons Mills, died last June in a hit-and-run accident on Route 28 that had nothing to do with moorings. It took state police six weeks to track down the driver, a personal-injury attorney from Boston's North End with no other ties to the Cape beyond a weekend party in New Seabury.

What is relevant about his case is how rapidly rumors spread throughout Barnstable that Hamblin, who was first on the waiting list for a town mooring in Hyannis's Eel Pond, had been knocked off by someone further down the list so the murderer could get Hamblin's mooring in Eel Pond.

The motivation behind such falsehoods is this: The supply of available boat moorings is virtually nonexistent, while demand for them is almost limitless. Supply is zero because the Cape's harbors are full and towns have stopped opening new mooring fields. Most waiting lists for moorings whose owners have died or moved are so long they have been closed, or else the waiting lists have waiting lists. And demand is huge due to the fact that so many Cape Codders live here because of the unique access to pleasant navigable waters the Cape's harbors provide.

As the peninsula gets more and more crowded, and its open spaces are increasingly built up, taking a boat into Nantucket Sound, Buzzards Bay or Cape Cod Bay has become the only reliable way to experience the kind of peace the Cape enjoyed in the past. With marina rentals prohibitively expensive, and launch ramps badly congested, a mooring is the only way most people can afford to own a boat any bigger than a dinghy.

As a result, mooring rights have become precious as gold. Families and friendships have broken up over who has rights to a mooring. And now a "mooring revolt" calling for mass installation of pirate moorings and displacement of legal ones has apparently resulted in the immobilizing of the Eel Pond police boat and the sabotage of 32 legitimate moorings—and yes, renewed rumors of a murder with moorings as motive.

© *Cape Cod News Online*

Murdo deepens the lines that frame the composition then settles down to details. He shades in portions of the coal stove, cutting tiny scores in areas that, from memory, were poorly lit. Boy watches him work, head cocked, then picks up a pencil and after a few tentative tries, still watching Murdo, starts drawing longer and longer lines on the paper covering his copper sheet; too long, god knows what he is doing. The lines are regular though, which is encouraging.

"Those're like cattails," Murdo tells him, "like the grasses in the marsh. Is that what you're drawing?" And then as the thought strikes him: "Is it true you go hide in the marsh sometimes? Swear told me. You go see him?"

"The mahsh," Boy says, nodding. "Swebajuk house."

"What?"

"Swebajuk," Boy repeats, nodding, and then adds, "My friend."

"Oh, right—Swear Bjørken?"

"Swebajuk."

Murdo turns away again, filtering out everything but the play of shadows on a woodstove on a barge. He realizes that he has not finished sketching Noble's studio and never mind how Boy reacts he must go back to the barge, which he does, not looking at the kid; climbing with his plate and needles up the ladder to the scow's cabin, settling at the easel once more. Hefts the needle in one hand, rolls it in his fingers, adjusts the light. He cuts in directly the fussiness of the coal stove's clawed feet, the flowers carved on the bunks' side-rails and cabin wainscoting. The fantastically dense graininess of Noble's waterfront prints, composed of thousands of tiny scratches that convey with breathtaking precision the convex surface of a mast, the reversed curve of a ship's tumblehome, are the net expression of a technique Murdo hugely admires.

The darkness he takes from Noble's war prints. These are distinguished by great tracts of shadow that remind him of Giorgione, or Titian, but which he believes were truly generated by the smoke and night of Omaha Beach, of Avranches and the Ardennes forest, where Noble sketched combat scenes for the Army newspaper, *Stars and Stripes*. These sketches he later turned into prints.

Using the rigging knife again he scratches a triangle of darkness to one side of Noble's easel; the port bulkhead of this deckhouse, near-black as well, make the artist's features shine in contrast like those of a martyred Byzantine. Somewhere in there a scrabbling intrudes, something thuds on deck. The narrow, scaramouche face of Pancho peers through an open porthole; then comes the overweight body of his raccoon, chirring greetings. Pancho hops on the bunk, cleans his whiskers with his paws, and falls asleep.

What is it about today, Murdo wonders, that everyone in his life except those he most wishes to see has turned up at his workshop? But he keeps on working.

Later, the regular whine of the power drill, the thumps against the lower hull that once more had syncopated Murdo's work, come to a halt. There is little sound in the cabin. A mosquito whines. The light transit of his etching tool as it draws lines through the waxy ground—the wax makes virtually no noise, maybe a "wissp" two decibels over human silence as the tool parts ground—fills his ears. The tip of his instrument actually touching copper generates even less sound, a tiny grinding. In the absence of workshop noise Murdo hears only "wissp" and the tiny grind and he delights in them, they are rich to his ears. He has finished shading in the cuffs of Noble's shirt, rolled up as he works, and his denim too. Murdo is good at drawing the folds of denim, maybe because he wears it all the time himself, and leather boots.

Still no sound outside. The mosquito whines closer, the bugs get through holes in the screen, he will have to patch them before more get in. Murdo picks up the copper, holding it by the edges, and examines it in the glare of work light, making sure that all his lines are crisp and well cut, the ground not blurred or over-ploughed so as to create foul-bite—areas where the acid will eat past lines he drew—but where the hell *is* everyone? He rests the plate carefully on a settee and opens the cabin door.

Below, in the knot of comfort afforded by an old futon couch, office chairs and gas heater, two hooded figures lurk like figures from *Game of Thrones*, from all the wizard-school blockbusters: Daisy and Boy bent over what looks like, what, *all three* of the copper plates he cleaned? Murdo, hand over hand down the ladder, almost stumbles at the bottom. Three plates total, at seventeen dollars each, fifty-one before tax. Daylight shot through the nearest window makes deep contrast of their features under the hoods: Daisy's victim-lips, Boy's cheeks.

"You taped the paper on?"

Daisy nods. Her eyes glint against the poncho's darkness. She lifts the hood clear of her forehead. Her earphones are off. On her laptop's screen, cities burn still. A flying piano shoots a projectile that vomits spiders and butter. On the table stands a bottle of Olde Bilgewater, more than a quarter empty. "They're pretty amazing, eh?"

"Good?" Boy asks her. "Good?"

"Yeah, Boy, I guess. Good."

Daisy gets up halfway to unstick a plate from the workbench, hand it to Murdo, and her hood falls back. In that position, head tilted upward in the light from higher windows, she forgets attitude, Murdo thinks, she looks quite lovely; the discovery makes him uncomfortable. It opens up the possibility that he has missed other, more significant details here. And how did she find his hootch?

Murdo looks around for Dog. The cabinet that hides his whiskey hatch is half-open, what the—of course Dog knows where the padlock key is kept—he looks down at the tracing paper covering Boy's plate. Though Daisy did a good job of taping the paper he expects nothing, kid scrawls, what the hell can a mentally challenged ten-year-old sketch out, houses with x-ed squares for windows and a squiggle coming out of the chimney, a stick mommy, a smiling sun with big rays of light? But no, whatever this is has been worked and reworked, hundreds over hundreds of lines in patterns and coordinated swirls, they resemble nothing but they are swirls that flow neat and parallel to each other. The complexity of it shocks him. He looks at the second plate. The swirls vary but the work's the same, lord the effort this kid put in here, Murdo is not sure what this is or if he likes it even but it has definitely been worked hard.

He looks at Boy, who has taken the woodchuck/beaver/whatever out of his hoodie pocket and is examining its belly zipper most carefully. The forelock falling over his forehead obscures his eyes. Murdo looks up at the workshop clock: 1:13. More than two hours he was up there. On the scow, three of the new strakes are in, the steambox forms one more; a day's work done, that would have taken Speed a month.

"My god," he says aloud, and then, to Boy, a little grudgingly, because he has to go out and spend fifty bucks on new plates now: "Hey, good job there."

"You have to mean it."

He looks at Daisy.

"But I do."

Now the kid is twisting his stuffed animal's head, making it check the clock as Murdo did.

"I'll print these up? A couple anyway. I mean—he really worked at these, right?"

"My Dad," the boy says, still aiming his animal at the clock—"I know," Murdo interrupts, "he showed you."

Daisy touches her upper lip with one finger.

"I had some whiskey," she says. "Dog, he showed me." She does not mean this cruelly.

"I can't believe," she adds, "you make this stuff. Moonshine, hootch, white lightning? The still an' all." She's watching the laptop, lifting the hood of her cloak/poncho from her forehead, letting it fall again; a thing she does.

"Where is Dog anyway?"

"Just left. Got a phone call. Why don't"—she looks at him briefly—"why don't you have a dram?"

A dram, he thinks, and his first reaction beyond his usual irritation at her British-isms is, Whaddya, nuts? It's barely afternoon. But she keeps talking, this black-cloaked woman who never speaks: the still, and how she's always been fascinated by moonshiners for some reason, the idea of a holler in the Virginia hills, stoking fires at midnight under machinery jury-rigged from oil barrels, car radiators, irrigation pipes, all stuffed to the gills with a stinking mash of Blue Ridge maize and sugar. Without thinking about it much he shoves the cabinet all the way aside, opens the hatch underneath, plugs in hook lamps that shine in the old root-cellar—how different the laboratory ware down here, what he gets through Bud Amaral, the clean glass boiler and valves and coils, a tight seal of silicon. "The stench though," he says, "you got that right." He has to make up mash in his parents' old barn, way off the beaten track in West Barnstable, no one to smell it but coyotes. Murdo's parents rarely visit the barn anymore, doing their own thing as always, last he heard renting a trailer off Prince William Sound; they always wanted to live in Alaska, his given name is testimony to that, and now they mostly do.

He closes the hatch, scrapes the cabinet back on top; picks up his etching, then Boy's, and lines them up near the sink, next to basins into which he'll pour acid to dunk the prints. He lines up bottles of hydrochloric acid and the clamps that will hold etching plates. He turns on the vent, takes out rubber gloves—then puts them back on the shelf. Restless. He returns to the print table, picks up the bottle of Bilgewater and finds, at the same time he remembers how it pulsed in him, it's gone: that sense he's had of waiting for something to happen.

He still has no idea what it was though he knows it wasn't good but it was always there, 24/7, the waiting, some phantom worry he could not let go of for weeks, months even: a dark force in these rafters? The final implosion of his marriage? A mooring revolt? And what zapped it now, and why—was it going back to print work, or introducing Boy to art? (*Filho da puta!*)

A slug of moonshine in the middle of the day?

Whatever it is, or was, and whether or not it's gone for good, he fills a water glass a quarter full of whiskey and silently toasts its departure—and Daisy, thinking he toasts her, raises her glass to him and looks at him with red-rimmed eyes. The boy is watching, clearly anxious to be included. Murdo casts around, finds a glass, washes it out and fills it with orange juice from the pocket fridge, probably been in there three weeks but it hasn't gone off or not much by the smell.

"Cheers," he says and Boy repeats, as he tends to inaccurately, "Cheese, cheese."

Murdo smiles, refills his glass. He needs to taste the hootch again. This is the Number 6 from two summers ago, it did not explode like last year's, it had a slight afterburn of maple.

He looks in the back of his printing workbook. The front lists details of ground, ink, and print-runs; the back holds, in weak code, whiskey data: percentage and origin of fresh corn, and sugar, and that time he threw in elderberries—elderberries! He forgot about those. Bitter but smooth as well, the third glass goes down fast, both his and Daisy's and pretty soon time becomes whiskey time, which is what he likes about moonshine, he is sitting sloshed with Una's kid sister on the reject futon and Boy is putting his fucked woodchuck carefully in his pants—not in the pockets but tucked in front, its amorphous head lolling over the boy's belt. Dragging a mountain bike gone red with rust from behind the broken band saw, he bumps it over the lintel of the people-door. Hey! Murdo yells after him, but Murdo is half drunk already and maybe that's why Boy ignores him. What happened, maybe what he was waiting to have happen, was this surrender to his own hootch, this let-go at the wrong time, with the wrong company, of the work he has waited so long to do—is he ditching it precisely because it is so rare, because it both results from and causes so much pressure, which makes the releasing that much sweeter?

His eye falls on the plates Boy made. He gets up, already he must do this carefully so as not to sway. He takes the plates one by one, his one and Boy's three, and lays them on the workbench next to one end of the flatbed press where he can scan them better under a work lamp.

Daisy rises from the futon, glass in one hand, and stands beside him as both examine the patterns on ground and copper.

"I can't figure him out," he tells Daisy. "He comes over here same time every afternoon, does the same things, uses the drill, sweeps up; yeah, sure, I exploit him a little. And suddenly he shows up in the *morning*—and freaks out! ... And then, he does this."

"That was my fault." She puts her glass on the workbench. "The freaking out. I shouldn't have let him—oh, you know," she turns to look at him directly. "It wasn't even him, it wasn't really his fault the sector went down."

He looks back at her as if he knew what she was talking about. Her mouth drags on both ends.

"Nekropolis. You've got to rebuild the city, you have to defend it from the Megorg. This time they got in through the data tunnels." She looks away, and back at him. "And you know," she says, with sudden fierceness, "you know who pulled scout-bots back from that tunnel? You *know* who did that on fucking *purpose?*"

"Fifth column?" he ventures.

"Fucking *Cooch.*" And all at once she is crying, really crying this time. A leap in his throat and chest: awe, shock? The last tears he saw came from Boy. In memory they were identical to Daisy's, rolled out against the plane of cheek and painted the color of light outside, which is gray-violet now. It reminds him of the underside of a blue crab's big claw, that shading into darkness, a speckled indigo. The weather has turned, day is fading.

"Daisy," he says uncertainly, "I." She turns toward him and folds into the side of him, it's as if different parts of her body, shoulder elbow neck forehead, the tumblehome of waist, have come unhooked, need reassembly like her game-city. She has found assembly in the side of him, which he knows is not much more cohesive but might be more cohesive than hers. He has no option but to lift his right arm and bring her in all the way.

"It's not *him,*" she says, "I'm not sad about Cooch, I didn't even trust him at the end, and respect?" She sniffs, wags her forehead against his shoulder, she is wiping her nose on his sweater for chris-sakes, the gesture is so innocent that he feels a sudden and quite novel wash of fondness for her: which translates, kidbone connected to boybone, boybone connected to heartbone, heartbone connected to armbones, into the language of holding-close.

Translation goes on in her as well. She lifts her head and looks at him. Her eyes aren't brown, he thinks in mild surprise. They are gold and black with brown flecks like oiled teak; like jimmies, the candied micro-sticks you shake over ice cream cones. The extra tearwater in them brings other colors out. The map of territory between Murdo's mouth and Daisy's carries mileage like the Pacific, like the distance separating two sides of a straight line. Leaning forward she crosses it, chin rising to kiss him softly on the lips. He can see her mouth, the upper lip that always looks bruised and drawn down over the wound of speech, OK he can't see it, it's under his own, but in his mind he sees it and that vision has connected straight to his crotch. He is all at once so hard it hurts. Tied in by the denim of his jeans he shifts; by a different physical process, a plate tectonic of internal quake and chasm, *this* brings his tongue into her mouth and both their arms wrapped blindly round each other.

It's been so long since he has kissed and been kissed like this. It has been so long since his body has felt such give against it; her lip, and her turn of waist which is almost as smooth and soft, like an expression of acceptance and ripe fruit and lust and the inward curve of Eby Noble's schooner hulls, the curve they call "the buttocks:" that low after-section between waterline and keel.

She breaks the kiss first and dips her head into the turn of his neck. Her neck smells of strawberries, sweet and dry; berries in September hay.

"Jesus," he says.

"Has nothing to do with it."

"I'm not sure—"

"This is a good idea?"

"We're not married, I don't think you should be completing my sentences."

He has not let go of her.

She looks up at him. She is shooting him with those rods and cones, a thousand jimmies of chocolate.

The Origin of Jimmies

Controversy arose in the "diversity"-crazed 2000s over the suggestion made by the kind of people who live in Cambridge, Massachusetts, that the term "jimmies," as used in Massachusetts as well as parts of Rhode Island, New Hampshire, Pennsylvania and Oregon to denote the tiny, hard, colored candy bits shaken over an ice cream cone, had racist connotations.

The reasoning behind that was based on the use of "jimmies" to indicate dark, all-chocolate candies. The association with "Jim Crow" was cited but never proven, as was the attribution of the term to white, racist, Irish-Bostonians. The confectionery is known as "sprinkles" in much of the rest of the country and as "hundreds and thousands" in Britain. However, "jimmies" in most parts of Massachusetts is used indiscriminately to mean any color of such candy. When specificity is needed, the two varieties are referred to as "chocolate jimmies" and "rainbow jimmies."

Two apocryphal stories attribute the name to different "Jimmy's": the first, Jimmy O'Connell, worked at a New England ice-cream store in the 1950s. The second, Jimmy Bartholomew, operated the machine that made sweets at the Just Born Candy Company in Philadelphia, Pennsylvania, in the 1940s.

Just Born's patent on the term "jimmies" is still in force.

From *Waffle or Sugar? A History of the American Ice Cream Cone*, by G. Fenton Hardy, Americana Press, Dayton, Ohio, 2012

"I won't tell," she says, "it's just a kiss."
  "It's jiss—"
  "For now—"
  "Or what—"
  She waits. As if she senses his distrust of her speed.
  "Una. Christ. Your sister, I mean."
  He wants the whiskey glass. He does not want to let go of her. This may not, it most likely will not happen again, he does not know when or if he will ever visit this universe of softness again.
  "My wife ..."

"You know the saying," she says, "about the goose?"

He does not hear that—not really. To the extent that he does, he doesn't make the connection up front. The curves of her seem to have ganged up on him, the arc of her buttock lines, the angle of her hip against his side. The thinking and memory part of his brain —the zones of gray matter devoted to loyalty, promise, trust, his wife—are overwhelmed; in that second he pulls Daisy closer and sideways toward the front of him. She holds back for a beat, then lets herself be pulled. Kissing again, her tongue in his mouth, he leans back against the flatbed press till he is half standing, half sitting on the press's bed. She lifts one knee so she is riding him, her crotch pressed against his. His hands touch her breasts, thumbs plucking at the bumps of her nipples and she makes a sound like the wind in a thick spruce; reaches down in turn and touches him, fumbles at his belt.

Like Murdo, she knows jeans. Not much in his head now, hew to stereotype he thinks, open the guy's zipper and watch his brains fall out; nor does he give a shit. Some elements have come together here—his gut loneliness, the line of her nose, eight months of rejection and unwilled abstinence and the way Daisy kept her face hid in the living room. She pulls his jeans down, he arches his back to free them, sits back on the bed; she touches him between his legs, holds him. His dick is happy. He puts his hands under her too-big sweater, rucks it up and tweaks her nipples directly. He wants to warn her, this is nuts, the door is unlocked, Boy could come back. He doesn't heed his own warning, he has reached down to pull up her skirt. She shifts, opening her legs, and she is guiding him, north and a little west to clear the band of her underwear; they are lace panties or some kind of frill that scratches him. It surprises him, as women always do, the fussy aesthetics of even the tougher ones. But now he's inside, in the warm, into the wet, into the resolution of all seventh chords, all the twists and turns and discoveries within her; there's a sort of double chamber his dick opens into, a darkness he can only imagine, but this one is soft and warm and flowing and in his mind, another cliché he

87

supposes but does not care, it is life itself, the very opposite of wrong.

He puts his hands on her buttocks and leans further back on the printer bed, carrying her with him onto the bench beside, kicking his legs so his jeans fall all the way off, shifting sideways so he and Daisy lie lengthwise. He is conscious even now of Boy's prints at one end, a delicacy of whorls that must be preserved. Murdo uses his heels to shift away from them. Her weight shifts as his does, and she lies on top.

Now he feels the end of the chamber inside her, it's as if he is touching something much deeper, more secret, risky for them both. Her head is bent, that wind in the trees, stronger now, it's a summer wind for it brings waves of heat, he is not sure if they come from her or him or both. The waves increase in sync with her movements, her black hair washes back and forth. Her eyes, looking at him, have changed color, gone almost completely gold; she utters a cry like a seabird in a storm and pushes hard against him. He wants to come with her, he is too late and disappointment happens; but that is soon washed over, as his concern about Boy's return was flooded over by the lust in him, the need for obsessive, quickening rhythms that bring this wave, this series of waves he floods her with, that now floods back into his brain with the image of her hiding, face obscured in a black hood, he looks for it but it is still hidden, her eyes and cheeks and mouth in the curve of his own neck this time. (Almost calls out, Una. No, Daisy! *Daisy!*)

Instead of her face and the grain and flow of her hair he sees the grain and flow of the drawings Boy made, now flat against his heels on the hard steel of the press. He bends his knees, drawing back again from that end of the print bed. This woman should be Una. Why does coming bring such disappointment? It is Daisy. Her shoulder is thinner, more pale, her body lighter than her sister's, her buttocks thinner, less soft. He holds her harder, squeezing out these thoughts.

The orgasm recedes, leaving him washed up on the beach of a

lake of sadness: for Una, for Daisy, for himself. That they should all end up like this.

What Daisy said about the goose hangs in his head without effort, it uses fasteners he did not know were there: the voicemail at CRAC, the follow-through of English verses, five syllables then six.

The way Una last touched him on the elbow, weeks ago, as if he was a stranger.

It is quiet in the workshop. The seawind is soft. The pocket fridge's compressor has shut off.

A mosquito whines, dives toward them, he waves it away. He must buy repellent, he thinks vaguely. She breathes more quietly.

His cellphone rings; two quick tones, text-message. He leans toward it but Daisy is still on top, he gives up.

"Saved by the bell," she whispers and leans sideways, she can just reach the workbench from here, to pick it up—only she does not pick up the phone but the glass of whiskey, which she hands to him, grinning.

"What's so funny."

"Your naked arse. It's a work of art. You must have sat on that when"—she gestures toward the practice plate he left on the press weeks ago, when he showed Boy how it worked.

So his ass, which just made love to her sister, now bears a portrait of his *wife?*

Blood rushes to Murdo's face. He closes his eyes. He takes a deep gulp of Olde Bilgewater and realizes in that instant he does not love Daisy: not yet, certainly not now. The space inside him that love for her could occupy is not cleared of Una, not enough to make room for Daisy's form, her hair, tempo of speech, angle of neck.

She leans over again and now picks up the cellphone, holding it up so he can see. He wonders at this, it could be Una, though she texts him less these days. Is Daisy making a point here? But the screen reads DOG.

In the same way the veins of a leaf mimic against their stem the angle of tree-branches to trunk, her eyebrows form the same angle to nose as her collarbones do to spine, under the rucked up sweater.

In 1930 and 1931 the slick, green, spearlike blades of eelgrass populating the intertidal areas of Hyannis's Eel Pond shoreline were decimated by a combination of higher than usual summer temperatures and an infestation of a saltwater slime mold called labyrinthula, to the point where almost none of the plants survived.

The eelgrass recovered from that epidemic, albeit slowly. By 2005, it had reoccupied half the terrain lost to labyrinthula, although it could never retake beachfront since occupied by docks and bulkheads protecting pricey real estate on the harbor side of Eel River's drawbridge.

The eelgrass, now protected by environmental regulation—for it provides, in turn, important protection and habitat for many forms of aquatic life—has declined by twenty percent since its peak in 2005. Scientists have variously blamed an offshoot of labyrinthula, a rise in mean ocean temperatures associated with greenhouse gases, a rise in sea level also associated with global warming, increased turbidity due to upstream construction, and nitrate pollution from various sources. Despite this attrition, half the shoreline of Eel Pond now carries copses of eelgrass which display different varieties of green as they are bent back and forth by wind in their stems and by salt-water washing in and out of their root system. Which is all pipefish would care about, had they wit enough to care.

The pipefish is a form of hippocampus, or seahorse: very long and thin, with a needle-like snout, a curled tail, an angular body and a dorsal fin that looks a little like a dragon's wing. It makes its home in eelgrass much of the year, swimming vertically, propelled mainly

by its dorsal fin, like a thumbnail filly sitting on its tail at the breakfast table.

Breakfast in the spring consists mostly of copepods. The little
seahorses blow water out of their snout and suck the miniature crus-
taceans in by forcefully re-inhaling the water. Despite abundant
supplies of phytoplankton on which copepods feed, fewer copepods
this year inhabit the eelgrass forests, and one reason for that might be
a simple preemption of space. The branches of a new weed that has
invaded a portion of Eel Pond's bottom, when dead or ripped up by
human activity, wash up against the eelgrass and are tangled in
their stalks like basketfuls of wilted orange salad.

Sufficient copepods nonetheless remain to feed the pipefish tribe
and fuel their mating, which starts in mid-spring. The females—
sensing from a mix of water temperature, moon pull, and genetic
programming that the time is right—belly up to the males, who open
a flap in their stomach area to receive the females' eggs and fertilize
them as they enter. The males then perform a weird contortion,
somewhat reminiscent of white men dancing to R&B, to wring the
eggs deeper into the pouch's bottom. The female pipefish repeat this
process a dozen eggs at a time until the males' pouches are full,
whereupon they swan off to find another compliant male.

The "pregnant" males now take over gestation, automatically
feeding the eggs through a lining in their marsupial-esque pouch in
which the larval offspring are stuffed.

Incubation lasts ten days. After that the sac enveloping the tiny
eggs is absorbed and the nascent pipefish swim out of the pouch one
by one and drift off, in most cases to become food for other fish.
Enough survive, however—and enthusiastically begin chasing copepods—to secure a future for the pipefish tribe within the dwindling
grass.

They find Dog pretending to look at mugs in the form of giant
breasts with the words "Living Large on Cape Cod" hanging in the

front window of a gift shop on Main Street. What Dog really watches takes place outside. He guides them in with text instructions, through a side door.

From this vantage point they have a clear view inside a cordon established by the Barnstable Police Department to block off a candy- and fudge-shop across Main Street. Cruisers section the street with Detroit steel and yellow tape. Their blue-white lights strobe epileptically. An emergency response team, fat with helmets and bulletproof vests reading SWAT and STATE POLICE, aims assault rifles from behind the county's armored car, squatting black and sinister in front of the candy shop. Two drones buzz overhead. A man in civilian clothes yells through a bullhorn. "DO NOT"—he pauses. "DO NOT!" Murdo reckons the scene feels familiar because of all the "reality" crime shows absorbed year after year, hundreds no thousands of times on TV and video-stream; *LA Counter-Terrorism, CSI Akron, Crime Scene Radiologists, America's Funniest Fatal Car Chases*. And the shoals of early-season tourists watching outside the cordon react lustfully to the sight of dramas from their laptops and flat-panels translated like this, *outside* the screen! It all reads, as a result, curiously fake. Does this mean that the little dramas of the screen—so Murdo wonders lightly—are what's real, their daily flash the greater truth of our hyper-mediated lives?

His thoughts are weightless larks with hooks on their wings that snag each other, loosely linking as they wheel and circle. Sex does that to him, cuts lines that anchored routine cares.

But what just happened with Daisy, maybe because of the many other lines of habit and allegiance it also cut or could sever, makes everything far spacier. His body feels as if it could join his thoughts, dance and fly and hook up, if only he allowed it to. He feels Daisy next to him, he senses the heat of her body just as the robots in her Nekropolis game register human heat as green in their sensors. The slight concave arc her nose makes is far stronger and more relevant to his life in that instant than the bizarre event unfolding beyond the lined-up plaster matelots and lighthouses and "My Mommy Went to Cape Cod and All I Got Was this Lousy T-Shirt!" t-shirts also racked in the display window.

And yet, and yet—that is Swear Bjørken's face just recognizable behind the fractal plate-glass of the candy shop: fringe of white beard, oxygen tube shiny under his nose. And Dog is saying, "He musta been tricked into this, it's not Swear's style. But those two other lowlifes, Ricci I went to school with and the other one I don't know. Cops were picking up the homeless—'

"They need a SWAT team for this?"

Dog nods. "Ricci's always had bad 'tude, he locked the doors, they got a counter girl in there with 'em. Hostage situation."

"*Hostage* situation?" Murdo repeats hoarsely. His voice doesn't work well for some reason, *Swear?* None of this fits with his memory of an over-the-hill alcoholic who apparently shelters Boy at his "house" in the marsh. Maybe, with an uncle like Danny Martin, Boy needs shelter. He sees them sitting around a campfire, he has actually spotted those campfires across Eel River at night. The Norwegian drinks and sucks at oxygen, and Boy, hood shadowing his face, adds driftwood to the flames because his dad "showed" him how—this mental excursion of Murdo's is brutally cut off by an SUV with a Kojak light that whines through the clotted crash-clothes of tourists to the cordon. Men with the cheap suits and hearing aids of Feds roll out, vector up to the bullhorn guy: Chief of Police Swallow, now standing beside Mike Connolly, the town councillor and real-estate agent who's also, Murdo remembers, on CRAC's board of directors. As if those political connections towed in others Murdo spots, beside a paddy wagon, Russell Cooper: the dark eyebrows, trim white hair at the temples, the fringe that hides the CRAC director's bald spot, a shirt-collar so sharp it could slice Gouda. Cooper stands slightly apart from both SUV and crowds, thumbing at a smartphone, smiling absently at Link Linnell, CRAC's "operations" guy. But Cooper's eyes, and Link's as well, are on the chief.

Murdo looks at Daisy. She does not look back. Her face seems very calm, at peace. He does not know what to think about this, he does not have the tools. Daisy is one bird, Una another—what Daisy said, what he and she did, all part of that flock of thoughts wheeling and chasing each other. The wetness of her still oiling his crotch, he must wash himself before going home. The logistics of adultery, he thinks, and hot blood once more washes the capillaries in his face.

But a stronger thought is this: Utter wrongness here, to put in the same ken a gentle inoffensive drunk and the statie M4s drawing scarlet laser dots on his temple. Using all the air between bird thoughts Murdo walks out of the shop's front doors, hearing Dog behind him, "Murdo *don't*," and Daisy asking, "Murdo?" Walks toward Swallow and the staties and almost gets there before two BPD officers notice him and, grabbing his shoulders, shove him back.

"Hey," Murdo says, "I jiss know him. The guy in there—"

"Get be-*hind* the *tape*," one of the cops says, not one Murdo knows, he doesn't know the other cop either, the BPD so big now. "This is an *ongoing* crime scene."

"But I know him, he's not a"—Murdo stops. He leans his weight against the cops, who push him again, much harder. The one on the left has a nose like a meat hook. "You don't get back, asshole," he snarls, "you're goin' to jail."

Without meaning to, Murdo starts to laugh. Meat hook stares at him in amazement.

"Jeez," Murdo says, regaining his balance. Suddenly he does not feel like laughing anymore. He takes his glasses off and pockets them. The second cop looks to Meat hook for guidance, I mean this guy is *laughing*, what do we *do*?

Something old and angry inside makes Murdo add, in the split moment while Meat hook figures out how to hurt this man who mocks cops, "Don't you guys have something useful to do, like hang at Donut Shack?"—wishing he could think of something more original. Balance regained, he shrugs off the coppers' hands.

But behind him the fates have placed another cop for backup, large and heavy. And the fates are not kind, for it is Gutzeit who kicks Murdo's knees into the shape of an angle iron while Meat hook drags him down by one shoulder and the other cop bars Murdo's throat with a nightstick. And before he can fully understand what has happened Murdo is prone on the tarmac, chill of handcuffs on his wrists and a knee on his right kidney. Hauled back to prayer position, forgive me father, nightstick still across his throat he's having trouble breathing and all the brain-pictures of people like him being choked like this flood his frontal lobes—

Then with the same kind of speed and lack of cause as when all this started the nightstick is pulled away, he is hauled upright. The cops hold him, waiting. Looking for orders up Main where Murdo sees the chief, one arm raised, talking to someone with a five-o'clock shadow, perfect triangles of white hair at his temples matching the triangles of his white dress shirt.

A few syllables on the radio, a muffled "Jee-*zuss!*" from Gutzeit, and his wrists are free, the cold cuffs gone.

The cops tell him, "Next time, asshole."

The cops tell him, "Get lost."

Book Two
Summer

The beach south of Eel Pond drawbridge twists around ripraps, stone bulkheads and jetties built to preserve new mansions from erosion and rising waters. In the course of these changes an area of dunes has formed between a parking lot dedicated to the late President John F. Kennedy, whose family summered only a short walk from here, and the bayfront beach. Shallow vales between dunes, sheltered by thickets of beach-grass, are colonized as the weather warms by people, mainly young, seeking to drink or grope each other in private; but from mid-May on they are taken over by a small seabird with pointed wings, a long tail, a black yarmulke, and a decidedly bad attitude regarding interlopers.

One could say the Arctic tern has a right to cop attitude. The mansions are inhabited by people who fly away during the winter but these migrations: to Palm Beach, or Portofino even; are nothing compared to the tern's. Every year it flies from feeding grounds in the Arctic to krill grounds in the Antarctic and back again, a journey of over 20,000 miles. It is the only creature in the world to experience two summers a year. To manage this round trip within twelve months requires not only stamina and a good sense of direction, but excellent timing.

More so than the most rabid sunbather's the tern's life is regimented by the rise and fall in sunlight's life and power, which regulate its ability to catch insects and shallow-feeding fish. In its head the duration of daylight is a prism, and that prism, of yellows and oranges shading to red, is calibrated as precisely as a spectrograph so that a progression toward the infrared side of the spectrum, past a very specific threshold, triggers a chain reaction: increasing activity, larger dinners to store fuel for flight, more social flying to round up other birds of the flock. And finally it will take off, to the north or south, on the next leg of its journey.

But now it's the start of summer in the northern hemisphere and a group of several dozen terns have come back to the dunes they usually visit in order to hatch. The birds waste no time in initiating the complex rituals of what ornithologists call high flight (female chasing male to altitude) and fish flight (wherein the male offers dinner to his mate). The couples circle each other, choose a patch of sand in which to nest and lay eggs; take it in turns, all puns intended, to brood. They also share defensive duties: When an intruder is spotted, whether it be cat, raccoon (there has been an uptick in raccoon predation lately), or human, the alarm call is sounded by every bird in the colony. Like Spitfire pilots at Biggin Hill airfield in 1940 they scramble at once; climbing twenty feet, they peel off and dive straight at the foe, screaming, pecking at the interloper's head and sometimes drawing blood, then soaring out of reach. If the enemy does not withdraw they repeat the attack with steadily increasing viciousness. When the chicks hatch the birds' nervousness and aggressions redouble. Only when the fledglings are able to fly on their own do the terns relax a little, and think of other things. Or of one other thing: the Voyage.

The idea of voyage at that point will become an ever-growing tension that can only be slackened by the first wing-flaps and a deep horizon to aim for. Now the tern remembers voyage is the other purpose for which it's made. When it reaches the next destination different concerns will chip in: hunger, nurture, self-defense. But amid all of these the tern never forgets the pull of light on the next horizon.

The tern always wants to leave.

The can marked Zap! is colored bright yellow. It bears, under the horror-movie font, a cartoon of a mosquito wearing a World War II era gas mask, coughing despite the protection. Fine print underneath announces clearly the use of dilethanophilezone 2/5, a substance that the finer print allows has been known to cause cancer in California rats but which kills bugs with such efficiency that the company manufacturing it, Cou-Yon Chemicals Inc. of Bayou Grand Caillou, Louisiana, has not changed its formula in years, despite having outsourced actual production of Zap! to Guangzhou; despite having recently been acquired by a Zurich-based multinational home-products corporation with a slightly greater degree of environmental sensitivity than Cou-Yon Chemicals.

Zap! is just *that* good.

The can stands in the "Seasonal Needs" shelf of the Samo convenience store at the corner of Old Colony and South Streets in Hyannis. It is there that Murdo buys it, along with a peppermint-chocolate wafer for which he feels, given the high-test emotions of the past few days, an almost physical desire.

He nibbles at the candy on his way to the workshop; trying, as he has been trying since his near-arrest, to avoid deeper thought. Deep thought areas include Daisy, and Una. Deep thought includes Swear, still held, along with low-life Ricci who triggered the "hostage situation," at the county jail on charges of kidnapping, extortion, resisting arrest. Deep thought includes the look on Cooper's face when he convinced Chief Swallow to let Murdo go.

Murdo squirms on the ripped seat of his pickup. He flicks on the radio; the down-Cape non-profit station plays a Clam Fetish song, "Proctologist Blues," it does not lift his mood. It requires all the zing of mint extract as well as active effort to keep his brain from going where it wants to and focus instead on the mosquito problem; as summer starts, bugs have proliferated in the salt marsh abutting his workshop on Fresh Holes Road. The Cape Cod Mosquito Control Commission is one of the most successful public works projects in New England; Dog even blames it for the overdevelopment of the Cape in that the near-eradication of stinging bugs has allowed the proliferation of human pests in coastal areas; but it cannot eliminate all critters all the time. Murdo has plugged the rips in his workshop's screens but more entry points exist. There are chinks in the ancient woodwork, in warped flooring, where bloodsuckers sneak in.

He vows, aping Churchill, "I shall spray them in the corners I shall spray them on their landing fields I shall spray even in spaces I cannot see, behind the scow, I will climb among the black and withered rafters and if I do not kill them directly I shall create such a noxious stench that they will think twice before flying in." So as soon as he gets back he starts spraying Zap! behind the scow—which is silly because the hull, thanks to Dog, is close to done, the boatyard has been hired to move the craft in four days' time and at that point all this area will be far easier to spray in. Still, clutching the can at arm's length, making sure the nozzle is not aimed at his nose, he directs a cone of mist between two studs of blackened pine into a hole of rust, cobwebs, nails, sawdust, and other detritus where he knows from experience the little fuckers hide. Even at arm's length the mist gets into his nostrils, sweet, citrus-scented, with an aftertaste of burnt aluminum and root beer. He shifts his stance to blast the next black joist.

He wonders, out of nowhere, what Una's doing now. He has seen even less of her since the bust. It bothers him that he doesn't know what shoes she's wearing and by extension, what mood she's in. Still his brain does not enter the portals of denser thought. But that mix of smells means something, it is stinging him in the memory banks like the mosquitoes it's supposed to kill, trying to wake the cobweb of nerves and blood, sodium and electricity, where that smell has already been secreted.

He relaxes his trigger finger, stops the spray. Realizing the memory has already been summoned, the currents joined.

The smell is Una's.

He has sniffed this exact mix: of citrus, aluminum, and root beer; for weeks, months even, on his wife. On her business jackets. On her hair. Yet she never uses bug spray, she takes the cancer warnings seriously. While sunbathing on the deck in summer she uses only an organic, animal-rights-approved, shade-grown, tea-tree-oil-based salve that smells of camphor—

Cooper.

Such thoughts do not present themselves in order at first. Conclusions happen like clouds or pressure gradients, they shift like weather till the sun shines, or storms happen; or lightning, sometimes, splits a tree next door.

Pressures regroup against stomach, chest. Corners of darkness appear in his brain, mimicking the workshop around him. Vacuum builds grief or is it the other way around, just as gut-changes seem to happen first although surely that cannot be because the idea that triggered them must have come before, and the story that envelopes it like a matrix before *that*—with who: with old lady Eugenia describing Russell Cooper? Was this the veiled thought he'd tried to shun?

"Never seen a man so scared of bugs, sprays everything with that spray, one with the gas mask on the mosquito."

And Joe Barboza answered: "*Zap!*"

Other stories must exist. Maybe Cooper pumps his whole office full of Zap! till everything in the CRAC suite smells like it. Except it doesn't, it can't, even Zap! is not that strong. And his wife, who doesn't like him to store sour mash in the cellar because of the smell, would never allow the odor of dilethanophilezone 2/5, though sprayed by her boss, to permeate her office.

Murdo smells his hand. Root beer, lemon, aluminum to the power of ten. He smells his shirt: sweat, sawdust, detergent. He rubs his hand against his shirt, smells it again: Root beer-detergent-lime. He takes off his glasses, the bridge of which cracked when the cops tackled him, and polishes the lenses with care.

He has no right to accuse her. Nine, no ten days ago he and Una's sister made love on the bed of his printer, not twenty paces away. "What's sauce for the goose," she said, though she didn't say it all the way. And finally he lets the saying run its course: *What's sauce for the goose is sauce for the gander*. So Daisy knew ...

And yet, all the time—for months now, even a year—he has missed his wife. Missed her with the strength and agony that comes when muscle tissue is torn from tissue. So that this proof: not court-room proof, but proof that turns gears in his stomach where the hundreds of other clues you've picked up, all unaware, suddenly join; her distance, her refusal to sleep with him, the unexpected tolerance sometimes, the half-smile on her face when she thought he was not looking—when all is said and done, this proof that Una is stepping out with Cooper does not have far to travel to come home.

With all his guilt, and hers, what he feels most bitterly now—standing in a dark corner of his workshop, gaping like a tourist at the toxic event of his own life—is the missing of her. The missing, and his wish that he could alter that life, with all the killing power a burst of Zap! visits on a bug, so he could go back to the way things were only a year ago.

Siraad, the waitress at the Over Easy, talks too much, but that's a characteristic Harold Crewe is used to; something he even welcomes after a long night at the Camp Street boardinghouse, those pre-dawn hours lying awake after he has given up on the TV snake handlers and God-hawkers and World War II superweapons shows, and lies with only the scallop-shaped nightlight and the snores of his roommate to keep the heebie-jeebies at bay.

That is when the years on Seaview Avenue, in Osterville, start to straggle past, like a whole country of refugees: Mr. and Mrs. Timoshenko and their daughter, Jasmine. The old questions are so familiar they have no shape anymore but come at him like mist rolling in from the Sound, ubiquitous, pervasive. Mist or not, they still have power to make him groan: Did they know how long he kept the house going, with his savings and what his father left him, when they were supposed to be paying *him* while he was working for them as butler, chauffeur, handyman—even, at the end, as nurse? Or did they calculate he would stay on when their funds ran out? Were they grateful ever, beyond the thanks that courtesy demanded?

All they had left, at the end, was their good manners.

He never hears from Jasmine anymore, but that was always unlikely. The Home took her, and institutions don't like letters, "triggers" they call them, he knows all the jargon from Jasmine, from when she used to let him visit. Anyway she stopped answering his letters years ago and finally he too stopped writing. The house on Nantucket Sound was sold when the parents died, and eventually knocked down to make way for one of those huge McMansions, ten-thousand-square-foot piles of clashing details: medieval turrets, plate-glass bowfronts, Palladian porticos, Ionian columns, five-car garages with Hawaiian arches. He loved the old house but then he loves most old houses, their weathered wood and creaking floors; how soft they are with lives lived, even the Camp Street boardinghouse that has been sheltering people like him, people with little money and no will to change, since the Korean war. It is a shame that the boardinghouse too will be closed three weeks from now—knocked down to make way, if what they say is true, for a steak-and-ribs franchise. Panic blows in his chest and his heart hurts, though he took his pills this morning.

He has no idea where he will go when the boardinghouse shuts down. He looks around for more coffee, hot coffee always helps with the fear, and Siraad is right there as she always is, her chatter whisking away the dust of his nighttime worries, his daytime panic. She talks in an accent that is half African half southeast New England as if it's all one sentence, "Well *there* he is, where your coffee Mister Crewe, no I getcha the usual, newspaper is ovah theah see now they talk about that new airport runway again but not one word anymoh about our Mistah Swear."

The Over Easy is usually half empty but this is summer and a full moon and Crewe knows, from what Jasmine said about the Home, how a full moon brings more motion and trouble too. Trippers are here from the early buses, squid-white bladders of fat lolling from bright shorts and shirts. They snap at kids, wolf griddle cakes, consult smartphones, tourist brochures. Archie wanders over to Crewe's booth, he is thin and hopped with anger as usual, not what Crewe wants with his first coffee. Archie is so angry that his arms, neck and face look like a web of overtightened cables on which broad nose, graying hair, small black eyes and rimless glasses are riveted. His hands move like mice, quick, paranoid. "Don't go out on Main Street, Crewe," he says, "it's finally happenin' brother, white people going to throw our ass out of town, like Swear."

"Isn't Swear a white man?" Crewe points out, staring at his coffee. And Archie, who over the last twenty years seems to have read only one book, *Soul on Ice*, by a black revolutionary from the Sixties named Eldridge Cleaver, goes on about how some white men are righteous, some are even honorary blacks because they are part of the same class of people who are always kicked around. Swear, who in the warm months sleeps in the same fold of the Eel River marsh as Archie and sometimes shares a bottle with him, counts as righteous: though his righteousness, Archie warns, won't shelter Swear from payback when the Revolution comes.

Crewe snaps his tongue, it's how he disagrees. He picks up the porkpie hat and readjusts the brim. This is another way he registers unhappiness. As Archie and Siraad are yakking to each other he has time to go back to the idea of Swear, which he now understands was what mostly kept him awake last night, old anxiety over the Timoshenkos striking chords with more recent worries about his friend in trouble, his friend in jail. Crewe has a little fund that he built up after the Timoshenkos died, he put it in condom companies when the AIDS started, in startups that made hand disinfectant when the critter flus began streaming out of Asia and South America; had it in gold when the stock bubble burst. He doubts it will pay for a lawyer.

He feels panic at the thought of dropping back to zero again. And he feels shame because he feels panic over helping a friend in need. Siraad refills his coffee and brings him his usual scrambled eggs with sausage and tiny vats of fake maple syrup for the sausage. Crewe looks around him as he eats: cheap lino counter, booths of poor laminate coming apart under the assault of Atlantic humidity. The wooden collages on the walls make silhouettes of docks, olden-time schooners, seagulls. He gets a feeling, as he eats, of how lives come together—Archie's face-cables, and the chain linking hand-cuffs around Swear's stick-like wrists, and the lines of distrust and envy that divide tribes and men and never seem to go away entirely. The invisible lines of moon pulling the tides, the new smell in Hyannis Harbor and how quahoggers don't spend money at the Foc'sle anymore.

The killing of that kid, and cops everywhere, and people moving across the common areas—through woods around the high school, Eel River marsh, the poisoned swamps surrounding those ponds near Industrial Park—on schedules, in directions he does not yet comprehend.

Lines of money always connect people: him with Mr. Timoshenko, Mr. Cooper from the CRAC with Michael Connolly, the town council chair whose daughter is a partner in Hallett-Connolly Realty, which manages four buildings on Main Street. They don't pay each other directly but Ellie Soares, who lives next door to Crewe in the rooming house and cleans CRAC's offices for minimum wage, has heard them talk about the jobs to which they'll steer each other later, all legal of course, their lawyers make sure of that. Ellie hears a lot since as a cleaning woman she is not only there every day but next-to-invisible to CRAC managers. Because she's Brazilian they think she doesn't speak good English and it's true her accent is thick but she speaks, and reads, the language well. Sometimes she comes across discarded memos, notes, that fill in what she hears, and she shows them to Crewe but to no one else.

All those high-pay jobs will happen once the boardinghouse is gone, when the homeless shelter is kicked out as they are planning; when people like Swear and Archie, Crewe and Siraad have been forced out of a town that's rich and rebuilt; when the houses around the Winterpoor and Stewart Creek golf course have been sewered and sold, and dives like the Over Easy and the Foc'sle are knocked down. And Siraad, oblivious to her fate, blows over as if the winds of cheap java have risen again, to freshen his cup. "Only half a cup down Mistah Crewe whatsa mattah you still asleep?" She fills him in on the pills she takes, or does not take, to sleep a full night, none of which she swears to god ever seem to work.

Time For a New Look At Housing

The scene was straight out of Afghanistan in 2018, or the Mexican drug wars. State police SWAT teams were lined up behind an armored car, their M4A1 carbines aimed at a store where three men appeared to hold a female shop-assistant hostage.

But this was early summer, and the place was Main Street, Hyannis. Luckily the incident turned out to be more farce than tragedy, and the shop assistant was freed without harm by the homeless persons who held her. Nevertheless we must ask ourselves what men who can terrify an innocent woman into believing she is being kidnapped are doing on the streets of Hyannis.

The answer is: They should not be here. The Mid-Cape Shelter for Homeless Adults and Families (MSHAF), where the men lived, and which is three blocks away from Main Street's prime tourist area, is slated to be moved to Industrial Park. This plan should be fast-tracked so that services the poorest Cape Codders truly require can be administered far from the temptations of our prime commercial area.

The increased presence of state and town police in high-crime areas is welcome, but it is not enough. The Cape Realtors Action Consortium's plan for boosting cooperation between police units and business owners in a zero-tolerance zone around Main Street must also be approved by town council in the shortest possible time frame.

Council should also greenlight as soon as possible the greater Hyannis development plan sponsored by CRAC, including the Winterpoor project, which would bring in upscale condominiums and cultural facilities to currently less advantaged areas on Sea Street, south of Main. Purchase of the Barboza property off Sea Street, which is currently being negotiated, should be fast-tracked also. That plan would also bring in more housing for responsible members of the lower-income community.

Approving sewerage of areas next to Eel River would improve the groundwater of that area by reducing nitrate levels. The fact that residents will have to foot part of the bill cannot be allowed to slow this civic endeavor. Already nitrates, according to a recent Center for Coastal Studies report, have facilitated implantation of non-native seaweeds in Eel Pond.

Only by raising the attractiveness and safety of the town as a whole can we put citizens beyond reach of all crime, including incidents such as the Main Street hostage taking. As zero tolerance programs in other communities have shown, cutting the rate of low-level infractions ends up reducing the rate of more serious crimes. The drug-related killing of Devan Douglas near Barnstable High School last month should remind us that Cape Cod is not immune to this type of tragedy.

© *Cape Cod News Online*

❄

She goes back to the workshop knowing he won't be there—stands outside for a half minute reading the notice:

HYANNIS WATERFRONT SCHOOL
AND WORKSHOP
EBY NOBLE PRINT WORKSHOP
will no longer be open at this
location starting 8/15
We will reopen in the near
future at new facilities at
THE ESTATES AT GOSNOLD-WINTERPOOR
Call (508) 333 7357 for details
www.midcapeCRAC.com
MidCapeCrac on Facebook and Instagram

A QR code is printed underneath. The sign is stuck to the metal sliding doors with transparent tape. A corner of the tape is not glued down, and Daisy grasps it between thumb and index finger and pulls. Half the notice comes with it, the ripping paper makes a sound like jets passing far overhead, and the sound touches her, inexplicably sharp, beneath her breasts somehow.

It feels as if she is ripping other things: her uncertainty about what she's been doing over the last few months, her anger at Una, the years with Uncle Rick and Aunt Janice in Silver Spring knowing she won't ever measure up to a sister who is always older, prettier, more charming, and on time; about Cooch and how he fell into it too, that time they flew back for the holidays and he went along with some remarks of Rick's, she cannot remember exactly what but it was in contrast to Una—"a high bar," he said, something like that, it wasn't Daisy's thing.

No it certainly was not, unless you were talking about Nekropolis, or pubs, which were her thing in Willesden at least. She rips down the rest of the sign and decides to move out of Una's house.

Murdo isn't here, anyway. Not in the house, or the workshop. There was a big blow-up, she was not involved—it's not as if they were exactly friendly before but he has treated his wife, they have treated each other like unexploded ordnance since that day his friend got busted on Main Street. That day—

She looks for the padlock key where he hides it under a shingle then realizes the lock's hasp is broken, the smaller door opens with a touch, she steps inside. A domain of shadow and vague memory, the smell of sawdust, ink, sea-mold. Her cowboy boots thud across the boards, the thuds ring hollow against contorted rafters, against the dark pine boards with felt-tip outlines where his tools once hung.

His printing press is gone, the worktable where they lay together is bare; the sink area's void of the jars and bottles that used to cover every spare inch. The space once occupied by the barge looks big as all the high moors of Scotland that she drove across with Cooch one spring. The whole workshop changed shape to accept the craft and now the shop has gone, it has changed back into something else—an emptiness, a waiting, like a woman who has given birth, whose stomach though shrunk still waits to hold a life that is no longer there.

She touches her stomach without thinking, and changes that movement into a thrust of wrist, a slide pocketward. She pulls out her smartphone: 09:27. Now school is out for summer, Dog says, the kid comes here every morning, even now the barge has left. Dog has been sleeping here, Daisy suspects, since the mooring foolishness. Though he is never here when she arrives his sleeping bag is always rolled up neatly where Murdo's printing press once stood near the northern window. And there's a coffee cup, unwashed, in the workshop sink.

The lack of printing press affects her more sharply than the sign did, and lower; she feels herself soften, and cry at the level between her legs. As if her uterus were mourning. *Stop* it, she tells herself, and not until something gasps behind her does she realize she spoke out loud. She turns, suddenly frightened by this place though she doesn't believe in spirits—having been, as a teenager, to several mediums, hoping to hear something, anything, from her parents, an explanation, a weird feeling even. This workshop, unlike the patchouli-infused fug of clairvoyants' parlors, feels heavy with unseen weight. She always thought it was the barge, the deliberate violation of a dead man's studio.

Still no one is here, the shop empty as the gorsy vales of Perthshire—only now something stirs beside the door, near the broken table saw, behind a tarp. Did someone sneak in behind her? "Dog?" she says. Her voice catches, and annoyance with herself rises a notch. But she is not wrong. The tarp budges; a foot, in trainers, sticks out from behind the Korean blue. Too small for Dog.

"Boy?"

He rolls out. He does not stand, but slides on his ass to the nearest wall. He draws his knees up and pulls his sweatshirt hood down in almost the same motion. She walks over and squats to look at him from his level. He stares downward, sheltering under the hood.

"Dog told me you'd be here."

He digs his chin deeper into his shirt and yanks the hood over his forelock. If he looked any lower his eyelids would shut. His mouth, which is half open on one side, top lip pulled down over lower, twists his whole face one way as if everything there had suddenly gone off balance, the way geneticists say happens to a face when the chromosomes are badly skewed, Y chromosomes warped to Z or whatever.

"Boy," she repeats, and reaches out with her left hand. He

shrinks away. She stops the movement, straightens up. Her under-wear is damp. Damn him, she thinks, damn her for all of this. She misses London all of a sudden with a ferocity that surprises her. Kilburn High Road on a winter's morning, the sting of drizzle, the seared-grease smell of her chip shop. Rock cod was what they called fried dogfish. The kid shifts, draws his knees closer together.

"I saw a thing at the town dock," she tells the boy after a minute or so has elapsed; turning away as if this were casual conversation, as if she hadn't come here at least partially for this. ... "A class, no not a class, a kids' event thing, you know, it'll be fun. About the harbor, and crabs 'n stuff. I thought—anyway, d'you fancy going?"

His face is still angled downward but his eyes look up at her or almost, a little to the left. He picks his nose, thoughtfully, and eats the snot. Daisy looks away, and back.

"They'll have fish tanks, you can touch the fish and crabs and snails 'n that."

"Lady?" he asks.

"What lady?"

"Crabs?"

"Crabs," she agrees.

"Crab lady!" he cries, and Daisy stares at him.

"I—guess?"

"I can *do* that," Boy says, but does not move otherwise.

It's less a path, really, than a system of paths that run through thin woods of scrub oak, scrub pine and poison ivy to the east of Barn-stable High School. It backs, at the eastern and northern ends, onto the yards of ranch houses built in the 1960s to last the length of their twenty-year mortgages. They have been slowly warping, molding, coming apart ever since. The system is known to genera-tions of high school kids as The Path, the place every school needs where kids can smoke, hold secret meetings, fight and fool around and fuck if they're brave enough, safe from the gaze of adults and CCTV.

Near the middle of the path, three years ago, some tenth-graders dug a pit. The idea was to make a foxhole for a paintball game but since then someone has excavated the pit to a depth of eight feet and scraped a shallow cave at the bottom. No one is sure who did that work, or why.

And someone, equally unknown, a few weeks back lured or chanced upon a 16-year-old boy named Devan Douglas and shot him in the chest and stomach seven times with a small-caliber pistol. Douglas' body—alive, according to the coroner, if only just— was then rolled into the pit, doused with gasoline, and set on fire. The pit is still ringed by yellow crime-scene tapes though no one guards it now, and high school kids have turned it into a shrine, a place to get high and scare themselves with horrors in which, despite the evidence before their eyes, they are too young to believe.

5:40 in the morning, way too early for kids, and they're on vacation anyway. It is not even light although the eastern sky is paling. The ranch houses, which in eight weeks' time will be visible through bare trees, are hidden by leaves.

A man walks through the woods from West Main Street. He wears the blue-gray uniform of a state police trooper under a nondescript nylon windbreaker and hood. When he gets to the pit he ducks under yellow tape and moves around the hole, aiming the narrow beam of his flashlight across the dried, much-trodden earth.

After two minutes of this he stops. He takes from the pocket of his jacket a pair of latex gloves and snaps them on. From the other pocket he removes a ski-hat, cheap and nylon. He squats, scrapes briefly at the clotted earth, then grinds the ski-hat hard into the dirt, twisting as he drives the fibers deep. When he has finished he pulls a large baggie from a different pocket, drops the earth-encrusted ski-hat in, and puts the baggie in his jacket. He straightens, looks briefly around, and flicks his flashlight beam among the silent trees. He takes off the gloves and pockets them.

Ducking under yellow tape once more, he leaves the same way he came.

When Daisy came to the workshop she had Boy in mind. When Daisy came she was also looking for Murdo and not looking for him too. She does not feel guilty, exactly, about having fucked him. She knows Una is fucking someone else, she knew even last year her sister had lost interest in Murdo and stayed with him only out of inertia, and a form of kindness; Una, to her credit, dislikes hurting people without good reason.

Perhaps Daisy feels more nervous because of other changes. Walking down Ocean Avenue she notices the tide is so high it floods the marsh. And strong weather is brewing. On TV the newscasters, looking disheveled with an excitement that is almost sexual, name this weather Ramón; they point to patches of warm water near the Sargasso Sea, further heated by global warming, which cook a low-pressure zone drifting lazily west on the Trade Winds, making it rise: at higher altitudes the zone's humidity hits cool air, condenses, and tumbles down again as rain. The cycle of air rising and rain falling is like the stroke and counter-stroke of pistons, one weatherman explains: a churning pump of air that feeds on its own power and, Englished by Earth's spin, begins to twist, and move with the jet stream; and before you know it a hurricane is on the way and given a human name.

Boy shuffles beside her. His hood has fallen backward, his mouth still twists to one side in that worried expression that breaks her heart, what has happened to this child to make him so? Clearly he is mentally challenged, or slow—"differn't" as her great-aunt Molly used to say—but she has known "slow" kids who were happy and calm. Timmy, who lived three houses down the lane in Silver Spring, was always hanging around like Boy, chattering though and friendly, even confident in a weird way. Boys on MacArthur Lane who harassed Daisy and her sister,

George Michelsen Foy

who lay in wait for them with mudballs, who chased cats; they all liked Timmy and waved to him and treated him with what kindness boys were capable of. But someone has whipped assurance from this kid, maybe not physically but mentally, emotionally. You can whip someone simply by withholding love, she thinks, and that act in itself can be as concrete and sharp as taking a bike chain to a naked back. She went to Boy's house three days ago to find his parents or the uncle Murdo told her about but no one was there at all. She asks Boy every day about his Mom and the answer's always the same: "Workin'. Not heah." (That accent they have! "Oh my goo-awd, I gotta go to the moo-all!") When she asks about his Dad she gets no reply at all. So who is heah, or here, she asks and he says, "My uncle," and that's it.

She wonders about this ability to put-up, in Boy; in Murdo too. He put up with a woman who has not touched him physically or emotionally for fuck knows how long. He tolerates this kid who bothers him, though he also takes pleasure in imparting what small skills the shop can teach Boy. At the same time he puts up with this living evidence of a royally super-buggered psycho-emotional situation at Boy's house. Who knows what forms of neglect are going on there? She's suspicious of the whole PC obsession with repressed memory, the default assumption of abuse, but she also sees something real going on with Boy. His hoodie probably has not been washed in a year and his hair often as not is filthy and greased out and his hands are always grubby and he won't look at her now. Too often he simply does not interact. Would Murdo be a good father, with this ability to endure things that are just plain wrong? She packs that thought away for future study.

Anyway by now they have reached the town landing, which lies next to one of the boatyard hangars. Noble's scow sits where it was moved when they closed the shop, on a cradle to one side of the round-roofed hangar: an ugly, brooding marsh duck among the shining Vikings, Hinckleys and other plastic yachts. Boy starts edging in that direction and she takes him firmly by one shoulder, guides him rightward toward the landing. He won't go at first, then his shoulders slump and he gives in.

An open, flat-bottomed fishing boat is moored at the town dock, another poster child for neglect she thinks. There's not an inch of this craft that isn't scarred or scuffed, paint flaked, the outboard cover is half cracked-off and repaired with duct tape; its owner is just as distressed, he is middle-aged with a beer belly that seems to move independently of the rest of his body, lines fissure his face like arroyos and his clothes are grimy and ripped. A large, rough-furred black dog of indeterminate lineage sits grinning in the boat's bow. The fisherman hoists gunny sacks of the purple-assed clams Murdo has told her are called "quahogs" and dumps them on the dock. A fish trap full of weed plus crabs and other assorted marine animals lies beside them. A woman in jeans, t-shirt and a strawberry-blond ponytail has the top open and is fishing out critters and dropping them in a glass tank, eyed by a half-dozen kids of different ages, the younger ones curious, a pair of twelve-year-old twins bored stiff.

A handful of parents with to-go cups of coffee stand next to their kids, and she feels the whinge, the Why-couldn't-*mine*-do-that plaint which happens automatically when she sees parents taking care of children who are the age she was when they vanished from her life. Normal anger, the shrink Rick hired told them, as if endless anger is normal. But she is used to it, and discounts the feeling as quickly as she discerns it.

"There's no razors in this one at all, Brian," the woman calls to the ancient mariner, who has stopped what he is doing and does not respond. Instead he eyes a white speedboat with the words TOWN OF BARNSTABLE DIVISION OF ENVIRON-MENTAL AFFAIRS stenciled on the side nosing through moored boats toward the town dock. A man in lifevest and camo baseball cap is ogling their group through binoculars.

With a curse the fisherman unties a line and leaps off the dock onto his boat. The dog jumps up, tail wagging, to greet him. A loudspeaker blats from the speedboat, a command: "Stop. *Stop!*"

and then a garbled sentence ending with words that sound like "Gotcha, haji!" The boat's outboard snarls, emitting oily smoke that sets the parents coughing and commenting; and the Ancient Mariner is gone.

"Are you here for the group?" the jean-clad woman calls to Daisy, who nods. She takes the stuffed creature from his hoodie—he resists, then lets it go, it is oddly heavy in her hand—and guides Boy through the parents to the half-circle of children. A woman with short dyed hair stands to one side, smoking a cigarette beside a ten-year-old with pig-tails and a sullen expression. The woman lifts the cigarette clear as Boy goes straight to her and nestles into her sweatshirt. She smiles at Daisy, shrugs.

"My foster kid," she calls, "once."

Closer to the children a trio of parents keep watch through designer sunglasses. They remind Daisy of Enforcers in Nekropolis; Yazzo, Kets and Lin5, who lured her avatar into the southern reclamation pits of Papa Sector. She still isn't sure how anyone cracked her avatar, she paid major credits for an identity-bleach, changed cyphers, appearance, new Tor circuits natch. But someone did and for sure she knows who, and therefore how: because in their last weeks together Daisy was playing with harmonic decryption, detecting patterns that lay behind uncrackable random ciphers. It was all in the context of Nekropolis: she was looking for rhythms, timing, the lengths between players' messages to determine not the encrypted message's meaning but the habits and ID of the sender, from which eventually she figured out what tactics her team would face.

Cooch is a git, she reflects, but he's brill at what he does. And he took her harmonic and turned it into a quantum homomorphic program that tracked encrypted data in the real world: something far, very far, from her original idea, which had come to her when they let a cottage in New Forest, watching the bees, wasps and spiders and how they moved in patterns. He loved honey from New Forest bees. She winces, frowns, shoves him out of her head, although the idea of rhythms—rhythms formed and broken, and how they interact with other rhythms, making an overall pattern one can read and predict once one knows the algorithm—has been on her mind lately. The way Boy always shows at various times, not visibly regulated by school or parents, but leaves exactly at 1:30, frowning as he deciphers the boat-shop clock. How the tides rise highest at dark, not full, of moon; how her own flows move at the same pace, or did. The way hurricanes track in response to jet stream pressures a thousand miles away; how Murdo pulls her at certain times, and at others leaves her stranded. Sometimes he has only to look at her and his eyes are so dark, like old cherrywood, and yet so full of hurt that she warms up at once—as if she wanted to bring him inside to protect. She wants to hold him, and cannot.

Sometimes his hands holding a fork affect her the same way, and his way of waiting before he answers, and how he gets edgy, almost anxious, when he starts to work. At other times he looks aside, or down—like Boy, she sees now. Arms crossed, shoulders hunched, he stands immovable, angry, at odds with his world and hers. Then she feels as if the temperature had dropped and she turns to dispense her heat elsewhere.

Daisy shifts on her feet, looking up and left. Though she is only half aware of it, this is the posture that she adopts when defensive. The whole Murdo thing has suddenly gotten much, much more complicated, and this is astonishing to her. Her whole life, which until a year ago was like Hampshire's countryside, green and tame, has turned into the jungles of New Guinea, wild and unmapped and hiding people whose language she cannot speak. She went to a shrink when things started to go south with Cooch and one thing Mr. Morecambe, PhD., told her which made sense was that she uses sex—her looks (not like Una's but still not bad); her physicality or more precisely the contrast between her black cynicism and the play of curves and embrace (now *there's* a fault-line, Morecambe said, that gives permission to come in, be taken)—she uses all of that to score attention she never got in Una's shadow. But hooked up to that like a rickety caboose is the corollary, that once she has used it the power wanes. She could map Cooch's attention as a function of his randiness. When he needed sex, once a week (he was a Brit after all), he got interested in her and what she did and thought. After they had fucked it was almost as if he forgot she was there although, being a Brit, he pretended; always with the fucking politeness, the over-the-top praise, the pro-forma humility, all the while lusting to drop her and go down the local to talk footie with his gaming mates.

But Murdo? She can't say his level of interest has ever changed. In a strange way it's as if he did not know she existed all the time she's been here until that evening the raccoons broke in and she started laughing and couldn't stop. The way he looked at her then —with surprise, and interest; yes, she would swear it was interest— it never left his eyes afterward. It was there when he came into her on the printing press. It is still there, though they have done nothing more, sex-wise. The steadiness is what surprises her ...

The Enforcers have turned sideways now, as Boy shrugs off his ex-foster mother's hand. They follow him with their eyes as she gives him a small, encouraging shove and he advances shyly to the half circle of children. She senses other rhythms; must she really thank Cooch for this, that week in the New Forest? She will not be beholden to him for shit. Still, she notices another syncopation here: how, exactly two weeks after Una told her sister she was leaving Murdo—well, Daisy and Murdo.

Fourteen, no fifteen days after that, Murdo moves out of his house, camping in the cabin of that barge he works on. And two weeks after *that* they shut down the workshop. Coincidence? Daisy asks herself, spoofing the crap conspiracies Cooch and she played out online, I don't *think* so.

The patterns of position the kids make are changing now as the marine biologist lifts various creatures from the squirming trap and deposits them—crabs, clams, cockles, a small and twisting eel—into the glass tank. Daisy realizes she knows this woman, she came into the workshop once, though Murdo claims he does not know her. She is pretty, Daisy thinks, in a freckled, Hebridean sort of way. The woman is reciting the names of animals she drops in the water and then asks the children, with a little but not too much of that sugary Waldorf School Mommy-voice Americans adopt when talking to kids: "What else do you think lives in salt-marsh water?"

Boy hops.

Oh, god, Daisy thinks. She wishes, for the first time in at least forty minutes, that she hadn't quit smoking. This is what cigarettes are best for: to have something to do when you're nervous.

He raises both hands.

The Enforcers' dark glasses zero in, lasers set to cauterize the unclean, the tunnel dwellers.

The marine biologist smiles encouragingly at Boy.

"Yes?" she says. "Tell us your name first."

"Boy," he says too loud. A couple of the children snigger. The woman only smiles.

"Boy," he repeats, and starts to hop.

Her smile wavers, but she maintains it gamely.

"Okay, Boy," she says. "What else lives in seawater?"

"FISH-SHID!" Boy yells, hopping still.

One of the Enforcer females gasps audibly. The children stare at Boy. A girl giggles. Daisy thinks, I will have to pull him out of here. But harder, stronger she wonders, What will this do to him: what further patterns of rejection, insufficiency, alienation will be razored deep into his psyche 'cause of this? She takes a deep breath, a step forward.

And the marine biologist says without missing a beat, "You're absolutely right, Boy. Fish poop. And what other kinds of poop go into Eel Pond?"

A long pause.

A girl with a page-boy haircut raises her hands.

"People?"

"Yes, sewage, nitrates, very good. What else?"

"Dogs," says a boy. "Well, like, not poop, 'cause I have to pick that up. But when my dog pees, on the ground, like it goes in the water?"

Boy watches the other boy with interest. He has stopped

hopping. Daisy lets out her breath slowly, thinking that maybe, just maybe, this is going to turn out all right, even though the Enforcers' eyes are still zeroed in; even though nothing is sure or predictable, rhythms or no-rhythms, in this or anything at all.

The mistake occurred a year earlier, inside an Asian wholesale warehouse in Edgewater, New Jersey, that sells Japanese products to sushi bars across the American Northeast. There, a small batch of a massively crossbred, orange-colored, live strain of undaria pinnatifada—an edible, kelp-like seaweed also known as wakame—was forklifted to stand beside a stack of boxes holding a more commonly used pickled green wakame. From their proximity the foreman assumed all boxes were part of the same shipment and the live wakame was sent, along with boxes of the pickled variety, to the Hokkaido Restaurant on Main Street, Hyannis. The cook immediately complained about the "slimy" and strangely colored wakame and the offending batch was dumped back into the wooden crate it had been shipped in and left in an alley outside for garbage collection. Before the garbage truck arrived, however, the crate was emptied and taken to a deserted area of Eel Pond marsh, to be used as kindling by a homeless man who lived under a tarp in the marsh three seasons out of four.

Not all of the orange wakame was emptied out. A few leaves and, more importantly, several sporophytes remained in the crate, and were drawn into the water when the crate drifted away from the campsite on the following spring tide. The weed settled on the bottom where the sporophytes, stressed by their travels, immediately morphed into spores, which begat gametophytes and then sperm and eggs, which in due course became baby wakame.

There—among the mud, sand, urchins skeletons, plant detritus, brackish water, and a powerful cocktail of nitrate from a golf-course fertilizer called TurfChow—the sporophytes found a fertile environment for reproduction and growth. By the end of that summer, by the time the sushi restaurant had fired half its staff in preparation for winter, a patch of upper Eel Pond bottom roughly ninety square feet in size was mostly covered with the strong ropes and Halloween-colored leaves of undaria pinnatifada: so much so that local varieties of seaweed such as bladderwrack, sargasso and sea lettuce were smothered and repulsed by the new weed and fell back, like a battered army, to deeper water. But the wakame followed them there, and by the time autumn came had established a foothold in the outer bay as well.

Murdo has left the building, he thinks. Murdo is walking up the beach because after a suite of muggy, overcast days the weather has turned fair and hot and going for a walk in nothing but t-shirt, cut-off jeans and flip-flops is, after all, what you do on a lovely day in summer on Cape Cod.

Murdo walks down the beach south of the drawbridge, slaloming between mounds of flesh, some burned, some carefully oiled with SPF 30; between scampering toddlers, coolers, beach balls, towels, volley-balling jailbait. Suntan lotion smells sweet but it's a good sweet, a coconut waft that registers evocative in his nostrils, pulling him back down a chain of aromatic molecules to days on the shore with his mother and Junie; to orange soda and baloney/mayo sandwiches and a little plastic motorboat that capsized disappointingly in the slightest wind. The sounds are the same too, kids' cries, pop music, even the occasional hurricane advisory broadcast on someone's portable radio. Scream of gulls, hush of wind, the happy applause of Nantucket Sound wavelets.

But Murdo is in this carnival, not of it. Murdo has left his house in disgrace because he went to pick up his reserves of Olde Bilgewater Number 7. Last summer's brew, the "premature ejaculation" whiskey Dog called it, has turned out to be even more unstable than he thought. It proofed out so strong that when he picked up one jug to place it in a cardboard box, accidentally tapping the neck against a table's edge, it blew up or more accurately the cork blew off but it was as if the whole thing exploded, homemade hootch jetting in gouts as gold and tan as the skin on some of these sunbathing teens. It startled him so badly he knocked over the next bottle which, after falling, did explode, adding glass shrapnel to the mix; knocking three more gallon jugs in a row, which rolled off the shelf, smashed on the concrete floor—and blew as well in a blitz of moonshine foam and suntanned booze in the dank dim cellar; plus more glass shards and Murdo blood from a slash in his calf, all flooding the freezer area, the washing machines.

Una was upstairs. Murdo suspected she was waiting to make sure he did not grab the Cahoon. He took what whiskey jugs were whole, swept up the broken glass, and left the details for her to clean up. All this will probably be used as ammo in a legal separation that was the one item they agreed upon in the days after he asked her about Russell Cooper.

Murdo walks below the tide line where odd algae have piled ropy branches and slimy leaves the color of pumpkins to the depth of a foot or more. The waves ambush his flip-flops, their rhythms choppy, inconsistent. The heads of parents jerk and swivel, tracking the odor of bourbon suddenly blended with that of weed. Sand hoppers spring in waves out of his path. He has been trying to drive his thoughts out of the corral of Cooper, not zero in on the history of Murdo and Cooper's family and what happened to Coop's sister, what Audrey's family did afterwards to Murdo's. Now his thoughts buzz straight back to Una's lover.

He wonders what Cooper does about sand hoppers when he goes to the beach. Though he read somewhere they are a form of shrimp, the hoppers look like bugs, with feelers, exoskeletons and long pale legs. And Cooper, Una told him, hates bugs. Does he Zap! them? No, Murdo reflects savagely, Coop would avoid altogether the beach and its insects, to bathe in swimming pools of warmed, filtered gentian water surrounded by the South Seas motifs he and Una both adore. Do they enjoy threesome sex with C. Westport or Fairfield or whatever his name is? Wearing leis as they embrace to ukulele tunes, licking mai tais off each other's chests?

Herring gulls hover and swoop among the swimmers, then fly off, the pincers of spider crabs hanging like bony linguini from their beaks. A mound of black and a couple of interested kids mark where a seal crawled out of the sea last spring to die. Only bones and hardened skin are left. A little farther down the beach, where short dunes have formed between two jetties creating a sheltered area that Arctic terns use to mate, a shrieking arises; a couple of teens have strayed into the zone of nests and the birds dive-bomb them, pecking at their hair. The couple flees, screaming in terror. Two single-engine planes fly single-file, parallel to the beach. Both drag publicity banners that shiver in the planes' slipstreams. The first banner reads:

DON'T DRINK AND DRIVE

The second one, in fat red letters,

PIRATE'S RUM — IT'S PARTY TIME

Murdo wants to laugh, though the thoughts he's been having prevent him. Then he does laugh. And almost immediately stops. He hasn't thought of Audrey Cooper in a while. But laughing feels like lancing a boil—pus everywhere but the pressure lessens, which cannot be so bad.

Fortes Beach ends at private waterfront and a row of McMansions that succeed one another from here to the Eel Pond drawbridge. Murdo has parked his truck in the public area south of here and he decides to leave it there, though the bed is filled with pirate hootch, covered by tarps. The bottles smell, they could blow up in the sun, he might get busted and this would have serious consequences; in the storm of what is happening to his life these days, it all seems of small importance.

He leaves the parking lot and walks across Ocean Avenue to

the boatyard. A man fishing on the drawbridge reels a twisting black wriggle toward the tip of his pole. An eel. Murdo notes this with interest: eels are growing rarer by the year in Eel Pond.

In the boatyard proper a group of kids with attending adults is gathered around the town landing between the boatyard's Quonset hut and a fried seafood shack. Noble's scow squats on the marine railway, an aquatic riddle, chunks of barge and equipment that are clearly nautical but assembled in ways that don't make sense.

Murdo pauses, spotting another pattern that seems out of place: Daisy's black ponytail, and the outsized dark blouse she wears when it's too hot for her poncho. He recognizes her way of slouching with all the weight on one leg, ass tilted downward toward the other, cowboy boots. She is watching the kids and when Murdo looks in the same direction he realizes one of the kids, engulfed in his vast hoodie, is Boy.

Murdo strides straight to the scow and up the ladder. Murdo is not allowed to live on the scow, for insurance reasons according to the luxury-yacht dealership that bought the boatyard six years ago. But people from the old yard still work there and Murdo has known them all his life. He has established a don't ask/don't tell policy, lubricated by Olde Bilgewater, with the forewoman. He also knows that as soon as the dealership finds out he'll be evicted but this is fine with him; it's a mini-version of what is happening to him, to the peninsula generally. In the mood he's in it can all go to hell.

Once in the barge's cabin Murdo does not hide from nor dwell on problems. The gear train he engaged days ago by working almost all day on the Noble print has been turning all this while—though some days, due to factors beyond his control, it runs slower than on others. But the wrench the Bell sisters threw into his life did not plunge so deep as to throw those gears out of sync. He thinks that they actually shift up, to a lower ratio more suited for long hauls, to compensate.

Today he switches on the desk lamp and examines the copper-plate of Speed silhouetted against the door of the workshop and the cattails behind. Two days ago he finished the actual sketching, adding at the last minute a figure in hooded sweatshirt on the pond's other side, one of the homeless in the marsh.

And yesterday, before they hauled his equipment out of the shop, he filled a tray with mordant, in this case a "Dutch" formula containing nine parts water to one hydrochloric acid, proportions he copied directly out of Noble's notes. Using pincers that hold the copperplate by its edges he lowered the drawing scratched in ground across its surface into the acid bath. He timed it exactly, using numbers listed in his prints-and-whiskey notebook that corresponded with the ground, giving it sufficient time for the mordant —the term, from French, translates into "biting medium"—to gnaw through lines he'd scratched into the exposed metal, but not enough time for the acid to settle or bubble into the boundary layer between ground and copper, a flaw known as "foulbite."

"I will have *no foulbite*," he muttered to himself contentedly as he worked. Although in truth one cannot not avoid acid creep, the idea is, keep it to a minimum. He liked the word and kept mumbling "foulbite" as he pulled out the plate and rinsed off the acid at the exact time called for in his notes, then rubbed away the ground with turpentine and rags.

Now, looking at the etched copper sheet, he sees more foulbite than he remembers from two days ago. And once again he wonders what was the magic mixture Noble found that reduced foulbite to near zero while preserving flexibility in the sketch? He puts the plate back down and pulls from a cabin bookshelf one of Noble's notebooks: the seventh in a row of twenty-four molded, brittle but still readable journals that someone, maybe even the old man, long ago stowed in a locker in the barge's galley behind a mound of dented cookware and rotted dock lines, then forgot about. Murdo has bookmarked an entry from 1926 about a chemical product of some sort called "cat fat" or "kal fat." (Surely not the fat of cats?) He is used to Noble's chicken-tracks but this scrawl is near impossible to decipher. Just like Murdo, if for different reasons, Noble was in a rush to fix his barge: overseeing installation of the Kaiser's cabin, screwing planks and water-proofing the gaps between.

Of his mixture Noble wrote: *The substance is very thick and dark but melts astonishingly fast when heated for a minute or two. Most importantly, when added to my base ground it becomes soft enough that I create smudge effect with a blunt pencil and yet, when I use my finest scribing tool, the ground holds the thinnest line with absolute precision. Perhaps I have got hold of some secret laboratory project of the kri* (illegible)—Murdo quickly puts the notebook back, shaking his head, he's been trying to figure out "cat fat" for months and he won't suss it out today and anyway this is absolutely not what he wants to do right now, he will go on no excursions now. He picks up the copper plate again.

The teamed scratches catch light and throw it back off-angle. Murdo chooses a Charbonnel black from a line of tins on a shelf at the forward end of the galley. The benches on the cabin's starboard side are where he mixes acids and inks, they're protected with wide boards and here the deck planks are covered in plastic sheeting. It's hot in the little cabin, he turns on the desk fan, opens two portholes. Puts on his work apron, fastens the ties behind his back, pours ink into a plastic tray. He selects a brayer, dips and rolls it in the ink, and wipes off the excess. Murdo loves the feel of these tools: the friction of the brayer's platen against its fork, the slip of ink. He loves the way he can hear both gulls and boatyard noises, and the creak of his brayer as it rolls—loves this place that harbors harbor, this sense of ocean lying, no limits and all-powerful, nearby, while sheltered by a turn of sand. Though not qualified he loves working on boats that are made to withstand oceans but which for now, whether hurt or whole, are safe and at rest in this spot where people who travel over water meet and speak in common languages because the mechanics of good passage, the workings of a spring-line, are a dialect known to all who ply a trade on salt water. Is this feeling sentimental? Of course it is, he reckons. Entire shops on the Cape are devoted to plaster lighthouses and "sea captains" in yellow sou'westers that exploit the archetype—his great-grandfa-

126

ther on his mother's side made a living painting mermaids, for fuck's sake!—but the business of boats and harbors is also real and hard and lonely and sometimes kills you dead.

Part of what he does, of what Noble did, is try to make the real parts visible.

He rolls a sheen of ink into the plate's face, then wipes it off with a different linen rag. A gull settles on the scow's roof, screeching. A forklift roars. Pancho is not around. Murdo barely registers the noises. Now the only ink left lies in tiny furrows the acid etched into metal through lines he scratched. He uses the palm of his hand to wipe at areas where he thinks too much ink has built up in a given set of lines, then wipes the hand on his apron. With the gears in him turning smoothly, small distractions fall away like smoke in a high wind, like smoke off the steam freighters Noble drew when he lived in New York, sculling a boat and sketching at the same time in the Kill Van Kull.

Bigger issues, while they do not go away, are shaped, processed and drawn into the rhythms of his work.

When the face of the plate is clean apart from desired lines, Murdo preps his press. He wonders if the hurricane they are tracking will come close, and if he will be able to protect this studio if it does. He turns to the flatbed, which is only a pace away; it takes up a good third of the cabin. He hoisted the press onto the scow at the last minute with the help of Dog and a winch hooked to the black rafters, before the boat hauler came, suddenly realizing that without a workshop or a house he would have nowhere to work; although of course he could have moved everything to his parents' barn in West Barnstable, which is where he will haul the still. But he remains director of this project, even if Cooper for reasons of sexual jealousy or of older revenge has thrown him out of the shop he was supposed to work in through the Christmas "watershed." The scow *is* the boat-school now, even if it's not ready; this equipment belongs on board.

As he wipes down the bed on which he and Daisy made love, Murdo continues to think of hurricanes. He has fallen in love three times: with his wife, with a girl at Mass-Art, with Audrey too; and because the first time happened during hurricane season he equates his emotions then and since with the formation and life of tropical anticyclones and all their categories of power: one, winds under 95 mph, swamping boats and felling trees; category three, winds between 110 and 130 that flood coastal areas, already vulnerable because of sea-level rise, and trash boatyards like this one. At category five, over 155 mph, all bets are off, white foam covers the land, people are whirled, still inside their cars, into the next county and the world you know if you live near the coast is gone, to be reborn quite possibly without you.

Murdo lays the plate on its bed and locks the keys that fasten it in place. Daisy at this moment is a tropical storm that, like Ramón, seems to be growing in might and headed in his general direction. He has no idea if she will become a hurricane although the sight of her, standing hipshot as she watched Boy, warmed his insides to the kind of temperature that would make anticyclones more potent.

He kneels to look under the portside bunk. Underneath, a series of shallow, wide drawers hold sheets of linen-rag paper. Some of the sheets are rough in texture like the sea's surface in harsh sun as seen from an aircraft. Some are fairly smooth though with the grain of mashed fiber still visible, an even, flat stipple.

All are thick, whether made in Belchertown or Bologna, and heavy. They carry tension across their surface when Murdo lifts them, forming resistant tori as cardboard would. He picks an Italian paper called *cu'bambino* and sponges it down on both sides. Then he places it, very carefully so as not to smudge, over the inked plate and covers everything with felt blotters and a section of blanket. Slowly he twists the wheel that turns gears that torque the printer's bed under the steel roller. With his other hand he bears down on the sandwiched paper to make sure it does not shift. As the bed moves the roller crushes blanket, felt and paper across the locked plate, evenly squeezing metal, levering ink from etched lines onto the *cu'bambino,* melding both.

The image brings in the memory of Daisy, her arms and legs around him on this very surface, wave and particle joined in the instant when everything dissolves into everything else. He shakes his head. It took him five minutes of hard scrubbing to erase the image of Una that got printed on his ass when he and Una's sister started to make love on the flatbed. Thoughts of sex though not unpleasant are too specific, they evoke liquids and rushes that reflexively induce action in his own body, they slip the gears of work.

When the roller has run its course he lifts away blanket and felt and carefully peels off the paper. He examines the result. The warmth that rises in him then is not sex or love, though strings of both are surely twisted into it. The ink is fresh and well defined. The etching is strong, sharp and balanced. The black around the door makes sky and cattails beyond look the way an end-of-classes bell sounds on a warm June day to an eighth-grader. In the print, Speed Herreshoff is controlled and present as he never is in real life; but the shadows overhead, where old rafters twist on the shop's north end, are not dark enough, he must have rolled the brayer there too hard, squeezed ink away. And there's a touch of foulbite blurring, ever so slightly, the garboard planks. He unkeys the plate and lifts it back to the scow's workbench.

Seventy minutes later Murdo has three separate prints and the last two are quite close to what he wants. He is looking at them serially under the work lamp when the ladder scrapes outside. Someone knocks on the galley door. Daisy's face appears, pale and half-mooned in the porthole. Now he gets the same lift from her as from the cattails in his second-to-last print—which makes no sense at all. He is still married to her sister, a wash of missing Una floods him when he thinks of her, a swirl in his chest that would stop him from working were he still working, which right now he is not.

But when he sees Daisy he feels this burst, this over-the-top fireworks burst of joy-freedom; and how can he be missing her sister at the same time?

Murdo, abandoning thought, opens the door.

"I saw you earlier, we were at the class." Daisy guides Boy through the narrow door into the cabin. She is holding a supermarket bag half full of beach shells. The kid goes straight to the workbench as if drawn by some fey attraction to what he could most easily hurt.

"His foster mom was at the class too. He went straight to her."

"Kathleen?"

"Yep. How come ..."

"I got no idea." Murdo's mind is still on the prints. Daisy observes him a few seconds more, then looks around her.

"I've never been up here when you could really see it, it was always dark before."

Murdo tells Boy to stand clear of the moist prints. Daisy tells him to wash his hands. Murdo pumps water for him in the galley sink.

He shows them around. There's not much to see—workshop, sleeping loft, hatch into the engine room, the tiny galley. Standing there, showing her how everything fits together, they face each other so closely it's as if they were two galley appliances themselves, formed around the stove on its gimbals, the mugs on their hooks, the memory of them together—so closely it takes no effort at all to lean a bit closer and kiss her. Boy is out of sight around the bulkhead. Murdo's tongue, as if animated by a will of its own, slips into her mouth. She responds, but does not close her eyes.

Their lips separate. "I have to tell you something," she says, and lets out her breath in one woosh. "Something important."

Now Boy comes into the galley. They jerk apart like guilty teenagers.

"Moodo?" The blue of Boy's eyes is strong under a sunray.

Murdo stares at him. Did he mean "Murdo"? Boy has never used his name before.

"Come," Boy says, and makes a "come hither" sign with one

hand. "Come, Moodo." He walks out of the galley, into the main cabin. Murdo follows him. Boy is standing by the press.

"Oh, no, Boy," Murdo says, "that is not—"

"I kin do it," Boy says.

"Boy, this is *not* like screwing in a screw. You know?"

"Boy." Daisy is standing at the galley door, her shoulder leaning against the jamb. "You sure you shouldn't be home by now?"

The boy ignores her. She insists:

"Why do you have to be home at one-thirty, most days?"

"Look," Boy says to Murdo, "I kin *do* it," and turns the flatbed wheel which he can indeed, no surprises there, turn himself. Boy rolls the bed back and forth five inches, grinning. Murdo winces inside. These are his most precious tools, not like the power drill, and sharing them does not come easy.

"He wants you to show him how you make the etchings," Daisy suggests quietly.

Murdo crosses his arms, looks down.

"It's not that simple," he replies just as quietly, though Boy is occupied with the mechanism and does not seem to pay attention.

"No?" Daisy sits on the cushioned settee that lines one side of the saloon. Then she lies down, on her back, her eyes on the skylight in the barge's loft. "It's harder than the electric drill? I'm not being facetious, I'm talking about motor control, so to speak?"

"It's not the same—"

"Not the same thing? But he must have seen you do it."

"Sure."

"Which is why," she continues patiently, "Boy thinks he can do it."

"I've seen someone fly a plane," Murdo says, thinking of Wrong-Way Warny Ormesson and Una, "but would you want me to fly you to Nantucket on the strength of that?"

"Una says the pilot you went with couldn't fly either."

"My point is still—"

"Valid?" Daisy interrupts. "Maybe. Although did you ever think, maybe flying stunts was kinda thoughtless, in her case?"

Murdo takes a deep breath. He was very conscious of the fact, when Una flipped out over Warny's tricks, that Una and Daisy's parents died when their commuter plane went down in the West Virginia woods on a long-ago Christmas Eve. He had not asked the pilot to fly stunts though given Warny's reputation he should have expected it. Before he can respond, though, Daisy continues, "But this is not flying, it's art. That's why you won't let him, right? Because it's your beautiful art."

Murdo blows his breath out in a sigh. He has no idea why, but they are close to fighting. "Dais—"

"Can I move in with you?" Daisy interrupts, still looking at the skylight. "I can't stay with Una one more goddam day."

Murdo stares at her. The heats and wellings inside him drop moorings, shunt around. Everything is moving too fast, Daisy and he are juggling elements that should take months to weigh, to measure, learn. Yet after a few seconds only, when they have started to settle: those heats and wellings, a novel temperature, the williwaws of psychic wind; the idea of her being with him all the time doesn't feel bad at all.

"Is that what you wanted to tell me?"

"No. Actually, it isn't. I don't really know, I—oh, shit. I always say the wrong thing." She glances at him, and away.

"Your prints, I—I think they're really good."

"You don't have to say that." He finds the decision is made, easily made. "Sure," he says.

"Sure what?"

"I'll let him try."

"That's not what I meant."

Her eyes are back on the skylight.

"What the fuck," Murdo says. He opens a locker overhead and takes out a bottle of Olde Bilgewater Number 6 and two glasses but Daisy shakes her head.

Murdo sinks a shot alone, trying to remember what he should be toasting.

An old man, very tall, almost six foot four, walks down Sea Street in the direction of the harbor. He is what most Americans would call black though his skin is light tan, his features more Latin than anything—hooked nose, strong cheeks, the kind of Latin that includes Arab, Turk, even Norman, a mix of the races that inter-killed and interbred for millennia throughout the Mediterranean. His eyes are of striking blue, the color of a kingfisher's tail. He is dressed lightly in green slacks, a tan windbreaker, leather hiking shoes. He wears no hat, though the weather has cooled recently and it's drizzling a bit. His thick hair, white as vanilla ice cream, shines with droplets of humidity.

Joe Barboza walks like a military commander, or some medieval count surveying his territory: deliberate and stern. Fifty yards short of the East Hyannisport Co-op he turns right down Ridgewood, which at this point in the year includes a dozen potholes that Joe will have to fill; left down Hiramar Drive, right again along Winterpoor Lane, the dirt road that gave the area its name. Winterpoor Lane ends at Lusitania Circle and Barboza will patrol the circle too; he is walking the bounds of his land, the land his grandfather bought with the help of a personal loan just after World War I, when tourism was rare in Hyannis and real estate was cheap.

Barboza examines the houses on Winterpoor Lane, which are mostly half-Capes; two diminutive ranches, asphalt-roofed, vinyl-sided. The Pinas, his cousins, live in one—Pattie Manley there, and Kathleen Duffy, who took in Boy, next door. Too much junk in the yards, third-hand cars, Kathleen's van still bearing the dents Boy put in. Lawns mostly unkempt, and Maureen's gutters are backing up again.

People with not a lot of money live on Joe's land; good people, most of them, with a few exceptions, like the low-life woman Jeff married, Maria-Luisa, in the farthest half-Cape on Lusitania, he won't use the term some people use for this woman but her morals are open to question, not to mention her drinking—which is how Sonny ended up like he did, fetal-alcohol syndrome one doctor called it, "We can't be sure" (he said) "but the signs are there." And Mari-Lu's no-good brother, What's-his-name. Joe shakes his head, his memory is usually good, good for a man his age anyway, he does not like it when he can't remember. *Martin*, that's it: Danny Martin.

Boy's—Sonny's—guardian. Joe shakes his head, continues walking.

He has been called a slumlord but that doesn't bother him. Everybody here makes out okay, he charges fair and takes pretty good care of his properties and with eight cottages rented year-round he is rich by local standards.

With the money the town and the Cape Realtors group say they'll pay him for the Winterpoor, he and his family will be rich compared to most people you'd care to name.

All his tenants here will have to leave. The homeless shelter which abuts the Winterpoor to the north will go too. But the town is building a new shelter and it has promised to put up several units of low-income housing on this land, it will be in the contract; some of Winterpoor's people will move to modern, clean apartments right next to the old Stewart Creek golf course.

And he is tired, Lord, he is tired. He thought when he sold the bar he could relax, but collecting rent and dealing with plumbing and repairs and smoke detectors and heat problems and tenant complaints wears him out more every year. It is not up to him to solve the world's woes or even the problems of his neighborhood. He will be 88 in June and has a right to rest for what time he has left.

He stops outside his house, looking next door at the cottage where Jeff lived when Boy was born, before Jeff waded into a flooded cellar containing a live powerline while working construction on that off-Cape site. Danny Martin's pickup is absent and the house is dark. He wonders where Mari-Lu has gone, she has not been around for weeks. He wonders almost automatically where Boy is. This is a problem that has been going on since the kid was old enough to walk and is not about to be solved but it has nothing to do with selling this land.

He has worked hard all his life, and fought for his country. He has lost one son and his youngest is in Orlando and Joe has his eye on an area of Jacksonville Beach where he can live and tend a small garden and not have to worry about potholes and ice and tenants; and maybe in that area he'll find some home or institution that takes care of kids like Sonny.

He has done his best, Joe repeats to himself, firmly. He has looked out for his people. It is time, no matter what Eugenia says, to look out for himself.

Yellowleg, flying between summer breeding grounds on Ellesmere Island in the Canadian Arctic and its winter haven in Honduras, is in a hurry. Always in a hurry. Hungry too. Sea, land, sea again; before sea resumes he spots a familiar beach between the tern colony and a green bridge. The inlet is thick with strange weed, orange, never seen that before. But the complex wrack below the weed line on the bayside, below the deserted colony, is mostly bladderwrack, and that means chow.

He's a gawky bird with a white rump and speckled brown feathers. His thin pointed bill is near as long as his legs. His legs, tan as much as yellow, are almost as long as his body. The legs are as important to him as wings. On them he can skitter around at great speed and find in five minutes what awkward gulls would take an hour to score.

The beach is devoid of humans, for high summer has been and gone, already the warmer days are numbered. Right on time, he is, at this beach; ready for a quick snack. He lands in the lacey swag of waves, picks out a hermit crab, winkles out the guts, lifts his beak and swallows. Delicious. He skitters on down the line of tide, stopping to stab at dead blue crab, live sand hopper—chases the fleeing waves to snatch a vagrant minnow, scurries shoreward as the waves roll back. At a reef of strangeweed he turns fast and skitters back the way he came.

But the light fades. The days, though not yet cool, are shortening, and he is in a rush. A stutter on sand, a flit of wings, and he is airborne: over Nantucket Sound, past the brown-edged trees of Martha's Vineyard, south and west.

The Eel Pond boatyard closes at 4:30, though the men start picking up around 4. On a clear day toward the end of summer dusk falls just after 7. A security light near the office switches on ten minutes later. Apart from sunset, road lamps and the security light, the only other illumination at that point comes from the portholes and skylight of a broad wooden barge with cabin stuck on top, a stovepipe chimney and another smaller cabin plunked on top of that, lying on a rusted carriage that runs on russet rails into the water.

Inside the scow's galley Murdo has opened and warmed the family-sized can of baked beans, with wheat bread and butter, that are all he has to offer for supper. After they have finished, Murdo and Daisy sit on the saloon settee. Murdo sips at another Bilgewater. Boy sits at the work table on which lie three prints all bearing the strong chiaroscuro, the detailed whorls of an etching he made a month before. He keeps both hands on top of the paper, as if a breeze might blow them away. He takes them with him when they leave: Murdo and Daisy in the pickup, Boy scrunched between them, the etchings held gingerly on his lap. Murdo drives out of town, ten miles to the Cape's north side, to a white-painted, wooden roadside shack on a dusty layby off Route 6A. A wooden sign reads ICE CREAM in large letters and in slightly smaller type "Clam Chowder." In a different, more somber font below is printed, *Wiinikainen's Funeral Monuments.*

"What is this place?" Daisy asks as they climb out. Late-summer tourists and aggressive wasps bumble around neon in the stand's service window. Though the buzz of wasps and the scritch of tree frogs are loud the night seems as quiet as it is warm. The smell of spilled sugar blends with the sweetness of mown grass. A whiff of raucous laughter and techno music fade in the wake of a convertible full of twenty-somethings speeding to a brewery-bar in Sandwich. A yellow cone of light from a streetlamp picks out arbor vitae, cedars, crooked tombstones in a cemetery across the road. It's a warm night in mid-September and it is vast with smells and stars, stolen kisses, the melancholy of passing things.

"This is the Finnish part of town," Murdo says. "It's called Shark City, 'cause it's full of Finns." He waits for Daisy to laugh but when she doesn't continues, "They sell good ice cream here. They don't make it themselves but it's good."

He takes a lick of his own ice cream. Rocky Road.

"They also control the cemetery business in this town; they make the tombstones. The town's cemetery department is mostly people called Wiinikainen, Saarinen, Ranta."

"Isn't that a conflict of interest?" Daisy tongues a cone of maple walnut. "Every cardiac case caused by, whatever, hot fudge sundaes, a pint of mint chip—another customer?"

"But," Murdo begins, and Daisy interrupts, "They'll get 'em anyway, I know. Shark City," she adds, and almost chokes. "Jesus. You're kidding, right?"

He puts his hand on her shoulder, keeps it there. She doesn't shrug it off.

Boy spoons from a bowl of quahog chowder. The chowder is thick and viscous and drips off the spoon. His hoodie is stained with it already. He sits at a picnic table next to a family from New Jersey. With his other hand he holds his prints out of the way of chowder drops. His stuffed animal hangs limply from the hoodie pocket.

"Boy," Daisy says, "it's almost eight."

He looks at her, then back at his sheaf of prints.

"You never told me," she adds, still talking to the kid. "Why you didn't go home today."

The boy smiles, looking to the left of her.

"Why do you keep asking that?" Murdo asks.

She glances at him, bites her bottom lip.

"Because he won't answer?" Daisy takes Murdo by the elbow and pulls him toward a stack of granite slabs, future tombstones lying under spindly locust trees by the driveway's edge. She slides her British Army bag off her shoulder and opens it cautiously so that even if a whole crowd of snoops were standing around only Murdo could see inside.

"What."

All he can make out is the geological strata of a purse: keys to old apartments, a cotton scarf, lip gloss, coins, ibuprofen. Mysteries of womankind. Daisy frowns, re-excavates. Murdo leans over to see better. She looks up at him.

Now on top of all the other equipment lies something shiny and metallic. Murdo meets her eyes, she looks back steadily. He has time to think that he loves the calm gold steadiness of her gaze. He puts his hand in and feels steel, cool and strange in the warmth of her purse; his thumb picks up the crosshatch of a grip, a stubby snout.

A gun.

His pulse accelerates. Night, locust trees, the lights of the ice cream stand seem to shift slightly and acquire different intensities and values. The peepers are much louder. It's what guns do, he thinks vaguely: change everything.

Now, in this moment, he whispers stupidly, "Fer chrissakes! Is that *real*?" Yet he knows it is, something about the mass and coolness of it, even though the weapon's small, belies the idea of play.

She nods.

"You carry a gun?"

"*He* had it," she hisses back, jerking her chin in Boy's direction.

"It was in his stuffed animal, in the pouch. Also this." She takes a slip of paper from a pocket of her purse, and angles it so Murdo can read. He peers at it, adjusting his glasses.

"It's just numbers," he says. "Lists of numbers?"

"Duh."

"But—I mean." Murdo makes connections: guns, the Winter-poor. That uncle with the bad attitude. "Numbers running?"

"Look at the digits," she says. "All eleven or twelve numbers, followed by four digits, then three or four. The last ones are secu-rity codes, the first four are month and year." Her mouth twitches, annoyed by his slowness. "*Credit card* numbers. Which means they're prob'ly nicked."

"But why—"

"Because he *sells* 'em." Daisy looks at Boy, who has put down his chowder and now has both arms around the prints, surrounding them without putting pressure on the rolled paper. The Jersey tourists sit angled away from him.

"Boy sells stolen Visa numbers?" Murdo asks incredulously, his brain zooming off on what Una would call an excursion: Boy on the phone to a Mob accountant, reeling off accounts; Boy idly loading and unloading his pistol. The vision pops like a soap bubble.

"'Course not," Daisy is saying. "He delivers 'em, it's gotta be for his uncle, the one you told me about. Who sells 'em to people who do the fraud, you know. He was probably selling the gat as well."

"Gat?" Murdo says. "Seriously? Jesus, how many gangster films—"

"Whatever." Daisy frowns. "Gat, shooter, rod. Piece," she adds, starting to smile despite herself. "Hog's leg."

Boy crunches up his styrofoam chowder bowl with one hand, muttering to himself. The tourists get up, not slowly.

Boy looks around, sees Murdo and Daisy and, leaving crushed bowl on slimed table, makes his way over to the shadows where they stand. He smiles in that cockeyed way he has, shrugging his hood lower over his forehead, still holding the prints close. They printed out pretty well, Murdo thinks as he watches. The kid's whorls, the concentration and intensity of them, are effective in this medium. He should frame Boy's etchings and display them with the ones he, Murdo, makes. Maybe Boy's will sell before his own do, and wouldn't Cooper like that. The kid stands before them now and says, "T'ank you. *T'ank* you."

Murdo looks at Daisy. She has shut her purse.

"Thanks for what, Boy?" she asks.

"Chowdah. Good chowdah." Boy nods. "But I can do good too; *bettah* chowdah. You'll see. With sausages, see? I can *do* that."

He looks down at his feet. He is gripping the prints so hard now that Murdo thinks they will wrinkle and puts out a hand to stop him but just then Boy looks up and the left side of his top lip is pulled down all the way to the bottom and the light from Wiinikainen's ice cream, chowder, and tombstone stand reflects at different levels in Boy's eyes—he is close to tears.

"You're—nice," he says. "*Nice.* Give me—chowdah, lemme screw."

He makes a small hop, a pale version of his usual enthusiastic jump. He tries several words silently, forming them with his lips but not voicing them, and then all at once in a rush he exclaims, "I can make dinner. Boy can make dinner, chowdah. Tomorrow. At my house"—he winces hard, as if forcing the words out were physically painful—"for Moodo, an' you, too."

He looks at Daisy, then back at Murdo. "You can come? My Dad," he adds, almost ritualistically, "he showed me."

"And 'genia," he adds. "She says, you *got* to eat."

Sounds like Eugenia, Murdo thinks, then says, "Shouldn't you ask your uncle if"—but Daisy interrupts him.

"Of course we'll come, Boy. Right, Murdo?" She looks hard at Murdo. "We'd love to come."

"Not tomorrow," Murdo says, remembering. "Not this week, we're launching the scow, remember Boy? I got way too much stuff to do this week, what about next week?" He doesn't want to see the tears get any thicker, breaking surface tension and coursing down the chowder-silted channels of Boy's face. He remembers, with a clarity clear as acid, what happened at the Mattapoisett Paint and Nail Factory. "Would next week be okay?" he gets in, before Daisy repeats, "We'd love to."

"Next week, okay. Any week, you know."

"We'll talk about it tomorrow." Daisy touches Boy's shoulder with one finger. "We'll find the best day."

Boy nods, whatever caused his tears forgotten now. He walks back to the table to unfold his crushed chowder bowl and dig around with a spoon, looking for the last few chunks of potato. Daisy and Murdo both watching him as a new round of tourists line up, favoring the cash register manned by Mary Wiinikainen's granddaughter, who is blonde and pretty. Tourists who have already ordered file by Boy's table, eyeing him sideways. Murdo and Daisy look at each other and say, at the same time:

"What're we—"

"What're you—"

Both fall silent. They continue looking at each other. Daisy thinks, I like the way he looks when he's confused; which is maybe why I like him, 'cause he's confused all the time.

Murdo thinks, She is so pretty, like the flower she was named for, and yet she dresses like an off-duty vampire and carries a handgun in her purse, though it is not hers.

"Don't wanna go to the cops," he says at last.

She asks why by the way she stands and holds her head. By the way she looks up, and leftward.

"Because"—he fishes for a reason. He doesn't trust cops, he doesn't trust Gutzeit after everything that happened but this is not the core of it. What he also remembers is how, when organizations of protection get involved, it's like living underneath a cloud of wasps. If they don't see or smell you, you can pretty much live as you please, but once one of them sniffs your scent the rest swarm around and they will sting you unconscious. He has seen it happen to Swear, to others like him; not homeless people necessarily but people with no money to fight, in this country where money is the one weapon, apart from guns, that reliably works.

It happened to his family because of Audrey Cooper. He doesn't want it to happen to Boy.

He cannot explain all this to Daisy now. "We just have to wait till," he begins, but she leans forward and says "Wait, Murdo, wait for what? Wait till things improve maybe?" She bites her lip, and winces.

"Things happen, love, whether you wait or not, you are too good at waiting"; you are too good and patient and a little lazy also I think, too ready to hide behind your art and your homemade whiskey; but Murdo, the world is not good or patient and it chews and spits up those who are.

Only IRL she doesn't say anything beyond "too good at waiting," the other words stay in her head. She closes her mouth firmly and turns away, hands holding her stomach which is curved only slightly but thinking: Waiting is what I'm doing, it's all I've got right now.

And Murdo, watching her hands cup her stomach, feels for the second time in ten minutes as if the lighthouses and fixed stars of his cosmos have shifted slightly, making connections clear that were before invisible.

"My god, Daisy," he whispers, "are you pregnant? *Are* you—"

And she whispers back, to the peepers, to the locust trees, to the family from New Jersey and the moths and wasps buzzing around the street lamp: "I think so.

"I know it's crazy, just that one time?

"But yes, it appears I am."

The two men sit in a late-model Range Rover parked a few yards west of the Eel Pond drawbridge. From this angle they can see across the channel to the boatyard, its buildings split by security lights into bright planes and shadow. On the far side of a Quonset hut the tracks of a marine railway lead from dark water to land; there, on an awkwardly wheeled cradle, sits a houseboat/scow. It is

11 at night and the scow's portholes and skylight glow the color of daffodils from lamps inside.

The man with the shaved head opens a nip of root-beer-flavored vodka and drinks half. He offers the rest to the driver, who shakes his head with a scowl of disgust.

"So he's living there now?"

"Yep," Cooper says.

"It's not zoned for that, it's not residential. We could get him thrown—"

"I don't give a damn about that."

Link's squint eases to his companion, back to the barge.

"I don't get it. Isn't the barge part of the boat-art school, which is s'posed to be part of the redevelopment project? And he's, like, on contract for—"

"That was *yesterday's* plan." Cooper sweeps one hand over the dashboard to eliminate dust. "We're working on a new version and that shit-ass antique artist barge, that low-rent school—no way. They don't belong here. Not on prime waterfront, anyway. There's already a maritime museum for Cape Cod, they have perfectly good exhibits, they do classes, who needs an art barge."

Link finishes his nip. "So what do—"

"He misses the next watershed, he's officially canned. The watershed is when that barge gets launched, when it's *floating*. Do I have to spell it out?"

Link works his tongue, tasting the root beer. "Why do I get the feeling," he says, "this is personal—"

"You're not paid to have feelings."

The sound of tree frogs living beside a strip of nearby marshland takes over the air for ten seconds, half a minute.

"I'm paid to do what you tell me." Link presses a button and the passenger-side window winds down. He flips his empty nip into the night. Cooper sighs.

"I wish you wouldn't do that."

"You know what I wish?" Link's eyes squint toward Cooper, and away again. "I wish you wouldn't interrupt me all the time."

They listen to the tree frogs.

"Just—use your imagination," Cooper says.

Chicks, chicks, look at 'em all, skittering over homemud as tide pulls out, pulls me. Spring tide and the last full moon of summer, blue-silver light and this is force! Power in the whiteness of the Mother Orb, power in its perfect circle and the way it pulls the pond almost to breaking point, farther than it ever goes the rest of the watercycle so that mudflats and then sandflats go on forever. Power in this right claw, yes size does matter ladies! This claw that is at least as big as the right claw of the guy in the next-door burrow and, by the way, my burrow is deeper than his, I have tunneled almost two feet into the mudbank, deep under the reefs of new weed and wrack, under the eelgrass and spartina roots: the safest, coziest place you could imagine to raise our little brood of fiddler crabs.

You there, with your small and dainty right claw, your opalescent carapace, those shapely legs, I wave at you and boom! I thump my claws and feet against the substrate. Look at my balls, my big balls of sweet mud neatly wrapped from all that burrowing; little balls also, that are what's left of all my dinners, scrumptious flakes of dead shrimp, moonjelly plankton and crab—cannibal? Why sure, who's fussy, it's all tasty and nutritious and dead; all fuel for those eggs you need fertilized, babe. Brilliant scavenger, that's me, one of the best, which you will need because this pond ain't what it used to be, there's less life in the upstream arc, the water stinks. My folks came from Brackish but we had to move. Let's not get negative here.

Boom! Boom! Bastard, get a-way from my burrow. Boom! (She's moving to my side. Yes!) Boom! Get the fuck back to your side, wimp! (Come on honey. Mind the big balls. In ya go. I'll even chase off that other chick for you, you're way hotter.) ... It's good to be a fiddler crab with a big claw and a cute little honey to lay eggs deep in my crib. I'll close our hole with a hatch of mud and goop, we'll rock all night! Crab sex, babe, come all over those eggs of yours 'cause it's good to be fiddler crab who is the darling of the moon, who submits to the moon perhaps but controls it too; all depends on attitude, how you look at it, right? Dark of moon, new moon, two weeks from no-moon then when tides are lowest, currents weak, is when me and my honey will come out and party. Then she will lay our eggs by the pondside and we'll say goodbye to our two thousand kids, because we serve the orb but we run things too, we know that these half-moon tides, these neaps, will treat our larvae with care, touch them only with their gentlest pull, float them the shortest distance possible out the cut and into the warm ocean, the Sound. Where they'll chow down at the copepod buffet.

Fiddler crab knows moon and tides and how to use them. Moon will come back, swing overhead, and all the power will return to wash our babies, now crablike truly, back through channels to Eel Pond, the gentle pond, the Home.

Tropical storm Ramón, supercharged by hot seawater between the Antilles and Bermuda, has by Saturday morning become Hurricane Ramón, a category two storm with winds reaching 108 mph. But hemmed in from the west by a high pushing seaward from Ohio and pulled to the east by an Atlantic low, Ramón merely boxes the ears of the lower Carolinas then roars off furiously into empty ocean, leaving the continent's east coast largely unscathed. A swirled trauma of clouds, a moist and strong southeasterly wind, and drenching rain are all that's left to mark its passing Tuesday.

On Wednesday only rain is left. A *Cape Cod News Online* reporter who shows up at 9:30 to photograph the launch of the "boat-school barge" as he puts it (reading from an assignment sheet) wears a bright yellow sou'wester and covers his gear with a box-store bag. "How did you find out about the launch?" Murdo asks the reporter, checking caulk is dry between the last planks Dog fitted to finally make her watertight. "It's not the official launch, we're just making sure it floats, it's not fully renovated."

"I just get the assignments," the photographer says, "you'd have to ask my editor." But Murdo doesn't have to ask, only two entities could have requested coverage, the boat school and CRAC, and since Murdo is sole employee and acting-director of the school, in name at least, that leaves only CRAC, and Cooper. He wonders why Cooper would want to blow some of the publicity value of a launch on this technical dumping—but now Daisy is here, with Boy; she took the pickup to fetch Boy from his house.

It is astonishing and somewhat frightening to Murdo how after one act of sex and weeks during which they barely saw each other, let alone dealt with what happened, they have moved in five short days to domesticity on the landbound scow. They make breakfast in Noble's galley, lie on settees on opposite sides of the main cabin, Murdo sketching, she involved in dark battles that, illegally streamed through the boatyard wifi, play out on her laptop screen. She uses his soap, his shampoo; unlike other women he has known she owns few toiletries of her own. They have made love three times, twice on the thin mattress in Noble's sleeping loft and once in his parents' barn in West Barnstable.

Murdo is not sure how long this can last and if it does he's not sure he's ready for it. He has only recently separated from his wife and part of his character, the marauding Y chromosome he supposes, insists that he should not tie himself down again so soon to one woman; should instead cast his seed far and wide, or flirt with girls in tourist bars at least.

But most of him feels good. The lack of readiness, paradoxically, fits like a tenon into the mortise of his life, which has never seemed prepared enough to grasp all variables. A related character trait, he hopes, is a not-unhealthy aptitude for change. As for Daisy's baby, their baby, which is now real—she ignored her first missed period, and doesn't seem to be affected by morning sickness, but has pissed on a stick three times since and every time it came up pink—from what he's been told by friends who've had kids there is no such thing as being ready.

They talked about it, once.

"I'm gonna keep it, Murdo," she told him, with that look she gets when the Enforcers are crowding around her in Nekropolis, "even if you don't want it, even if we're not together."

But he suspects on balance he does want it. And the idea of having a kid with Daisy makes him feel curiously calm, almost fatalistic, as if he has entered another level of being where not being ready doesn't matter anymore, because what happens now is up to whatever gods made all this happen to begin with.

The scow, on the other hand, *is* ready. Murdo has drawn up checklists for engine, hull, and deck and gone over every one with Dog and Claire Crosby, the yard forewoman. They went down the lists Friday, after Murdo and Daisy moved to West Barnstable. Now, with the boatyard tarmac gleaming like a seal's coat with rain and the scow's scuppers hosing out water, Claire and Murdo, Daisy and Boy congregate in rain gear by the diesel winch that drags the wheeled cradle up and down the rusted railway on which Noble's scow has sat for the last couple of weeks. Old-fashioned tech for a retro scow; because of changing sea levels the average tide in Eel Pond rises five inches higher than it did a decade ago and two-thirds of this marine railway's tracks lie too deep to be of use; plans are afoot to rip them out altogether. The modern plastic speedboats that make money for the dealership are launched differently, on a travelift, a giant motorized mobile hoist in the form of two upside-down "U"s that scoops boats in and out of a special dock, on canvas slings.

Grip, a red-haired twenty-five year old, climbs into the scow so he can monitor the stuffing box, which seals the propeller shaft and always leaks at first as the hull goes in. Murdo checks depth of water. The lagoon around this railway has silted up. "It's six feet," he tells Claire, "almost a full-moon tide, we'll never get better depth."

"Storm tide," Claire says, "this pond gets really deep, that's the only thing would be better.

"So we're ready to go," she adds, looking for some reason at

Daisy, who is looking at Boy. The wind gusts, rain falls harder, raising a billion silver pimples across the surface of Eel Pond.

"Just a sec," Murdo says. He takes from behind the baulk where he hid it earlier a bottle of Olde Bilgewater Number 7 and walks toward the barge's wedge-shaped bow. "That's right," Claire calls, grinning, "christen 'er!" The photographer gets excited; there will be some sort of ceremony after all. He runs around between water and barge and aims his camera at Murdo, who holds the bottle by its neck over one shoulder, as if it were a Molotov cocktail —and hesitates.

He had been going to christen the scow the *Eby Noble*, though he has not consulted Cooper or anyone about this. What stops him now is not the fact that he hasn't consulted anyone, but the name, which suddenly seems all wrong. The *Eby Noble* sounds like what you'd name a destroyer, or a supertanker, not this bizarre floating art studio. "What do I call it," he yells to the group.

"You haven't picked a name yet?" Claire says, "Wow!"

Daisy is grinning, both her hands on Boy's shoulders because he is hopping and straining toward Murdo. "I can," he yells, "I can *do* it!" And Murdo, adrift in the lack of control over his own life; stung by Daisy's accusation, only ten days ago, that he spends his time waiting—and in truth, he tarried too long in deciding what to do about the gun in Boy's Stuffy, till Daisy finally opted to hide it, and put a note in the Stuffy saying they would go to the cops if Boy was again used for illegal schemes—decides he *will* decide, for once. Doubly easy to decide this because CRAC will have their own ideas anyway and they'll probably scrap any name he chooses but this can be their private name for the scow, for now, and why not give a little pleasure at the same time.

"I christen thee," he yells, "*Noble Boy!*" And smashes the bottle against the flat bow, shading his eyes with one hand in anticipation. Sure enough the bottle explodes, so hard that glass and whiskey rain over his oilskins as well as across the scow's fresh white trim. Daisy stops laughing, thinking maybe this name is not a good decision given what he told her about the CRAC and Cooper. Then she smiles again, and whispers to Boy; who hoots in delight, and puts both hands on the brake lever Claire is holding.

"Whoa," Claire says, "this isn't for kids." She looks at Daisy again, then at Murdo as he rejoins the group. Claire is calm and assured in all things.

"What you *can* do"—she takes Boy's right hand, places it on a second lever. Boy's hands twitch and his eyes follow her movements like the eyes of a cat watching a chickadee.

"When I say so, you push this lever down, it releases the pawl, see? Down—an' that allows me to let go the brake so the boat can go in. Ready?"

Boy nods repeatedly. Claire winks at Daisy. "Okay, push"; Boy thrusts down with all his might on the pawl lever, and Claire pushes her own lever. A vast metallic groan rises from the rusted gears. Slowly the cradle's wheels start to turn, and the scow, *Noble Boy*, rolls slowly down the track toward rain-pocked water. The cradle on entering makes swooshes in the water that march in slick platoons across Eel Pond. The hull should begin to float when two-thirds of the cradle is underwater. It stays fixed in the cradle and Murdo wonders if it's not stuck there by a brace or chain that they neglected to loosen.

Then it makes a movement, independent of the railway, slight and vertical. The stern lifts, the hull comes level.

It makes Murdo happy, in some pocket of his being that believes in balance, to see the scow's waterline rise, dip, and hold almost exactly parallel to the water.

"It's free," he calls. He trots along the dock to grab one of the long mooring lines that were previously strung from the barge's bollards to the wharf. A second boatyard hand, who was watching from the shelter of the office stairs, tails onto another line. Together they haul the barge off its cradle, flipping lines over vertical struts that held it in place.

It's heavy as a contrary sow, Murdo thinks. Every time he leans back and pulls the barge his boots slip on the slick planks of the wharf. Someone shouts, "Stop! What the fuck?" The shout comes from the scow. "Stop!" again, almost a scream.

Grip pops out of the studio door, fast and abrupt as a Punch and Judy character. "It's sinking!" he yells at Claire, "fuckin' thing's sinking!"

Murdo stops breathing. He is so used to thinking of this barge as a pig, a problem, a bolt-hole that replaced his living space, that he is staggered at how much horror the idea this pig might sink summons inside him. He takes a breath now and calls, "Is it the caulking?" but Grip is too busy yelling "It's sinking!" to hear him.

Murdo steps dangerously from the dock to the barge's stern. The sole of his workboot slips on the gunwale's slick paint and he only just manages to avoid a fall, hanging on to a strut, his body at an angle to the water until he pushes himself backward, falling pathetically on the scow's deck, on his ass but safe. Muttering *filho da puta* he rushes into the cabin and down the ladder to the engine-room. He hears water gushing strong, in the confined space it sounds loud as an open hydrant, but it doesn't come from the engine area or the stuffing box, it's forward. Still, Grip is right, at this rate of flow the barge is going to sink. Water already licks the floorboards. Nearer my God to Thee, Murdo thinks to himself, stupidly.

He climbs back topside, his ass and back aching from the fall, and onto the wharf. With Claire, Grip and the other hand all hauling on various lines, they drag and twist the scow, its waterline already submerged, back toward the cradle bed. The barge is deep enough that it hits the cradle's middle brace and prevents them from hauling it further. If the hull sinks much more it will not slide far enough up the cradle and the craft will slip off and founder where it lies.

Claire drops her line, runs back to the winch and lets the cradle roll out as far as it will go; this time the scow's bow catches on the brace then releases, and they pull the hull landward far enough for the cradle to hold three-quarters of it.

Enough.

Grip and Murdo tie lines from barge to cradle. Claire starts up the winch and drags cradle and scow fifteen feet up the rails till the hull is resting out of the water and out of danger. Water rinses off the barge. It is gushing from every through-hull valve the hull possesses.

Murdo looks around him; at Claire and Grip, panting and grim; at where Boy would be if he were still at the winch, which he is not.

Daisy, standing by the winch controls, stares inland toward the harbor road, and Murdo follows her gaze.

The gray hoodie is hard to distinguish among the thin spears of rain but it moves as fast as Boy can run toward the Winterpoor.

Something is wrong here, something has definitely gone awry, though on the surface nothing has changed in Eel Pond. The water on a calm morning is flat and shiny as a dance floor. The tide swells to full, gulls wheel and screech, the fish hawks that live in a nest atop the chimney of a McMansion to the east (to the fury of its owners, who now cannot use the fireplace, nor evict the nest without a conservation easement) still cruise the marsh, uttering their shrill cheerk! *to each other as they search for snapper blues, the juvenile bluefish that swim into the coves at autumn's start. One of the ospreys tucks its wings and dives. Coming up with a snapper, it flaps mightily to take off, the fish jerking in its talons, leaving a staple pattern from wing strokes in the water.*

Horseshoe crabs, their mating done, amble the shallows like brown, archaic battle tanks. Scup fin above them, lunging at plankton and minnows, being lunged at in turn by the hungry blues as they crowd in on the flood.

This is normal, it's all well and good and such activity, this strong, regular pulse of estuary life, goes on for half the area of the lagoon.

In the northwest stretches though, where the water shallows into mudbanks and the lagoon narrows to the creek that feeds its head, life slows.

A diver swimming into the area sees a sudden thinning out, a dip in rhythms. If the pond had a pulse it would be weak here. Suddenly there are no fish. Zero. What bottom is visible looks like a cemetery in a zombie movie. No hermit crabs or scallops are there to eat the dead, and so the dead have taken over, blue crab and sea urchin shells mostly, piling up exoskeletons that in these places of low tidal flow are not polished and clean but take on a dark mascara of mud and other rot.

This graveyard is only visible in spots for the wakame spores sown last summer around its initial patch, bulimically devouring the nitrates that flow so plentifully down Eel River, have flowered. From ninety square feet at the start of summer, the weed now covers a third of an acre inside Eel Pond, in areas where tidal flow is weak. And it has expanded its colony beyond the drawbridge, into Hyannis Harbor. On Eel Pond's bottom it blossoms and sends out more spores and when it dies its leaves combine with oxygen in the water to rot and become part of the detritus of which the bottom of the lagoon is made. The process absorbs almost all oxygen in that tranquil corner of the lagoon, creating anaerobic pockets: dead zones where no other organism can breathe. Alewives heading back to sea, exhausted from spawning, have blundered into such a zone and drowned for lack of oxygen, adding their own corpses to the process that killed them. Horseshoe crabs pass out and die. Near shore, at low tide, a few surviving soft-shell clams poke their snorkels out of the muck, gasp deeply for air.

The water, paradoxically, grows clearer where life fades. Strong winds disturb the lagoon, and decomposing shrouds of wakame are washed into shallow waters and pile up against the eelgrass. The rotted weed does not smell like normal death. Mostly because there is so much of it, the undaria concentrates its own stench, a mix of methane, fish shit, and the staleness that happens when not enough air exists to foster normal decay—"the rot of hell" is how the marine biologist thinks of it, smelling it even through her mask as she digs glass beakers into the mud for samples she will study later.

The rot that happens when death itself breaks down.

Murdo on the beach once more, this time at night.

He is half-drunk, and holds a bottle of Bilgewater Number 6 in one hand. No moon, and only the last and hardiest of necking teens occupy the beach parking lot, along with their packaging: barbecue chips, beer cans, the torn envelopes of condoms, all dusted with sand.

He walks south with deliberate care, anticipating the slackness in his reflexes, placing his heels exactly, as far as he can tell by the glim of stars and beach-road lights, into tracks made earlier by sunbathers. He only trips occasionally; once over a couple so intricately involved that they barely protest (he thinks of Daisy, briefly, but sex is low on his list of concerns right now); over a ride of weed, a piece of dinghy broken earlier by seaborne assault.

Drifts of blue crabs, all dead. A blown-out beach chair. He stumbles on what feels like, and is, a body—heart blamming, breath hurting his windpipe. It's only the dead seal he spotted last time he was here. He trips over a log thrown clear by the gagging sea, and picks it up.

That the sea is gagging is something of which he is sure for the smell here is strong and bad. It's not bad with seal, which mostly dried; nor is it bad with the rot of open sea, for that is not bad, Murdo thinks: Rot is work the sea performs in its salt chambers, it steals the death and sickness of its citizens and employs their energy, distills it to a different spark—food for life, made new and clean again.

That's what Noble saw in the decay of coasting schooners. How in the act of dying they wrote a new and different poetry. How nostalgia means nothing to the ocean, though one might love its previous forms, because what the sea does best is change.

But the stink here is so strong, so altered, that Murdo wonders if something has happened that for the first time has killed Nantucket Sound's ability to change, to assimilate and cleanse everything that dies. Just as inside himself he wonders if the angers have piled up so high they might make him incapable of finding his way back to balance, to the flex and tides of reason and happiness.

Murdo takes another swig of Bilgewater, he uses the kick of liquor to torque his thoughts.

The barge is a wreck again. Even if he and Daisy wished to return it is uninhabitable, canted in its cradle. It was thought best to let water drain to one end while pumps there emptied the hull. Uneven though their lives are anyway, he and Daisy could not adjust to fifteen degrees of tilt.

He kicks a section of two-by-four free of dead crab and adds that to the fascia of wood under his left elbow. He has already found a plastic milk jug, gallon size, which he stashed in a shoulder bag. The wind is from the east and chilly but the chill will not last, for Murdo has a plan. He kneels in a clear patch of sand and scrapes a shallow hole..

What Claire and Grip found, once the water had gone, was that the hoses for every drain and intake to the scow—galley sink, head, engine coolant, a wash-down port, four deck drains—were removed. Not just unclamped but deliberately pulled clear, then lightly rested on the pipes that led through the hull. And the valves, the seacocks, that should have closed those pipes were open so that once the barge was launched and the through-hull fittings were underwater, salt-water displaced the loosened hoses and spurted into the hull.

The day before the launch, Grip had checked the seacocks were shut and the hoses clamped on, though he had neglected to double-check just before launching.

The boatyard's closed-circuit television showed a man in jogging clothes climbing into the barge the night before the accident. The figure was unrecognizable, his face obscured by a pandemic mask but Murdo thought he recognized the crew cut, the tall frame of Cooper's operations guy.

The outrage that surged in Murdo over it all surprises him, he had not thought he cared so much. Water hurting the hull that Noble worked on feels like a hand laid on a child, a wildflower stamped on without heed or need. The anger he kept at bay with thoughts of Noble and sea change and the effect of walking, now clouds up his mind the way an octopus dyes its neighborhood with sepia. Murdo takes from a shoulder bag a handful of supermarket flyers (Hanger Steak! Special Two-Day Sale!), scrunches them, and lines the hole he dug with paper cabbages. He chooses the thinnest, driest pieces of driftwood and builds a grid over the paper, placing the heavier wood on top. He takes out a box of matches—it's from the Tashtego Grill, a restaurant where he and Una once ate in Nantucket—and on the fourth match gets the newspaper to light.

The flames, cowed by wind, spread slowly. Murdo sprinkles an ounce or two of Olde Bilgewater and the fire leaps like it's been goosed, turns blue. More paper catches, then kindling. Heat feeds on heat, light unwinds from the firepit and makes a larger cave of orange yellow in which Murdo and his anger crouch, black trolls against the fire, waiting.

They come at once. Sand hoppers, drawn by heat that reminds them of the sun that woke them from their larval sleep, advance like a horde of mini-guerrillas on pogo sticks. They are half-inch long, beach-versions of shrimp and their shiny albino carapaces glint in the fire's light as they hip-hop and slide on crystals of sand. They pause, flex their long pale legs, jump closer. Dozens, then hundreds of them. As they climb over the sides of his fireplace Murdo traps them in one fist and dumps them in the gallon jug.

The sand hoppers are just as numerous and alive as the blue crabs are numerous and dead along this beach. Murdo wonders about this, and the anger in him examines this question, turns it over the way Pancho turns a sweetmeat he is not used to, looking for a link to what he understands. It takes twenty minutes to fill the jug to a depth of one or two inches: eighty, a hundred hopping insects, he reckons. More than enough. He caps the bottle, kicks sand on the fire, gulps down the dregs of whiskey. Then he stashes the jug full of hoppers in his shoulder bag and walks back, less carefully—swerving a little, toward the parking lot.

He drives by his old house first, no cars are parked in the drive. Eight-foot lengths of four-by-four tarred wood, are stacked by the driveway; the tar smell is strong through his open window. In the security lights he sees the horizontal thrust of Una's lanai is half finished now. Something moves in the stacked wood: a pair of eyes gleam in the lights. An animal waddles out, muzzle down, ass high, long tail dragging, the typical raccoon walk.

"Pancho," Murdo calls.

The raccoon stops, sits back on its haunches, and makes a chur-ring sound. Its mustache is very white under the blackness of its mask. "Yeah," Murdo says, "nice to see you too, ole buddy, but I got stuff to do."

Murdo turns back onto Old Colony Road, then right on Shaughnessy toward Hyannis Harbor and the larger houses—mansions only slightly smaller than the ones beside Eel Pond's drawbridge. A sign reads, The Gardens at Ripple Cove Estates – A Private Community. Security lights blink on, then off, as he drives in. Lawns are wide, smooth and black as licorice, swimming pools glow a weird cobalt, like containment pools for plutonium.

The fifth house on the left is Cooper's. Three cars stand in the drive. Una's Swedish car, an American SUV, and Cooper's German convertible. One light is on upstairs. Outdoor spots shine at the house's front, the driveway's half in shadow. Murdo parks on the street a few yards past the drive, in the shelter of a tall rhodo-dendron. He is sober enough to think of cops at this point, and CCTV, but drunk enough that the effort it takes to keep a straight line—in walking, driving, and intent—feels like its own surety. With this much momentum, the whiskey says, he can't be stopped. If he is, he can talk his way out of it, and if that doesn't work, well— the worst will happen later, after the buzz, so what the hell.

He gets out of his truck, taking the milk jug with him, and

walks slowly, calmly, around the bush, over a strip of lawn to the driveway, to Cooper's ragtop. A dog barks, but Cooper has no dog. A little faster now, his breath and pulse are starting to speed, Murdo takes out his rigging knife, opens the main blade till it locks and holding it Hitchcock-style, blade down, stabs the point into the vinyl roof, making little *Psycho* noises as he works—*"Eee! Eee! Eee!"* —giggling to himself.

The top is triple thickness, tougher than he imagined. But Murdo is a craftsman and keeps his blades well honed. Sawing back and forth, he opens a rent three inches wide over the driver's seat.

He looks around. The dog has stopped barking. Something moves in his peripheral vision but it is only the rhododendron, swaying in breeze. At 3 a.m. all is quiet in Ripple Cove Estates. He folds the knife, pockets it, uncaps the jug and jams its neck into the vent he made. Thinking of Cooper's face when he discovers his precious convertible hopping with beach bugs, the face contorted—

He yanks the jug neck out.

Murdo fits the cap back on and stands straight, heart pounding, looking at Cooper's house, where Cooper no doubt is sleeping with Murdo's wife.

Cooper, Una's lover.

Cooper, Murdo's boss—who planned *Noble Boy*'s sabotage, which surely is grounds for vengeance.

But Cooper is also Audrey's brother.

Thinking of his face twisted in anger as he contemplates his car filled with the kind of creatures he loathes—a plague not even gallons of Zap! could fix—builds a bridge, feature to feature, to a fifteen-year-old boy, twenty-odd years ago, the same dark brows and close-set eyes brought closer in a scrunch of pain, and of fury. Audrey's parents and her kid brother sitting close together on their living room couch as Murdo tried to find words to say what language ultimately could not encompass. Even now he can remember the hydraulics of shame pressuring his blood vessels.

He remembers his fear also, as he tried to talk and found he just could not. The couch was a pink flowered print. The Coopers' house had a wall full of photographs of their family, at the Grand Canyon, at an amusement park in Florida. Murdo's parents sat behind him and said almost nothing. He sweated then, the way he is sweating now from the effort of sawing at the ragtop's roof. That grotesque pink couch, the thought of Cooper's face, act on him like a drug that fries neurotransmitters.

It scrambles communication with his hands, and now he is unsure what to do with them. He stopped giggling long ago. He holds the sand hopper jug very still, though his arm muscles are bunched with effort, as if fending off a strong opponent who seeks to force him to do something he doesn't want to do. But freezing his arm muscles finally allows his brain to pause as well; halts that memory vector, that "excursion"—and he is back in Cooper's driveway, the boy grown up.

The effort of stopping makes him sweat more freely. Sweat drips off his nose, it soaks his underwear. The whiskey turns inside his stomach, from something that warms into a substance whose effects are dubious. Nausea blooms in his esophagus.

Murdo bends to look through the driver's window. The inside of the car is very dark but he sees, or thinks he sees, a couple of albino flecks on the driver's seat.

One hops, and is gone into the space between two bucket seats.

"Ah," Murdo whispers. "Ah, *vai-te foder.*" Vomit rises in his throat and he retches but nothing comes out. Swallowing hard, straightening, he upends the plastic jug over the driveway and shakes the remaining sand hoppers out.

He stumbles back to his truck.

On an overcast day in autumn's youth, with temperatures not particularly cold but containing harbingers of frost in their back-drafts, two thirty-foot trucks grunt and sneeze into the parking area of the Mid-Cape Shelter for Homeless Adults and Families, or

MSHAF, known colloquially as "Em-shaft"—as in "shafted," which is how Main Street businessmen see the shelter, something that drives customers away; as in "shafted" for the residents, many of whom feel, rightly or wrongly, that they have gotten a crummy deal from the town, the county, from society at large.

MSHAF is a neat, gray-painted triple-decker sitting behind spare, trimmed bushes off Sea Street, on the north end of the Winterpoor: two blocks from Main Street, five from the candy store where Ricci and Swear Bjørken allegedly injected terrorism and hostage taking into the labile bloodstream of Cape Cod's housing problem.

Though it is only 7:40 in the morning MSHAF is not asleep. A number of residents wearing nylon sports clothes sit on the shelter's steps, smoking, watching the trucks.

"That's them," says a young and restless man with a thin beard that does little to disguise his acne.

"I know that," an older man in a sheepskin-lined vest tells him. Ink on his left bicep reads "Birdie," presumably to match the tattoo of a drunk-looking canary grinning below.

"Yep," a large woman in turquoise slacks agrees, nodding so vigorously her thick ponytail of platinum hair swishes like a palomino's mane.

"Well, they're late," the young man says.

"Only five days," Birdie replies.

"You complainin'?"

An older black man with thick glasses and a careworn face comes out of the office, glances at the trucks, and says, "Okay, boys." He goes back in.

They watch the trucks in silence for a while. One of the men takes a cigarette from his neighbor's pocket. The ponytailed woman falls asleep, snoring gently. Men step down from the nearest truck's cab. They walk up the steps and into the office.

"Still hurtin'?" Birdie asks the younger man, who has straightened out his left leg in front of him, propping it on the steps. He holds his knee with both hands and laughs instead of groaning.

159

"It shouldn't hurt like that," the older man says. "I mean, they're s'posed to give you meds."

"They gave me meds."

"What'd they give you?"

"Percocet."

"Percocet's shit."

The truck men come out of the office and roll open the first truck's loading door. The platinum ponytail wakes up.

"Percocet's okay," she says. "I like Percocet."

"Percodan's better," Birdie says.

"Percodan never lasted for me. A couple hours, with a bad infection, you don't feel anything different—"

"Isn't that what you want, Brenda?" the young man interrupts. "Not to feel anything?"

"I said anything *different*."

"Percocet's shit," the older man repeats. "What you really want is the 'codone."

"You guys don't get it," the young bearded man comments. "The drugs make you *forget*."

"Forget what?" the large woman, Brenda, asks. "Forget who?"

"Rich people." The young man waves his hand as if to take in the rest of the Cape. "People who run things. Same people evicting us."

Silence greets this comment.

"Best thing I ever took," Brenda offers finally, "was Dilaudid."

"Oxycontin and a good belt," Birdie says enthusiastically, punching the air. "Now you're talkin'!"

"Hillbilly heroin." The young man folds his knee back carefully.

Birdie's fist drops. "We're not hillbillies," he says quietly. "We're not junkies. Not one person here got into drugs 'cept to take care of the pain."

A very pregnant woman in maternity jeans that read "Streetz" in silver studs down the seam comes out the MSHAF door and walks down the wheelchair ramp, holding tight to the railing. She is followed by three other women, all but one pushing strollers. Two are visibly pregnant. Two are somewhere between seventeen and twenty-five. Three of the women have hair the color of polished brass, three are either smoking or rummaging through handbags for a cigarette.

There is no apparent correlation between tobacco use and hair color. One of the women has very dark, close-cropped hair. Another sports red tights, a patterned miniskirt, and curls so savagely permed they resemble the dessert known as "baked Alaska." She also possesses broad shoulders, thin hips, a five-o'clock shadow, and stands over six feet tall.

The woman with short dark hair stops, brakes her stroller. She stares at the trucks, then at the older man who has come out of the office again and is looking at papers the truck men have brought.

"You movin' us out, Lou?"

The older man waves without lifting his eyes from the papers. One of the truck drivers stares at the woman with baked-Alaska hair.

"You know we don't even know where we're going yet? Lou!"

"He's busy," another non-blond woman says, fiddling with her baby, who has started whining. "Louie's got *papers*." She says this as if she always says this, which is in fact the case.

"We got the new shelter," says a girl who looks no older than sixteen.

"It won't be ready till a month from now," the dark-haired woman says. "*And*"—she raises her voice—"it's somewhere in Industrial Park, hel-*lo*?"

"We're going to a motel first."

"Who's got the lighter. Sally, you got my lighter."

"I gave it back."

"I don't think so."

"If it's the Mid-Cape Motel," the dark-haired woman insists, "it won't have kitchenettes. Most of us have kids, or we're gonna have kids. What're we supposed to do when we heat up formula, call room service?" She laughs hoarsely.

Lou turns and looks at her.

"We're working on real apartments," he says. "Funding is slow, is all. You know that, Gina. We got a whole motel in the meantime. Swear is there now, it's where they put him after—"

"In Industrial *Park.*"

"Whachoo looking at," the baked Alaska woman says to the truck driver in a gentle but loud baritone.

"Swear doesn't have kids," the dark-haired woman says. "All *he* needs is a package store."

"We can't even walk to the shops from Industrial Park, gotta Uber or—"

"Not much," the truck driver replies, grinning at the other driver. The baked Alaska woman walks over, raises a hand the size of a salad plate, and slaps the driver across his grin, so hard he falls backward.

"*Bitch,*" she says.

The other driver takes two steps toward the baked Alaska woman but she is four inches taller, fifty pounds heavier, and is glaring at the second driver, reaching into her handbag at the same time.

The driver stops, and turns to help his partner.

"Jesus, Amarilla," Lou says, "you didn't have to do that."

"Way to go, Amarilla," Sally says.

"They're just trying to get rid of us, like they got rid of Swear and Ricci," the dark-haired woman says.

"Ricci got rid of himself," Birdie replies, "but now—"

Sally's baby is crying energetically, and with a thrust of her hips she pushes her stroller into gear. She moves out of the parking lot in the direction of Main Street, toward a convenience store that sells coffee, cigarettes and diapers. One by one the other women peel off, move from the handicapped ramp and follow her. Amarilla brings up the rear, swinging her hips and thrusting her chest forward in defiance.

Finally only Gina is left in MSHAF's driveway, with Birdie and the rest of the men. Her child heard the unhappiness of Sally's baby and is starting to whimper as well. The woman's shoulders round downward, half in defeat it seems—half as a way of shifting her weight low enough to shove her stroller in the same direction as the rest.

Murdo and Daisy crouch side by side in a root cellar. Two hook lamps are clamped to an overhead beam but they are not lit. The only light is flat, shivved through the rim of a hatch above their heads. A neon camping lantern Murdo has set on the floor beside him glows a feeble honey color. The walls are made of stacked flat stones, the floor of packed dirt. The cellar smells of mold, damp, and sour mash. Murdo gently unseals a flange from a large glass pot and unships the attached tube, which is also of clear glass, three feet long, enclosing a much narrower glass tube twisted in the shape of a corkscrew. He places the tubes carefully in a box lined with bubble wrap.

"That's called the worm," he tells Daisy. "Where it condenses down."

Murdo touches the big pot.

"Here's the first distillation. You boil the sour mash, boil it forever, and you measure temperature carefully. What comes out at lower temperatures is acetone, methanol—shit makes you go blind. You dump that, obviously.

"The ethanol," he continues, "what you want, comes between seventy-eight and eighty-two degrees centigrade and you keep that, it runs through a tube to this"—now he touches a stainless steel canister, also sealed with corks—"which is filled with the run of sour mash, what came before. It's still pressurized, so the alcohol, here, well—"

The apparatus, its coiled glass pipes and pot-bellied retorts, is hooked together and supported by steel legs and bolts over a system of burners, rubber tubes and propane canisters. The still takes up three-quarters of the small cellar. Murdo, to move at all, has to inch around her where she crouches by the thump pot. His arms slide around her waist and his crotch fits to the curve of her buttocks; seizing the moment he pulls her close and kisses the nape of her neck.

"Murdo," she says.

"Sorry."

"Don't apologize."

He lets his hands slip upward to touch her breasts.

"I thought you said we had to do this fast."

"We do."

"Well make up your mind then. You were busy mansplaining. Anyway you'd have to practically become part of that machine to fuck me."

"Which might be interesting?"

"Grow up," she says, but smiles. He shifts his jeans around, takes the rest of the still apart, placing gear in boxes and grunting them through the hatch. While he climbs to the workshop floor to hump the dismantled still to the pickup she notices a small wooden chest in one corner, almost invisible under a coating of dust.

"Hey."

He leans over the hatch edge.

"What is this?" She has opened the box and is poking around the contents: objects like greenish sticks and bits of shell, except for one piece that has a hole on one side and two parallel slits separated by another, thinner shell.

"Bones," he tells her.

"Bones?" she repeats, stirring them with one finger. "Not *human?*"

"Maybe. Probably."

She withdraws her hands, looks up at him. Her face is very pale against the root cellar's gloom.

"So—your old girlfriends? *Now* I find out?"

"I didn't like them like I like you. Okay, okay"—he holds up his hands—"bad joke. ... But there's a note in there somewhere, with dates? The bones might be Indian—Wôpanâak, the local tribe— they found 'em when they dug the cellar ..."

Daisy is motionless.

"My dad had a Wôpanâak grandfather," Murdo adds defensively, "you could say it's a family thing"; but she shakes her head, staring at the bones.

"An Indian burial ground," she whispers finally. "This place was built on a fuckin' burial ground for Indigenous people—and you never gave 'em back?"

She whistles between her lower teeth.

"And you wonder why the *Noble Boy* sank?"

Excerpt from Eby Noble's notebooks, 22 October 1944

It is very hard to write this.

I wished to join. I wished to fight this war. I thought our cause was right and I think so still—our enemies have caused too much pain for no good reason, they and their mad rulers must be stopped. I even tried to enlist, though I was close to the age cut-off. When I was classified 4-F because of tuberculosis scars I almost wept.

Yet after two months of fighting, or rather, two months of sketching soldiers as a civilian artist attached to the U.S. Army's Twelfth Regiment, Fifth Armored Division— drawing them as they fight, as they are wounded, as they die —I find I do not wish to see fighting anymore at all. This is not because of fear although I must confess, with neither humility nor shame, that I am afraid almost all the time. I am afraid of dying, of being crippled or mutilated. I am terrified of never being able to see my children again, of not being able to make prints of the sketches I have done here.

What causes this revulsion, though, is more the scale of the pain that we are suffering, and inflicting too. Except for their uniforms, the bodies of dead Germans—even some of the Liebstandarte Adolf Hitler SS units that caused so much harm to our troops here—look no different from the bodies of dead men from Minnesota or Oregon or New York. The cries of the wounded sound alike, in German or English or French. Men in agony bear the same rictus, the language of fear is universal, the faces of refugees must show the same blank numbness in Malaysia and Italy as they do here in France. The countryside of Normandy is green and lovely as we advance but by the time we have passed through it is scarred and in many places churned black and brown from shelling, tank treads, fire. Forests are turned into black skeletons by high explosive, hedges are smashed, wheat fields become acres of mud punctuated by huddled corpses, burnt machines.

I am sick of it all. I think of coastal Massachusetts, the peace of its marshlands, the gentle meadows rolling to the sea, the sweet-smelling forests of pine and maple and yellow seagrass reflected in the still waters of Eel Pond. I imagine what a war like this one would do to the places and people I love. And I realize I cannot associate myself with such destruction, no matter what the circumstances. ... I know this is trite (three lines blacked out in the text) ... a C/O argument. It would put me in the stockade were I to voice it aloud. And the MPs would be right to arrest me, it is not fair to these men to question their cause, since doubt might add hesitation and therefore risk to their world. Yet does there not come a point when a being blessed with intelligence makes the decision that destruction such as this, pain such as this, are far too monstrous to be condoned in any way at all? War cannot halt war in the end. Only when men decide that they will never, under any circumstances, bear arms will we truly prevent such horrors from recurring, again and again.

The quickest route to Murdo's parents' barn runs down Iyannough Road—past the Donut Shack, with its usual pair of squad cars sixty-nined beside—past the malls, the airport runways, through the new, expanded building lots of Industrial Park. As they drive through the park Murdo notices a squat man in a porkpie hat and thin overcoat walking the other way along the verge of a four-lane road not built to accommodate pedestrians; the hat and the calm in his way of walking as much as the khaki tone of his skin trigger a pattern of reactions in Murdo's brain. "Crewe," he exclaims, "hey I know that guy."

He slows the truck.

Daisy glances at him. Her hands are folded over her belly. This is how she often sits now although the swell in her stomach, while greater than it was a month ago, could still pass for menstrual bloat, or a summer's worth of beer. Her eyes seem as calm and deep as Crewe's and maybe it's this concordance that encourages him; or maybe he's simply reading her better, understanding that she will not object, as Una would, if he offers Crewe a lift. The sense of freedom that realization gives him is out of all proportion to the thought's apparent weight. He pulls a U-turn at the next stop sign, draws up alongside Crewe, who leans down to peer through the open window.

"You're the friend of Boy's. McMurdo?"

"Me, too," Daisy volunteers. "I mean, I'm a friend of Boy's, too."

"This is Daisy," Murdo says. "I saw you at Joe Barboza's. I used to see you at Twin Joes' all the time."

"I remember," Crewe says. "Black Russians, right?"

"Not anymore. Where you goin'?"

"I'm not sure, really." Crewe takes off his porkpie hat, adjusts the brim, fits it back on. "Direction ain't too big in me right now."

Daisy stares at him. Murdo has to keep himself from smiling.

"Well, I can take you back to Hyannis."

"You weren't heading that way."

"We're going to West Barnstable, but it's no trouble to take you back to Hyannis."

"Northside would be fine. I don't have much to do either place."

"But don't you live in Hyannis?"

"They closed down the boarding house." Crewe nods as if he were talking about a particular bird, or a film he's just seen. "They shut down the shelter too, put us all in this motel. But there isn't anything near there, the motel I mean."

"You're in the motel in Industrial Park?" Murdo jerks a thumb in that direction. "The Mid-Cape? But that's for truckers."

"They put Swear in there too," Crewe says, "when he got out of jail."

A rumble becomes a roar that shakes the car. An airplane fills the sky overhead. It is taking off: sharp-nosed, twin jets, no logos—the reason town council wants a new runway, Murdo remembers, is to handle private planes owned by billionaires on Nantucket, where there's not enough room to park the aircraft.

"It's got roaches," Crewe adds when the jet has become a dwindle in the sky. "They call it 'Roach Motel.'"

"Nice," Murdo says, and then suddenly: "You wanna come with us to West Barnstable? I mean, if you have nowhere to go—"

The idea makes no sense, it fell out of his brain like a pie filling that has been baked so long it loosens and pulls away from the crust. Then again—and this calculation happens over a second or two, as everyone avoids looking at each other, digesting the proposal—the feeling Murdo had before, that his life is so unpredictable as to mesh only with more unpredictability, makes him in some fashion welcome this development.

He thinks it meshes with Daisy's getting pregnant, and her

moving in, and his discovery about Una. Though he suspects he has felt unsettled: as if things were in great flux, a momentous event always about to happen; for much longer. Like a boat adrift on Nantucket Sound, mooring lines cut, anchors gone, swanning east then west with the tidal currents, waiting to fetch up on one of a hundred shoals. This is how he has felt since last winter at least.

Murdo suspects Crewe feels adrift also. He knows how Crewe feels about Olde Bilgewater.

"Ah, come on," he urges. "We got whiskey, we got food? I'll take you back to the motel when you want."

Daisy slides sideways on the bench seat next to Murdo, who has time to register, again, how cosmically different is her reaction compared to what Una's would have been. After a few seconds' hesitation Crewe takes off his hat and climbs in carefully beside her. He opens his mouth as if to say something, glances at Daisy, nods. They drive through Industrial Park to 6A, to Popple Bottom Lane and the turnoff that leads to the Peters' barn.

The barn is not much: thirty feet by sixty, roughly built of spruce joists, heartpine planks and shingles. It was once a real barn with stalls where Murdo's great-grandfather, an Azorean who lived to be 98 years old and taught the young Murdo how to swear in Portuguese, raised chickens; a corner is still devoted to coops and wooden runs. His son added a makeshift bunkroom on one end and used the stalls and hayloft areas for storage.

The barn sits on an acre and a half of land which abuts on one side a catchment zone owned by the town's water department, and to the west a parcel of conservation land belonging to the Barnstable Land Trust. This is all wooded, as is most of the next-door acreage to the east, the owners of which are Boston finance people with disposable income. On several occasions they have offered to buy the Peters' land, raising their bid each time they were refused. In the meantime they keep as much woodland as possible between the two properties to shield their pool and lawn and their passive-solar, massively windowed, triple-turreted, column-fronted, steroid-injected manse from the Swamp Yankee hovel next door.

All this is fine for Murdo's purposes. He mixes sour mash in a large stainless steel cauldron he warms on the bunkhouse wood-stove. The mash makes the whole barn smell of corn syrup, old hay and vinegar and the stench as the mix ripens wafts through cracks between barnboards to the outside. But the barn is far enough away from the baronial house that hootch-smell can't make it off the property.

Murdo has not mixed mash in months, which is why his reserves of non-exploding Olde Bilgewater are so low. The barge deadlines kept him from whiskey chores at first and then he was tied up with moving out of the house plus lawyer appointments as the divorce from Una took shape and became solid; became some-thing he will wake up to one day and discover is real. It has caused him not only to lose interest but to forget, most of the time, that he has a hobby, and a profitable one at that.

He can only pray Una will not use the moonshining as a weapon in court.

In the last two days he has taken a 1950s-era electric stove, half its burners broken, from the kitchen and dragged it to the porch; he'll need help to lift it into his pickup. He has replaced it with a three-burner propane camp stove. He has hauled a mattress into the loft and fixed up a couple of battered armchairs, an Ikea couch, and a fake Danish-Modern dining table which were stored in the chicken area. The main section of the barn seems almost homey if you don't look too closely at the spider-hung corners, the dust-drenched coops; at the wooden outhouse, set twenty feet into the woods, its doorway sagging ten degrees off-center.

It was only last year that Murdo, feeling a somewhat delayed guilt over dumping raw waste, however rarely, forty feet from a town wellfield, propped a chemical toilet on top of the wooden seat. Daisy, when she first saw the outhouse, started humming the banjo-laden theme of an old TV show, the premise of which was that a family of Appalachian white trash struck oil on their land and moved to Beverly Hills. Now she hums it every time they arrive at the barn. And yet she likes the place, she told him so and he believed her.

Crewe insists on helping them unload. Murdo keeps him from tackling the heavier boxes so Crewe carries the light, delicate containers the still is packed in. The older man holds them carefully and doesn't drop a one.

When the truck is empty Murdo opens one of the last two cases of Olde Bilgewater Number 6, uncorks a bottle and hands Crewe a glass, which the old man takes, without saying anything portentous for a change, walking through the open barn door to sit on a short ramp over which cows were once led. There he sips whiskey in a wedge of watered sunshine.

"He looks content," Daisy says. Her laptop is open. She stopped playing Nekropolis after moving out of Una's, partly because the boatyard's wifi was too weak to play properly, but she kept in touch with her guerrilla group. The barn, oddly enough, has cable and internet—installed when Murdo's parents, in a fit of homesickness, spent a summer in West Barnstable before going back to the west coast—and recently she has gravitated back to the game.

He tries not to resent this although the way she plays, hunched into the screen with big sound-damping headphones on and the hoodie hiding her face, clearly excludes him, as it used to do at Una's.

Murdo is cleaning out the back end of the chicken coops. Behind stacked perches is room enough, he reckons, to set up the still while keeping it concealed behind chicken wire, thus evading detection should a stranger enter. He finds a quilt of his mother's, moth-chewed, and throws it over the boxes of tubing and retorts.

The printing press has its own corner to one side of the barn door. The copper plates, grounds and inks are lined up on a card table next to the press. Noble's notebooks stand in a row on a pine shelf hung nearby.

Murdo, looking around the barn, gets a feeling that tastes like the mash he should already have made up a month ago, with the last of the summer corn. It's a taste both sweet and vinegary: sweet because for the first time in years he has gathered all of his ongoing life in one place, as opposed to some here, some at his old house, part in the workshop, part on *Noble Boy*—which still sits on the marine railway, repairs stalled, deadlines busted; always vulnerable, Murdo reckons, to sabotage.

But now all of Murdo's gear is here, the printing, the moonshine, Daisy and the family he still has trouble imagining but yes, it is a family he will have, they will have, in six months and change.

End of February, the doctor said.

All within the drafty, uninsulated, cracked-pine walls of this barn.

The vinegary taste comes from the backside of the same elements, because he has no idea what he will do for work now. An email from CRAC's accounts department has informed him that, given damage to the barge and resulting inability to ready the craft by contractual deadline, Murdo is no longer employed by said nonprofit. This is hardly unexpected but the fact that Cooper is certainly behind his firing and probably responsible for sabotaging the barge as well injects a bolus of black anger beneath the money worries: anger he must ignore, since he can prove nothing and the only options for revenge could land him in jail.

Unemployment benefits will barely cover copays, even on the state's cheapo health insurance, which he requires now for Daisy and the baby. He will have to get another job, of any kind. He taught art for four years on a Sea Education Association schooner out of Woods Hole, it was how he qualified for the boat-school job and SEA might take him back but he can't leave his family so that's out. He does not know whether he'll have time to go back to the printing, even to that limited effort he rebooted on the barge: One print, or rather three proofs of the same etching, is all he's been able to finish in three months.

He does not see how any of this will improve soon. The barn is too drafty and cold to spend the winter in. Murdo, flexing his hands as he thinks of the prints he has not made, almost drops the box of glass tubes he has been holding. He places this carefully atop the biggest box, which he knows contains the thumper, the principle of which only an hour ago he was explaining to Daisy: bubbles of alcohol from sour mash swimming up through a second bath of the mash he made for the previous batch, synergy you could call it—masturbation you could also call it, Daisy remarked, a circle-jerk of alcohol. He smiles at the thought and frowns a little also because it reminds him of a similar process, of circular use, one that has no specific name or handle to it though he has come across a reminder of it—something associated with his old workshop, he held the taste of it in his mouth, the smell of dust, withered oak and caulk: the rounded, paint-stippled, tool-scarred planks where the barge used to sit, and where he fell on his ass, the day he first met Boy.

He gives up on the thought, wondering where Boy is now, in special ed. school of course, but the association does not come from Boy—

"Murdo?"

He startles slightly. Off on another excursion? Una would say. Except it's not Una, the voice is similar but lower.

"*Murdo.*"

Daisy is standing at the big doorway, leaning on the jamb. An axe-head of sun chips the room, splitting it into black shadow, sculpted light. She is in the light zone, her poncho very dark in shade, almost white in the sun's rays. He walks over.

She points outside, at Crewe, who is lying, legs sprawled off the ramp, back leaning against the partially closed barn door. Sunlight has warmed the flaking paint of the door to the point where Murdo can smell the green, sweet with oils and shellac. Crewe's whiskey glass has toppled into crabgrass. His eyes are shut. He lies quite still.

"Crewe?" Murdo's voice judders, and his heart cracks as he thinks, he doesn't want to think, Crewe's heart must have done just that, crack, oh *shit*—

Daisy puts a hand on his arm.

173

"No, wait. I was wrong.

"Listen."

She beats her finger to a slow rhythm. After a few beats Murdo hears it: a minuscule snore that happens, he notices it now, as the angle of Crewe's hat shifts very slightly. Crewe's head nods, almost imperceptibly, as his chest rises with each long-drawn breath.

"Shit," Murdo says again, and lets his own breath out. He leans against Daisy. She moves behind him and puts her arms around his waist so that they meet over his stomach. Her lips touch his neck, find their way to his right ear. She sticks her tongue inside, tasting earwax.

"Jesus."

He twists and puts his own arms around her.

"Tit for tat," she says. "You started the fear-thoughts, in the Indian burial cellar."

"Those weren't the thoughts I remember."

She drops a hand to his crotch. "If only," she says, glancing at Crewe.

He looks at her. He feels as if his chest has all at once changed, maybe gotten smaller, less certain of its function.

"Come on," he says, "lemme show you something."

A Good Week for Hyannis

The final approval Thursday by Barnstable town council of the town's airport renovation plan, as well as the long-delayed transfer of homeless services to new sites away from the town's commercial center, should finally convince doubters that Barnstable's government is up to the challenge of revitalizing Cape Cod's largest town.

The ongoing plan to purchase the Winterpoor property and build high-quality housing as well as several lower-income units there also seems on its way to realization. Sources tell the *Cape Cod News* (See *Winterpoor OK'd*, p. 5) that a closing on Winterpoor, following last month's funding approval, has been scheduled. The sale is expected to go through before the end of the year.

Add to that roster of excellence the expansion of police patrols on Main Street and around the high school on West Main. State police spokesman Tim Ryan also told the *News* yesterday that a breakthrough has occurred in the Devan Douglas case.

Homeless Man Arrested

A homeless Hyannis man has been questioned in connection with the case. Ryan stated that Brad Ricci, 27, who was already in custody for his role in the alleged abduction of a shop assistant on Main Street last July, supposedly to protest moving the MSHAF shelter, is known to have links with alleged credit fraud kingpin, opioid dealer, and fugitive Lariat James Wilson.

Ricci, who allegedly has an alibi for the actual shooting of Douglas, is thought to have knowledge of motives and suspects behind the shooting. We can only hope that the state police, who are focusing on a possible tie-in between the Grace Winslow disappearance in Wellfleet two years ago and another alleged person of interest who moved recently from Wellfleet to Hyannis, will have similar good fortune in solving that long-standing mystery.

All in all, it's been a good week for Hyannis.

He leads her down the shitter path. The path dips slightly behind the outhouse, narrows and grows sandy. The trees change from scrub oak and maple to white pine, pitch pine; then thickets of juniper, poison ivy, and bayberry take over. Even in the cool air, the scent of resin and moss is strong and fine.

The trail dwindles and vanishes. Daisy hesitates, unsure of where they are going, or what he wants, though she has a good idea; Murdo takes her hand and leads her through a stand of bayberry and stunted cedar. He is taking care to guide her around the worst thorns and ivy, though brambles still scratch her legs; past a final screen of vines to a rough hexagon of ground, surrounded by white pines, that is covered only with sand, moss, and the buff rug of pine needles.

A kingfisher, startled, takes wing in a flash of blue.

One corner of the hexagon is dyed to jade and yellow by the sun. He turns now, looks at her for a second, then puts his arms around her shoulders, pulls her close. She looks up at him, and wonders at the depth in his eyes, a depth that implies strength when he is so uncertain in other ways, so unsure of his own agency. His pupils are the color of pine bark in summer and suddenly she wants him as much as he seems to want her.

"Is it safe here?"

"There's no one for miles," he says. "Well, almost a quarter-mile—"

She kisses him, her tongue roaming deep inside his mouth, wishing she could reach everywhere in his face, his eyes. He opens her poncho and slides his hand low, under her sweater hem, up to her breasts, which are heavier now. She likes their heaviness. He pinches a nipple, softly, and she says, "Ah."

He starts to take her sweater off but she says, "No no, Murdo, cold." He is kneeling now, taking his jacket off and laying it next to her. She unbuckles his belt, pulls down his jeans and, kneeling beside him, pushes him gently onto his back. She bends down and takes him in her mouth, and gently pumps him with her cheeks, her tongue seeking out each detail of the geography of his dick, until he groans and says "No," and pulls away.

She sits then, and kicks off her boots. Her legs in the weak sunshine, against the sandy soil and dawn-hued pine needles, are pale; they almost startle her, as if they had without her knowledge pulled in the force needed to maintain such ivory smoothness against the texture of coastal woodland: curve vs. angle, softness vs. thorn, skin as opposed to bark. She lies beside him. His hands follow the scantlings of her thigh, smoothing the reverse curves that end in the keel of her. He bends down and tastes her, running his tongue up the seam between her legs, drinking in the wetness like a cat. Then unfolds himself on top of her, lets his crotch take over the task of tracing and running the lines he followed with his fingers and tongue, tracking her bilge like a vessel being launched, and how ridiculously à propos are these images tacked to his daily obsession. But this is not the time for self-reference and Murdo lets the images declinate, blur; lets himself float, into the high head of a harbor that widens and goes deeper and soon tightens, and his lines all released.

Daisy gasps softly. Her hands fold over his ass to pull him deeper inside. Her gasp somehow increases the temperature in him. He reaches downward with one hand, to elicit another gasp; to show her also, perhaps, that he has the craft, he is no male egoist indifferent to a woman's pleasure. The awareness of her pleasure increases his. He feels the tiny skeg, pushes up and smoothes it downward as if he were comforting an aquatic creature for whom fins were vital. She says, Ah, again, and ah, quicker; he wants to hold back, hold on to land a little longer before being pulled out to sea, he would shun this image too but he is too wound up, it has been too long, and he lets himself slip at last, no choice against this suck of water, into the ebb of her, the warm riptide to sea past groves like this, miles of cattails and spartina, millions of loving molluscs, the stands of pitch pine and shadblow, the currents full of fish whose desires he cannot guess at, currents of golden-black, the eyes of this woman he has launched himself into, floated with, journeys with.

She does not come when he does, does not come at all, the wave is close to breaking but it doesn't. As he stops moving and collapses on top of her she pulls him tighter in. She feels as if she has absorbed him, the weakness and the strength, the cum and cross-sections of Murdo; the warmth inside her, from him, from her womb, is as great as the sea is great around this peninsula, it has risen in her to a depth that can drown all the crossed ideas and helpless treacheries of this man, of all men; and the sense of fullness meshes with the ongoing knowledge of the micro-life inside her, the life this man fathered, and Daisy feels so hot and full that she is convinced, all of a sudden, she has come apart, floated into the pines above and the bushes around and the moss beneath, they are as much a part of her as she is of them.

"Did you call me 'scantling'?" she whispers.

"What?"

"Scantling. I thought I heard—"

"I don't think so? I ..."

They fall silent, the wind seems noisome to them both.

"I bet I'm not the first girl you brought here," Daisy says, when their breathing has slowed.

He considers this. He has learned enough about relationships over the years to understand that there are many levels to the truth one tells to a lover; that which level is more important can vary with age, with gender, and you have to be aware of all of them when talking with a woman whom you don't know so well and even with one you do.

"You're the first in a long, long time," he says finally.

"Una?"

"Una?" He grins. "Can you imagine Una here?"

She doesn't laugh, just looks sideways, as if it isn't inconceivable. But when they met, Murdo and Una both had their own places, she a condo in Hyannis, he a hobbit cottage in Cummaquid. And truly, cavorting in the woods was not Una's style.

"In high school," he says, "my girlfriend then."

"What was her name."

"Ann."

"Were you in love with her."

"I thought I was."

He should tell her about Audrey, who came here also. He gave her a charm bracelet as they lay together in the grass, the last time. A cheap one, brass not gold, but still. It's been a long time since he thought about that bracelet. He can't bring himself to tell Daisy, the habit of avoiding Audrey has grown too strong. In any case he is tired of how the memory of her twists the actions he considers; sick of how history warps the Now. He wants a chance to mold his perception of all this: Daisy, the baby—corny as it sounds, a new life—for just one brief, pure moment before memories of his childhood, his parents, and all the mistakes and screwups and disappointments he continues to live with fuck it all up again.

The bayberry shirrs as wind rises. A chickadee sings in pitch pine. She pulls the corner of her poncho over his buttocks.

"Maybe we should bring Boy to the barn," Murdo says. "He doesn't know where we are anymore, anyway he can't get here on his own."

She places her left hand on his forehead and pushes his head upward from hers to look intently at him. The left side of her mouth is caught in her teeth. Looking at her eyes he gets the same feeling he had coming into her, of being launched, of finding water to float.

"We're having dinner with him," she says, "remember?"

"Omigod," he says. "I forgot, we've put it off for so long."

He thinks, it was still summer when Boy first asked, and both fall silent for a while. He rests his head between her cheek and her shoulder.

"He didn't seem to mind though," Murdo adds.

"His dad died," Daisy says after another few seconds have passed. "Did you know that?"

"Boy?" He lifts his head. "Boy's dad? How do you know?"

"Online. How do you think? Stalked his family, local paper, court reports, all that."

"My Dad, he showed me," Murdo whispers. "Poor little kid." He feels a flood of pity for Boy, and watching Daisy's eyes he thinks he sees the same emotion reflected in the depths of hers. Her corneas now are more brown than gold. His dick has shrunk and now falls out of her, releasing a back-eddy of warm liquid from inside her. The emotion he feels for Boy melds with the warmth he feels for this woman and she seems to respond to this, for she holds him closer; they are lovers, they are pleased with the depths of their emotions, and though he knows a lot of this is self-indulgent, a glorying in how good they feel, it still somehow comes out OK.

After a few more minutes have passed they stand up, hoist and straighten their clothes. Brush needles off each other. To walk the narrow path they must go single-file but they manage to hold hands at the same time, one towing the other. It isn't easy. They move through colors of wood-fire, marigold, cedar-bark, pumpkin, all cousins of the flora here: hues absorbed into dying leaves through the grace of weak sunshine and acid soil. Among these colors appear the silvery gray of the barn's shingles, and a reflection, shiny and long, of something that does not belong.

A few more steps. Murdo walks more slowly, Daisy treading on his heels. As he approaches the outhouse, blue and white pixels come together through the intervening branches, along the length of a late-model SUV. The word POLICE in large letters. The Barnstable Police Department is here, Murdo thinks; BPD for Borderline Personality Disorder they used to say in high school when cops were by definition the foe. An officer sits in the driver's seat, another man rides shotgun. When Murdo comes out of the woods the driver gets out and stands by his car.

The trees, still making leaf noise in the breeze, sound good to

Murdo in contrast to what cops always make him feel like: Victim. Prey. Unclean.

The officer, though, is not Gutzeit. He is thirtyish, athletic in build, with a square face and big ears. Ray Leblanc. Murdo drops Daisy's hand.

"Ray," Murdo calls, "isn't it kinda late for you to be staking me out?"

Ray is the child protection officer. Murdo was in the same grade as his older sister, he even went out with her for a while. She was a field hockey star. She was not, he is quite sure, one of the girls he led down the path behind him.

More to the point, he knows Ray is not the brand of cop who's in it for the M9 and the opportunity to legally bust heads. Murdo always figured he got into children's protection to stay away from that kind of police work.

They used to hang out a little, while Murdo waited for Rosie Leblanc to get ready.

In high school, Gutzeit liked Audrey Cooper. There's another memory from the vault, Murdo thinks; and the implications of it for what happened, for his understanding of it, make him feel as shaky as thinking hands-on about Audrey. This is pure Cape Cod, he knows, the old Cape of incestuous relationships, the sweaty-close connections. Boy, he thinks suddenly, god I hope nothing's happened to Boy?

The second man gets out of the cruiser. He is in plain clothes, much thinner than Ray, older and shorter. He has close-cropped brindled hair, short sideburns, a lean face with a nose that is small and pointed; his button eyes behind large glasses remind Murdo of something, which it takes him only seconds to recall: the mosquito on the Zap! bottle, staring through a gas mask. When he frowns, his mouth somehow frowns as well.

"Hey," Ray says finally, "Murdo," and nods but does not smile.

Murdo stops. Daisy walks around him, into the barn. Ray watches her go. The lean man says, "Are you McMurdo Peters?"

Murdo starts to ask, What's this all about—but using the cliché, it feels to him, would pull him into the script he's seen on every streamed drama, each film with police in it. So he says nothing, wondering instead how Ray knew he was here. The existence of the barn is no secret and he supposes, given that he's twice had to quit his usual lodgings, it's the first place a cop who knew anything about him would look.

He wants to ask if the kid's in trouble again but something holds him back. And then he remembers the whiskey.

The image comes to him of Rosie Leblanc, slightly plump, very pink and naked in her bed, one Saturday when her family was away. He wonders if her brother knew. He wishes now, before making love with Daisy, he had better hid the distilling gear. The plainclothes man says to Ray, "Is this him?" and Ray nods.

"We understand," the squinty man says, and pauses for effect. "You have been, erm, consorting with a minor?"

Murdo stares at him. The whiskey narrative: rumors, complaints, and now, after three clean years, the bust—was already starting to unpack in his consciousness. He has to make an effort that feels near-physical to wrench himself from that story.

"I—what?" he says at last, to Ray. "Who is this guy, anyway?"

"The officer confirms your identity." The thin man's mouth returns to a pucker at the end of every sentence. He reaches into the cruiser, pulls out a folder, opens it and produces another folder which he also opens. He hands Murdo a thin sheaf of papers; these Murdo, reflexively, takes.

"My name is Barbier," he says. "I'm an investigator for DCF. A complaint of sexual and physical abuse of a minor has been filed against you. A Department of Children and Families team has investigated the, erm, circumstances. Unfortunately the evidence we have screens you in."

Barbier does not sound like he thinks this is unfortunate.

"We believe you have consorted with this minor—"

"What minor," Murdo interrupts, loud and suddenly. "What are you talking about?" But a second story, the real story apparently, is forming inside him and it has shadow, it casts a bleak kind of sense.

"Who made the complaint?"

The thin man says, "All complaints are kept confidential." His mouth unpuckers. "Do we have permission to enter the premises?"

"No you fuckin' well do not," Murdo says, "not unless you have a warrant—"

"What we have," Barbier interrupts loudly, "what you have just been served with, which, erm, as witnessed by this Barnstable police officer, following a 51-A complaint, erm, is a temporary restraining order. This prohibits you from consorting with, speaking to, or approaching within three hundred feet of a ten-year-old male named"—he sneaks a look at his file—"John Joseph Barboza, Junior."

"Boy," Murdo says. He glances at the papers he holds, crosses his arms. "You think I hurt *Boy*?"

"A boy," the thin man agrees, and his nostrils flare as if he smells something bad. He squints at Murdo. He has gray eyes that glint like marbles behind their folded lids. His mouth now reminds Murdo of a bug's anus. "A ten-year-old male—a boy, if you prefer—"

"Boy's his *name*," Murdo says. "Well, his nickname. If you knew anything about him you'd know that. And his uncle" ... He can feel the fright in him, it's like a twisting, a black re-twisting of the lust he felt only, what, twenty minutes earlier? A sensation of incongruity, various strong feelings not fully meshed. Where lust was warm this is cold, it separates with frost what should be joined, yet builds a bridge of ice to when this happened last: the investigators, Audrey's father—and Russell Cooper at fourteen years of age.

Murdo says, "It was that uncle, wasn't it? He's a—Daisy!" He shouts. "Daisy?"

She doesn't come out immediately. He is about to shout again when her form appears at the barn door. He wonders where Crewe is. He supposes Crewe, like most of the Main Street bunch, becomes hard to find when the Blues show up. But Daisy comes out of the shadows into the broken sun. She moves like a colt, half gawky half graceful; and the consistency of her, and the fact that she came when he called, melt the frost a little.

"Someone made a complaint," he says.

"That's a 51-A?" Ray asks the DCF man quietly. "Never seen one processed so fast."

Barbier buttons his jacket tighter and does not look at Ray.

"What about?" Daisy asks. "The complaint."

"Boy," Murdo says. He uncrosses his arms, takes off his glasses, and starts polishing the lenses on his shirtsleeve. "They're saying I abused him, molested him, whatever, *vai-te foder*"—he takes a deep breath.

Daisy stares at Barbier.

"It was the uncle," she says. "Boy's uncle, he's a criminal, he's doing it to protect himself, well."

"You know what we found in," Murdo begins, but Daisy interrupts, suddenly and fiercely, "You can't say anything." She walks down the ramp and stands very close to him, looking Murdo steadily in the eyes. "Not till there's a lawyer."

"We found—"

"No!" Daisy almost shouts.

Murdo stares back at her.

The four of them stand on junk grass, on the chickweed of early fall, on crisp-fried leaves. The wind picks up, unsheathing a tiny knife of winter, and some of the people in the tableau shiver just a little bit.

Book Three

Autumn

una@CRACcapecod.com
murdo???!!!
(sent from my Smartphone ©)

coop@CRACcapecod.com
O'Neill says
(sent from my Smartphone ©)

una@CRACcapecod.com
ADA oneill? must b mistake

coop@CRACcapecod.com
Good thing we canned him.
Can't keep a child molester
at the project.

una@CRACcapecod.com
no way murdo is that. he is not

coop@CRACcapecod.com
He's nailing your sis!

una@CRACcapecod.com
thx. thx! but not kids!

coop@CRACcapecod.com
Not the point. Now he is out
need to totally rethink school.
Pirates are popular, Eby Noble
way less
LOL

una@CRACcapecod.com
no room @ gosnold-w'poor,
not 4 both schoolz + pirate relix

coop@CRACcapecod.com
Barge is on hold anyway

una@CRACcapecod.com
kid thing is not fair

coop@CRACcapecod.com
you're very forgiving. Know what
the dealer wants to replace my car roof?

una@CRACcapecod.com
dunno was him

coop@CRACcapecod.com
BS. And I hear his buddy Dog Snow
cut my boat loose

una@CRACcapecod.com
this about diff-abled kid?

coop@CRACcapecod.com
yes

una@CRACcapecod.com
Why not let him finish barge
at least?

coop@CRACcapecod.com
Did you check the traps?

una@CRACcapecod.com
no. ck 2nite

coop@CRACcapecod.com
You have to check, if that raccoon gets
out, he'll trash your house again :(

coop@CRACcapecod.com
meet me BAR-ista at 6

una@CRACcapecod.com
Can't. Have 2 finish grant proposal

coop@CRACcapecod.com
Tomorrow. 6 at BAR-ista

una@CRACcapecod.com
7

coop@CRACcapecod.com
i'll be buzzed already :)

una@CRACcapecod.com
roflol

coop@CRACcapecod.com
love you tons

una@CRACcapecod.com
me 2

coop@CRACcapecod.com
:) :) :)

❄

The East Hyannisport Co-operative Market and Package Store is crowded. Though Daylight Savings Time has not yet ended, most rides from work now take place near dusk, and darkness falls soon after. In early autumn the days seem to shorten particularly fast so that 7 p.m., which last Saturday was still twilight, is now dark. The change has affected customers, made them conscious of the need to stock up on food, and drink, yes, lots of drink. Stefan is kept busy ringing up flavored vodka nips, six-packs of beer, pint flasks of brandy. He hums songs in Macedonian as he works.

Dog Snow comes in for beer and winds up talking to Joe Barboza, who is warily examining linguiça from the deli's fridge. Swear Bjørken has invested in a pint of the Wolf Paw port that Stefan thinks of privately as alky syrup and is one of his biggest sellers. Swear asks after Crewe but Stefan has not seen Crewe for a few days, not since they shut down the boarding house. They shut down the shelter too but Crewe wouldn't stay in the shelter. Stefan is glad to see Swear, who he believes did not do what the cops said he did to end up in jail for a week. Stefan remembers the SDB, the secret police in Macedonia, when it was part of Tito's republic; he's not sure policemen are so different here, especially the state police, who have been more present in Hyannis since last summer. He says, "It is good to see you, Swear," and the old Norwegian nods shyly and looks away, fumbling with the straps of his oxygen tank.

The bell on the door jangles. One of the inmates from the Old People Institute trembles in. He will shuffle and dither for ten minutes and buy, with shaking hands, one Snickers bar. In his wake kids enter wearing Halloween masks—a vampire, a monster of some kind. It is almost two weeks till Halloween but Stefan has placed plastic pumpkins lit from within, and a drugstore witch with a plastic broom and cauldron, in the front window. On the counter he has placed a Chinese-made vinyl ghoul that blows fake smoke. He has lots of Halloween candy but he knows these kids, forget the masks he knows who they are and they'll buy a stick of fifty-cent bubblegum each, he wonders why he bothers with this Halloween *gomna* sometimes. Some of the kids will stuff candy in their pockets if he's not looking and on the night itself they'll foam his windows and toilet-paper his bushes, they do it every year.

"I ain't in the mood this year," Mildred Sweeney says, looking at the kids, and Stefan replies fervently, "You read my mind."

"Those kids run wild," Mildred adds and Stefan nods although now that Mildred is saying what he's thinking he is not so sure he wants to think those things since Mildred is the worst kind of whiner, the worst kind of gossip.

"Wasn't that a cop I saw at your place," she continues, looking at Joe Barboza, who has turned away from the fridge. Joe, who does not care for Mildred either, frowns and says, "Weren't any cops at my place."

"Your daughter-in-law's place, maybe?" Mildred insists.

"Saw no cops that I know of," Joe replies. He picks up a *Cape Cod News*, the headline of which reads: *New Leads on Pit Murder*, with a subhead that adds, *Soil Test May Link Homeless to Crime Scene Hat*.

Though most of the homeless population of Hyannis have at one time or another frequented Stefan's market the guy the cops are accusing did not shop here, or at least not regularly. On the other hand the papers say the suspect, Ricci, is the same man who dragged old Swear—who to Stefan's knowledge has never raised his voice in anger, let alone harmed or even threatened anyone— into barricading himself in the Main Street fudge shop. If Mildred makes that connection they are in for twenty minutes of harangue.

But now Joe places his package with some finality on the counter next to the smoking ghoul.

Outside, Dog and Swear are sitting side by side on the bench to the left of the door, they better not be drinking Stefan thinks, he's not licensed as a bar; he leans over the counter to look, and sure enough Swear is holding the paper bag with the bottle in it, the paper all scrunched up at the neck.

Stefan sighs, and hands Joe Barboza his change.

Gan'pa at the co-op. There's not linguiça, not enough; got to have more sausage, Boy likes sausage in chowder. Not like chowder in Moodo's ice-cream place. That chowder is not as good as Boy's, he'll show them! Yah!

(The boy stirs a large aluminum pot so hard that liquid slops and spills onto the stove. Smoke rises from the ring element. Cream, quahog meats, cut-up sausage, onion and potatoes steam into a burnt-out fan-shape on hot enamel.)

Daisy and Moodo—*love* this Gan'pa place. Better than Boy's, better than Uncle. Boy can show them—*his* family, not Uncle.

But Moodo likes Boy anyway, Moodo lets him work on the square boat. Moodo lets him make pictures on the ink machine. Moodo gets mad a little, like when Boy spilled the burning stuff, but he is Boy's good friend, he and Boy are good friends. And the pretty lady Moodo likes, she likes Boy too, she is Boy's friend also. Daisy. She hugs Boy like hard, she touches his hair and pushes it back like Mama. Like Mama, and Gan'pa, she likes Boy. *Not* like Uncle, not like Justin or Cody at the special school, not like kids

190

who call him: Mow-ron. Ree-tad. Fee-by. Moodo never would say that, not Daisy too, they are Boy's good friends.

Boy had My-Dad, but My-Dad left, Gan'pa says he had to go somewhere better and can't come back. And Boy had Suzee, and she was a good friend, but one day they played games and she said he hit her. He didn't, Boy never hit Suzee! After that her Mama wouldn't let her play with him, she said they're not friends anymore ever.

(Boy wipes his nose and eyes. Mucus, and a trail of moisture from the corners of his eyes pasted on the inside of his hand, are transferred to the ladle with which he stirs. Joe Barboza comes in, puts a package of sausage on the cutting board, slices up linguiça. Boy makes a cup of his hand and Joe ferries sausage into the cup. Boy adds it to his chowder and stirs it with a ladle.

(Joe Barboza looks at the pot and goes over to the kitchen table, which is set with plates, spoons, glasses and a large plastic bottle of diet root beer. The tablecloth depicts elephants of different colors, all smiling. Joe rearranges the settings then stands, a little stooped, watching Boy.)

"Did cops come here, Sonny?" he asks. "Policemen?"

(It's the first time he has spoken. The boy looks at him and smiles. Joe repeats the question.)

"Cops?" Boy says.

"Anybody. *Qualquer um. Policia.* People," Joe says. "*Perguntas,* asking questions."

Boy squints. He reaches back, grabs the hood of his sweatshirt, and pulls it over his forehead, almost over his eyes.

"A man," he mumbles. "*Não policia.* He ask Boy?"

"What. What does he ask, Boy?"

"Jiss questions." (Boy waves one hand, abruptly. The hand knocks the ladle, which flips out of the pot; chowder splatters over the table and floor. Boy cries out, grabs a dishrag, and starts to scrub the tablecloth so hard the cloth moves and a fork falls to the floor. Joe shakes his head, takes the dishrag from him, rinses the cloth, wipes and rearranges the settings once more. Then he looks at the wall clock, which reads twenty-six minutes past seven. He stands straight and still for a few seconds, then musses Boy's hair with one hand.)

"I've got to go see Eugenia. I'll be back at eight. Eight." (Out of long habit, he goes to the clock and puts one finger on the "8".) "When the little hand gets here. It's seven-forty now."

"Okay, eight," Boy says. "Okay."

"Chowder's ready, don't touch the stove anymore. Got that?" (Joe touches the pot, turns off the burner.) "Uncle Danny's at your house. I told him you had your dinner, he won't come by. But if you need him he's there."

"Mama call?" Boy asks, stirring the pot again.

"She calls Sundays, Sonny. You know that's when she calls."

Barboza leaves.

❄

If it's seven with the big hand on eight, and the little hand almost there, Boy knows that's after seven-thirty. That's *late*. Boy told Moodo seven. Boy goes to bed after eight and Uncle watches naked people shows at eight and he gets mad if Boy's not in bed. If it's little-hand-on-eight, Boy has been stirring a long long time of it.

Moodo is late, okay. Sometimes Moodo isn't in the square boat for a long long time when Boy is there. Boy said, little hand at seven. So Daisy is late too. Maybe they had stuff to do on the square boat Boy helped them fix.

(Boy looks out the window to make sure his grandfather is gone. He turns the burner back on till the electric element turns a glowing orange-gray. He sits at the table. From his pocket he takes out the stuffed rodent. He unzips the pouch and pokes his fingers inside the empty compartment. He pulls the animal's ears. He picks up one of the bowls and dips it in the chowder and puts the bowl in front of him; he props the stuffed animal at the bowl so it can eat.)

Daisy said it wasn't Boy's fault, with the square boat. Moodo did not talk to Boy but he smiled.

But Moodo got mad about the boat, when he gets mad he *fala Portugues* and that's why they are late maybe to punish him. Because Boy helped move the boat and it sunk. Not Boy's fault! Not!

Someday Boy will show them he can move the boat, he can fix the boat and move it too. Though he spilled the drink that burned in the place that makes pain and nails. The fac-tree.

That man who came asked if Moodo was his friend, and Boy told him, Yes, *good* friend. And the man asked if Moodo hurt him, and he told him about the burning drink, but that was Boy's fault.

The man asked if Moodo touched him, and he said he let him screw.

The man said he should not see Moodo now, Moodo is not his friend, and Uncle says that too. But Uncle never liked Boy or his friends. Boy does not believe Uncle, Boy does not believe the man.

Now the little hand is on the eight. Maybe Moodo and Daisy are still mad and they don't want to come to Boy's dinner anymore. Maybe they aren't his good friends anymore, like Suzee.

Boy does not want to cry. Girls cry. The other boys laugh at him more when he cries. He shouldn't throw stuff either. He shouldn't throw Stuffy, who is always his friend even if he works for Uncle. And now Stuffy is dirty. Uncle won't like that. Uncle will smack him like last time when he brought Stuffy back and he was empty.

Boy wipes his nose first, then his eyes.

Stuffy is dirty. That is Boy's fault.

He picks the stuffed animal off the stove, wipes him on his sweatshirt, and places him back at the bowl.

In November the Earth, its northern half tilting away from the sun as it spins toward solstice, sheds warmth in ever-growing increments

from that hemisphere. Flatlands cool faster. The colder, denser air rolling over the Great Plains forms pools of high pressure that with time will be nudged by Earth's rotation, like hurricanes but in the opposite direction, so that their winds start moving clockwise as the front advances over the Snake River.

In Nebraska and Iowa, ten days before Thanksgiving, the temperature dips to sixteen degrees Fahrenheit at night; and the high pressure area, riding a fast jet-stream, tracks hard on the heels of a mass of warmer, low pressure air that has already started to turn, as low-pressure systems will, counter-clockwise, in opposite rotation to the high.

A day later, revved by the steep pressure gradients across its relatively limited area, the circular flow of wind in the low has increased greatly in strength, reaching speeds of over fifty mph in the northwest wedge of its circle, over southeastern New England.

The winds there, still moving counterclockwise around the low (now located east of Cape May) blow locally from the northeast. The high-pressure system to the west, rotating clockwise, further crowds the low so that northwesterly winds in the high's seaside quadrant approach northeasterly winds in the low's inland sector. If these two systems get closer they will merge into a flying wedge of strong northeast to northwest winds that spells real trouble—or so the weathermen, with professional Schadenfreude, warn—for coastal areas between Point Judith, Rhode Island and Cape Porpoise, Maine, and for all ships at sea in that area. A freak nor'easter, Bob Miller of Cable Weather News intones gravely, trying hard to keep his delight from showing. Residents of southeastern Massachusetts, Cape Cod and the Islands, and Boston's South Shore should expect strong northeast to northwest winds, heavy surf, coastal flooding, erosion, and power outages. After that, coat-tailed on the high, will come temperatures that Bob Miller calls "unseasonably cold."

In Hyannis the impending arrival of the first nor'easter of autumn is not marked with fanfare. Temperatures rise slightly as the low fingers the area. Southerly winds increase to thirty knots, back westerly, pulling in a skyful of iron-gray clouds that look heavy, as if aching to drop their racks of rain. The lids of garbage cans fly and roll with a crash like cymbals. Brian Fuller, waiting till Macabru is off watch, moves his oyster skiff to an illegal mooring near the head of Eel Pond, and curses as the mooring pennant comes over the gunwale dripping slime, its diameter doubled by barnacles and a cargo of the foul-smelling orange weed he has come to hate.

Claire Crosby sends crews to check what few boats remain moored to the yard's floats and docks. The boats, double-tethered or not, stir restlessly in their berths, like corralled sheep smelling wolf. As afternoon draws to a close the light takes on a sheen of fish-nacre and black-eye blue before fading into dark.

Murdo parks his pickup in the space he always parked it in, the driveway of what used to be his *hapa haole* house. The house that soon, the lawyers tell him, though he has not yet formally signed off, will be entirely Una's.

He has not parked here for months. No other vehicles are in the drive and except for a lamp that Una leaves on in the living room to foil burglars the house is dark. When he gets out the wind gusts and slams the truck door shut for him.

Murdo walks around the lanai. It's still at the stage it was in when he came here looking for Cooper last time. A stack of planks lies to one side, covered with a tarp that flaps in the wind. The smell of tropical wood, oily, sweet, touches his nostrils, and is yanked away by wind. Satisfaction rises savage in Murdo. Perhaps Speed, despite his fondness for Una's cocktails, is running true to form—starting off with OKs and energy then disappearing without a trace. Half a lanai in what, six months?

His impulse to smirk is hobbled by the doom-sense that brought him here, something niggardly (a sand-flea biting at his psyche) that suddenly has swelled higher than his cheap satisfaction over the unfinished lanai; higher than the Fijian diagonals of his own, or rather Una's, house. The nudge and might of that growth, he thinks, stem from his being oppressed for so long by a similar feeling: of doom, of catastrophe lurking in the dark rafters of his workshop; which suddenly vanished—he is not sure how or exactly when—but it left well before the aborted launch of *Noble Boy*, sometime in the summer.

Now it's back, softer than before but growing: a recurrent worry that something vast and horrid is set to happen, something worse than the temporary restraining order and all this implies, only it may not happen soon, or ever, he might grow gray in the waiting, he simply does not know.

He thinks—and this is new, it has something to do with Daisy, her being at the barn and waiting for him—it is time he dealt with that dark architecture once and for all; time he embraced and figured it out, got rid of it forever. But now is not the time or place.

Murdo moves away from the lanai, searching under the sand cherries and shrubs that shield their house from the road. He finds it roughly where Dog, after spotting it on his way to the package store, told him it was: under the dogwood. It is the mesh rectangle of a humane trap, with a black bulk inside that's visible even in the gloom under the bush. Murdo lifts the trap and the bulk does not move, it possesses an uncompromising stillness. He slips two fingers through the mesh and gently prods the animal. Its fur is soft but the flesh is firmer than it should be, and colder. Nothing "humane," Murdo thinks savagely, *filho da puta*, nothing non-lethal here!

He opens the truck's cab and, sweeping tools and papers onto the floor, places the cage on his passenger seat in the umber wash of dome light. He is reluctant to look. That sense of black expectation primes in him the certainty of Pancho's death.

It is, as Dog said, a raccoon. The animal lies on its side, mouth wedged open, a yellowish foam caked around its muzzle. Salmon-hued portions of fish with which the trap was baited hang off the wire strands.

But this 'coon has a broader face than Pancho's, and it's definitely smaller. Relief surges in Murdo, and he's ashamed of the feeling. This is not his friend but rather one of his friend's cubs, or his mate, he cannot tell for sure. Do raccoon families stay together? He isn't sure. Is this the critter that free-climbed his pantry shelves?

The relief gives way to sadness that in a bizarre way—loss hooking up once more with loss?—seems part of the same emotional liquor brewed when he was told he could not see Boy again. Not that Boy is dead, of course; but the space Murdo has made for boys, human or not, with all the hungers and curiosities of that age; the appetite for seafood, the lack of caution, the "I can *do* that!"—he almost hears Boy say it—he almost hears this young, dead raccoon think the same way, and it all rings with loss.

And so, once more, the rage. Murdo yanks the cage back out, places it in his pickup's bed, and again drives down Shaughnessy to Ripple Cove Estates, to Cooper's house. He has nothing left to lose, no job, no wife, it's time they had it out. But Cooper's driveway is as empty as Una's except for the four-wheel-drive that is Cooper's backup vehicle. Are they drinking together in a Main Street bar? Traveling even? In some swank Kauai hotel, pretzeled naked on a king-sized bed?

Murdo walks around the house, debating with himself where to place the trap so they know he's been here, so they read this as a warning. He looks for security cameras and once again sees none. Coop's swimming pool would be perfect, if he threw the trap in they would have to empty and disinfect it, but it has been drained for the off-season. Thoughts of Audrey won't stop him now. This has gone too far and anyway Audrey might approve. She loved animals, Murdo remembers, or dogs at least.

She also, not parenthetically, thought her brother was a jerk, although on some level of course she loved him too. That memory seems distant, diluted, compared to the solid blackness of his current rage.

Finally without pausing for thought Murdo pulls the trap up and back, high over his head, and hurls it overhand into a plate-glass window facing the harbor. But the mesh just bounces off the double-panes, bounces back onto the lawn. The dark body rolls within its cage, flopping like Boy's stuffed creature. Murdo returns to the truck, finds a tire iron amid the junk in his cab, drives one end of it through the thick glass, knocks out jagged shards to enlarge the hole. The crash and music of glass breaking is only slightly dimmed in a sough of wind. He was expecting an alarm but the only sound is wind.

The room inside must be the den. A flat-panel television is lit, its too bright colors show a scene paused in the middle of a film or serial: a woman looks at the camera, mouth open to speak, her eyes tragic. A man stands behind her, hands on her shoulders. When Murdo shoves the cage and dead raccoon through the hole into the den behind, his action finally triggers motion detectors and a modulated siren starts to whoop. Murdo leaves fast, gunning his pickup at first, then slowing to a less suspicious pace as he follows the back lanes out of Ripple Cove Estates.

Murdo has no desire to go anywhere.

He doesn't want to go home. Like others before him who've lost destination in their day-to-day, he ends up at the Foc'sle. A pair of fat road bikes are lined up next to pickup trucks outside the bar's low, shingled front, its neon beer signs. A circling light from the airport control tower down Iyannough Road imparts an aura of *Casablanca* to the scene. And who, Murdo wonders sourly, holds the letter of transit that will take him from here tonight?

Inside, bikers and would-be bikers play pool. The long bar of polyurethaned pine is lined with regulars: a nondescript, over the hill bottle blonde (there is always one) with tabloid eyes and a glass of something syrupy; Hawk, who once ran a contracting firm and now hands out business cards that claim he manages country-western bands. The tall, thin guy from the Hill, across the tidal creek from Winterpoor Lane; the guy Una claims was once a writer and who never seems to do anything but watch others working; sits on a stool in the book nook looking puzzled, as if he has no clue how he ended up in this place.

Swear, of course, occupies his corner, the bottle of oxygen in a rolling caddy at his side. He eats the bar's free popcorn without pause except to lift a glass of house-grade brandy to his mouth. The plastic tubes that bring him oxygen shine long, short, long as his jaws open and shut, moving the nose harness up and down. His white beard shines as well, with popcorn grease.

Next to Swear sits another refugee from MSHAF. His sweatshirt, under a sheepskin-lined denim vest, is carefully rolled to cradle a hard-pack of Manly filters and to expose the bright-yellow tattoo of a canary.

Murdo takes a stool not close to Hawk, who tends to not shut up. Bucky draws him a pint of Fat Tire that Murdo sucks down fast. His hands are shaking slightly from the tension of his deed at Cooper's, the hangover of his rage. Glad he did that. Worried about what Cooper will do now. *Glad* he did that, *filho da puta!* Worried about Pancho, and how Cooper will now fuck even more with the raccoons—is there a way to move Pancho and his surviving brood to West Barnstable? Would it be ironic, or just what Una planned, if Cooper's plot resulted in Murdo's doing what Una begged him to all along?

Because Una did not put poison in those traps, Murdo is sure. She dislikes, even fears Pancho, but she will not harm or kill spiders or flies even. He does not even believe she would wish to harm him, the husband, soon to be ex-, now living with her sister. Though they do not officially talk, Una called Daisy after she heard about the TRO, to offer help if Daisy needed it. (He wonders, now he thinks about it, if that gesture was as selfless as he at first assumed.)

She'd stood on the bed once, when a field mouse broke in around this time of year, fleeing the cold; screaming at Murdo to do something—screaming at him also, when he tried to step on the tiny animal, not to kill it. "Wrap it up!" she yelled, throwing a shawl at him. "Are you *scared* of the stinking little thing?" Her hair awry, cheeks pink with panic, eyes that deep blue-gray they went when she was mad. And, he's pretty sure of this, though it's been so long now he can no longer know for certain, when she was physically aroused. How different from Daisy's eyes, that turn brown-gold with sex. But though the colors are different they both have that ability to change color in coming, as if the heat in Una's womb and in Daisy's could reach a level to alter pigments. He feels it in his stomach, this loss of his wife. It is jagged as iron shards and the ale will not dull it.

A missing, too, of Daisy, who in the brownness of the stout and his memory of that gold stewing in her eyes feels like a harmonic of her sister, different in notes and register but needed, for music, to strike chords with the first.

He drinks, shocked by the power of color to link two sisters who no longer speak, the memory of whose regards has aroused him now, squirming on this vinyl-covered barstool: the yellow-gold of varnished bar, the darkness of the Foc'sle's corners and rafters, which like his old workshop seem baleful in the horrors they hide: a stuffed cobra, a ship's model with cobwebs so thick they look like Spanish moss in the rigging; the forty-year-old license plates from Nevada and Vermont reading SNATCH and BEER, preserved barracudas and beach gewgaws and Cape-Cod-cracker bumper stickers: "MARY-JO KOPECHNE LIVES!", "HEY LEFTY – FREED TIBET YET?" and "ENDANGERED SEA TURTLE: TASTES LIKE CHICKEN." Everything covered in shadow, old tobacco, bad dreams. Long ago one of the Foc'sle regulars willed that his ashes join the collection in the bar's rafters, but the last time anyone checked they couldn't find the urn; it too had been absorbed into the dusty, nicotine-browned depths.

All these hues as he downs a second pint grow warmer, less distinct, and blend, as happens in sex with Daisy—as happens also in a process he knows well but which is not sex.

But which is what?

He puts down the pint glass, adjusts his jeans again.

Something blood-brown you push into a crack but that is not sex.

Caulk.

Not cock but *caulk* (though it's pronounced the same); same stuff Dog wedged in cracks between the strakes and planks of Noble's hull to seal them when they swelled in water, to make her tight.

That harden when exposed to air.

Murdo hunches over the bar. What he imagines now is not brown and carries no hints of gold, although it is tan: sandy-tan like the pages of Noble's notes that describe the day he found the One True Printing Ground.

He's sure those notations were in a section written while Noble was repairing the scow—screwing in new planks and caulking them, just as Dog did more recently. *Cat fat, cow fat*, a word like that, though for some reason he's sure it was not animal fat, even if tallow does show up in standard etching grounds to soften it. But Noble stirred that other substance into his "true ground" and, abracadabra, it hardened without delay to the precise consistency he needed: soft enough for a pencil to mark and wash, but also firm enough that it would take a scratch of finest needle true and neat and allow no foulbite when you bathed the plate in acid.

Something like marine caulk in both color and consistency.

The Foc'sle beer is cold but when it reaches his gut it now warms him in other places.

Murdo orders a Black Russian and downs it, fast. He pays for his drinks with two bills that represent almost the last of his bank account and drives home smoothly in the buzz booze brought. Leaves, russet and black and umber, are flung at his windshield by the wind. His truck shudders every time it gusts and when Murdo reaches the turnoff he finds a fallen branch of spruce has blocked the drive. He gets out, drags it aside to pass. Against the dim glow of the barn's windows the trees now shake their manes like angry mares.

Daisy has lit the woodstove. The smoke stings Murdo's nose even before he opens the door. Though it's only in the fifties outside she switched on the space heater too. The wind combs through every crack, a bouquet of sea heather Daisy picked on the marsh shifts as if it still swayed to saltmarsh drafts. She sits in the armchair, a blanket over her knees, the eternal laptop over that.

"Hey," he says, kissing her.

"What happened?"

He finds he doesn't want to talk about it. He doesn't want to worry about raccoons, or have his thoughts track back, like earlier, to Boy. He wants to find these notes, this word, *cat fat*—

"It wasn't Pancho," he says, "maybe one of his kids or girl-friends," and a brief wash of sadness rinses him again, then dwindles as he walks to the shelf beside the door where he lined up Noble's books. Barge-school property: three days after he was "let go," the lawyer for CRAC sent him an email demanding the notes' return.

Murdo never responded.

He leafs through the books. Even now when he is buzzed, excited, furious, sad to some extent—worn out a little by all that's going on—even now he is conscious of how well these notebooks were made, of thick linen rag bound with cotton string and glue inside leather covers. The paper was clearly bleached since it has turned the color of weak tea from reaction to air but Noble's notes and sketches, drawn and written in India ink, still stand out well. The slipping sound of page sliding against page is just audible above the rant of wind. Under hook lamps lighting his press he searches for the passages he remembers, when the barge was on the hard, in 1925 or '26. "I have an idea," he tells Daisy to explain his inattention to her, "of what made that etching-ground, Noble's I mean." He falls silent once more as he concentrates. "Had to be on Staten Island," he mumbles. "It had to be when he bought the superstructure for the scow, and got it lifted off that German yacht they were breaking up."

Noble sketched the placement he wanted for the new loft and skylight, as well as deck beams he wished to add, and the galley, and where an access hatch to the scow's innards would lie. His notes are full of boatwright's terms and accounts related to repairs. "2 x 8 x 8 oak: 80 cents. Paint, 5 gallons, $2." Those were the days, Murdo thinks, though he also reckons "$2" was a fair chunk of change back then. He searches this section twice but finds no mention of caulk. As he is casting forward and back in time, more desultorily now for he is less sure of what he's looking for, Daisy says, "You still didn't answer."

"What?" he grunts, still scanning pages.

"About Thanksgiving."

He looks up at her. Both her hands clutch the laptop, their knuckles pale. Her face is pale also, and Murdo suddenly feels remorse, and a great pity for her—because Daisy is cold; because she has had to sit here alone when he's out, since Crewe went back to the Industrial Park motel days before. Sitting alone with her wifi connection while he hares off searching for murdered raccoons. Stuck in a West Barnstable barn as he obsesses over lost formulas for an archaic art form ...

He wonders, not for the first time, if this is not the core, the true ground of Murdo Peters: to bury himself in the arcana of etching mediums or whiskey stills so he doesn't have to deal with the hearts of the people who love or loved him.

But looking at Daisy he feels that notion of anticyclone stirring warm in his gut and he puts the notebooks down and kneels by her chair. Her hands are cold too. Wind rattles the barn door and he looks at it, then glances at the autumn garland she hung over the dining table; at the small and somewhat corny arrangement of miniature pumpkins and apples in a bowl.

"What about Thanksgiving? I'm sorry, I didn't hear."

"I said, your parents. Shouldn't we invite them."

She is looking at her hands, which he lets go of now.

"No."

Getting to his feet, he goes back to the notebooks.

"Why not?"

"I'm not even sure where they are."

"But—that's not really answering my question, Murdo." She looks up at him now.

He sets the notebooks down on the press. He is surprised at the strength of his anger. Does anger feed on anger? Sure it does, he thinks. Feeling that and recognizing it seem to ease the draw of anger from other sources.

"They'd never come. They're just not interested, I tole you that."

She shrugs, shoulders high and hunched. Another trait, Murdo thinks, she shares with her sister.

"You said that before, but you're wrong." Now her hands, consciously or no, stray to her belly. "Of course they're interested, they're your mum and dad—"

"They never were before." He slides the notebooks against each other like playing cards. "Interested, I mean.

"They're a perfect couple," he continues. "What interests them is each other. Teaching. Camping in Alaska, holidays in the Azores. Little presents for each other, you know, nicely wrapped. A teapot. Flowers. And walks. All my life"—Murdo takes off his glasses, polishes them on his shirtsleeve, puts them back on—"they were just like that." (He crosses his arms.) "When I was in grade school I used to bring 'em stuff I made, you know, typical kid shit: awkward pottery, drawings with houses 'n stick figures 'n sailboats. They smiled and put 'em away somewhere and kept on giving each other flowers 'n books and, ah, recipes for elderberry *wine*.

"I don't mean to sound sorry for myself," he adds. "They did everything they were s'posed to do, kept me in clean clothes, went to school art fairs, you know. They were *nice*. But they were just going through the motions. With Junie too.

"When I went off to art school it was the best gift I ever gave them."

As he stops talking wind fills the silence, blowing b-flat in the eaves, dropping in pitch. The Audrey incident, he thinks, should have brought them all closer but it had the opposite effect.

"When my parents died," Daisy begins, but Murdo interrupts her.

"I'm sorry, but you just don't know. They cared for you, your parents, and then they died, I know how you and Una feel. But imagine—"

"It's not as if *your* parents died," she replies hotly.

"But imagine if your parents lived, and didn't give a shit?"

She shakes her head.

"I can't."

He turns back to Noble's books. He wants to add, when his sister left she had it figured out; Junie went to Colorado and that was the last they saw of her. Though Daisy is also right, it's not the same as having your parents die in a plummeting commuter plane.

His hands are shaking again and he drops a book. When he picks it up he sees the spine has cracked. He spits out *"Foder,"* puts it down, walks over to the chicken coop and lifts the tarp that now covers the still and the last bottles of Olde Bilgewater Number 6.

He takes one of the bottles to the annex kitchen, uncorks it, pours whiskey into a water glass. The wind rams smoke back down the stovepipe and he coughs from the acridity of it. He walks back into the main barn and Daisy does not look at him. He goes to the printer, picks up the notebook. Takes a gulp of whiskey.

"I'm sorry."

She does not respond.

He walks over to her and, putting one finger under her chin, lifts her face upward. She resists, turning her face away. Noticing the computer, which is still lit, he says, "Is it that game again?" He touches her lower eyelid. "What did he do this time?"

She stares at the computer screen.

"It's just a game, Daisy?"

"You don't get it."

"Try me."

———
———

"He got to my friends," she says, finally. "He did everything he could to me, fair enough, but now he's got to my *friends*.

"And it's not just a game, you really can't understand it. There's real people behind the avatars. Mates of mine."

She wipes her nose with the back of one hand, a childlike gesture. The hand returns to the laptop automatically, fingering the keys without pressing them.

"Cooch found them," she continues, "one by one—he figured it out from the fuckin' algorithm, *my* algorithm.

"Then he told the Enforcers."

She lifts her hands from the computer—pulls them apart, fast, as if to release something held inside. "Poof! Five years of gaming, of friends and allies and trust. And of course, since he worked for GCHQ ... Now no one in Nekropolis will even speak to me." She smiles wanly.

"I thought it was personal—we were having problems—but it turned out, it was all about the harmonics. Cooch wanted to kick me out so the coding was just his, so he could sell it to his spooky mates in Cheltenham. As if I *wanted* to be part of his fuckin' spyware."

"But you can explain, you can ... contact them in other ways, like email—no?"

She shakes her head. "You still don't understand. It was where we—how we interacted. We *lived* in Nekropolis. Except for a couple in Willesden, a guy in Brussels, I have no other way of getting in touch. And now they won't want to anyway."

"I'm sorry," he says again, and lets his finger move down her cheek, lightly.

"I'm not. I killed my avatar this morning, I'm over it."

"Then what's—"

"It's, I feel *alone* so much, Murdo. There's you, and there was Crewe for a while but *Murdo*"—she lifts her eyes to his. The brown is magnified, refracted. "I miss *Boy*. We saw so much of him, and now this!"

He kneels beside her armchair. She puts an arm around his neck. The feeling he had before, sitting beside the dead raccoon, comes back without friction or delay. "Lost boys," she mutters, and he thinks she is talking not only about Boy but also the raccoon, even about himself, though he doesn't feel lost.

How he feels, like her, is lonely. He's lonely for Pancho's son, or girlfriend; lonely for the bumbling chubby kid with the killer squint who could sink a screw in garboard planks at the end, at the beginning even, much better than Murdo. Though garboard planks—

"That woman called," Daisy says, sniffling, and passes a finger across her nose again to catch the snot. "Boy's foster mom? She says she wants to talk to you. She says she knows how they work, the social service people, DFC or something, she knows the uncle and she thinks he's a prick—"

"No shit?" Murdo agrees, though his attention is wavering again. (Those garboards—)

"She said exactly the same thing I told that guy—the uncle's trying to blame his shit on you. Shit he did. She says he's violent, thank god you didn't tell them."

"Tell them what?"

"The gun! I *told* you: The cop would've had to bring you in for that."

"I hope he's okay," Daisy continues, and pauses; for Murdo has gone back to the notebooks, muttering, "Garboards, garboards—"

"A later notebook," he adds, riffling. "He was fixing up the scow in Staten Island. There was a passage, I think, Noble was talking about his ground, and he was working on the barge then—"

Murdo finds the page:

They have replaced the port garboard but when we launched the barge to move to the South Channel it took on water, long after it should have swelled (illegible). *I never had problems in that area before. The barge had been hauled Thursday, and the yard crew dragged the German cabin on thick* (words crossed out.) *Of the ka fat I found in the stern locker enough remains* ... (the next words are blurred by water stain) ... *fix the garboard I think.* (Murdo's heart pumps a little faster.) ... *more Katfet* (Murdo reads, or *"Kalfet"?* Two paragraphs later): *The mixture is very thick and dark but melts astonishingly fast when heated for a minute or two. Perhaps I have got hold of some secret laboratory project of the kri* (illegible). *At any rate I will tell Spinelli to add* ...

He traces the long, looping letters of Noble's handwriting. This isn't the page he remembers, nor is the next. Three pages later, however, he finds another passage where Noble used what he now reckons looks like "kalfat." *"I used the Kalfat, a 20 percent mix ... This works perfectly as* (illegible)."

If Noble found "kalfat" or "katfat" in the cabin he pulled off the Kaiser's yacht the word might well be German. Murdo remembers looking for it in an online dictionary when he first came upon the reference. He found nothing, but at the time he had no idea what to look for.

This time he checks three different German-English sites online. He finds no match. Does it mean *"Talfahrt"* ("downhill voyage") the Cambridge dictionary asks helpfully, while *"Kalifat"* (an Islamic political entity) is proposed by AI-Thesaurus.de.

On his fifth attempt, however—on a German site called "Pons —*Hallo, Welt!*"—he finds the phrase, *"etwas kalfatern,"* which the dictionary lists as "NAUT.: To caulk (something). From *Kalfat* (caulk)."

He closes the laptop. A cricket of excitement chirrups in his gut.

Caulk is what Noble was applying to the scow's garboards, and caulking compound is exactly the kind of product Noble might have discovered in a half-used tin on an abandoned wooden yacht from Germany. Typically it's a dark, gooey gunk; but diluted in spirits, heated, and maybe mixed with other components, it might just turn into the sort of versatile workable medium that makes for perfect printer's ground.

Daisy is gone from the armchair when he turns around. Holding his whiskey in one hand he looks for her in the kitchen annex. She is standing at the woodstove, her back to him. He was planning to tell her what he might have found, but when he approaches she seems so small and frail—is it by contrast to the wind, that seems to have risen even in the forty-five minutes since he came in? Or in relation to the life inside her which, though minnow-sized in the third-plus month, continues to curve her stomach outward, past the beer-belly stage now—a curve of power in a light structure, though still noticeable only to those who live nearby? This seems to register less as thought than as action. He moves close to her from behind and puts his arms around her, across her breasts, then sliding lower, his hands meeting over hers, over her stomach, warmed now from the stove she stands beside.

Some years are good for the bay scallop, some years are bad. Larval development depends on a complex array of factors including water temperature, salinity and turbidity (the amount of floating matter in a given unit of liquid). The number and strength of storms, the prevalence of predators such as blue crab, starfish and herring gull, the strength of tidal flow and presence of favorable habitat—in particular, eelgrass—play a part as well. The eelgrass blight of the 1930s, for example, practically wiped out the population of bay scallops in New England because the shellfish larvae had far less fauna on which to stick and grow and in which, as adults, to hide from enemies. In Eel Pond, as in any ecology, the various factors affect each other. Increasing turbidity from runoff and especially from nitrate runoff up Eel River damages eelgrass beds and reduces the water's oxygen content, making it harder for spat to thrive.

This year, though, a number of more positive elements have conjoined, and in most Barnstable bays the flats are thick with bivalves. Their ridged shells present horizontal, linear patterns among the vertical thickets of eelgrass and seaweed. The thirty-two blue eyes of each scallop peer, register strength of light, and send a message to "shut shell" if a shadow moves across their line of sight. The shells snap closed, open, snap shut again, fast enough to propel the shellfish by jet propulsion away from advancing starfish, though not fast enough to escape the scallopers.

Brian Fuller, who moved to Barnstable from Wellfleet with his oyster skiff six months ago, finds he needs little local knowledge to fill his dredges with scallops, although he did waste part of an afternoon dragging the top end of the pond, where it meets Eel River, finding nothing but drag-fulls of bad-smelling empty shells and a weird, orange, kelp-like weed the likes of which he has never seen before this year.

The work has been hard, even with a power takeoff that allows his outboard to turn a winch that hauls the heavy metal drags—like a big rake with a chain receiving-basket—into the boat and over the culling board. For eight hours of daylight he has hauled and dumped the dredge, shoved detritus overboard, unloaded bags of shellfish. At twenty-five dollars a pint for the pale adductor muscle each bushel of scallops nets $200. He's been doing all right, well enough to bring back a pint or two to the woman from whom he rents a room.

"They're already perfect, Kathleen," he tells her when she wants to bake them in a casserole with cream and breadcrumbs and cooking sherry. "You don't need to do anything with 'em, just heat up some fresh butter in a frying pan. Roll 'em around. Sprinkle a little salt and pepper. I sprinkle in a little rum, too. That's my brother's recipe." (He pauses.) "Lorenzo loved rum, anyway;" Brian opens his hands, which are clasped together tight as a scallop shell. "Keep testing 'em to make sure, and soon as they're almost cooked, just shy you know? Take 'em off the heat. And that's it. They'll keep cookin' for a minute or two. A little lemon, maybe a fresh loaf of brown bread and butter. There's your meal."

It's night in the Winterpoor. Kathleen's house is overheated. Brian's clothes throw off a faint odor of seaweed. A state police cruiser slides down Hiramar, a light goes dark in Danny Fernand's house. A twelve-year-old girl, one of Kathleen's foster children, bursts into the kitchen screaming that someone has stolen her tampons. Kathleen gives her a fresh box of tampons and a time-out and the girl retreats into the bathroom, still screaming. Her screams seem of the same register as the strong northeast wind now playing the gutters and eaves of Kathleen's cottage like a penny whistle.

Brian wonders if he should check his skiff again, but he knows it would be futile, since he already secured the boat on a 500-pound mooring and lengthened lines against the storm. Anyway it is getting colder outside and Kathleen's house is warm and with a glass of rum under his belt already he finds it easier to stay in.

When the cellphone rings part of Murdo's mind is mumbling "What?" but part feels as if it was already awake, nervous on some caveman level about the wind, which muffles the sounds of predators and sometimes sounds like a beast itself. It blows at the house, a demented architect wanting to shift walls around, picking at a loose shingle on the north side, testing glass panes in their frames. (He fields an image of Cooper's plate-glass window, smashed on the lower right-hand side, the rain blown in. Would the cops *call* instead of coming over? Would Una?) He gropes beside the mattress, picks up his cellphone.

"Murdo?"

A woman. Not Una.

"Um," he says. Clears his throat. "Claire?"

"The barge," she says impatiently. "Murdo—you didn't launch it, did you?"

"Huh"—he sits up. Daisy stirs beside him but does not wake. Skeins of meaning, combed by storm, snatch at his brain, release. "Launch the scow? No. Of course not—"

"Well someone did." (The line crackles.) "... Grip ... cradle, 'n untied the mooring lines." (In the pause that follows he hears the wind in stereo, from the house around him in one ear, from wherever Claire calls from in the other.) "It's gone," she continues, "... in the office an' I don't even see it in Eel Pond, though I can't see shit" (more crackling) "wind northeast like this, through-hulls shut so it'll float off ... would have drifted straight into the bridge. Plus the tide? ... see *shit*, with this rain!"

"You know," Murdo says carefully, "I'm not involved anymore, in the scow I mean. I was fired."

"... again?"

"They closed the contract," he says, "I'm gone."

More static. He waits for the static to subside. As he waits he realizes that it doesn't matter if he was fired or not, he will have to go and see what happened.

"Who else 'm I gonna call," Claire says, in a sudden lapse of noise.

"Yeah," Murdo agrees, "I guess." After a few seconds he adds, "Thirty minutes."

Daisy is awake. She has not moved but he can sense a different tension on the mattress beside him.

"Someone launched the *Noble Boy*. I think"—Murdo fumbles for his glasses, prongs them on. He was going to say it was Cooper trying to get back at him but he has neglected to tell Daisy about the plate-glass window. He hesitates to tell her now. Under the whip of storm his action seems so puny, so much a response of the weak.

"Boy," she says, and sits up suddenly beside him.

"What I said."

"Not the *Noble Boy*—Boy!"

"Boy? What about Boy."

"He did it."

"No way," Murdo says. "It was Cooper. He tried to sink it once already, opened the seacocks—"

She snorts. For some reason this pisses him off.

"I threw the 'coon through his den window."

He makes out the shape of her face, pale and angled in his direction.

"Whatever, Murdo," she says at last. "It's that guy's barge, though, Cooper? It's not yours anymore, so if something happens, it's on him."

Which is true, Murdo thinks as he gets up and dresses. He doesn't switch on the bedside lamp, so she can go back to sleep, but Daisy gets out of bed anyway. He has time to appreciate the shape of her body, pale S's and darker ovals against the gloom.

"What're you doing?"

"Coming with you."

"It's not Boy, he could never—"

"You didn't see him," she interrupts. "I did. He was watching every move Claire made. He was *dying* to launch it."

"In the middle of a nor'easter? In the middle of the night?" But he remembers then Boy's squint, and the curious concentration of which, never mind his IQ level, the kid is capable. He has a vague memory of Claire suggesting something when they tried to launch the scow the first time—something about storm tides, which might well be happening now. Although surely Boy would have no idea of what a storm tide is?

At the same time Murdo knows in the sump of him that Cooper, irrespective of CRAC's side-projects, would happily get at him through *Noble Boy*. He has the old reasons, of course; and he's got that rooster rivalry going, because of Una. And now he can refer back to Pancho's comrade, oozing bodily fluids on the pristine shag of Cooper's den.

Thinking Cooper might know how much he cares for the scow—thinking that history, like what happened to Audrey, is quite capable of twisting men's motivations into perverse action, forces Murdo to realize that he truly has become attached to that awkward, box-shaped excuse for a seagoing vessel.

Makes him see, also, that everyone has realized this except him.

More branches have been knocked down, and it takes him five minutes to haul them clear of the driveway. Wind buffets the pickup as they drive across the tree-free stretches of Industrial Park. Traffic lights dance the Beaufort tango. Leaves, twigs, box-store packaging, shingles litter the roadway. With the storm blowing from the northeast, Eel Pond and the bay beyond, on the Cape's south coast, are sheltered by the peninsula's land-mass, they are not the collage of raging surf they would become in a south-westerly gale. Still, in the absence of trees to cut its power, wind will be strong across the water.

After Main Street the streetlamps have gone out, power is out generally. Sheets of rain, swirled by convection, appear to be waving, gesticulating around the moving circle of dark that surrounds his headlamps' beam.

The boatyard spotlights are dead, the only color comes from the running lights of an eighteen-foot workboat at the gas dock. Daisy slips on slick planks as they board. Murdo catches her arm but she has already regained balance and shakes him off impatiently. Claire, gleaming in a yellow slicker, is sheltered under the dodger, yelling into a cellphone to make herself heard. "I did," she says. "Nah wait, he's here now."

She starts the outboards and he casts off. Wind pushes the boat away from the dock as if the heavy craft were made of styrofoam. A clutch of clam skiffs, rigged with davits and heavy dredges for scal-loping, seesaw back and forth at their lines as if wishing they could leave as well. The tracks and cradle of the marine railway that held Noble's scow are underwater.

Murdo watches the drawbridge loom, its black machinery taking up space that sky should take. And without any friction he is back, excursion and relevance for once in synch—balancing on the roof of the bridge attendant's cabin. Showing off like an asshole for Audrey Cooper. "Yaah, Audrey!" (Subtext—look at me *now*!) Audrey watched him leap way out, clear of the bridge pilings: the brief passage of wind and night and freefall, heart on hold for that time. Then a curtain of ivory foam, an explosion of liquid noise near 1 a.m. in the deepest part of the channel. He was naked, daring her in more ways than one, though by that time they'd already had sex twice.

The other kids who started out with them had lost interest, one girl had to get home, her boyfriend and another girl took a ride with her. The bridge-cabin's roof is a good twenty feet above the water's surface, the concussion of his contact with water splayed his butt-cheeks painfully, punched his balls, slapped his head to one side. The harbor was all the night's blackness in liquid form, despite its initial solidity it did not hold him as he went in, its dark cool plasticity took over his life, then released it. He kicked upward, feeling the tide pull him toward the bay; surfaced laughing, shouted for her.

Audrey, stripped to bra and panties, was a white ideogram climbing the cabin rungs, hesitating on the gutter. "It's plenty deep," he called, "just jump way out!" He had done this a dozen times before, he could impress her with his savvy. She stood still for a moment longer, then screamed, not a real cry, a fun-fair scream as she jumped. Her flesh streaked against the obscurity of harbor, well to one side. Much too close to the pilings, he thought at first, and something cold touched him deep in his chest, but the explosion of water came more or less on cue and the cold turned warm and he was sure she was fine. He swam, fighting the tide, which was concentrated and strong around the pilings, to where she'd gone under. After a few strokes, he began to call her name.

He remembers the time, marked by his panting breaths, the slap of small waves, the buzz of beer; time stretched like an elastic from waiting, to that instant when the amount of seconds underwater seemed a little too long for the half-circle in space, time and water needed to recover from a jump in current; to the first dog-teeth of panic nipping his stomach lining.

Suddenly from not coming up at once she was not coming up at all, despite his own circle in the water as he dog-paddled, and dove, and dog-paddled again, trying to spot her pallor against dark water, aching to touch her. He cried no longer for Audrey but for help, help from anyone, from people, from angels, for a reversal of that elastic stretch, for time to go back to before—"before" was not that great, not even sweet, only buzz and horniness and the edge behind, but just then the notion of before seemed like very heaven.

He dived for her deep, and deeper, his ears popping with pressure, back into the cool hug of tide, hoping with every cell of him for something, anything, a lightening in the liquid black that would be her face, her underwear, a foot. Sobbing now into the brine as he came up for air, bubbles of guilt, this was all his fault, he should never have dared her to jump, she had never done it before.

Gutzeit came, a rookie cop working the worst shift of the week, alerted to the bridge-jumping not by Murdo's cries but by Chet, who owned the boatyard then and lived beside the bridge. Chet had heard the cries, he did not like bridge-jumpers.

The Coast Guard had a boat in the harbor in those days and the fire department launched their rescue skiff. Blue lights, red lights flash, searching the harbor farther and farther down-tide—it feels to Murdo now as if the lock of time that fastened on him when Audrey drowned has clamped on him again, terrible in the lack of hope implied in such duplication.

He is cursing under his breath as the yard boat moves into the harbor. Claire shouts into the VHF's mic. Over the splash of wake, the mumble of outboards, just louder than wind, news comes back: countdown to inevitable, relayed by a buddy of Claire's on the EMS squad.

Grandfather reports the boy has been missing since 8 p.m.

A cop saw a kid matching his description walk down Ocean Avenue toward the boatyard around 10 p.m.

And finally, from the fire department inflatable, word that they have located the "craft," washed up half-swamped on Great Island: on Point Gammon, against a stone jetty. "Lucky the tide was coming in," the radio squawks, "with this wind, shoulda ended up in Chatham. ...

"No one visible aboard."

Murdo sits on the bench forward of the console, wiping spray from his glasses. Claire speeds up, steering through thrusting gusts, the whitecaps, toward a spackle of lights off Great Island. Freezing spray flung from the boat's bow stings their exposed flesh. His glasses are streaming and he unbuttons his jacket, wipes them on his shirt. Daisy, bent double, holding tight to the aluminum armrests, crabs around the console to sit next to him, puts her arms around him. Murdo does not respond. She unlaces her arms, uses them to hang on to the armrests.

The heart shape of her face is pale against the darkness of her poncho hood. A portion of his being wants to fold into her, into the comfort of her; Daisy's lean softness, the heat of her breath, the feeling he believes she holds for him.

And he feels as if to do so would put her at risk, for what is he after all deep down but someone who, through various gears and camshafts of ego, drives people to their deaths in water? It does not make strict sense but part of him is sure he must not get as close to her as he wants until he understands how he puts people in peril this way. The thought of hurting someone as warm as Daisy—a woman who wants to hold someone as sullied and dangerous as himself—allows him to recognize, now that he rejects it, how he has come to love her. The feeling is a patch of sunlit grass above the dark shoreline, above the poisoned black waters he imagines himself, he imagines Daisy too, moving through.

Despite the angle of his thoughts he leans back against her slightly. The smack of the boat's hull turns a lean into a rhythmic touch. He expects her to refuse, he has just indicated after all that he does not want to be touched, and she does not lean back for twenty seconds, a minute. Then she does, absorbing his weight more firmly when the boat shifts them together. They are, after all, both cold. He does not put his arms around her though he longs to. He must not let her get hurt. She has followed him onto night water and the risk, however slight, this entails has put their child at risk as well. Their other child—the compartments in his brain that carry Boy's face and memory are built just like the compartments in which he stores the idea of this baby he and Daisy wait for. He thinks of Boy as a father would and somewhere deeper than his guilt, deeper than his contempt for what he has done, a pocket of pressure is uncovered, released; it's a pocket where doing something that his own father could never do vouchsafes some heft.

The workboat pounds harder and harder as the increasing fetch of harbor behind allows wind to pile up the harbor waters. Claire cuts their speed, the engines' whine sinks to a lower register. The wind is strong enough now to make it hard even to yell. Now searchlights pin details of the scow's cabin, the flat sides of the *Noble Boy,* water smacking cream-white over them. It has gotten colder as well. "Look ... that weed," Claire yells, "it's all piled up, they can't bring the boats close." Even thirty yards off, Murdo makes out swags of sodden algae against the scow's cabin, a low wall of it against the on the beach. Against the nearby jetty waves kamikaze themselves into pale streamers of spray.

They are close to the fire department rescue boat, a large, semi-rigid inflatable with an aluminum cabin, standing off the larger, spotlit shape of *Noble Boy.* Two flashlights jig down the beach. Another rescue boat works up the shoreline, also thirty yards off. In Murdo's field of vision the wind-ripped waves alternate with scalpels of hard light from rescue boats. A figure now stands on the barge, readying lines. "They'll try towing it off," Claire shouts, "Good luck, half aground in this?"

Murdo yells back, "Can we"—he is on his feet, holding on to the console windshield for support as their boat, now broadside to the waves, lurches heavily, "Can we do what they're doing?"

"What?"

"Search down the beach?"

"Have to stay off," she shouts back, and points at a dial on the console's dash, a temperature gauge whose needle nudges the red. "Shit-weed's gettin' sucked into the port engine." But she punches the throttles, alters course to parallel the shore.

The anti-cyclone passes east of Cape Cod around 4 a.m. but as forecasters predicted the high-pressure system has edged so close to it, moving east also, that anti-clockwise winds from the low's rear wedge now mesh near-seamlessly with clockwise winds from the advancing high; their compound winds blow together from the northwest. In Hyannis Harbor they strengthen to forty, sometimes gusting to fifty. Since the high-pressure zone's winds conceal in their gut the chill of Western plains, they are cold.

And the rain becomes sleet, the sleet becomes snow squalls that score the night in white diagonal rods. The temperature slides to thirty degrees, twenty-eight. Rescue boats continue their search patterns but the occupants of Eel Pond yard's workboat lack the thick sou'westers of the professionals, and they are very cold now. Daisy has laced her arms around Murdo again and this time he responds straight off, leaning into her hard. It feels to him as if the imperatives of survival have thrown emotional gears into neutral. They are both soaked in freezing spray, both shivering. He is holding the portable searchlight and it takes real effort to keep it straight against the shaking and focus it on the beach. He has taken off his glasses, which are useless because of the rain. All they see anyway is snow, black water, weed, an occasional scoter duck riding out the storm, and styrofoam and other junk.

When Claire finally yells, "We're gettin' low on gas, I'm goin' in," neither he nor Daisy object, although the pit of horror that has been sucking at Murdo's stomach grows stronger as they turn northwest for Eel Pond. "We can't be sure he was on it," Daisy says into his ear, but he doesn't believe that and he knows she doesn't either. If Claire doesn't want to take the workboat back out, he decides, he will buy gas, find warmer clothes, and go out on his own.

It is not dawn yet though to the east the night is clearly thinking about retirement. Murdo does not look up at the bridge as they pass underneath. The echoes of engine noise magnified by the murderous abutments of stone and steel seem to boost the trembling in his body.

He focuses instead on gradations of darkness beyond, the pale coating of snow, light but falling still—dark water and blacker docks of the yard starting to reflect a thin glow to the east. The land around Eel Pond feels like hostile country, a line of scrubby trenches holding ground against a horizon only marginally less dark. The power in Hyannis is still out.

He wonders if this is what it felt like to be an invader: Verrazzano's men, perhaps, or Champlain's, scrutinizing a shoreline no European had seen before. A hostile land—they knew the tales of attack, and flying arrows, and English or French bodies buried hastily on the beach as their shipmates fled—as the peaceful Wôpanâak looked on, amazed.

No one lives where he's looking of course, for most of the land bordering Eel Pond is saltmarsh. No one except Swear, in "Swebajuk house." He almost smiles, thinking of Boy, of Boy's take on where Swear sleeps rough.

Abruptly, Murdo stands. His teeth chatter from cold, his heart thuds to a rhythm a beat slower.

He helps Claire tie up the workboat then runs as fast as he can on stiff legs to the pickup. He has the engine running and heat feathering from the vents by the time Daisy gets in. He moves off before she has swung her door shut. She doesn't object—another difference from her sister, she likes moving fast like this.

"Fire," Daisy grunts, "heat," her teeth chattering hard as his. Her cowboy boots are soaked. But he does not turn up Sea Street for West Barnstable, instead crosses the drawbridge and hits 50 heading west down Ocean, then slows immediately for a troop of men with flashlights walking along the beach road. They are too much of everything: too thin, too fat, too stooped, too gimpy, too slow in their walk. Their hair is gone, or white, the flashlights waver madly, they are all over the road, he has to drop to a crawl to weave around them. The Old Folks Institute, alerted to Boy's disappearance by a police scanner the ancients listen to 24/7, is joining the rescue effort. "Christ Jesus," Murdo says, "they'll end up having to be rescued too"—understanding from how he phrased this, by adding the "too," how fast hope came back. How desperate is this hope, as well.

"He goes there when he's in trouble, the marsh"—Murdo points to the right now. "He's done it before." Turns right up Greenwood, right again down a side lane; between two houses he finds a dirt track through a cut in a canyon of cattails. The track ends at a small clearing thirty feet in.

"You think, really?" Daisy asks. She's not doubting him, by her tone, just surprised that anyone would go to ground in such a deserted place.

Under the dome light she looks small, tired, hugging herself against a cold that dug into her body mass and resists the hot breeze coming from the vents. He turns the fan to maximum. "Don't get out," he tells her. "Keep warm. Leave the engine on.

"I have to check," he adds. "I know it's a long shot, I *know*"—rummages around the cab but can't find the flashlight he once kept there.

Because of the dome light his night vision is gone. The path at the trail's end is like a tunnel now, the cattails, the invasive reeds behind them, are so high and thick. The path narrows and he pushes himself into the grasses, bending the woody stalks to each side so that they rustle and click; slipping in thin snow and thick mud, stumbling over roots and invisible junk. The light of the truck's headlamps paints the top half of the grasses starkly yellow, then fades as what path there is twists left. The footing grows wetter, more uneven and after only a few paces his foot is twisted sideways by a balk of something hard and pain shoots from his ankle. He steps more cautiously; the rolled ankle hurts when he puts weight on it, but takes the weight. He carries on.

The smell is bad: low tide, rotten fish, and a sickly, overarching odor that he is coming to recognize as the smell of what Claire calls shit-weed. The reeds thin, giving ground to shorter, lighter stalks of spartina grass. Then he hits the weed itself, a rampart two feet high of decomposing slimy ropes and leaves raveled in the tide and washed up at wrackline. He turns right, then left, searching for the delta of a small creek defined in part by pitch pine copses where, when he looked out from his workshop, he used to spot the home-less, Una's "wrecks."

Finally—it is not by dint of searching but because daylight, albeit diffused by wind-strung clouds, has made it possible to distinguish more than varied tones of chiaroscuro—he spots the patch of sand, the rough structure made of driftwood and a piece of ripped tarpaulin that indicates human presence of some sort. But Swear's "house," if that's what it is, looks dark, void of life.

The hopelessness that flooded into him when he first heard about Boy and the scow, that receded against his better judgment when he thought of the marsh, soaks him once more. He trudges on more cautiously, watching for driftwood. The ground here is littered with it, clearly accumulated for later use. A circle dusted with snow and surrounded by half-burned logs indicates where Swear lights his campfire. A milk crate holds a clutch of liquor bottles, mostly Wolf Paw port, all empty. "Hello," Murdo calls; it comes out more as a grunt. "Oh fer godsake," he calls, more loudly, "is someone there?"

Sure now of the answer, or rather lack of it.

At the foot of the reeds, in the complication of whatever shelter this structure affords, what light exists is once more reduced to shades of charcoal under the frayed tarpaulin. Bending down he sees only logs rolled together, though one of them reminds him of something else, in part because of shape, partly because of folds in its bark or fiber.

It moves

Logs do not move.

Or fold.

"*Filho da*," Murdo gasps. He clutches at his glasses, he has star-tled up and sideways, dislodging them from his nose. A shadow behind the moving log stirs also, bending upward, turning out of the tiny V-shaped shelter. It pushes one of the smaller logs, which glints metallically.

"Swear, is that you?"

Murdo crouches. The oxygen bottle makes the question moot. But the shape crawls backward now, he has never seen Swear move so quickly, never seen him back up at all. The Norwegian's butt seems too small, and his hoodie also, his hoodie—

"Boy," Murdo yells. "*Boy!*"

The figure sits. The hood half falls over paler features. Murdo is on his knees before him, halfway under the tarp, clutching the shape, which does not resist—Murdo pushes back the hood, throws his arms around the kid's neck, tension that he'd forgotten was there spiking in his chest, his throat, "Oh, *Boy.*"

Then he sits back to take it in, what he can see in this light. The half-lit mouth, the hair falling over one eye, buck teeth biting down on the lower, left-side lip; even in the half-dark his uncertainty, the sense of a question that will never find reply. "Boy. I— *Filho da puta.* I mean, are you okay?"

He lunges forward again, losing his glasses, thinking it's good DCF guy is not around, hugging Boy hard to hide the fissure in himself, the stuff that comes out of those fissures, memory and inarticulacy and also snot and salt to add their rot and wetness to this place so full of both; the urge to conceal it is instinctive, something he did because his parents found emotion distasteful but for once he does not give a damn about the history, he will not go on that excursion. This stuff will come out because he is too full of it.

Boilers blow if they're not bled.

He lifts his head, the wet on his cheeks burning in the cold and shouts, "Daisy! *Daisy!* I found him, he's here"—half-laughing— "he's *here.*"

"Moodo," Boy says. He wrenches away and crawls, fast as a puppy, back into the tarp's shelter. Murdo retrieves his glasses then lifts the edge of tarp, yanking out a couple of logs that served to hold it down against the wind.

"You can't stay here," he says, "you don't have to worry, Boy."

Rainwater has puddled in the hollow where Boy lay beside a log—only this, too, is not a real log. Now the tarp is lifted he sees the second huddled shape in sweatclothes, a shape that has no face, it has a wisp of white that could be a beard from which twist the twin plastic snakes connecting Swear to his oxygen.

Swear does not move when Boy clings to him. Murdo kneels again, in the puddle, feeling along Swear's shoulder and collarbone to touch, beyond the wadded sweats, his neck. The man's skin is cold. He feels a flutter, very faint, under the skin but no movement otherwise, nor response to his own touch.

He slides backwards from the confines of the makeshift shelter, gets to his feet. Telling Boy to wait, he stumbles off through the reeds and cattails, heading back to the pickup truck, to Daisy.

The fire department ambulances get there first, their red and white bubblegum machines making candy stripes of the cattail jungle. Daisy stands by the pickup to guide the EMTs. Because of Nekropolis she possesses a keen instinct for systems of repression and she urged Murdo to leave and go home in the truck before the cops got here but he refused.

"If I hadn't shut you up about the uncle's gun you'd be in the nick now, for possession," she reminded him, her voice low as it tends to get under stress. "Now *listen* to me, you're violating a court order."

He doesn't listen though. He is high with finding Boy; confident, despite his own experience, that this success and his clear concern in searching for Boy will negate, for the authorities, the false charges that have been filed against Murdo. Surely emergency allows a bending of the rules, any judge or DA will see that. He disappears into the cattails again.

A cruiser slicks up four minutes after the rescue squad arrives. The officer is large, fat, in his mid-forties. A man sits in back, behind the security gridwork, shoulders forward in the attitude people adopt when their arms are bound behind their back with handcuffs.

The cop gets out but does not walk after the EMTs though the searchlight of his patrol car points a rod of brightness down the cattail path. Daisy, watching from the pickup's cab as he gets back in the cruiser, chewing gum and talking on a radio microphone, wonders if he is not too fat and unfit to negotiate the track. The rubber ducks tied to his rearview mirror dance as he shifts in his seat. The person in back, a black man with a graying Afro, shouts something that the cop ignores. His radio squawks, he taps a sentence into the car's laptop.

The snow stops suddenly, as if a switch in the weather had been flipped.

Daisy checks her army bag. Only after rummaging in the bag for ten seconds does she realize she's looking for the cigarettes she gave up nine and a half months earlier.

A few minutes later splits and scraps of a light that is clearer than dawn play among the cattail stalks. People appear, moving carefully, efficiently. A medical technician walks in front, but backward, playing his flashlight on the path before the feet of two men and two women carrying a stretcher. A fifth holds an IV tree over a shape mounded under blankets and tubing on the stretcher, that pitches and rolls despite the EMTs' efforts to steady it.

Behind them a fireman walks with Boy, who wears a space blanket around his shoulders and shuffles proudly, his eyes focused on the spaceship lighting of the rescue truck that lights them all, intermittently, in shades of blood and plasma.

And finally Murdo shows up, an afterthought hunched in a soaked jacket, still shivering from cold, from the backwash of adrenaline. He walks past the pickup and stands to one side, his eye on the EMTs. The policeman says something into a shoulder mic then heaves himself out of his cruiser. Daisy sees him, in the multiple blinks of light, stand in front of Murdo. He puts his hands on Murdo's shoulders, turns him roughly around and in a swift, almost graceful motion snaps handcuffs on his wrists. The EMTs notice but they are too busy to care, fiddling with oxygen and IVs, sliding the stretcher gently into their rescue truck— hooking up wires to screens. Medicine has taken Swear Bjørken.

George Michelsen Foy

Daisy almost falls as she jumps out of the truck, calling out
"Murdo! What is going on?" though she is pretty sure she knows.
She stands in front of the cop, reading the name tag on his
jacket: GUTZEIT. She lifts her poncho hood to look at him
straight.

The cop tells her, "Back off, missy."

"Daisy," Murdo says, and his eyes, dark-socketed against the
lights, seem exhausted, drained of spark compared to just a few
moments ago. "I'm *abusing* Boy now, maybe we both are, right? Ah,
by trying to rescue him ..."

"The rescue part?" the cop says, chewing at gum, "dunno, but
the abuse part, we got a history with that, don't we Peters?"

"That's *bull*-shit," Daisy says angrily.

"I told you, back *off*," Gutzeit tells her, more loudly than
before. The wind has picked up again. "Wanna go to jail too?"

The EMTs have slammed the rescue-trucks' doors. Their
diesels roar, a siren winds up that drowns the wind's whine; the
ambulances reverse single file down the track, beeping angrily, into
Greenwood Lane, then roar off toward the Cape Cod hospital
complex. It is then Daisy understands they took Boy as well. No
doubt they will give him warm fluids at the hospital. They will
examine him too, as the manual insists, for signs of rape, of hurt.

But she backs off as the copper suggested, forcing herself to not
stare at him, to look upward and left. It is useless to confront
Enforcers, she thinks, though she has sworn to stop thinking this
way, to avoid seeing her world through the prism of Cooch's game,
of Cooch's victory over her. Or at least—the thought slips out
despite her—you don't attack them head on.

Gutzeit leads Murdo to the cruiser and, gripping him by the
shoulder with one hand, the other on the butt of his pistol in case
Murdo should dare to resist, guides his prisoner into the back seat.
He chews mightily at his gum, and each chew seems to hold a
smile. The black man shouts, a sentence beginning with "White-
ass motha-*fuck*—" that is cut off as the door slams.

Yo, Archie, Murdo thinks to himself, chill out.

The rear-view ducks cavort as the policeman settles into his seat.

Murdo's head turns against the dark inside to look at Daisy as the cruiser backs up, turns, then speeds away.

She stands huddled in her spray-soaked poncho, among ruts the rescue trucks made, staring after him into the half-dark for a good half-minute before her own trembling, and the ever-present worry that abusing her body too much might have some effect on the smaller body starting within her, drives her back into the pickup—the engine of which has been running all this time, stuffing the little cab with heat.

Excerpt from Eby Noble's notebooks, 14 December 1952

The living quarters of this studio that I work in, that now floats peacefully at its mooring in the calm of a lagoon in southeastern Massachusetts, was once the home of Tillison Gorton.

Tillison was from the Yellowstone Valley, a mule-skinner by trade, and he could neither read nor write. Through the turnings of a long life he ended up as night watchman in the disused coal docks on the Arthur Kill, on Staten Island. I would not say Tillison was the happiest man I ever met but he was, I think, content because he expected little from life and got pretty much what he expected. And he had a surprising eye for quality, and fine workmanship, which are one and the same I believe. This dictated his choice of lodgings, the elegantly wrought cabin of an imperial yacht.

I sometimes think that for all my art and education I am not unlike Tillison Gorton. I have lived in Paris and New York and had articles written about my work but here I am in the

---

autumn of my life living under the same roof he lived under. My wife has gone to New York to live with another man, my children are grown and moved away, but I am largely satisfied by the work of sketching the ships and work-craft of another era that have been abandoned here to die.

Like Tillison, I am left to guard what no one wants anymore. Like Tillison I honor the grace of my wards, the centuries of knowledge that went into the schooners of the Eastern United States. Those ships were beautiful as a woman is beautiful because her curves are made to fit, with a lover, a child, a landscape even. Their arc, the way they reverse into and echo each other, reflects a ratio and a rhythm so basic to our world that she has no choice but to move with grace, to meld with other curves, to harbor.

And I have drawn women—I drew hundreds of sketches of Penny—but the bulk of my work here has been to preserve in paper and ink the curve of sheer and deckline matched underwater by the garboards, by the arc of canvas pushing a hull not against but with the turn of waves. How the tumblehome of the upper hull echoes flare by the bow, how spanker jib bellies with mainsail, how pintle fits into gudgeon. I have loved these ships and boats as I have loved the men who worked them because they were all built for a task and the task was a good one that meshed with horizon and clouds, with the hardness of the coal or paving stones they carried, with the seacoast they belong to and in their souls must honor.

To move with a landscape, to possess such skill that one can work together with it, whether this be tacking to make the tide in Vineyard Sound, coaxing apple trees to bear fruit on a rocky hillside, moving a platoon of infantrymen through a valley within range of hostile fire, is always beautiful—even if the last example includes much ugliness in context. The work of the observer, I sometimes think, is to find loveliness, though it be in places of decay and sadness. Brueghel—I am not comparing myself to him, only noting a detail—painted a boy relieving himself against a wall and that was part of "Children's Games" and both its familiarity and vulgarity add to the depth of the whole. My last sketches of Penny, though I did not notice it at the time, traced the lines of fatigue, of anger, that living with me brought out, but in those sketches she is still lovely and the lines change her prettiness, make it deeper, make it earned. She and I earned much in our years together and in a strange way the joy fitting together as a family gave us was made sharper, even in a curious way stronger, by the terrible strains of separation.

The prints I made of the schooners left to rot in Staten Island, in Hyannis Harbor, show how the balance of those lovely ships shifts with rot, changes with age, until a different loveliness emerges, an altered but still valid truth, one that encompasses all of existence: the suffering as well as the joy, decay as well as growth, death as well as life.

The schooners are gone now. Even their wrecks have been taken apart, or burned by rampaging boys, or finally sunk into the harbor bottom. A marina has been built in the inner harbor where they used to dock. Of the last schooner left here, the "Zebulon," only a few black ribs remain, rising from cattails and black water like broken monuments from a forgotten civilization.

Only I remain, an old man in a fixed-up scow, as they call it here, to mark this passage. It amazes me that I am not bitter, nor twisted from the loss of much that I have loved. It surprises me sometimes that I am glad to be alive when a

*new morning—and every morning is new—pulls colors out
of the harbor and the trees surrounding and the crowds of
brash new motorboats that dot this small lagoon. Perhaps,
like Tillison Gorton, I have learned to be content with workmanship wherever I can find it.*

Perhaps, for any life, this is enough.

The Hyannis field office of the Department of Children and
Families of the Commonwealth of Massachusetts takes up a
portion of a mini-mall that lies at the intersection of Main Street
and High School Road Extension—occupying, appropriately
perhaps, space previously leased by a chain that sold children's
shoes made by low-wage workers in China.

Beyond a blue canopy and two pairs of glass doors the decor is
state institutional, one can find the same scheme in Registry of
Motor Vehicles offices and state police stations: tiled floor, walls of
light blue gray (of the same color as troopers' uniforms), wood laminate in the receptionist's booth.

The only unusual touch here, painted on the wall to the right
as you come in, is a rough mural depicting in cheerful hues various
types of marine life—whales, jellyfish, eels—drawn on a dark blue
background behind the waiting-area chairs. The fish swim in and
out of a forest of kelp and other kinds of weed. The weeds are black
as trees, almost threatening in their solidity.

Kathleen Duffy and Joe Barboza sit opposite each other. Both
of them stare at the fish and the weed. Finally a man and a woman
enter the waiting room from a door in back. The woman
announces, "Joseph Barboza?"

A telephone rings.

Joe gets to his feet, followed by Kathleen. She gives her name
to the DCF woman, who consults stapled papers, frowns, nods.
The man opens a door to one side and switches on the light. The

walls of the hearing room are of the same statie blue. The room is small, nearly filled by a round table surfaced in bright yellow formica. The DCF woman stands by the door as the others choose seats from five chairs at the table. After half a minute a uniformed Barnstable police officer walks in and takes the remaining chair, and the woman closes the door.

Kathleen fishes a notepad out of her handbag and places it, closed, on the formica. Joe Barboza puts his hands on the table. They are large, wrinkled, and seem to take up too much space. The DCF woman is plump as a pudding, with rounded features that look as if they are waiting for raisins to decorate them. Her colleague is good-looking in a tight sort of way. His nose and mouth are well shaped but small, his lips seem to exist under high tension. After working as a foster parent for almost fifteen years Kathleen has met a crowd of DCF people but she does not know these two.

The cop is Ray Leblanc, from the BPD juveniles division.

The woman says, "As you know, we're here to proceed on the case of Joseph Barboza Junior—after, uh, this case was screened in on a 51-A complaint—"

"I'm sorry," Kathleen interrupts immediately. "I thought this was on a petition to confirm Joseph into foster care, into my custody as a foster parent again."

The two state workers stare at her.

"Let us finish, please?" the tight-mouthed man says. He wears a plastic tag that says BARBIER. The plump woman wears over her left breast a smaller tag that reads "Ashley" under a smiley face of the same color as the table formica. Under the smiley face, in Bodoni Bold, are printed the words "I Care." She picks out a document from a sheaf she placed in front of her.

"Erm," Barbier says, opening a folder, "we found sufficient cause for further investigation, and for a restraining order to be placed on the, erm, alleged abuser, a mister McMurdo Cahoon Peters? Who lived formerly at 15 Harbor Way in Hyannis, and now resides at his parents' property at 178 Popple Bottom Lane in West Barnstable."

"I'm sorry," Kathleen interrupts again. "I have a babysitter for my two current kids at home, plus Joseph Junior, and I was asked to come here only yesterday—"

"You were asked, erm, in your capacity as potential permanent foster parent for Joseph Junior," the DCF man says, talking loudly to drown Kathleen's voice. "It seems to me—"

"Ex-*cuse* me," Kathleen says, sounding angry rather than apologetic. "I have done this for a long time. I know DCF backwards and forwards. I know—I know—" she talks louder in turn as Barbier starts to talk again, "I know you have a tough job sometimes and you try your best but frankly I think you're coming at this problem from the wrong end, which would not be unusual."

"Now wait a minute," Barbier says.

"Now how did we get here?" says the social worker, Ashley, frowning so her doughy features dimple in odd places.

"I think," Joe says, moving his hands toward each other across the table. He has a voice that is soft but also quite deep and partly because of this, and partly also because he is a tall, older man with a calm way of looking, everyone falls silent and looks at him.

"I think this situation right now is bad. I don't know about this Murdo guy, he came to my bar but that is not always a good way to know people. What I do know is, Sonny seems to need care he is not getting." Joe smoothes the top of his head with the palm of one hand. The hair is white and oiled and it shines like pond ice after he strokes it.

"His father, my son, died four years ago in a construction accident. His mother works in New Hampshire and his uncle, he was supposed to take care of him, well I'm told he is not responsible sometimes."

"We got a call from the mother," says Ashley. "She said she could not attend this meeting without being let go?"

"The restraining order was violated five days ago," Barbier says. He closes his lips between each sentence and his mouth gets round and tight. "Following a flight incident. Flight and vandalism of some kind of, erm, houseboat belonging to, erm," (he checks his folder) "the Cape Realtors Action Consortium?"

"Can I say something?" Kathleen asks. Barbier ignores her.

"And it's partly to protect the juvenile from Mister Peters that we put him in emergency care with you three days ago."

"He needs his mother," Joe says. "She could not find good work on-Cape."

No one speaks for twenty, thirty seconds.

"I've had Boy in my care before," Kathleen says finally, "and I've noticed a change in him this time round. He seems very depressed."

"It's a common effect of abuse," Ashley remarks.

"Well, yeah," Kathleen says. "But he's also fixated on this Murdo guy and his girlfriend. Apparently he was showed how to screw—"

Barbier glances at his colleague—

"I mean, screw *in*, like, planks." Kathleen tries not to smile at her mistake. "On this boat they're making. He showed him, I mean Boy, I mean *Joseph*; Murdo showed him how to make etchings."

"Oh dear," the DCF woman says, rolling her eyes. Kathleen is not smiling now. Her eyes reflect the awful glare of neon with an intensity that makes Barbier look away.

"*Real* etchings," Kathleen insists. "He's a printmaker. An artist. I guess that's what CRAC hired him for.

"Boy tried to make dinner for them," she continues, "but they slapped the TRO on Murdo and it got him upset. Boy, I mean."

"That's true." Joe nods.

Kathleen continues to look at Barbier. "I can't say for sure this Murdo guy didn't abuse him, but"— she leans back in her chair— "if I were you, if there is abuse at all, I'd focus more on Danny Martin. The uncle."

"Now wait a minute." Joe raises one hand and turns to stare at Kathleen. "Just wait a minute. Sonny's uncle is not the abuser here, he is not that kind of man."

"This is not within the scope of this inquiry," Ashley remarks.

"Why are you holding this hearing here, anyway?" Kathleen asks. "It's usually in the courthouse. And why the police?" She glances at Ray, who starts to speak but is interrupted by Ashley.

"The courthouse was overbooked." Ashley picks up her sheaf of stapled papers as if for comfort. "Officer Leblanc was a witness, it's a new policy, anyway the uncle is not the focus, *placement* is the focus. Protection of this child is the focus. You don't seem to realize, this Mister Peters, this *artist*, his profile you need to look at here, he has prior record."

"Well," Kathleen says slowly, "that's different. What kind of record?"

Barbier opens another folder. "Criminal negligence," he reads, and looks up. "A girl died."

"A girl died," Kathleen repeats. "When was this?"

"Apparently," Barbier reads as he talks, "Peters encouraged her to, erm, dive off a high drawbridge? He did two months in juvenile. And he was sued by the parents of the girl, for negligent manslaughter."

"Juvie?" Kathleen says. "So he was underage. Diving—but that's not abuse, is it?"

"It all fits," Barbier insists, "it's a profile."

"Maybe," Kathleen interrupts, leaning forward. "But this Danny Martin? Everybody knows him in the neighborhood, he's a bad actor—"

"Would you please not interrupt when—"

"I *have* to interrupt." Kathleen turns toward Joe. "I'm not saying he's an abuser, Joe. Your in-law, or whatever he is. I *am* saying Martin's capable of making that kind of charge to cover up something that happened because of, I dunno. He has gangbangers over, you know he does, they deal in all sortsa shit. Everybody in the Winterpoor knows that. They are not pretty people, Ray here can vouch for that."

Kathleen looks at the policeman, who has been following the conversation but with his chair pushed well back and legs stretched, out of the way both physically and in terms of the discussion. Now he gathers his legs under him and holds up both hands, palms out. "I'm only here," he says, "as a witness, like she said. I can't comment on any of it."

Kathleen looks at Barbier, then at Ashley, who flattens her hands protectively on her papers.

"I think you should either confirm the placement with me," Kathleen says softly, "or place this kid with another parent, stat. Get him out of reach of both his uncle and this Murdo guy.

"But every instinct I have," she continues in an even quieter voice, "tells me you're missing something that's key here."

Barbier says, "We'll take that under advisement."

Ashley says, "We'll call you."

Kathleen says, "That's it?"

Barbier says, "Given the tone of this hearing, my colleague and I need to—"

"What do you mean, tone?"

"Your attitude—"

"You know where you can stick my attitude," Kathleen replies. "I've been taking care of foster kids for fourteen years and I know what I'm doing and I know a toxic family situation when I see one."

Joe gets to his feet, leans over the table and offers his hand to Barbier, who shakes it without taking his eyes off Kathleen.

"I've had it up to here," Kathleen says, getting up also and picking up the notepad, which she never opened.

"We know what we're doing," Ashley says. Her tone is suddenly conciliatory. "We're the ones fighting for the kid, we're the ones trying to get him a better deal."

Kathleen puts the notepad in her bag.

"That's what you people always say," she replies, looking at Ashley. "And sometimes it's true, I guess. But in all the time I've been doing this, the only thing I see that gets consistently better is your pension plan."

Barbier's mouth has gone so small it looks like a keyhole. Ashley shakes her head, tiredly, setting her jowls a-wobble.

Joe Barboza holds the door open for Kathleen as she walks out; then follows, limping slightly, leaving the two DCF officers and Ray Leblanc sitting silent inside.

Murdo has trouble parking his truck. The main Cape Cod Hospital parking lot is full. Finally he parks it at the south end of the compound, next to the psychiatric wing. As he parks, a sedan screeches through the Gleason Street entrance, much too fast, into the emergency room access lane.

From the docks a ferry moos. Murdo watches its mast and funnel, over bare trees and a motel rooftop, inch toward the harbor mouth on its run toward Nantucket.

Murdo thinks, a century ago this part of the Hyannis Harbor would have looked like a forest of masts from all the schooners docked here. He ignores the sirens, a flurry of sudden activity at the ER entrance as the erratic driver is subdued and cuffed.

Intensive Care is on the third floor. The waiting room is well lit, its chairs are upholstered and the wall paintings are full of cheery colors. A ceiling-mounted TV shows an all-news channel. The volume is off but subtitles appear as the anchors speak. Murdo checks in as required with the ICU receptionist, who looks up Swear Bjørken's information on a computer terminal before her.

"Are you family?" she asks.

"Nephew."

"He has a lot of nephews."

The receptionist doesn't smile. She says she'll call him when the nurses allow a visit.

An elderly woman in blued hair and golfing clothes sits in a corner reading a paperback titled *Why Women Rule the World*. A younger woman with long blond hair tied in a ponytail sits on the edge of her chair, watching the TV. She wears lavender polyester slacks, a gray sweatshirt, and track shoes with chewed up heels.

Murdo sits opposite the old woman. Two nights ago he spent

twenty-four hours in the tank at Barnstable police headquarters after he was caught within 200 feet of Boy and this, for all its glossy magazines and paintings, feels similar; a place you can only leave with permission. He supposes, for patients here, it is exactly that kind of place.

A man comes in. He is maybe 50 years old and wears a sheep-skin-lined denim vest that looks older than he does. He nods at Murdo who, recognizing him from the Foc'sle, nods back. The man's t-shirt sleeves are rolled up; a tattoo reading "Birdie," with a drunk-looking canary underneath, adorns his left bicep. The odor of tobacco drifts behind him. The receptionist looks up sharply.

"Were you smokin' in the men's room?"

The tattooed man grins at her. "Me?" he says. "I would never do such a thing."

The receptionist frowns. The TV screen shows the United States Capitol. The closed caption reads, YOUR SURE, JANET, THE LEDGER STATION. I MEAN WELT THE CENTAURS PAST. Murdo, reading the caption, watching the walls, feels a whiff of nausea coming on.

"What the fuck," the ponytailed woman comments.

Everyone but the older woman and the receptionist watches the screen. Murdo unwraps a chocolate-peppermint candy he bought at the hospital shop and chews it. Against the deadness of filtered air, the sting of mint feels fine in his mouth and nose.

A short, plump woman in scrubs and plastic clogs comes in and talks to the receptionist, who looks up from her screen and says, "Mister Peters? You can go in now."

Murdo follows the nurse through doors that open automatically when the nurse thumps her behind against a big aluminum button. The ward consists of cubicles defined by curtains and pain. They are stuffed with equipment: chromed steel poles, clear bags of fluid, chunky plastic displays full of blinking lights; pumps, tubes, wires, sensors. In each cubicle the equipment circles a hogged and railing-protected horizontal machine, also hung with wires, tubes and remotes. Everything is wired to mounds covered with blankets atop the horizontal machine at the center of the sensors' hub.

Beeps in different keys sound rhythmically from all directions. The nurse leads Murdo to a cubicle on the far left. A sign reads BJORKEN, SVEN SWARSTAD. The blanket-covered mound seems oddly shrunken and short but it has a head that, as Murdo approaches, resolves into features he recognizes as belonging to Swear(508)—thick nose, brushy yellowish eyebrows, sparse white hair. The features were wrinkled before but now it seems to Murdo that the wrinkles have taken over and the recognizable parts of the old man's face are mere additions to wear-and-tear. Much of the face is obscured by an oxygen mask, and what he can see of skin is white as paper. A hint of blue registers through eyelids so folded they resemble crumpled tissue.

"Swear?" Murdo leans over to see him better.

"Just five minutes, hon'," the nurse says cheerfully, and stabs a readout on a pole holding plastic bags. One set of beeps stops dead.

"Can you see me? It's Murdo. I'm the friend of Joe Barboza."

"I think Mister Barboza was in earlier," the nurse comments, and leaves.

Murdo looks around for witnesses, then pulls from an inner pocket of his jacket a pint bottle that he earlier filled with Olde Bilgewater. He waves it near Swear's head, taking care to avoid the tubes and wires. The old man's eyes open wider, and his pupils track the moving bottle.

"It's my whiskey, Swear," Murdo says. "I can't give it to you now, but when you get out—"

"You can't give him that at all."

It's a different nurse, younger and thinner than the first. She steps inside the cubicle and puts her hand out for the bottle. Murdo shoves it hastily back in his jacket. A groan, so soft that Murdo barely hears it, rises from the oxygen mask.

"What is that?" the nurse demands, frowning at Murdo's jacket.

"Whiskey," Murdo tells her. "I wasn't really gonna give it to him."

"You want to kill him, go ahead and give it to him." She starts pulling at tubes that lead from under the blankets to plastic bottles full of yellow or pinkish fluids. Another set of beeps joins the beep chorus already in cry. "You'll have to leave anyway, I have to check his stent. Mister Buh-jerken," she calls loudly. "I have to check your stent, I'm gonna raise your torso a little bit?"

"Can you tell me how," Murdo begins, but the nurse cuts him off.

"I can't tell you anything, you have to talk to the Attending."

"Well, can I—"

"Talk to the desk."

In the waiting room the man is flexing his bicep in front of the old woman in golfing clothes to make the tattooed canary flap its wings. "Tweet," Birdie says, "see? Tweet."

"That's very impressive." The woman keeps her eyes on *Why Women Rule the World*.

The woman with the ponytail is still staring at the TV.

"I can't believe who writes this shit," she says. "I read perfectly, I always have, right? But you write something like 'unrest in ashcan, Stan,' well it just makes no sense."

"It's a machine that does it," Birdie says. "AI, voice recognition, but sometimes—"

"I don't care if it's all of Harvard University that does it," the woman retorts, "it still sucks."

Murdo, sitting, unable to focus on *Golf Monthly* or *Cape Cod Home & Garden*, for the first time looks carefully at the artwork on the walls. He feels a combination of disgust and irritation that seems to boost, and might have caused initially, the nausea he has felt since entering the ICU. The images are silkscreens in faux-naïf style, all primary colors. They depict pretty mermaids, quaint seaside hamlets, shingled boutiques, smiling flounder, cavorting whales and scallops; around their edges, on ornate banners, are written in block capitals legends such as "Cape Cod Girls Have No Combs, They Comb Their Hair With Codfish Bones."...

The paintings are not Cahoons, Murdo realizes. They are not even reproductions of Cahoons, but rather pastiches in the style of Murdo's great-grandfather on his mother's side.

School of Cahoon. All quaintness, Ahoy there! and tourist kitsch.

The woman who disapproves of closed captioning looks at Murdo curiously.

"You here to see Swear?" she asks suddenly.

Murdo nods.

"You know him from the shelter?"

"No. Just a friend."

"He's got lots of those," the woman says. "People love ole Swear." She sticks out her hand assertively, and Murdo shakes it.

A deeply pregnant woman in scrubs with a stethoscope looped around her neck walks out from the unit proper.

"You wanted to talk to me?" she says to Murdo, who stares at her. Her voice is so high and nasal that he imagines, for a split second, it is the tattooed man imitating a bird.

"Oh, yeah," he says stupidly.

"You are Mister Peters?" the woman says. When Murdo nods she adds, "Let's go over here?" She walks down the nearest hallway to a set of windows facing a brick wall and aluminum HVAC vents. The brick is blurred with dots of white. It is starting to snow again, Murdo realizes; it's the first time snow has fallen since he found Boy and Swear in the marsh.

"I'm Doctor Boudreau," the pregnant woman says. "His attending. Mister Buhjokin has given me HIPAA to talk to you?" (Murdo tries to control his facial muscles. Her voice is, if anything, squeakier than before.)

"What is HIPAA?"

"Privacy permission. Seems to give it to everyone."

He's probably happy anyone cares enough to inquire, Murdo thinks, but doesn't say it.

"There's not much to say anyway?" the woman continues, and since she ends most sentences on an up-tone as if it had a question mark at the end, her words disappear into frequencies so high they would be perceptible only to a dog. "He's suffering from exposure? He has emphysema, and borreliosis? And he's diabetic, of course, which is why the necrosis?"

"Necrosis?"

"Yes. You know about his feet?"

"His feet?" Murdo closes his mouth. He feels as a child must feel—like Boy, perhaps—utterly helpless before this squeaking doctor and a horde of machines he does not, cannot understand. The woman brushes a strand of hair out of her eyes.

"We couldn't save them. He came in with point-four-three blood alcohol, which constricted blood circulation in his extremities? So both feet had to be amputated, along with two of his fingers?

"Even so," she continues, "he was lucky. Hypothermia had set in so far he was close to renal failure? He's still on dialysis but we have some kidney function back? That's the good news. His liver"—she shakes her head. "The floor nurse tells me you tried to give him alcohol?"

"I didn't try to give him any damn thing," Murdo says. "I showed him the bottle, that's all."

"You're not allowed to bring alcohol in here."

Murdo crosses his arms, and leans forward. Dr. Boudreau looks at him levelly.

"You know," she says, "the shape he's in, Mister Buhjokin, well he's got maybe two years to live? Three if he's lucky, if he gets good care and shelter. But if he starts drinking again, he won't even have that?"

Murdo meets her gaze for ten seconds, fifteen. Then he looks away. Boudreau's belly, its deviation from normal bellies, catches his attention. The doctor has been pregnant much longer than Daisy.

He finds that he wants to see her, to be back in the barn with

Daisy, far from this place of blinking lights, rhythmic beeps, cold machines—and that drive seems fully as strong and concrete a feeling as was his hatred, three nights ago, of being trapped in a jail cell. Murdo lifts his eyes from the doctor's midsection and looks around him. The walls of this hallway too are hung with fake Cahoons. The nausea clouds his gut, recedes. He fights an urge to burp.

When Murdo is sure he can speak without making other noises he says, "I guess, given where he was a few nights ago, even a year is gonna look pretty good to Swear."

Murdo talks fast and low and maybe that's in reaction to Boudreau's mousy squeak. More likely it's a function of the irritation in him that has risen to a point where he must call it anger. He isn't sure where it comes from—the fake Cahoons are part of it certainly, but so is the feeling of lost control that has not left him since he was first placed in handcuffs—hell, since Barbier found him and Daisy at the barn.

He thinks of Swear, his feet now gone, huddled in that machine-bed next door.

Murdo's arms hurt. He uncrosses them slowly.

"What I really hate about these things," he tells Boudreau, pointing at the nearest silkscreen which depicts a snowbound Cape Cod harbor with Christmas trees and lights and the usual whales and dancing mermaids, "is how they lie? They paint everything so cute and folksy, with lights and presents and, and happy fish, I mean look; but that's not where we live, is it? That's sure as hell not where Swear lives?"

He shuts his mouth hard. Dr. Boudreau's up-speak, he realizes, is catching.

"So I got to tell you, Doctor," he continues, making sure to end each phrase as affirmation. "I got to tell you. If he feels like drinking again, I ain't gonna be the one to stop him."

They stare at each other for a few seconds. The doctor's face twists, as if she had a stomach pang. She shrugs, turns away. Murdo turns also, walking toward the elevators, which five minutes and several corridors later he discovers lie in a different part of the hospital entirely.

Eel Pond at the winter solstice looks less tamed, more as it might have looked like a century before. That's mostly because the pleasure boats that broke up its expanse in summer are gone, their mooring buoys exchanged for winter-sticks, two-by-four markers that poke up, like masts of forgotten wrecks, into the air of what now looks like a real cove, a serious expanse of salt water, something cold and deep; not as cold or deep as Lewis Bay or the Sound outside the ramparts of Hyannis Harbor or the ocean beyond that, but plenty cold and deep if you have to cross it or deal with it in any way except to look.

Brian Fuller's battered quahog boat swings to a borrowed mooring, as do Jensen's mooring hauler and a pair of boatyard floats rough enough to withstand winter ice.

The old scow that the boat-school was restoring until it was turned adrift by a kid in the November nor'easter and nearly sank on Point Gammon hunkers again on the boatyard's marine railway. The bright varnish of its cabin is clawed and dirtied and the decks are still covered, sometimes to the depth of a foot, in orange seaweed. It looks, in other words, right at home, another workboat much the worse for wear, another chunk of flotsam that the harbor painted in its own colors. The same weed that covers the scow's decks has built up around the lagoon's landward side, and this is different from last year, but it stinks less in the colder air. And the rest of Eel Pond seems the same as always: clean and gray with cirrus sheetrocking the sky and the wind whispering phone-sex to cattails and eelgrass.

In the lagoon's center several flocks of seabirds: eider ducks, scoter, merganser; have settled in drifts across the water. A solitary loon lurks nearer the western shore. All the birds are black and white and look, to humans observing, like graphic design, hash marks on a lithograph, an Escher pattern scattered to reinforce a point made in deeper text.

And there is text, deeper down. On the shallower mudflats, in drowned earth, it looks as if someone has written the epilogue to a testament in cursive script. A dozen eight- and nine-year-old eels, more sensitive to dropping temperatures than the rest of their peer group, have lit out for the ten-fathom mark; in wiggling snake-like across the shallower flats, between weeds and rock and oysters, they leave a farewell note scrawled in linked "S" shapes on the mud, pointing toward the lagoon's mouth, signing off in deeper muck beneath the drawbridge.

The farewell is forever. At their lives' end the eels are heading back to the Gulf Stream to finish the current's cycle, riding it past Iceland, and Portugal, to the Sargasso Sea where they were born. Just before they die the females will hatch the only clutch of eggs they'll ever bear. Then the baby eels, the elvers, will ride the Gulf Stream north to Eel River, to start the cycle anew.

One of the S-marks left by the eels swipes a hint of metal where a girl's charm bracelet lies, its bronze tarnished to green, only a hint of clasp and a metal dolphin showing; something the tide happened to latch onto and lick free, for now.

In the black mud Maginots of the harbor's sides the fiddler crabs have locked themselves in their bunkers. On the withered eelgrass that roofs these redoubts the moon jellies, now morphed into clear polyps, cluster up and down the green stalks. The water is clear, although the intake of nitrates from all sources increased this past summer, yet again.

A family of raccoons parts the stalks of spartina, then eelgrass, and finds a bed of mussels. The paterfamilias, a medium-sized animal with a patch of white fur under his muzzle, looks suspiciously left and right, eyes glinting in his Movietone mask, before fitting his black front paws around one of the shells and worrying it free of substrate. A smaller, feisty 'coon hops into the mussel-rich water next to the paterfamilias and is warned away with a cuff, a grouchy churr.

The mussel shells are glossy, indigo. Clouds from a cold front moving in from the west conceal lavender within their gray. The facets of water, slapped up by wind, are deep blue with hints of violet and black. Few greens of summer are left in the grasses. The spartina, cattails, even the invasive reeds that ring the lagoon have turned albino, with highlights of tan and gold; of umber, ochre-brown, russet as well.

The great democracy of coming cold has paled the overall palette, and the brute Komissar of winter will seek to impose an icy conformity, even among things from other places: wakame, drift-wood, the hapless scow; till everything finally looks as if a bad artist has scraped pale light off the ocean horizon and used it to scumble Eel Pond. All this will only get more-so until, well after the winter solstice, the days grow long enough to warm the water past fifty degrees, to unleash once more the verdant jacqueries of spring.

Book Four
Winter

Eugenia Gomes is making coffee in Joe Barboza's kitchen when Joe gets back from the bank. She spoons instant crystals from a jar into a glass pot and fills the pot with boiling water. As she waits for the crystals to melt she gazes over the kitchen sink, out the back window, watching crystals of snow fall on a vegetable patch in which tomato plants lean crucified on sticks and twine. The patch is wedged between a pair of thief pines that separate Joe's house from a clutch of dead lawnmowers and a wading pool on the next lot. The snowflakes are large and fluffy; they fill the pewter sky above the pines with white, and hit the ground like thoughts on a hot mind, vanishing where they touch.

And yet, it's getting colder. A few houses over, a blue spruce, the only tall tree left in the Winterpoor, wears shawls of white on its dark, broad-spread needles.

She hears him come in but does not turn and Joe says nothing when he sees her. They were lovers once, after Joe's wife died but while Eugenia was still married, and though it has been years since they slept together or even spent a full day with each other the shared assumptions, the hangover of familiarity, persist. Joe always leaves his door unlocked, mostly for her.

He hangs up his coat in the hallway and walks into the living room. He takes money out of his wallet and puts cash and checkbook in the ancient register that once sat on the bar of Twin Joes' Villa. He checks the bottles behind this bar—he is almost out of the moonshine Boy's friend, the boat artist, makes. He thinks back to what is going on between his grandson and the boat artist and Boy's uncle but he doesn't think hard. Joe thought about that before and also during the meeting with the DCF people and he always finds it better to compartmentalize; to think about a given subject and act on it if possible and, once action is no longer relevant, put it aside like a book he will finish later.

He takes out his bar book and makes a note about the whiskey. He switches on the TV, leaves the sound off, and sits in the wicker armchair, putting his bad leg up on the next seat, enjoying the resignation of cushions that have had the gumption worn out of them.

Eugenia comes out of the kitchen with two cups and hands one to Joe, who nods. The gas heater switches on, blows warm, lightly perfumed air through the hallway vent.

"Another winter comin'," Eugenia says, after a while.

"Cold getting to your bones?"

"Don't you worry about my bones."

The blower switches off. In the sudden silence the snow makes noises like teeth clicking against the living room windows. Eugenia takes a sip of coffee.

"How's he doing?"

"Who?"

"Who you think."

Joe, uttering a grunt he tries with only partial success to conceal, gets up from the wicker chair. He limps behind the bar again, grabs a dish towel, takes a beer glass from the shelf.

"At our age, Eugenia, could be any number of people. Half of 'em sick of one thing or another, the other half dead."

"I know you went to see him earlier."

Joe rubs at the glass, slowly.

"Not so hot," he says finally. "I thought *you* were going to go see him."

"I thought so too. But I can't—oh! Not since Lenny." She shakes her head, hard. "I can't bring myself to go near that goddam place."

"It's gotten better," Joe says.

"What has?"

"Cape Cod Hospital, Cape Healthcare, Corporate Wellness, whatever they call themselves now. They don't kill so many people anymore."

"Can they give Swear his feet back? Can you *ever* get something back, once it's gone?"

Joe puts the beer glass back on the shelf, then takes it down again. He holds it up to the light, rubs a smudge away from the glass's lip. On the TV screen a handsome young white man and a pretty Latina woman sit at a desk together, laughing at each other's comments but gazing at the camera the whole time.

"Let's not go into that again," Joe says finally.

"You say that." Eugenia sticks a thumb in her mouth, takes it out again. "You say that 'cause you don't want to admit you're wrong."

"I'm not wrong."

Eugenia puts her cup down. She folds her hands across her stomach and looks at him.

Joe frowns. He knows that look well.

"They closed the shelter, Joe. First they made it smaller, and finally they closed it."

"It didn't close, they moved it."

"Moved it! Moved it to Industrial Park. There's nothing there, Joe! That's why Swear didn't go there, and Crewe won't stay there either. And you know," she continues, "they're only gonna build eight units of affordable housing on the land you're selling them. But if you *don't* sell all of it—"

"I told you, I don't want to talk about it." Joe frowns harder, squints across the room, at the small rectangular windows set on each side of the front door. A knock sounds at the door. He comes out from behind the bar, strides across the room with only a hint now of limp in his leg. When he opens Crewe and Dog walk in, followed by Ken-Ken. They slap at the snowflakes already melting on their shoulders. erwinrommel collapses near a heat vent and, with a sigh, returns to the task of keeping his balls clean. Dog wears his usual paint-stippled Carhartt, Ken-Ken an English waxed jacket; Crewe wears a worn raincoat with large pockets out of which he pulls a pint bottle of Wolf Paw. He places it on the bar counter. He removes his coat but not his hat and sits on the wicker couch, on the left-hand side by the end table, his accustomed spot.

The right-hand seat, where there is no side table, is where Swear usually sits so he can park his oxygen bottle beside him.

No-one looks at the right-hand seat. Eugenia fetches the pot of coffee from the kitchen and pours two more mugs. The pot is still half full. Joe, watching her, says, "Why do I get the feeling this is not a coincidence?"

"Cuz it ain't," Eugenia says.

Daisy picks four logs from the dwindling stack on the barn's south side, cradles them in her arms. It is still snowing and she pauses to look around her, at the flakes falling against a darkening sky; on oak trees, barn, on rough grass in between. Each fat white dot wavering downward seems to cut the usual lines of topography, of gravity, of perception even, making the world—making her—as tenuous as a dream you don't write down.

She shakes her head, quickly walks back inside, kicking the door to behind her. She dumps the logs by the woodstove then squats, opens the stove's hatch, and crams a log into orange glow. Heat scours her cheeks and she keeps the hatch open for a few seconds, soaking it in.

She feels, sometimes, as if she never fully warmed up from that panicked boat ride in the storm, during the night when Boy launched the scow, when they were certain he had drowned.

Restless, she returns to the armchair, to her laptop. She will not go back to Nekropolis, not ever, and she clicks back to the project she has just started, that she wants to surprise Murdo with. But for once the coding eludes her, she doesn't have the patience, she's too anxious for no reason she can figure. Clicks to the Craigslist/Cape and Islands job posts but this is the third time she's looked in an hour and there was nothing worth pursuing to begin with and nothing has changed since.

She wonders yet again how they'll get through the winter, with a baby on the way and no money coming in. Murdo has his severance pay from the CRAC, which is what they're living on, and he'll get half the value of his and Una's house when the divorce comes through, but that won't be for months. They have filed for Mass. Health, and Medicare—or what's left of Medicare after the latest cuts—and have yet to hear if their application has been confirmed; and she is sick of this uncertainty, sick of not knowing whether they'll have enough firewood this winter. Not knowing if their baby will get the care she, or he, will need.

Daisy shoves that thought away like pushing a log into the fire. She never suffered much from morning sickness but her hormones are still running hog-wild and if she lets these thoughts race she will end up a sobbing pathetic heap on the hook rug, it has happened before.

Abruptly she shuts the laptop and walks to the kitchen for coffee, then decides she's had enough caffeine. The baby books she's been reading recommend cutting down on that, on booze—on everything, she reflects sourly, that she likes. It's a good thing she already gave up cigarettes, mostly.

Back in the barn proper she walks to the bookshelf but the handful of Lovecraft novels and travel guides there don't interest her. She runs one finger down the rows of ancient books that hold Noble's notes on etching. The barn is silent except for an occasional crack of hardwood burning in the stove, the keen of hot air escaping up the pipe; her finger makes a tiny thud against each notebook spine, then bends against anomaly—a notebook also, bigger than the others, ten by twelve when the others are mostly five by seven.

She pulls it off the shelf. The cover, of tan cardboard, is illustrated with watercolor flowers, faded but well drawn. She opens the book.

8 August 1989, she reads. *15.3 gallons of blackberries. Obtain molasses sugar from Boston Monday + 2 quarts honey from Annie's cranberry hives.*

1989? Daisy thinks. This can't be Noble's.

Among the pages she finds a neat sketch in ink and watercolors of a mason jar holding a dark maroon liquid next to a bunch of branches, leaves and berries. There's a signature in the right-hand corner that looks like "Bob (or Rob) Peters." A few pages on, a pen-and-ink sketch of a glass tube with the notation: *Anne ordered the wrong hydrometer from Bradford's! Will taste-test sugar content of elderberry ...*

A winemaker's record: kept, she has to assume, by Murdo's father. Every entry is written with dark blue ink in a neat, even painstaking hand. The information is extremely detailed: *22 lb. 7 oz. of Wellfleet blackberries added to the redcurrant must. Tartaric acid, 2.18 oz. September 18.* A column of numbers follows.

In between the notations and watercolors of winemaking are quick sketches of a dark-haired woman pouring juice, stirring jars, picking berries. These are freer than the more technical images but accomplished with similar skill and attention to detail. The book is almost 100 pages long. The notations and drawings go right to the end, implying there's at least one volume after and, given the expertise that speaks of long habit, probably one or more before as well.

She checks the dates: 6 July 1989 to 12 March 1990. Murdo was born seven years before this book was finished, and his sister, Juneau, a year earlier. Daisy looks at each page, expecting at every turn to find a drawing or mention of children. She finds not one.

She slaps the book shut, replaces it on the shelf, and walks to the window. She looks at the snow without seeing it. Tears are running down her face almost before she realizes she is crying and a sob escapes her chest the same way, before she is fully aware. It wrenches her rib cage, it feels as if it's allowing the escape of a sadness so big her entire body cannot contain it.

"Fucking *hormones*," she whispers and punches the window frame with her fist, so hard it hurts; so hard that paint flakes off to the wooden planks beneath in blue mimicry of the flakes still tumbling downward on the window's other side.

The snow is long gone, the powdered-sugar effect transient as cupcakes in kindergarten. A week after the nor'easter a warm front showed up and stalled overhead, bringing four days of daytime highs in the 60s that got people talking of global warming with approval. Now December has dug in with its usual lack of imagination, drizzling on and off, clouds like steel bulkheads to shut off sky, heavens sandblasted by westerly winds that drag temperatures down, if shy of the freezing mark.

But this afternoon, this late afternoon, the temperature dips to 28 and the road from Mattapoisett to the Cape Cod Canal is slick with a first notion of ice. Drivers, not yet used to winter conditions, slow to speeds a well-fed pony could keep up with, then stop altogether where a Honda driven by a retired pharmacist has skidded into woods from which it is being hauled by a tow truck.

Murdo, frustrated, pulls off at the Wareham Diner. He sits at the counter and orders a coffee. The diner is warm and, twenty minutes from closing, almost empty. A waitress sips soda and flips through a wrestling magazine in one corner. The television has just been turned off. The cook sluices his grill down and scrapes at slurry with a steel spatula. Steam rises, bearing the odor of soggy ground-chuck. Murdo takes from his jacket a sample bottle filled with thick, brownish liquid. The label reads *murdo/noble mordant*

George Michelsen Foy

#17 w/ kalfat-mittel [*Möller Gmbh*]. The liquid is the same color as the diner's coffee. Murdo places the bottle next to his cup, there really is almost no difference, he thinks, and when he turns from the stove the cook confirms this, saying "Bring yer own? Don't blame ya, ya got the last of the last."

"Could be worse," Murdo says.

"Come back tomorrow morning, it'll be fresh."

In fact it seems okay to him, both the coffee and this compound, which mixes German caulk into one of Noble's mordant recipes and which on a square of steel he used as a test plate, firms up to a consistency ideal for etching. "Can't believe," Bud said, shaking his head at a printout from the gas chromatograph, "what's in this shit: not just caulking compound but damar resin, lye? An' olive oil—there's fuckin' *soap* in here—and a tree, it's called yellow meranti, I had to look it up."

The ground is thin but not too thin, resistant but not overly hard, and most of all when cooled it takes the tiniest lines scratched by the point of a needle, or a pencil, with none of the burring or undercut that might spawn foulbite. At least it shows none that Murdo can see, looking at it as closely as he can with a magnifying glass and his glasses freshly wiped. He will never be sure, not one hundred percent, but Murdo has a feeling in his gut that he has found Noble's "true ground"—the one that "held" his line yet took a rub like soft ground when desired.

He sips at his coffee, wondering how it would taste if he made a mistake and drank the *kalfat* medium instead. Probably not much different. It's the heat of coffee sluicing down his throat that gives him pleasure.

He is amazed at the lack of elation in him. He has researched Eby Noble for almost thirty months, ever since the barge-school job opened up. He was curious about "true ground" almost from the start, when he happened across the first mention of it in the notebooks. He should be celebrating: Bud, who got the German caulking compound express-mailed, at the factory's expense, from a chandlery in Kiel, broke open the Olde Bilgewater Number 7

254

Murdo had brought to toast their success, since he was out of Number 5. He wanted to throw a mini-party in the paint lab, though a third of the Number 7 gushed all over his workbench as soon as it was opened; Murdo took only a few sips of his. "You're on the wagon?" Bud asked, frowning, and Murdo shook his head, not wanting to go into what he can't explain even to himself.

Maybe too much has happened over the last ten days. Murdo has had to withstand what he came to think of as the Attack of the Acronyms, CRAC, BPD, DCF; the TRO, that restraining order the state hit him with. In the midst of all this legal trouble the storm happened, and with it the certainty he had lost Boy, when the kid launched the scow.

That was the worst, when he'd thought Boy had drowned off a drifting scow under the same bridge that killed Audrey Cooper; with the same processes at work since both, albeit in different ways, were following Murdo's lead. Two kids, over twenty years apart, dead because of him. Remembering the black gears of the drawbridge's workings, the smell of weed and whip of wind, Murdo squirms on the revolving counter stool, which squeaks.

He told Daisy about Audrey the night after Boy was found. She said he was a fool for beating himself up about an accident. Her eyes were full of gilt surprise and he assumed that the surprise was because he was still screwed up over Audrey; he resists the idea that she was taken aback because he is not the man she thought he was. Not careful, not competent the way a prospective father should be.

That line from *The Godfather*: "Children can be careless, but not men."

He drains his coffee, trying to flee the quote, and asks for a refill he does not want—and waits. The cook is trying to demonstrate that service, even for rotgut coffee, is truly over for today. The waitress won't look up from her magazine. Murdo massages the area around his wrists where the handcuffs gripped. Gutzeit was not shy about hauling him around by the cuffs' chain and even ten days later the skin is still bruised and raw.

But Boy came back.

Murdo only realizes he said this aloud when the cook, finally refilling his cup, looks at him with an expression in which puzzlement and impatience are mixed.

Boy came back, and for a while—even in the drunk tank, where they locked him up for violating the restraining order—Murdo felt as if he had, on some cosmic scale, started to make up for Audrey's death. That's an illusion, of course: another "excursion," which likely explains why it did not last. Why Murdo, drinking shit coffee in a closing diner, feels as if he has nowhere particular to go right now, and no desire at all to go there.

Why abruptly he wishes he could stay in this diner all evening, all night, all week; even if the coffee sucks.

But the waitress has put down her magazine and is stacking chairs upside down on tables. The cook is turning off the lights. ...

Instead of driving straight back to the barn Murdo takes a long detour past Hyannis Harbor to see what is going on with *Noble Boy* but nothing has happened—the scow still squats on the marine railway where it was hauled up, like a naughty kid dragged to detention, once the fire department got it towed. A ladder stands propped against its starboard gunwale. The yard is shut, it's almost 5, dusk is setting in.

The scow's deck is still piled thickly with weed. One of the cabin windows is broken. If the waves got that far, Murdo thinks, the damage inside must be great.

It's not his problem now.

It hurts, nevertheless.

Murdo returns to the barn well after nightfall. Despite its draftiness, poor insulation, and general unsuitability for freezing conditions, the barn is warm enough tonight. The smell of woodsmoke is strong and a small fan that pumps in air from the kitchen shed, where the stove resides, spins at full speed. Murdo looks around, surprised: Daisy has been decorating. Sprigs of holly are fastened to the stalls, on what's left of mangers, to four-by-four joists that hold up the hayloft. Cheap cardboard reindeer and elves are tacked between the branches, and a garland of white Christmas lights is hung between two adze-hewed beams. The old dining table has been invaded by cut branches of white pine underlying a papier-mâché Santa Claus she must have bought when she took the truck shopping earlier yesterday, and has hid from him since then.

For a second Murdo is at loss to explain why this all seems so strange to him. Then he remembers how Una refused to put up any Christmas decorations since they were associated in her mind with losing her parents. They never put up Christmas trees or lights or wreaths in all the years he and Una were together, which did not bother Murdo because his own parents did almost nothing for the holidays beyond a plastic tree, drugstore lights, a couple of discount-store toys each for himself and Junie.

It hits Murdo then, not for the first time but for the first time this strongly, how predictable it was for him to take up with Una's sister. What a waste of opportunity not to branch out and become part of a new family with fresh traditions and none of them sad! The thought whips back on him though, because it implies if that had happened he would not have Daisy now—and he misses her, all of a sudden, quite savagely, for she is nowhere to be seen. The fierceness draws strength in a circuitous way from the source of his earlier fear; from his memory of the night in which he searched for Boy amid the love-shredding mayhem of a storm.

He was unable to touch her on the yard boat at first. To do so seemed wrong, because he did not deserve her, because she needed someone who did not cause others to die.

But when they found the barge, and he truly believed Boy had drowned, she came close to him again, and the warmth of her body felt like a mooring to keep the beat-up craft of his own life from being broken on the shore the way the scow was being wrecked.

Then the gleam of her face in the glow of searchlight seemed the only thing in the world that held and harbored value; the one force against which all darkness in his mind, all the black and haunted fears that hid in rafters and bridge pilings, possessed no agency at all.

For a second, standing just inside the door of the barn, he runs excursion. Daisy has left, finally. She understood that this is wrong, will never work, she packed her laptop and took the next bus out. Or maybe something happened with the baby—*Daisy!* he yells, suddenly panicked—and she answers in a calm voice from the kitchen.

In that calm his fears fade like B-movie vampires when touched by sunlight.

He finds her sitting at the breakfast table next to the camp-stove, bent over her laptop. The screen is filled with carets and brackets, "ifs" and "thens," the symbols and numbers of computer coding.

She toggles a key and an image replaces the coding: a harbor with a boatyard, a drawbridge, an old-fashioned sailing ship anchored in the middle. An animated man rows toward the ship, quite realistically, though he's not getting anywhere.

Murdo bends his head into the curve between her shoulder and neck. Daisy smells of soap, woodsmoke, strawberries in hay. She raises a hand to touch his face.

"That don't look like Nekropolis," he says, straightening.

She smiles, her eyes still on the screen.

"I got an idea for a game. A harbor—fishermen, smugglers, pirates. Schooners, too, like the ones Noble drew. Indians and gangs, ghosts and brothels, right?"

"That's not a schooner."

"Don't be a pedant, it's just a placeholder."

"What's the quest, buried treasure?"

"Oh, puh-*leez.*"

Murdo walks back to the main room. He places the flask of what he believes to be Noble's *kalfat* mixture on the shelf with the other grounds.

The farmhands' workbench is clear, boxes holding pencils and etching tools, jugs of acid ranked on their shelf in Prussian orderliness above Noble's notebooks. Sheets of paper, too wide for the shelves, are piled on the floor to one side of his American-French press.

The press itself is clean, oiled, and protected from dust by the tarp that once covered the broken band saw in his previous shop.

Murdo experiences the same feeling he got from looking at the new ground which is to say he feels nothing—no joy, or desire to work, and little curiosity about how it might feel to draw with pencil or needle on Noble's secret compound. The lust he felt only a few weeks ago for sketching small details of his world is largely gone. So is the physical pleasure he garnered from touching paper made of linen rag, or wiping from the russet shine of an etching plate all ink that would not be caught in lines of image.

Murdo sighs. A wedge of light shifts across the workshop. Murdo goes to the window, expecting to see the lights of a car. The wind has risen, wet leaves blow from the gutter, rain stipples the pane. No headlights mar the outside dark. Murdo turns, thinking he'll see Daisy carry something shiny that might have caused reflection. He feels cold blow through the uncaulked doorframe, on his skin. He turns. His eyes fall on the stall and the tarp behind that hide the whiskey still. Abruptly Murdo walks to the stall and pulls the tarp away.

Return of the Winter Doldrums

Only last summer it seemed to this newspaper that Hyannis was on its way to a long-awaited rebirth. A new plan by the Cape Realtors Action Consortium together with the Barnstable Police Department to clean up Main Street was approved by town council.

A new shelter for the homeless of Hyannis was built in Industrial Park. The purchase of the Stewart Creek golf course, the so-called Winterpoor tract off Sea Street, and the planned construction of a modern condominium complex there, together with eight units of affordable housing, would anchor a revitalized vision of downtown Hyannis from the West End rotary to the proposed airport flyover. A recent, tragic murder near the high school was on its way to being solved.

Sadly, most of this progress has been stymied. The Winterpoor purchase was called off last week by the tract's owner, Joseph Barboza. The homeless have largely rejected the new shelter, and some are spending their days on Town Green, to the consternation of local merchants. And the Devan Douglas murder, along with its possible drug-ring connections, remains unsolved after the prime suspect (still under investigation) proved to have an alibi.

"We will keep trying our darnedest," CRAC spokesperson Una Bell said in an interview yesterday, citing the construction of a new commercial complex on the old Camp Street boardinghouse site, and a possible bid for the golf course by a private academy for differently abled teens. We can only hope that the New Year will smile on her efforts.

© *Cape Cod News Online*

Una watches the silhouette of her husband fill the small window next to the barn's door, slope sideways, disappear. He is still her husband, she reflects, and will be for another two or three months until the papers go through. Something about his slouch, his way of turning, touches her. It reminds her of the months they spent in each other's company when the other's idiosyncrasies were sources of affection, amusement even; not anger, not despair.

On the other hand this falling-down barn on a dark and godforsaken piece of land, this branch-strewn, like, *track* the Peters call a driveway, depresses her and always has. His pickup is more beat-up than ever and what is that to one side of the barn door, swaddled in the tarps Murdo uses to protect gosh-darn-near everything —a stove? They keep *appliances* outside the barn? Is this a friggin' *trailer*-park?

The windows of the kitchen annex are brightly lit. Una bites her lip. She supposes Daisy is in there, by the stove. Daisy is like a cat, she always finds warmth to curl up around. Part of the reason Una stopped the car short and turned off the lights instead of driving bravely to the barn is Daisy. Una still doesn't know how to deal with this, all right she cheated on Murdo first but *still*. The thought of her sister is like the thought of a foreign city, a place she has visited often but could never call home. She grips the wheel harder, leans her forehead against the cold plastic.

Damn it! She will have a great life. Russell Cooper is the man she always wanted and needed and darn it—*darn* it—*deserved*: none of this artistic hooey.

Una straightens. There are two kinds of people, Coop says: those who get things done, and those who whine about what's wrong with the world because they can't survive making whatever pretentious, unprofitable product they think they're entitled to make.

That kind makes babies casually, by accident, like catching a cold.

She knows which side she and Coop belong to.

And yet—she will talk to Murdo, because this has been on her mind. Tell him she'll volunteer as character witness should he need one to fight that lowlife's accusations. There are lines Una is not prepared to cross, no matter what Cooper says, no matter what her soon-to-be-ex-spouse did or did not do to Coop's den with the dead varmint. The accusation that Murdo molested a kid is too ridiculous, too unfair, for words. Even if—

Her smartphone rings the overture to *Tosca*. Email. She should check emails. What she will do is *text* Murdo. Una has the smartphone in her hand before she has even formulated the thought. She clicks to messaging and highlights his name on the list. Her fingers are stiff, the car is bleeding heat. Her thumb halts, hovers.

She wants to *see* them.

She will walk across this rough-cut brush, this savanna of torn leaves and fallen pine needles and crabgrass, and knock on the door of the barn where her husband and her pregnant sister live together.

Una replaces the smartphone in her bag and smoothes her hair, flipping down a little vanity mirror concealed behind the sun-visor. Her eyes are better than Daisy's, she thinks, her mascara just right today. Her scarf is silk and she put on one of her newest pairs of shoes, the Alfonso Putana: Italian leather, blood red with violet trim, dagger-sharp toes and piano-wire straps and heels just shy of stiletto. Dangerous, she looks, in the Putanas—but how the heck will she walk across this, like, *wilderness* in them? What in heaven's name will she look like when Murdo opens the door, what will she say to them, to the child they're expecting; that she'll bear witness for their swamp-Yankee lives and the little food-stamp family they're starting here?

That she'll vouch for his relationship with that differently abled, trailer-trash kid?

Una snaps the sun-visor back into place. No, she decides. If she sees them, if she bears witness at all it will be on her own terms. Not in this barn. If it must be done it will be done in the courthouse, which is majestic and old, of granite and varnished panels, a colonnaded mansion on a hill in the county seat of Barnstable.

Una turns the ignition key. Warm air from the heater washes across her face. She wipes her face again. After ten seconds, or maybe twenty, she twists the wheel left and drives. Once the car is pointing in the direction from which it came she switches on her headlamps and the drive appears out of night, half-bare branches arching overhead as if to salute the decisions she has made, in life as in fashion; in love as in driving away.

Murdo is having trouble with the seal on the lyne arm that leads from distilling pot to condenser. The pipes are connected by collars of thick plastic tightened with screws, but the screws are tiny and don't thread right. He finds himself wishing, fiercely and unexpectedly, that Boy were here to help him. After cross-threading a screw for the fourth time Murdo suddenly shouts *Cu da tua mãe!"* and flings his screwdriver across the barn.

The thud as the tool hits barnboards wakes Daisy, who has fallen asleep on the couch. Murdo walks over and retrieves the screwdriver. He also picks up her blanket, which has fallen to the floor. He pulls the blanket over her and she smiles without opening her eyes. He strokes her hair, very gently, and goes back to the lyne arm.

A half hour later he is still trying to connect the collars when a wedge of light passes across the window near the door; this time it brightens, slides horizontally, brushing barnboards with a hint of straw.

Cops, Murdo thinks. His stomach hollows. No one is supposed to rule on his violation till next week but the DCF, he has been told, is unpredictable and so are the courts unless you have a fancy lawyer and Murdo does not have a fancy lawyer, he doesn't have a lawyer at all unless you count a public defender who does not look old enough to drive and who missed their first appointment anyway.

He walks to the window. A van is drawn up near the big doors. It doesn't look like a Black Maria, it is not blue and white. A woman of medium height and build comes around the driver's side of the van, and then the passenger door opens and a smaller figure gets out that side.

It is drizzling, the woman wears a scarf over her head and the passenger has a sweatshirt that is too big for him, or her. The hood of it falls forward over the eyes. The figure stands hunched in jeans and trainers, looking back at the woman, and somewhere in that sequence of details Murdo knows.

The kid looks up. The hood keeps him from seeing anything so he pokes it upward and to one side. That gesture, too, feels like a key unlocking a hatch in Murdo's memory. The eyes glint in bright light spilling from the van.

"*Boy*," Murdo whispers, and thrusts open the door. He strides to the van and stands in front of the child but does not touch him.

The rain is cold and stings his face and hands.

"Oh fer chrissakes," the woman says, taking an unlit cigarette from her lips to say it, "go ahead and hug him, I already violated nineteen laws just by driving here."

"This could put me back in jail."

"I don't think so." Her voice is what finally makes the connection for Murdo—the tone of it, which allows no time for shilly-shally. This is a woman who made up her mind on any given decision the week before last. This is Kathleen, whose van Boy keyed, it seems like eons ago, though the van from this angle looks unhurt.

She takes a drag of her cigarette. When she talks again her words come out mingled with the steam of breath and a haze of tobacco smoke.

"Your case is under review," she says. "TRO's still on but that DCF woman says they're gonna pull the 51-A as 'unsupported'."

Kathleen takes another drag and flicks the glowing butt into sodden grass.

"Suddenly there's *way* more information about the guy who filed the complaint."

Boy shifts his weight from side to side. Sparse light from the door makes the hollows under his eyes and cheekbones seem blacker than Charbonnel ink. Murdo wonders, all of a sudden, why he never made a sketch of Boy.

"He's in my care again," Kathleen adds. "I been putting up with it for days, Moodo this, Moodo that, yesterday he takes off and walks to that place you used to work? On Fresh Holes Road? So finally I said, fuck it. I told him, what the hell.

"I called your wife, she told me where you were."

Murdo stays where he is, not moving. He thinks, never mind what this woman says, they'll nail him for violating the order twice and this time the judge won't release him on recognizance. Boy drops his eyes to Murdo's left hand which still clutches the Phillips screwdriver he was using, ineffectively, on the still's connecting collars—

"I can do that?" he says, more hesitantly than he has ever said it before.

The door behind Murdo slams. He turns. Daisy is shielding her eyes with one hand against the rain. "Boy," she says, and then, louder, "*Boy*"; she runs across the piled needles and dead leaves and puts her arms around the kid and, bending downward, folds her head into the crook of his shoulder, the way Murdo did with her only a little while ago.

"Seems to think you have a job for him," Kathleen says.

Murdo, watching Boy wrap his arms around Daisy; feeling the hollowness in his stomach fill slowly, as if he has been gutshot and this is blood filling his stomach, only the blood is painless and good; says, "Yeah, I do.

"I got work Boy can do."

With recent rain, and temperatures near freezing at night, the water in Nantucket Sound has dropped to 55 degrees Fahrenheit. The moon is new and tides are strong in the sandy underwater valleys between Horseshoe, Half Moon, and Tuckernuck Shoals. Winter flounder, flattened against the bottom of those valleys, pick up the signal; some hook in their genes and neural ganglia, latching onto nerve-loops of tide, moon and temperature, triggers the lust of flatfish.

They start to move. It is December now and the dragger captains from Hyannis, New Bedford, and Point Jude, aware of the patterns if not the lust, are waiting. They shoot otter trawls and drag the passages flounder follow to return to their spawning grounds in Hyannis Harbor, East and West Bays, and Popponesset. The "legs" of rope pulling the nets troll ticklers, chains that scour up sand ahead of the trawl's mouth to scare flounder off the bottom where they might well be missed or crushed by the heavy net as it churns across the whorled ground.

Flounder are not sentimental, they do not mourn the disappearance of their mates. Once the net has passed and sand has settled the survivors return to bottom, smelling water and the tides; analyzing, in ways that are not understood by them or anyone else, the data of bottom, of Earth's magnetism, of planetary transits. They figure out where they were headed and resume their trek.

A knot of these fish seek a precise cocktail of information that includes brackish water as well as a unique mix of eelgrass and bladderwrack, mud and crab shells, the resin of pine twigs and a type of clay that occurs in the upper stretches of Eel Pond. The cocktail this year is not strong, it has been diluted by the stink of a new weed, but it doesn't matter. The females are heavy with eggs; a single, three-year-old lemon sole can carry two million of them. She is eager to find the harbor to drop this load and the males who accompany her focus only on their role in this: the spurt of milt, the sense of losing themselves in something greater—the crazy whodunnit of ovaries, spat and future.

Up the channel then, under a drawbridge, into the weed and mud and ah! the mix they sought. The females circle, it takes them longer than usual to find a patch of white, weed-free sand, but a handful of patches remain. Here they will drop their eggs when moon, temperature of water, and slip of tide, feel right—sometime in February.

For now, the sun rises late and sets early, the water tastes increasingly of frost. The flounder settle on the mud and sand, their eyes aimed upward at the dwindling light.

the end

Acknowledgments

My intent in writing *The Winterpoor* was to give voice to the vulnerable, threatened inhabitants, both human and animal, of Cape Cod and its surrounding waters. Readers, especially those who know the area, will recognize that I have drawn an alternate, composite map of the Cape and its denizens that is true in spirit if fictional in names, specific characters and details. ... I was helped in writing this novel by Eileen Chace, David Chaffetz and Ginny Christensen. Susan Nickerson at the Provincetown Center for Coastal Studies and Sandy Macfarlane, formerly of CCS, helped check environmental details; Lane Myer and Andrew Raftery at RISD were invaluable when it came to verifying the etching tech; the John A. Noble Collection at Sailors' Snug Harbor on Staten Island also provided inspiration in that department. Dr. Nuno Matos kindly advised me on the Portuguese, and my cousin Torbjørn Rasch Pettersen on the Norwegian. Eugenia Nordskog did a fine job of checking the manuscript from the depths of a Minnesota deep-freeze; to Mary Petiet at Sea Crow, deep thanks for understanding what the novel seeks to do, and for shepherding it to publication. I am deeply grateful for the expertise, advice and assistance provided by all the above; any inaccuracies or awkward tweaks are my fault and mine alone. Finally, my family as always provided a deep and long-term structure of support for someone involved in the solitary, obsessive, sometimes maddening trade of writing, especially in the case of a book that took almost fifteen years to finish: my gratitude to them is unbounded, heartfelt and permanent.

About the Author

George Michelsen Foy is the author of 14 published novels: the latest *The Last Green Light* (May, 2024) with Guernica Editions; other novels were published by Viking Penguin, Bantam Double-day, University Press of New England (as GF Michelsen), Éditions Globophile (Paris); and three works of nonfiction with Scribner and Macmillan. His long-form nonfiction has been published in *Harper's, Rolling Stone, the New York Times,* etc.; fiction in *Notre Dame Review, Ep;phany Journal, Washington Square Review,* etc. He has worked as illustrator and editor (for the *International Herald Tribune* and the Cape Cod *Register,* among others); also as merchant marine officer, commercial cod-fisherman, lobsterman, construction worker and factory hand. A native of Cape Cod, he was educated at the London School of Economics and Bennington College's MFA program, teaches creative writing at New York University, lives in Barnstable County, is a recipient of an NEA fellowship in fiction and other awards, and finds writers' biographies amusing.

About the Press

Sea Crow Press is committed to amplifying voices that might otherwise go unheard. In a rapidly changing world, we believe the small press plays an essential part in contemporary arts as a community forum, a cultural reservoir, and an agent of change. We are international with a focus on our New England roots. We publish creative nonfiction, literary fiction, and poetry. Our books celebrate our connection to each other and to the natural world with a focus on positive change and great storytelling. We follow a traditional publishing model to create carefully selected and edited books. In turbulent times, we focus on sharing works of beauty that chart a positive course for the future.